Praise for *Mariana*

"An intense and gripping novel that is almost impossible to put down. The reader would be well advised to seek out a comfortable chair to experience an exceptional read."

— *The Winnipeg Free Press*

Praise for *The Splendour Falls*

"This action-packed mystery-romance, set in a medieval French town, shows the same deft plotting that won Kearsley the Catherine Cookson Prize for her earlier *Mariana.*"

— *Chatelaine*

"Thrilling, haunting, and deeply romantic."

— Rachel Hore, best-selling author of *A Gathering Storm*

"Like something out of the pages of Daphne du Maurier."

— *Daily Express*

Praise for *The Shadowy Horses*

"Part ghost story and part romance . . . beautifully imaginative with a dream-like quality."

— *The Bookseller*

Praise for *Season of Storms*

"If you liked *The French Lieutenant's Woman*, you'll love this suspenseful, often better, novel."

—*Romantic Times*

Praise for *The Winter Sea*

"A deeply engaging romance and a compelling historical novel . . . Susanna Kearsley has written a marvelous book."

—Bernard Cornwell

Praise for *The Rose Garden*

"This colorful romance peoples both the past and present with characters worth swooning over."

—*Kirkus Reviews*

"Kearsley beautifully evokes the wild landscapes and history of Cornwall in this pleasant time-travel romance."

—*Publishers Weekly*

"A thrilling, haunting, and deeply romantic story powerfully told by an engaging heroine."

—Rachel Hore, author of *A Place of Secrets*

ALSO BY SUSANNA KEARSLEY

The Rose Garden

The Winter Sea

Every Secret Thing

Season of Storms

Named of the Dragon

The Shadowy Horses

The Splendour Falls

Mariana

The Firebird

SUSANNA KEARSLEY

A Touchstone Book
Published by Simon & Schuster
New York   London   Toronto   Sydney   New Delhi

Touchstone
A Division of Simon & Schuster, Inc.
1230 Avenue of the Americas
New York, NY 10020

This Touchstone export edition April 2013

TOUCHSTONE and colophon are registered trademarks of Simon & Schuster, Inc.

For information about special discounts for bulk purchases,
please contact Simon & Schuster Special Sales at 1-800-268-3216
or CustomerService@simonandschuster.ca

Designed by Akasha Archer

Manufactured in the United States of America

10 9 8 7 6 5 4 3 2 1

ISBN 978-1-4516-7382-1
ISBN 978-1-4516-7384-5 (ebook)

This book is for Lee Ann Ray,
who first suggested I give Robbie his own story.

Though I am old with wandering
Through hollow lands and hilly lands,
I will find out where she has gone . . .

—W. B. Yeats, "The Song of Wandering Aengus"

chapter ONE

He sent his mind in search of me that morning.

I was on the Tube, a half a minute out of Holland Park and in that muzzy not-awake-yet state that always bridged the time between my breakfast cup of coffee and the one that I'd have shortly at my desk. I nearly didn't notice when his thoughts touched mine. It was a rare thing these days; rarer still that I would let him in, but my own thoughts were drifting and I knew that his were, too. In fact, from what I saw of where he was—the angle of the ceiling and the dimly shadowed walls—I guessed that he was likely still in bed, just waking up himself.

I didn't need to push him out. Already he was drawing back, apologizing. *Sorry.* Not a spoken word, but still I heard the faint regretful tone of his familiar voice. And then he wasn't there.

A man sat heavily beside me, squeezed me over on the seat, and with my senses feeling raw already, even that unwanted contact was too much. I stood, and braced myself against the bit of wall beside the nearest door and forced myself to balance till we came to Bond Street. When the doors slid open I slid safely back into the comfort of routine, my brisk steps keeping pace with everybody else as we became a texting, talking, moving mass that flowed together up and out and through the turnstiles and emerged onto the pavement where we went our separate ways, heads down and purposeful.

The morning was a lovely one for August. The oppressive sticky heat had given way to fresher air that promised warmth but didn't threaten, and the sky was a pristine and perfect blue.

I barely saw it. I was thinking of that shadowed room, a greyer light that spoke of clouds or maybe rain, a hand that had come lazily in view, to rub his eyes while he was waking. It had been his left hand, and there'd been no rings on it. At least, I didn't think I'd seen a ring on it.

I caught my thoughts before they had a chance to wander further and betray me. *Doesn't matter*, I reminded myself firmly, and to make quite sure I heard myself, I said the words aloud: "It doesn't matter."

I could feel the glances of the people walking closest to me, wondering if I were off my trolley, and I flushed a little, tucking my head well down as I came round the corner and into South Molton Street, a little pedestrian haven of upscale shops, cafés, and galleries. Everything always seemed quieter here, with the mad rush of Bond Street behind me. I carried on down past the graceful old buildings with beautiful doors to the one with the freshly white-painted facade where an expensive-looking brass plaque with fine lettering read: GALERIE ST.-CROIX, FINE RUSSIAN ARTIFACTS AND ART, THIRD FLOOR.

The naming of the gallery had been one of Sebastian's little vanities—in spite of his French surname he was English through and through, born of a line that likely traced its Hampshire roots back to the Norman conquest. But Sebastian knew his business, and to art dealers like him it was essential to create the proper image.

I was part of that, I knew, because I had the proper look, the proper pedigree, the right credentials, and I always dressed to fit the part. But when he'd hired me two years ago, he'd also made no secret of the fact that it had been for my abilities—not only that I held a masters degree in Russian Studies and the History of Art, but that I spoke fluent Russian besides, my organized nature appealed to his strong sense of order, and I had, what he'd called then, "potential."

He'd worked to transform me, to mentor me, teaching me how to get on the right side of the bid at an auction, and how to finesse our more difficult clients. I'd come a long way from the rather unworldly young woman I'd been when he'd taken me on.

He had transformed the gallery building as well. We were on the third floor, in a space that today was as richly detailed as a penthouse. Even the lift was mirrored, which this morning didn't thrill me.

I was frowning as it opened to the elegant reception room where a flower-seller painted by Natalia Goncharova hung above the desk at which our previous receptionist had sat. She'd had to leave us unexpectedly, and I'd been interviewing this past week to fill the vacancy, while Sebastian and I shared out the extra duties.

It was not an easy thing to hire a person who could suit Sebastian's tastes, aesthetically. He wanted something more than simple competence, or class. He wanted someone who embodied what the Goncharova painting did—the painting he had hung above that desk, where it would be the first thing noticed by each customer who stepped into the gallery.

He'd had offers for it. Several of our clients could afford to pay a million pounds with ease, but then Sebastian didn't need the money.

"If I sell the thing," he'd told me once, "then I'll have only satisfied one client. If I leave it where it is, then every one of them will think it can be theirs one day."

It didn't only work with art. It wasn't a coincidence that many of our loyal and best customers were women, and they looked upon Sebastian as they did that Goncharova flower-seller, as a prize that could be won, with time and effort.

In fact, as I passed by his glass-walled office on the way down to my own, I saw he had a woman with him now. I would have left them to their business, but he saw me and beckoned me in, so I pushed the door open and joined them.

Sebastian's smile was all professional, with me, and even if it hadn't been, I would have been immune to it. He was too rich to be my type. A gold watch flashed beneath his tailored sleeve as he leaned forward, looking so immaculate I half-suspected that he had a team of stylists working on him every morning, from his polished shoes right to the tousled toffee-coloured hair that had been combed with just the right amount of carelessness. "Nicola," he introduced me, "this is Margaret Ross. Miss Ross, my associate, Nicola Marter."

Miss Margaret Ross was not what I'd expected, not our usual sort of client. For one thing she was plainly dressed, but dressed with so much care I knew she'd taken pains to look her best. And although I was usually quite good at guessing ages, I had trouble guessing hers. She had to be at least a decade older than myself, so nearing forty at the least, but while her clothing and the way she held herself suggested she might be still older, there was something in her quiet gaze that seemed distinctly youthful, even innocent.

"Good morning." She was Scottish. "I'm afraid that I've been wasting Mr. St.-Croix's time."

Sebastian, ever charming, shook his head. "No, not at all. That's what I'm here for. And even if it can't be proved, you still have a fascinating story to tell your grandchildren."

She cast her eyes down as though she were hiding disappointment. "Yes."

"Tell Nicola." Sebastian's tone was meant to salve her feelings, make her feel that what she had to say was fascinating, even if it wasn't. He was good, that way. To me, he said, "She brought this carving in for an appraisal."

It looked to me, at first, an undistinguished lump of wood that curved to fit his upraised palm, but when I looked again I saw it was a small carved bird, wings folded tightly to its sides, a sparrow or a wren. Sebastian was saying, "It's been in her family . . . how long?"

Margaret Ross roused herself to his smooth prompting. "Nearly three hundred years, so I'm told. It was given to one of my ancestors by Empress Catherine of Russia. Not Catherine the Great," she said, showing her knowledge. "The first Catherine."

Sebastian smiled encouragement. "Peter the Great's widow, yes. So, the 1720s, sometime. And it very well might have been." Holding the carving as though it were priceless, he studied it.

Margaret Ross told him, "We call it the Firebird. That's what it's always been called, in our family. It sat under glass in my grandmother's house, and we children were never allowed to come near it. My mother said"—there was the tiniest break in her voice, but she covered it over—"she said, with Andrew gone—Andrew's my brother, he died in Afghanistan—with him gone, and me not likely to have any family myself now, my mother said there was no point in the Firebird sitting there, going to waste. She said I should sell it, and use all the money to travel, like I'd always wanted to do."

"Miss Ross," said Sebastian, to me, "lost her mother quite recently."

I understood his manner now, his sympathy. I told her, "I'm so sorry."

"That's all right. She had MS, it wasn't the easiest life for her. And she felt guilty for having me there to look after her. But," she said, trying to smile, "I looked after my aunties as well, till they passed, and she was my own mother. I couldn't have left her alone, could I?"

Looking again at her eyes I decided their youthfulness came from the fact that she'd never been able to live her own life as a woman. She'd put her own life into limbo while caring for others. I felt for her. And I felt, too, for the mother who'd hoped that her daughter would sell their one prized family heirloom, and finally have money and comfort to live just a little. To travel.

"The thing is," Sebastian said, kindly, "without any documentation or proof, what we dealers call provenance, we simply can't know for certain. And without that provenance, I'm afraid this poor creature has little real value. We can't even tell if it's Russian." He looked at me. "Nicola? What would you say?"

He passed it to me and I took it, not thinking, forgetting my mind had already been breached once this morning. It wasn't until I was holding it, light in my hands, that I realized I'd made a mistake.

Instantly I felt a warmth that had nothing to do with the carving itself. I closed my eyes to try to stop the vision, but that only made it worse. I saw a slanting fall of light, with fine dust dancing through it. Two women, one ageing but lovely, with heavy black eyebrows; the other respectfully bent, perhaps kneeling, her young face upturned in uncertainty. "My darling Anna," the first woman said to the other in elegant Russian, and smiled. "You were never a nobody."

I opened my eyes quickly, maybe a little too quickly, but to my relief no one seemed to have noticed. "I really don't know," I said, giving the small carved bird back to Sebastian.

He looked at it with a commendable blend of admiration and regret.

"The trouble is," he told our would-be client, "it's so difficult to date this sort of thing with any certainty. If it *is* Russian, it was very likely peasant made; there is no maker's mark or factory stamp to go by, and without any documentation . . ." He raised one shoulder slightly in a shrug that seemed to speak to the unfairness of it all. "If she had brought you back an icon, now, this ancestor of yours, or some small piece of jewellery—*that* I might have helped you with."

"I understand," said Margaret Ross. Her tone was bleak.

Sebastian turned the little carving over in his hands one final time, and I knew he was searching for some small thing to praise, to let this woman down as gently as he could. "Certainly it's very old," was what he ended up with, "and I'm sure it's had a few adventures."

Margaret Ross wasn't sure about that. "It's been sitting there under that glass for as long as I've known it, and likely it sat there a good while before that."

The twist of her faint smile held sympathy, as though she knew how that felt, to be there on the mantelpiece watching the bright world pass by, and I saw the small sag of defeat in her shoulders as, accepting Sebastian's return of the carved bird, she started to carefully wrap it back up in its layers of yellowed, creased tissue.

Impulse drove me to ask aloud, "What was her name?"

She looked up. "Sorry?"

"Your ancestor. The one who brought your Firebird back from Russia."

"Anna. That's all we know of her, really, we don't know her surname. It was her daughter married into the Ross family, that's how the Firebird came down to us."

Anna. Something tingled warmly up my arm. *My darling Anna . . .*

"Because maybe," I suggested, "you could try a bit of research, to establish some connection between her and Empress Catherine."

From Sebastian's glance I couldn't tell if he was grateful or annoyed, but he chimed in with, "Yes, if you were able to find proof of any kind, that would be useful."

Again that faint twist of a smile that spoke volumes about how much hope she held now of discovering that. She admitted, "My granny tried once, so she said, but no joy. Common people, they don't make the history books. And on our side of the family, there's nobody famous."

I saw the warm smile in my mind. Heard the voice. *You were never a nobody.*

"Well," said Sebastian, beginning to stand, "I am sorry we couldn't be more of a help to you. But if you'll leave us your address, we'll keep it in mind, and if ever a client requests something like it . . ."

I felt like a traitor, as Margaret Ross stood, too, and shook both our hands. The feeling held as we escorted her back out into reception, and Sebastian, with full chivalry and charm, gave her his card and wished her well and said goodbye, and as the lift doors closed he turned to me and, reading the expression in my eyes, said, "Yes, I know."

Except he didn't.

There was no way that he could have known. In all the time I'd worked for him I'd never told him anything about what I could do, and even if I'd told him, he'd have rubbished the idea. "Woo-woo stuff," he would have called it, as he'd done the day our previous reception-ist had told us she was visiting a psychic.

"No," she'd said, "she really sees things. It's this gift she has—she holds a thing you've owned, see, like a necklace, or a ring, and she can tell you things about yourself. It's called psychometry." She'd said the term with confident authority.

Sebastian, with a sidelong look, had said, "It's called a scam. There is no way that anyone can be a psychic. It's not possible."

I'd offered him no argument, although I could have told him he was wrong. I could have told him *I* was psychic, and had been for as long as I remembered. Could have told him that I, too, saw detailed visions, if I concentrated on an object someone else had held. And sometimes, like today, I saw the visions even when I didn't try, or concentrate, although that happened very, very rarely now.

The flashes of unwanted visions had been more a feature of my childhood, and I had to close my eyes and truly focus now to use my "gift"—my curse, I would have called it. I had chosen not to use it now for years.

Two years, to be exact.

I'd chosen to be normal, and I meant to go on being normal, having the respect of those I worked with, not their nudges or their stares. So there was no good reason why, when I sat down at the computer in my office, I ignored the string of waiting emails and began an image search instead.

I found three portraits, different in their poses and the sitter's age, but in all three I recognized the woman easily because of her black hair, her heavy arching eyebrows, and her warm brown eyes. The same eyes that had smiled this morning in the brief flash of a vision I had viewed when I had held the wooden Firebird.

There could be no mistaking her: the first Empress Catherine, the widow of Peter the Great.

"Damn," I whispered. And meant it.

S ebastian had noticed. "You're not even listening."

Bringing my thoughts back to where they belonged, I gave him my attention. "Sorry. You were saying?"

"I've forgotten, now, myself."

It was later on that afternoon, and he and I were clearing up before the workday's end. I found it calming, the routine of putting everything in order, going over both our schedules for the next day, sharing any needed details.

After frowning for a moment at his mobile, his face cleared. "Oh, right. Next weekend. Thursday week till Sunday. Have you any plans?"

"I don't, no. But I'm sure you have some for me, since you're asking."

"Well, I rather thought I'd send you to St. Petersburg."

He had my full attention, now. "St. Petersburg? What for?"

"To view an exhibition."

I could tell, from how he watched me while I counted forward silently to figure out the dates, that he was waiting to see how long it would take me to put two and two together.

Next Thursday would be the second of September. "What, the Wanderers exhibit, do you mean? The one that's coming from America?"

The Wanderers, or Peredvizhniki, had been a group of Russian realist painters whose liberal political views set them at odds with the Academy of Arts, so in protest of what they deemed the uselessness of "art for art's sake" they'd broken free of the academy and formed their own group aimed at properly reflecting the society around them, warts and all. True to their name, they'd taken their exhibits on the road, across the country, through the end of the nineteenth century and into the beginning of the twentieth, and it only seemed appropriate that now their works had ended up in far-flung places, from the Netherlands to Tokyo. The exhibit had been in the pipeline for a few years, ambitiously gathering paintings on loan from museums and private collectors and galleries, and more ambitiously making arrangements to tour it from New York to Paris to Sydney. But first, it would have its grand opening months in St. Petersburg.

"Got it in one," said Sebastian. "Yuri's one of the curators. You remember Yuri? And he tells me Wendy Van Hoek will be there for the opening."

I waited for the rest of it. "Yes?"

"And I'd like you to do a deal with her."

"I've never met Wendy Van Hoek," I reminded him.

Sebastian counted that as a point in my favour. "She's rather . . ." He paused as though searching for a way to put it politely, finally settling on, "Formidable. But then I'd imagine one can't be a Van Hoek without having that attitude. God knows her father was even more frightening to deal with."

Her father, I knew, had been one of the greatest of private collectors in Amsterdam. I'd never met *him*, either.

I told Sebastian, "Surely you should be the one to do the deal. She knows you."

"She thinks she does, yes. But unfortunately, what she thinks she knows, she doesn't like," he said. "We don't get on." He paused at the expression on my face, and asked me, "What?"

Drily, I remarked, "I didn't know that any woman could resist your charms."

"She isn't any woman."

I had never seen Sebastian frown like that about a woman. It intrigued me. "So, what is this deal you're wanting me to do with her?"

"She has a Surikov. I want to buy it. It's in the exhibit, you'll see it."

"And who is it for?"

He said, "Vasily. He's set his heart on it, and you know Vasily."

I did. A lovely man with quiet charm that masked a fierce tenacity, he was, hands down, my favourite of our clients. He'd suffered, as his parents had, under the Soviet regime, and had been tortured in the Lubyanka prison, though he rarely ever spoke of that. Instead he seemed determined now to focus on the beauty in the world, and not its ugliness. It made a difference, knowing I'd be doing this for Vasily.

Besides, I liked St. Petersburg. I'd done a term of study there, at the St. Petersburg State University, and knew the city well.

"All right," I said. "I'll do my best." I made another mental calculation of the time remaining and the things I'd need to do. "I'll have to get myself another suitcase, though. My old one's broken. And I ought to go and have a chat with Vasily, beforehand."

"Go tomorrow, if you like. In fact, why don't you take the day?" he offered. "It's Friday, you could start your weekend early. Get some rest."

The way he said that made me raise my eyebrows. "Do I look as though I need rest?"

"I don't know." He looked me over and pronounced, "You're not yourself." And then he said, "Oh, hell, is that the time? I'm late for drinks."

"With whom?"

"Penelope." He stopped and stood a moment near his desk, expectant. "Jacket, or no jacket?"

"For drinks with Penelope? Jacket."

"I thought as much. Damn. Where's my tie? Is that it on the chair, just behind you?"

I crossed the few steps to look. "No, that's a scarf."

"A scarf?" He frowned. "You're sure?"

"Of course I'm sure." A woman's scarf, in shades of blue, the colours of the tie that I caught sight of now, coiled tidily at one end of the bookshelf. "There it is."

He looked where I was pointing. "Thanks." He threaded it into his collar, flipped it round and over in a Windsor knot. "How's that?"

"It's crooked."

"Could you . . . ?" Standing with his chin angled slightly to the ceiling, he glanced sideways at the blue silk scarf still hanging on the chair. "It must be hers," he said. "The Scottish woman from this morning. Margaret . . ."

"Ross." I fixed his tie as I had done a hundred times before this. I had a brother. I was good with ties. "I don't remember her wearing a scarf."

"Well, that's where she was sitting. And apart from yourself, she's the only woman who's been in here today."

"She left her address, didn't she? I'll put it in the post to her."

As I stepped back his hand came up to smooth the finished tie with satisfaction. "Thanks. You're all right locking up, then?"

I assured him that I was. Alone, when he had gone, I took the blue scarf from the chair and brought it out to the reception desk, to put it in an envelope for posting.

It was, I thought, the least that I could do. No matter what my day had been like, I knew Margaret Ross's had been worse. She must have been so hopeful when she'd woken up this morning, still believing that her carving could be traded for the means to buy a little bit of happiness, a little bit of life. And we had killed that dream and stomped on it, and that seemed inexcusable.

The scarf was a designer one. My fingers touched the label. Hermès. Not an inexpensive, everyday thing, but a rare indulgence— something that the woman I had met today could ill afford to lose.

I found the address she had left Sebastian, and I copied it with care onto the envelope. And then I took the scarf and started folding it.

I shouldn't have.

My visions, when I concentrated, started out more cleanly. Though I didn't ever fall into a trance in the accepted way, the concentration brought a sense of calm, a peaceful deep awareness not unlike the way I sometimes felt relaxing in the bath. Then gradually, against the void, I saw a small parade of moving images, projected like a filmstrip running past until one image grew to blot out all the others, and I viewed it much as I would view a film at the cinema, observing what was going on.

This vision wasn't clean, like that. It came on as a random flash, the same as I had felt when I had held the wooden Firebird, the same as I'd so often felt in childhood, but the end result was much the same: I saw a glimpse of Margaret Ross's life.

I saw loneliness, drawn in her silent and dreary surroundings, a chair by a window that looked on a small narrow garden with walls, and a clock ticking somewhere, relentlessly counting the slow-passing minutes. In all that drab room I could only see one bit of colour—a travel brochure from a cruise line, the white ship enticingly set on an ocean so brilliantly blue that it dazzled the eyes.

And then that scene grew smaller as another rose to take its place: a window and a desk . . . a doctor's consulting room, I thought. And Margaret Ross herself, much as she'd been this morning, sitting in a chair, her shoulders sagging with dejection. I could hear the doctor speaking, and I caught my breath because it seemed so cruel, and so unfair.

I pulled my mind back, made an effort, and the visions stopped, but there was no way to unsee what I had seen, or to ignore what I'd learned.

It was still very much on my mind the next morning.

I met Vasily early, for breakfast at his favourite restaurant, the St. Pancras Grand, on the upper concourse of the train station. He liked the retro English menu, and the elegance of the place with gold leaf on the ceiling and dark wood and leather bistro-style seating. We had a lovely chat about the Surikov, the painting he was keen to have me buy for him while I was in St. Petersburg, but it was what he said as he left me that changed the whole course of my day.

He ordered a takeaway meal at the end of our breakfast, another whole plate of eggs Benedict, and so I teased, "You'll be putting on weight, if you start eating two breakfasts."

"It's not for me," he said, "it is for the old man at the end of my street. He has no one to live with him, so he eats poorly some days. I have seen it. Whenever I come here, I bring him eggs Benedict."

"You're a good man, do you know that?"

He shrugged it aside. "It's not good. It is right. When a person needs help, then you help them. What else would you do?"

I thought about that, after Vasily left. From my handbag, I took out the envelope that I'd brought with me to post back to Margaret Ross, and I looked down at the address a long time, and then I walked from the restaurant and round to King's Cross and I bought a return ticket up to Dundee.

Because he'd been right. Margaret Ross needed help. I could help her. The truth was, I couldn't *not* help her. I'd never have lived through the shame.

What Sebastian had told her was perfectly true: There was really no way, by conventional means, to determine her Firebird's provenance. But if I were to hold it again, and to concentrate, I might find some information imprinted upon it to help me know where I should look for the proof that the carving had once been the gift of an empress. In less than a week I would be in St. Petersburg, there on the ground, where the first Empress Catherine had lived, ruled, and died, and where Margaret's mysterious ancestor, Anna, had most likely been in that flash of a vision I'd seen. I'd have time, then, to dig around, learn what I could, ask my colleagues who worked in the Hermitage . . . there were a number of ways I could try to help.

Starting with holding the Firebird.

Nobody needed to know, I assured myself. Not if I simply asked Margaret Ross if I could look at the carving again, maybe study it privately, just for a moment. She'd see me holding it, no more than that. No one needed to know.

And secure in that reasoning, I started north on the train.

The doubts didn't start to creep in for a couple of hours. I had been going over the plan in my mind when I'd suddenly noticed a hole in it, and having noticed that hole, it had seemed to grow larger until it was all I could see.

Empress Catherine and Anna, I suddenly realized, had lived nearly three hundred years ago, and since that time countless people would likely have handled the carving, obscuring those earlier imprints with later ones, clouding my readings.

The vision I'd seen had been something spontaneous, something I hadn't controlled. If I wanted to be any help at all to Margaret Ross now, and given I might only have one chance to hold the carving, I'd have to be sure I could sift through the levels and layers of time to arrive at the right one.

And that was why, when my train slid into Waverly station at Edinburgh, I didn't change to the train for Dundee, as I ought to have done. I stepped right off the platform, and walked up the ramp from the underground dimness to daylight, with Edinburgh castle set high on its unyielding rock just ahead of me. It was why I walked the busy length of Princes Street, and turned towards the river, and was heading down the hill now to the one place I'd been certain I would never go again.

chapter THREE

The house looked like all of the rest of the old Georgian houses that ringed the small private park, making a circle around the tall trees that were fenced in and gated and rimmed by a hedge of dense holly. The houses rose four storeys tall, all with similar rows of large white-painted windows set into their grey stone facades, and high steps leading up to their similar doors with arched transoms above.

No one would ever have guessed that the house I was standing in front of was one of the foremost centres for the study of the unexplained: the Emerson Institute of Parapsychology, named for J. Norman Emerson, the Canadian archaeologist who'd pioneered the use of psychics in his expeditions in a quest to study what might lie beyond the limits of man's current scientific understanding.

I had never heard of Emerson, or the institute, until four years ago. My elder brother, Colin, was the one who'd put me on to it. One morning he'd come down to breakfast looking even more thoughtful than usual. Giving a nod to the stack of brochures at the side of my plate he'd remarked, "You've decided on Edinburgh, then, for your masters?"

"Yes," I'd told him. "Russian Studies and Art History."

My mother had smiled. "Russian Studies," she'd said. "You can study a Russian for nothing, at home. Just look there." And she'd given a nod to our grandfather, reading his newspaper at the far end of the table. He'd remained dignified, as though he hadn't heard, but he had folded his newspaper down for an instant to let his eyes smile at me.

Colin had continued, "Then you might want to get to know these people." He'd handed me a page he'd printed out from his computer, all about the Emerson Institute. He'd watched me while I read it through, then added, "They do studies there, real scientific studies, that might help you understand that thing you do."

The air had stilled and thickened in the kitchen. And my grandfather had set his paper down. His eyes had lost their smile. "You don't ever tell anyone what you can do, Nicola. Do you hear? Always I've told you, since you were a little girl. Never tell anyone." And when my mother had tried to placate him he'd lifted a hand. "No. This is not for argument. I know," he'd said, in a tone harsh with feeling. "I *know* what can happen. You keep this a secret. You tear up that paper."

My brother had calmly remarked that this wasn't the Soviet Union, and the researchers in Edinburgh were not the KGB, who had done God knows what to my grandfather back in the sixties, when they'd learned through his neighbours that he had . . . abilities.

What he had undergone in their intelligence program had been so traumatic he never had told us the details, but I'd felt the depth of his pain and concern as his eyes had met mine down the length of the table that morning. "Nicola," he'd said to me, "tear up that paper."

I'd done as he'd asked. But I hadn't forgotten. And then in my final year, when I'd come back from my term in St. Petersburg, I'd seen an ad in the paper for volunteers—anyone, just normal people, not psychics—to help take part in a new study the Emerson Institute was just beginning. No risk, I had thought. I could see what they did without ever revealing what I could do.

So I had answered the ad.

I cut those memories off, deliberately. At the edge of the green park I stood for a moment and gathered my courage, then drawing a steadying breath I crossed over the road and went in.

The receptionist was new, but the other woman standing with her back towards me, leaning on the tall reception counter, was no stranger.

Dr. Keary Fulton-Wallace wasn't psychic. She'd had no clue I'd be coming, and when she turned round her features plainly showed her surprise. I'd never known her age. I knew she'd told me once she had been a researcher for over twenty years, and so must be approaching fifty, but she had a youthful energy that made that seem impossible. She would have made a perfect Peter Pan, I thought, in pantomimes.

Tossing her bright cap of auburn hair out of her eyes, she recovered herself and smiled at me. "Nicola! How wonderful to see you." Just like that. As though the past two years had never happened.

I hovered. "I'm sorry, I ought to have rung first. Is this a good time?"

"Yes, of course. Come, let's sit in my office."

Her office still looked the same. Only the calendar over her desk had changed, no longer seascapes but views of a garden. She shifted a pile of papers from one of the chairs at the side of her desk. "Let me get us some tea. Do you still drink the green kind?"

The prodigal son must have felt like this, I thought—relieved and embarrassed and touched by the fuss being made.

"Nonsense," was her answer to my protests that she didn't need to wait on me. "You're very welcome company today, and I was just about to stop and take a break myself, at any rate."

She fetched the tea, and a half-plundered packet of Hobnobs, and settled in as though I were an old friend stopping by to chat. She'd made me feel just this relaxed and this welcome two years ago, when I had first ventured in, all uncertain, and she had explained what they did at the institute.

"Parapsychologists don't try to prove extrasensory perception exists," she'd said then. "We test hypotheses, like any other scientist, and our test results here have shown overall evidence that would support the hypothesis that ESP does exist. So we form more hypotheses, run more tests, try to find out—if it's actually there—how it works."

I'd taken part in two studies she'd led. The first one, where I'd hidden in among the normal people who had volunteered. And one more, after that.

"I had a question," I said now, "about the psychometry study."

"Oh, yes?"

The question made more sense, I reasoned, if I backtracked just a little and explained about my job now, and the fact I had a carving that I wanted to authenticate. "I thought I might try using my . . . I might just try psychometry, and see if that can lead me somewhere, help me find the proof of where it came from."

She thought that was a very good idea. "You know me. It's the practical applications of ESP that interest me the most. How can I help?"

"Well, to properly do this, I need to be able to zero in on one particular person who once owned the carving," I said, "and I thought I remembered you saying there might be a way to improve . . . to get better at doing that."

"You did rather well at it, as I recall."

"Did I?"

Lifting her brows at my tone, she said, "Nicola, you had the second-best scores in the study. Or you would have done, if you had . . ."

"If I had finished it."

"Yes." It was simply a statement of fact, with no judgement attached. "I could look up your actual scores, if you like. I still have them on file." With a swivel and roll of her chair she pulled open a drawer in her filing cabinet and drew out a folder, then opened it up on her desk and examined the papers inside. "Here it is," she said, passing it over.

I looked at the scores and I knew they weren't high enough. Not to do what I would need to do. My disappointment must have shown, because she reassured me with, "But it appears to be a skill that can improve with practice. Some of our subjects who started with scores rather lower than yours averaged nearly that high by the end of the study. You might have done better yourself, if . . ."

I said it again for her. "If I had stayed."

She'd never asked me why I hadn't, and I knew she wouldn't ask me now. Her scientific need to know was tempered with an empathy that seemed to make her understand my conflicts. "Never mind," she said. "You can practice it anywhere, really."

Except, I thought bleakly, I didn't have time. If I were to help Margaret Ross, I'd have to find a quick way to improve, or . . .

I gave a nod down at the file on her desk, and said, "I know you're not allowed to tell me how anyone else did, but can you just tell me . . . the highest score, was it . . . ?"

"Yes." Her lively green eyes plainly showed she knew *I* knew exactly whom she meant. "He scored direct hits, every time." She did give in a little, then, to curiosity. "Do you still see him?"

"No." It wasn't a lie, I decided. Not really. I didn't see him in the sense that she was asking me.

"Well." She defused the moment deftly with a smile. "I'm very glad you thought to come see *me*. Another biscuit?"

"Thanks, but no. I should be getting back up to the station."

"What time's your train?"

I wasn't altogether sure. I'd seen a couple of later Dundee trains listed up on the departures board at Waverly, so I knew that my odds of catching one of them were fairly good. But not wanting to let Dr. Fulton-Wallace know that I'd been so haphazard with my travel plans, I made up a time. "Six o'clock."

She stood with me. "It really was lovely to see you. I'm glad that you're doing so well down in London."

I thanked her and turned away, stopped at the door. And because I felt I owed it to her, I looked back. "I'm really sorry," I said, "that I didn't stay and finish what I started."

Her eyes were understanding. "It's never too late. Anytime you feel ready, come back and I'll finish your testing myself."

But she probably knew from my face that I wouldn't be back.

It was good to step out in the sunlight where lengthening shadows walked with me back up to the still-crowded pavement of Princes Street. It seemed a short walk back to Waverly station. The woman at the ticket window gave a dry nod as I showed her my ticket and told her, "I missed my connection."

"Aye, so you did. That train to Dundee left two hours ago." Squinting down at her schedule she told me, "I've one at 18:18 that'll get you there at 19:44. Would that suit you?"

I didn't answer straight away. My thoughts had slipped backwards to yesterday morning—the dim, shadowed room with its grey light that might have been filtered through clouds, or through rain, that I'd viewed through the eyes of a man waking up in his bed.

He'd scored perfectly, so Dr. Fulton-Wallace had said. Every time we'd been given an object and asked to zero in on just one person who had used it, he had done it. Every time.

I wavered.

Only for a moment. Then I roused myself and faced the waiting woman at the ticket window. "Actually, I've changed my mind." I put the Dundee ticket in my pocket, and breathed deeply before telling her, "I'd like to have a single, please, to Berwick-upon-Tweed."

chapter FOUR

Finding a taxi in Berwick was much easier than finding one in Edinburgh, and the driver who sped me the short distance northwards and over the border again into Scotland was a friendly man with tattoos and a thick Geordie accent, who'd spent his life working "off shore." Throughout the swift ten-minute drive, he kept the conversation going.

". . . and they have an accent all their own, do Eyemouth folk," he commented. "But likely you'll know that already from living there."

Not sure why he'd think that, I said, "I don't live in Eyemouth."

"No?" His eyebrows lifted slightly in surprise. "I've never known a woman yet to travel with no suitcases," he told me. "You're my first."

We'd reached the fringes of the town now, where elegant-looking Victorian homes perched on steeply banked tidy front gardens, with lights coming on to glow warmly in windows against the descent of the dark.

I closed my eyes a moment and reached outwards with my thoughts, a little hesitant from being out of practice. Not that it would matter, I felt sure. He was better at this than I was, his own thoughts so strong that unless he was actively blocking me, it would be like hearing somebody shouting at me in a room full of whisperers. And even if he blocked me I would "feel" the block—a solid wall of static.

I felt nothing. That might have discouraged me more had I not been aware of my limits. He might have been able to reach me in London, and do it without really trying, but I'd never managed that kind of a range.

I was trying again when the driver asked, "Where would you like me to drop you, then?"

I wasn't altogether sure. Where did one get dropped off in Eyemouth? I wondered. It wasn't a large place. On inspiration, I turned to him. "Do you know where the police station is?"

His eyebrows lifted higher but he gallantly said nothing, only took the necessary turns and stopped outside a cream-painted stucco house trimmed with red brick, that looked just like an ordinary house till I noticed the blue POLICE signs. The lights were on here, too, and my driver remarked, "You're in luck. It's not always manned."

And that was all he said about it, as though it was commonplace for him to drive young women with no suitcases to places where they didn't live, and drop them at police stations. I tipped him very generously.

The wind was fierce. It struck me full on as I climbed the few steps to the marked public entrance that bade me to PLEASE KNOCK AND ENTER. Inside, the small reception room was clean and warm, with nobody in sight behind the glassed-in service counter. I felt ridiculously nervous, so much so that when a friendly young constable came out from the back room to see what I wanted, I stumbled on the words. "I'm looking for a man." Then, as *his* eyebrows started to rise, I collected myself and explained, "A policeman. He works here, I think."

"Oh, aye?"

"Yes. Rob McMorran."

The constable's grin was good natured. "And why are you looking for him, then? I'm clearly the better man." But through the teasing I knew the first part of his question was valid, and needed an answer before he would help me. After all, for all he knew, I might be intending to lodge a complaint.

I smiled back, in an effort to show I was harmless. "I'm a friend of his."

"Oh, aye?" he asked me again. "Not a local one, though, or I'd surely have seen you."

I said, "I'm from London."

"From London? A long way to travel to visit a friend. Did he ken you were coming?"

I shook my head. "That's why I'm trying to find him."

The constable studied me closely a moment, then seeming to reach a decision he picked up the phone. "He's not working the day, but I'll see if I can't hunt him down for you."

"Thank you."

I waited.

The first number he dialled got no answer. "He's not got his mobile. I'll just try the flat." When that didn't work either, he frowned for a moment, then tried a third number, growing so purposely charming that I guessed it was a woman he was talking to. After exchanging a quick bit of banter that I couldn't follow because of the accent, he said, "I've a lady from London here with me who's wanting to find Robbie Keenan. Would ye ken where he might be?"

"It's McMorran," I corrected him. "Rob McMorran."

He gave a nod to reassure me as he listened, then he thanked the woman and rang off. "He's on a shout the now," he told me, "with the lifeboat, but Sheena says they're on their way back in, they'll not be long, and if you've a mind to go down to the Sole she can give you a meal while you're waiting."

I absorbed all this as best I could. "The Sole?"

"Aye, the Contented Sole, down by the harbour. Just go down this road here, the Coldingham Road. There's a church at the bottom. You keep to the left, it'll take you right down to the harbour. The Sole's at the far end of that, you'll not miss it."

"Thank you."

"No problem. A word of advice, though," he said as I started to leave, "when you go into the Sole don't use the same first line you used with me, and tell them that you're looking for a man." He flashed the friendly grin and said, "You'll not get out again."

I didn't actually see that many men about, when I reached the harbour.

Narrow and long, it still looked to be a working harbour, with several small fishing boats moored at the walls, but I remembered Rob telling me once that the fishing was done, or as good as; that government quotas and standards had killed off the whole way of life, and his father had sold his own boat to a big corporation and bought a much smaller boat so he could go for the lobster and crab, like the rest of the few men who'd clung to their trade here.

The seagulls had not given up, though. They wheeled and shrieked everywhere, hopeful, although at this hour of the night with the dark coming on there were probably no scraps around for them.

Even the long covered building that must once have been the fish market had found a new purpose as part of a Maritime Centre that loomed overhead at the edge of the harbour and had been designed to look like an old seagoing frigate.

I passed a white pub with a sign that proclaimed it the Ship Hotel, and at the door of the public bar two men *did* turn from their talk to regard me with curious interest as I walked by, but I carried on briskly a few buildings farther until I caught sight of the Contented Sole.

It looked much like the other pub—plain and pale walled, standing square at the edge of the dark road with space for a few cars to park at the front, its windows spilling warmly yellow light across the pavement at the water's edge.

I'd nearly reached it when I saw a boat slip boldly through the breakwater that stood against the sea. About the same size as the fishing boats, this one was dark on the bottom but painted bright orange above and marked with the distinctive emblem of the Royal National Lifeboat Institute. More gulls had come in with it, fighting the wind as they cried their displeasure at not being fed, but the crewman who stood by the rail in the bow took no notice. Wearing his bright yellow kit with a full life-vest harness strapped round it, he was readying the mooring rope, it looked like, as the lifeboat started turning to reverse into its berth along the harbour's far side.

I stopped walking. The wind blew my hair briefly into my eyes and then whipped it away again, stinging, but I didn't move.

The crewman stopped, too, with his back to me. Angled his head very slightly, as though he'd just heard someone calling his name. And then he looked straight back and over his shoulder, directly at me.

"Hi," he said. He didn't say the word out loud—there wasn't any way I would have heard him at that distance—but his voice still resonated clearly in my mind, as though he'd spoken. It's a hard thing to explain to anyone who's never carried on a conversation that way, but for me it came as naturally as breathing. It was how my grandfather had realized I'd inherited his "gift," when at the age of three I'd answered him at table, "When I'm sleeping," and my mother, glancing up, had smiled and asked me what I meant by that, to which I had replied, "Granddad asked me if I ever would stop talking." I could still see their exchange of glances; still recall the silence that had followed.

Now I met Rob's gaze across the harbour. *Hi.*

I've got to finish up here. Can you wait?

Yes.

He sent me an image of warmly lit comfort, a cozy room with pale green walls and polished dark wood tables. *Upstairs,* he told me.

I nodded. *I'll get us a table.*

Thanks. Turning away with the rope in his hand he went back to the business of bringing the lifeboat in, and I uprooted myself from the pavement and walked the few steps to the door of the Contented Sole.

Inside, I had to climb a flight of stairs to reach the dining lounge, but I didn't need to see the pale green walls or dark wood furniture to know that I was in the right place. This room already felt familiar, from the glimpse of it he'd given me. I knew there'd be a tartan carpet woven in deep blues and greens, and flowers on the tables, and a deep-set window looking out towards the harbour, flanked by high-backed benches that formed cozy-looking alcoves in the corners.

I sat in the nearest alcove, drawing a few curious glances from the people eating at the other tables—a middle-aged couple, three elderly men, and a young mother keeping her eye on two toddlers.

The waitress came over and shot me a friendly smile, setting two menus down. "Heyah. You've just come from the police, then, have you?" The curious glances intensified as she went on, without needing an answer, "The lifeboat's just come in, he'll not be long. He always comes in for his supper Fridays. Can I get you a wee drink while you're waiting?"

A drink suddenly sounded like a very good idea. "Can I have a dry white wine, please?"

The wine helped. It went straight to my head and relaxed me, so that I was feeling remarkably calm by the time I heard the footsteps coming up the stairs.

I'd rehearsed this scene, with variations, all the way from Edinburgh, perfecting my dialogue based on the things I felt sure he would ask me, but all of that went out the window the minute he took the seat opposite, leaning back easily into the bench as though these past two years hadn't happened. In that heartbeat as I looked across at him, I could have made myself believe they hadn't.

He looked just the same, with his almost too-perfect face. When I'd first met him I'd thought he looked French from his bone structure—straight nose and boldly drawn eyebrows and deep-set blue eyes, and that sensual mouth that could suddenly change from its serious line to a quick boyish smile more in keeping with the black unruly hair that always flopped onto his forehead. At the moment his hair was damp, trying to curl at the ends. In a gesture I remembered well he pushed it back and nodded at my drink. "You want another one of those?"

"Please."

"Right."

He didn't need to call the waitress over. She had seen him coming in and was beside us in an instant. "So you've found each other, then."

"We have, aye. Sheena, this is Nicola."

She gave a nod of greeting and assured him we'd already met. "George sent her from the police station. I'd just heard it on the radio that you were on your way back in. Everyone all right, then?"

"Aye. It was fairly straightforward, a couple of fishermen taking on water. We gave them a tow back to Burnmouth."

"Better than Tuesday's shout," Sheena agreed. Then, to keep me included, she told me, "A couple of tourists capsized off St. Abbs, Tuesday morning. The woman was nearly done in when the lifeboat arrived, and she'd have likely drowned if not for Keenan, here. He'd seen it already, up here," she said, tapping her temple, "and he'd telt the coxswain who did a phone round so the crew were all kitted up and on their way in the lifeboat afore the call even came in." She winked at me. "He likely kent that you were coming, too. That's why he's dressed so nice."

He said to her, drily, "There are other places to eat in Eyemouth. I could take her to the Ship . . ."

But Sheena only grinned and told him, "Never. Did you want a pint of Deuchars?"

"If you think that you can manage it. And one more glass of wine, please."

As I listened to their easy-going banter, I was trying to imagine how incredible it must feel to be living in a place where everybody knew—and from the sound of it, accepted—that you saw things that they couldn't see. Small wonder Rob McMorran was so well-adjusted.

And he *was* dressed nicely, now I noticed it. His fine knitted jumper of deep navy blue looked like cashmere, and followed the breadth of his shoulders and chest in a way that looked tailored without being tight. He kept his head bent as he studied the menu, but from the quick glance that he gave me I halfway suspected he'd noticed me noticing, so I looked down myself, reading the menu without really seeing it, trying to summon up small talk.

I could start by asking why everyone here called him Keenan, I thought.

"It's no Keenan," he answered my unspoken question without looking up. "It's 'Keen-Een'—keen eyes—from my having the Sight, ye ken."

"Oh. So it's a nickname."

"My bye-name, aye. Sort of tradition in Eyemouth, it helps sort us out. In a small place like this with so many old families it's nothing to find a few men with the same name—a few David Dougals, say—so we use bye-names to tell them apart."

"And how many Rob McMorrans are there here in Eyemouth?"

"Only me." He looked up then. "But I got my bye-name from some of my dad's friends the summer I went to the fishing with them, when I turned twelve, and it's stuck." His blue eyes smiled the way that I remembered. "Go ahead."

I hadn't noticed that the waitress had returned, but now I turned to her and ordered. "Can I have the chicken curry, please, with rice?"

"No problem. Keen-Een?"

"Make it two. With chips for mine." He thanked her as she took the menus from us, then he raised the pint of dark ale that she'd brought him as he settled back and faced me as before. "So."

Breathing deep, I echoed, "So. It's good to see you, Rob."

"It's good to see you, too."

"I'm really sorry—"

"There's no need," he cut me off, and took a drink before continuing, "I told you at the time I understood your reasons. I still do."

He very likely understood them better than I did myself, I thought. I cleared my throat and said, "I've been to Edinburgh this afternoon."

Whatever else he knew, it was apparent that he hadn't known that, because he lifted his one eyebrow in the way he always had when I'd surprised him. "Oh, aye?"

"Yes. I went to visit Dr. Fulton-Wallace."

When I hesitated, not quite sure how to proceed from there, he sent me a lopsided smile. "Is this a twelve-step program that you're on then? Making peace with all the people from your past?"

His tone was teasing, but I shook my head with an unnecessary force. "No, it isn't. I . . ." I faltered, not sure how to ask this question.

Rob said, "Of course I will."

"Will what?"

"Come with you to Dundee."

There was no need for him to ask if that was what I'd wanted; I had always been an open book for him to read. Too bad it didn't work the other way around, I thought. I tried to read him now, and met a stubborn wall of static as his blue gaze levelled calmly on my own.

I took a long drink of my wine. "I suppose that you already know all the details."

"No," he said, "but you've had a long day, it'll keep. I've the day off tomorrow, we'll drive to Dundee in the morning, and on the way up you can tell me the whole story. Suit you?"

It suited me fine, and I said so. "Rob?"

"Aye?"

"I am sorry."

The warmth of reassurance wrapped around me like a hug, so nearly physical I couldn't quite believe he hadn't moved. He looked away. "I ken fine how you feel," he said, and moved his pint of ale aside to make room for the plates as Sheena brought our meals.

When Sheena brought the final bill she set it on the table so it was beyond my reach and said, "You see that Keen-Een pays that now, when you've come all this way to visit. Where's he disappeared to?"

"He thinks he left his mobile at the lifeboat station," I explained. "He's gone across to look."

She smiled. "I'm that surprised he disnae keep a room there. He was all about the lifeboat from the time we were at school. If they'd not let him join the crew we'd all have raised a protest, for there would have been no living with him."

I didn't know too much about the running of the lifeboats. "It's a volunteer thing, isn't it?"

"The lifeboat? Aye, they do it for the love of it, or from the wish to help. It isnae everyone could wear that beeper, let themselves be dragged away from anything and everything, and wakened at all hours. Myself, I'd never last a week."

I doubted I would, either. I didn't know how Rob could find the energy to serve as a policeman and be at the lifeboat's beck and call as well, but Sheena, when I said as much to her, advised me, "Never let him fool you into thinking that he's calm, it's all an act." Her tone was certain. "I've kent Keen-Een all my life, and I can tell you that it isnae in his nature to sit still, he's only taught himself the trick of it."

He certainly looked calm enough when he came back, his gaze shifting indulgently from my face to Sheena's as she asked, "Found your mobile then, did you?"

"Aye." Rob, without sitting, reached down for the bill. "If you've finished telling her my shortcomings," he said to Sheena, "we're away."

"Och, Keen-Een, it would take more time than this to tell her everything." The waitress went off with a wink and a smile. "Have a good night, the pair of you."

Thanking her, Rob took his wallet out, put down enough for the bill and a generous tip, and then tucking the wallet away, looked at me as I stood. "D'ye not have a jacket?"

I shook my head. "I didn't really think . . . I mean, it's August, and it's warmer down in London, and I didn't . . ." I was babbling again. I stopped myself and started over, more coherently. "This trip was a last-minute thing. I didn't plan ahead."

Rob hid a smile. "A first for you, then." Shrugging off his own dark blue windcheater, he held it for me. "Here, put this on."

The coat was lined with thermal fleece that felt blanket-soft on my bare forearms, and when I stepped from the cheerful pub to the dark pavement outdoors I was grateful for both the coat's warmth and the sheltering windbreak of Rob at my back. He didn't crowd me, didn't touch me, but I felt the force of his protection all the same.

Even though it was properly dark now, the cold wind roughening the water of the harbour so whatever light was coming from the fishing boats and those few windows on the black hill opposite reflected only briefly in a thousand scattered fragments that were swiftly doused in blackness, still the harbour was alive with people out to find their fun on a Friday night. As Rob shepherded me past the Ship Hotel, a trio of men stumbled out of the door to the public bar, where they'd apparently been for a while from the look of them, and from the loudness of their voices, cursing cheerfully and often.

One man staggered into Rob and let loose with an expletive before he noticed who he'd just bumped into.

Rob said, "Heyah, Jimmy."

The man, less belligerent, gave a nod. "Keen-Een."

Rob looked at the man's mates and said, "You'll be helping him home, will you?"

"Aye," said the nearest man, dragging his friend back. "We're gaun hame the now."

"See that you don't wander off into Armatage Street," he advised them. "I've been on a shout with the lifeboat the day, I'm fair jiggered, and getting called out to a housebreaking widnae improve my mood any."

The nearest man stared at him hard for a moment, and then his mouth twisted into something approaching a grin. "All right, Keen-Een. We're gaun hame, as I said." And he herded his friends away, all of them walking unsteadily.

Watching them, I asked Rob, "Will they go home, do you think?"

"Oh, aye. It spoils their fun," he told me, "when they ken I ken they're at it."

I imagined that the crime rate here in Eyemouth had gone down since Rob McMorran joined the force. Whereas I only "saw" things when I held an object, Rob's own gifts were greater than that, as I'd learnt in the short time I'd known him. He read people's minds with astonishing ease.

I remembered that talent now, trying to keep my own thoughts in control as I asked, "Do you live very far from here?"

"Not far at all." He nodded to a block of flats scarcely a stone's throw away. "I'm just there, Chapel Quay, but it's only a bedsit, and you'll get no sleep with my snoring."

His tone was normal, but I felt the line that he was drawing in between us, whether from his own desire to keep me at a distance, or to show me that he understood my coming back for help meant only that, and nothing more.

"I see. So then where . . . ?"

"You'll find more comfort out at the cottage."

"The cottage?"

My mind filled with images, swirling, receding—the brightness and warmth of a low-ceilinged kitchen, the edge of a lace curtain brushing the white-painted sill of a deeply set window with one cracked glass pane, a succession of snapshots so rapid and fleeting I couldn't catch all of them, blending to one strong impression of *home*.

Rob said, "I've rung my mother, let her know you're coming. You can sleep in my old room."

That seemed even more personal, somehow, than spending the night at his bedsit. "Won't your mother mind having a guest to look after?"

"My mother? She's probably baking something as we speak. She loves company." Stopping at a navy blue Ford Focus in the car park, he opened the passenger door for me. "It's my father you'll want to be keeping an eye on. He's aye had a liking for blondes."

It was only a short drive, not more than a mile or two out of town on a narrow road banked at each side with wild hedges that grew in the low, twisted way that things did near the coast where the salt wind was constantly beating them down. I could see the black tangle of trees to the left, and the dark rise of hills to my right, and a few scattered houses set back from the road as though wanting seclusion.

The cottage, though, sat at the road's very edge, spilling welcoming light from its windows. Rob turned in beside it and parked at the foot of a long private drive winding up through tall trees to a larger dark house on the hillside above. "Rosehill House," he supplied, when he noticed my interest. "The owners are away on holiday, just at the moment. My granddad was their groundskeeper, afore he retired, and my mother keeps house for them, off and on."

I was looking out my window past the line of trees that edged the low stone wall beside my door when Rob came round to help me out. I frowned. "That field . . ."

". . . was once a Roman battleground," he said with understanding.

Which explained the faint uneasiness I felt as I stepped out and stood, my gaze fixed on the night-black field that stretched beyond the wall. I almost heard the battle cries still hanging on the wind, the clash of swords, the frenzied galloping of horses' hooves that passed by in a rush and drowned the sound of marching feet . . . except for one lone set of measured footsteps, coming down the graveled drive towards us.

I couldn't help the tiny chill that chased between my shoulder blades, but when I turned to look I only saw a friendly border collie, black and white with one ear perked and one flopped over, long tail wagging as it trotted up to say hello.

Rob bent to give the ears a scratch. "Good boy. Come meet Nicola."

I loved dogs. "What's his name?"

"Jings." He smiled. "In Scots, that's what you say when you're surprised, like, and when this one was a pup he was forever underfoot, and my mother was aye tripping over him and saying, 'Jings!' until he thought that was his name, so we just called him that. We couldn't call him what my granddad said when *he* tripped over him."

I shared his smile and turned my collar up against the chill that brushed my neck as I bent down to pat the dog myself. I might have been mistaken when I thought I saw Rob give a nod of greeting to the empty air behind me. But I didn't mistake the short laugh he gave, low, nor the phrase he spoke, not for my ears. And in Latin.

I understood, then. I looked up, but the footsteps had started again, moving off and away from us, into the field. I gave Jings's head one last pat, straightening. "Friend of yours?"

Rob looked where the footsteps had gone. "Aye, a very old friend."

"Can you actually see him?"

He nodded.

I tried to imagine what that would be like, to be able to see ghosts. Converse with them. "He's one of the Romans, I take it?"

"Their sentinel, aye. Keeping watch, still."

A lonely thing, keeping watch over an empty field, night after night through the centuries. Having someone who could see him, as Rob could, must be a relief. I covered up my sudden ache of sympathy by asking, "And does he like blondes, as well?"

Rob laughed. I had forgotten just how great a laugh he had. "No, he prefers dark-haired women. You've nothing to fear from the Sentinel, Nicola."

Rob's father, though, was a charmer. He greeted me as we came through the low doorway and into the warmth of the kitchen, his accent betraying his Newcastle origins, more north-of-England than Scottish. He might have been anywhere from his mid-forties to late fifties, I couldn't tell. While his hair was a silvery grey, he was muscled and fit and the lines round his eyes seemed to come more from smiling than age. He was smiling now, white teeth flashing against his tanned skin as he said, "So you're Nicola, are you?"

I couldn't see any resemblance to Rob in his features, but he tipped his head sideways the same way that Rob often did and I caught the gold glint of a small hoop in one ear that gave him the look of a cut-throat, as did the tattoos snaking over the strong forearms showing beneath the rolled sleeves of his shirt.

He said, "Robbie was saying you came up from London?"

"I did, yes."

Before he could ask me more questions, Rob cut in with, "Where's Mum?"

"Making the bed up," his father replied.

I felt guilty. "I'm sorry to be such a bother."

His laugh was like Rob's, too. "You don't know my Jeannie. She lives for this, eh, Robbie? She's got biscuits in the oven and all."

Rob glanced down at me with an "I-told-you-so" look, and pulled one of the chairs at the old kitchen table out so I could sit.

I got feelings from rooms, sometimes, and the warmth in this one came from more than just the Rayburn cooker wafting strong spice-and-ginger scents into the air. There was love here—not perfect, but strong, and a kind of a peace that came with it and helped me relax as I sat, with the collie, Jings, settling under the table and coiling his warm body close by my feet.

Rob sat, too, taking a chair at one end of the table and rocking it back on two legs till his shoulders were propped on the wall behind.

"Don't let your mother catch you doing that," his father warned, good natured, as he crossed to switch the kettle on. "So, Nicola, where did you meet my son?"

Rob exhaled, weary. "Dad."

"I'm only asking."

Slipping off my borrowed coat, I hung it on the chair back and said, "Edinburgh."

Rob's father turned, with interest. "Oh, aye? When was this?"

"Two years ago."

"Two years ago?" His interest seemed to sharpen as he looked at Rob. "When you were at the uni doing all those tests?"

The look that Rob sent back to him was plainly meant to kill the topic, and his father shrugged and turned away again, returning to his role as host. "Will you have tea or coffee, Nicola?"

"I'd love a cup of tea, please."

His father's smile when he glanced round looked curiously pleased, and it was only when I saw Rob bring his own head round to look at me that I became aware of what had happened.

Rob's father's eyes met mine and though he didn't move his lips I heard his voice say, *Interesting.*

Even as I blocked him in surprise, he grinned and turned to Rob and said, aloud this time, "That's very interesting. Keeping it a secret, were you?"

Rob's expression didn't change, but from his eyes I guessed that he was saying something choice in private to his dad.

"All right, all right." The older man held one hand up, amused still, but apologizing. "No offence."

I sensed that Rob was trying to say something to me, too, but I had blocked them both out, still unsettled by the unexpected contact. Not once had it occurred to me that Rob might have inherited his psychic talents, as I had my own. I viewed his father with new eyes as he glanced back at Rob with an expression half resigned and half impatient, as though he were being lectured.

And he very likely was, if Rob's slight frown was anything to go by. Still, I felt the strong affection binding one man to the other, too—a deep affection that would not be shaken by small differences.

The kettle boiled. Rob's father made the tea, and said aloud, as though repeating something he'd been told to say, "I'm sorry, Nicola. I won't do that again, I promise."

Setting my tea on the table in front of me as a peace offering, he gave me a swift charming smile as Rob's mother, just coming in, asked, "Won't do what again?"

She was a lovely looking woman, feminine and small but with an air of capability. Her soft cheerful face seemed more freckled than lined and the highlights of grey in her chestnut hair might have been done for artistic effect by a stylist, they looked so attractive. But it was her smile that I noticed the most, it was so like her son's.

She came over to welcome me, toning her rich accent down in the way many Scots did when speaking to outsiders. "Nicola, is it? I'm Jeannie. We're so glad to have you. Now, what has my Brian been doing to bother you?"

Both the men had adjusted themselves to her presence. Rob quietly brought his chair back from its tilted position to rest in the proper way, with all four legs on the floor, while his father, too, made an attempt to look innocent.

I said, "Nothing at all. He's just made me some tea."

Her eyes danced. "Never defend him, you'll only encourage him."

Rob's father grinned. "Robbie's brought home a bird of a feather," he told his wife plainly. "He met her while doing those tests up at Edinburgh. I did a test of my own, that's all. Reckon I gave her a bit of a shock. And your son," he informed her, "has already torn me a new one, there's no need for you to do likewise."

Rob, at the end of the table, said quietly, "Nicola doesn't like using her gifts. Or discussing them."

"Well then," his mother remarked, "enough said." And she cheerfully shifted her husband aside on her way to the Rayburn. "Now, who'll have a biscuit?"

I could tell, before another half an hour had passed, just who was at the heart of the McMorran family. For all the affection I'd felt between Rob and his father, I sensed that what bound them together most strongly was Jeannie McMorran herself, with her quick easy laugh and her genuine warmth.

I'd have had to have been carved of stone not to like her.

And she made amazing ginger biscuits. Rob ate four of them, but even with all of that sugar and coffee to bolster his system he wasn't a match for the after effects of his time on the lifeboat, and what must have been a long day. When he yawned for a third time, his mother said, "Och, away home with ye, Robbie. You're dead on your feet."

"I am not."

"Away home, or I'm fetching the pictures of you as a bairn to show Nicola. I've got those good ones of you in the bath . . ."

Rob conceded defeat with a grin. "Right, I'll go." He stood, stretching, and said to me, "Don't let them push you around. I'll be back to collect you at eight."

"All right."

"Eight in the morning?" his mother asked. "Never. Let her waken when she wishes, and I'll give you a phone when she's finished her breakfast."

Rob knew better than to argue, from the look of it. Instead he bent his head and took an interest in his wristwatch. I walked with him to the door.

"You'll need your coat," I said, lifting it from the back of my chair to give to him.

He took it with a question in his eyes. *All right?*

His father was watching us. I gave a nod.

Rob unbuckled his watch strap and passed me the watch. *The alarm's set for seven.* He smiled and stepped out, letting cold in behind him.

Then Jeannie McMorran was there, spreading warmth. "You must be needing your sleep as well, after your travels. Come, let's get you settled."

The cottage was not large—the kitchen, a sitting room with a piano, and two bedrooms, one with the door standing open and welcoming. Rob's mother told me, "The bathroom's down there, at the end. Take as long as you like, we've a lovely deep tub if you're wanting a bath, and I've found you a pair of pajamas."

She'd done more than that. In the bathroom, I found a thick stack of soft towels, and new soap and lavender bath salts, a hair drier, toothbrush and toothpaste, all laid out with no questions asked, as though having young women show up on the doorstep with only the clothes on their back were an everyday thing here.

I took the advice of Rob's mother and ran a hot bath and sank into it gratefully, letting it soothe away some of my swirling, confusing thoughts. Rob was a part of the life I'd deliberately put in my past, and I had the irrational sense that it should have been somehow more difficult, this reconnection.

It seemed half surreal to be here in this house he'd grown up in, with his mum and dad drinking tea in the kitchen, and everyone simply accepting my presence as easily as they accepted the things I could do, things my own family virtually never discussed, or acknowledged. It had me off balance, a feeling that lingered long after the bathwater cooled.

When I finally ventured back along the passageway and into the bedroom that I was to sleep in, I found Rob's mum setting a water glass down at the bedside. She turned as I came in, and smiled.

"Those pajamas all right for you, then?"

I assured her they were. They were navy-blue flannel, a little too large, and too long in the legs and the sleeves, but I'd rolled up the cuffs.

"They were Robbie's," she told me, "when he was a teenager."

He must have had the shoulders even then, because they hung from mine with loads of room to spare. I felt a sudden urge to hug the flannel to my skin, but I resisted it and simply said, "They're comfortable."

"Oh aye, they were his favourites," Jeannie said. "I had a mind to make a quilt of them someday, ye ken, with some of his old T-shirts. Someone did that in a magazine I read once at the doctor's, that's what gave me the idea. But I've never yet got round to it."

A good thing, I decided. They were very warm pajamas.

And this room that she'd prepared for me was obviously Rob's old room. Not kept the way it would have been when he was living here, of course. They'd used one corner of the room for storage—there were boxes neatly piled along the wall, and stacks of clothes that wanted sorting. And a sewing machine, bright and purposeful, held court across from the bed on a large sturdy table with patterns and fabric scraps tidily organized down its long surface.

The bed, though, was still a boy's bed, with a bookcase built into the headboard and brown-and-white ships sailing over the coverlet. He would have taken all his treasures with him when he left, but there were still a few framed photographs of Rob at different ages smiling from the bookcase shelf. One was a formal police portrait of him in uniform, smart in his jacket and cap, deadly serious but for his eyes. There was one showing him and his father in front of a red-painted fishing boat, standing near its moorings in the full sun of the harbour.

"That's the *Fleetwing*," said Jeannie, when she saw me looking. "That was Brian's boat. And that," she added, nodding at the photograph beside it, "is what Robbie looked like as a lad."

He'd have been about eight, when the picture was taken. All elbows and knees, with a bright smile and freckles and big blue inquisitive eyes, kneeling down with his arm round a black-and-white collie with one ear flopped over.

I leaned in more closely. "That looks just like Jings."

"Aye, that's Kip. Jings's great-granddad. He was like Robbie's wee shadow, was Kip, always followed him everywhere. They couldn't bear to be parted. We buried him out in the field, when he passed. Robbie thought he'd be company for—"

She had caught the words, glancing at me as though wondering how much I knew, so I finished the thought for her.

"Rob's Roman ghost?"

"Aye, the Sentinel. He's introduced you, then?"

"Well, in a way." To her curious look I explained, "I can't see ghosts. I feel them sometimes, but I don't see or hear them. I'm not quite as . . . gifted as Rob."

Jeannie smiled at me. "Neither," she said, "is my Brian, so whatever mischief he got up to earlier, likely that's all he can do. If he tries it again, you've my blessing to belt him with something, all right?" Looking round, she inspected the room one last time and asked, "Now, d'ye have all you need? Right, then give me your clothes and I'll just bung them into the washer."

Like Rob, I could tell there'd be no point in protesting, so I complied. But I rescued Rob's watch from my jeans pocket first, and when Jeannie had left me I propped the watch up like a clock on the shelf of the headboard so that I would hear the alarm in the morning.

I hadn't really looked at it too closely until now, that watch, but suddenly it struck me that it looked just like the watch that I had given him two years ago—only that watch had just been a joke gift, a throwaway, bought off the counter at Boots when he'd turned up late one time too often. I'd said to him, "There, now you have no excuse," and he'd laughed as he put it on.

Surely he wouldn't have kept it, a cheap watch like that? He'd have chucked it away when the battery died, when the plastic strap broke. But it *did* look the same.

I picked it up, feeling the weight of the watch strap of durable leather, and folding my fingers around it I closed my eyes, seeking not a vision, but a memory.

chapter SIX

I remembered it was early in the evening. I'd been standing at the counter of the Boots on Princes Street, with my collection of small purchases: some nail varnish remover pads, a hair-slide and a toothbrush, and the watch. I'd found it last of all, that watch, reduced to ?4.99, and with a smile I'd picked it up.

He didn't own a watch. He used his mobile to tell time with when he thought of it, and since he rarely thought of it he usually was late. He was late now—that was why I'd come in here to kill some time while I was waiting. In the weeks that I'd been seeing Rob, I'd learned there was no need to wait in full view on the pavement. He would find me when he did arrive, and I would know the moment that he did. I'd feel that sudden tingle of awareness, as I felt it now.

I turned, and thought again that I would never tire of watching him approach like this: his easy stride, his boyish smile, his blue eyes warm and seeming to see only me. His voice as well, that deep Scots lilt, was something that I'd happily have listened to all day. He said, "I'm sorry to be late."

"What was it this time?"

"Inattention. I was reading."

"Well, there," I said, and handed him the newly purchased watch. "Now you have no excuse. It has an alarm you can set, see the button?"

He laughed as he took it and put it on, buckling the cheap plastic strap with one hand. "Thanks. That may be the best gift a girl's ever given me."

"Get them a lot do you, presents from girls?"

With a serious face he assured me, "Oh aye. It's continual." But those incredible eyes told me differently. He glanced at the items I held in my hands. "D'ye have everything you need, then?"

I had everything I needed in the fullest sense, but all I did was nod and Rob said, "Right, we should be on our way. We don't want to keep Dr. Fulton-Wallace waiting."

I rolled my eyes at him. "So it's all right to keep me waiting, is it, but not her?"

"I've no idea what you're on about." He raised his wrist and turned it so that I could read the digital display. "Can you not see the time?"

I called him something rude, then, and he grinned and caught my hand in his and out we went together to the street where the day's rain had finally dwindled to a windblown spray that made the pavement gleam beneath the lights just coming on against the gloom of a mid-January evening.

My hand in Rob's felt warm. I'd been so hesitant at first to let him touch me. I'd been nervous, given how intensely we'd connected without any touch at all the first time we'd been thrown together, without even being in the same room, for all that.

I'd been nervous then, as well. My very first week in the study at the Emerson Institute, and I'd been sitting in a soundproof room, reclining in a soft upholstered chair while Dr. Fulton-Wallace gently taped halved Ping-Pong balls across my open eyes to mask my normal sense of sight.

The test, she'd reassured me, was a simple one. The "ganzfeld," she had called it, was a traditional procedure meant to test whether my mind could "see" an image sent to me remotely by a person in another room. That person, whom I'd never met, was sitting somewhere else within the institute and similarly soundproofed, though with eyes and ears left open and aware.

The test's design was basic. In that other room, the isolated "sender" would be shown a video clip that a computer had chosen at random, and for half an hour he or she would sit and concentrate on watching that, while in my own room I remained immersed in my state of partial sensory deprivation, with headphones playing me filtered white noise—known as pink noise—and a red light shining down at my face to produce an unvarying glow through the translucent Ping-Pong balls. All that I needed to do, in that time, was to talk—make a running report of whatever I felt, and whatever I saw. At the end, I'd be given four video clips to watch, and I'd be asked to rate and rank each on how closely it matched what I'd "seen" in the ganzfeld procedure.

Dr. Fulton-Wallace, ready with my headphones, had said, "There's no need to worry. You'll do fine. We're not testing you, really. This study is meant to explore what the sender does. There's been a lot of debate and discussion within the field about the role of the sender, and whether a sender is needed at all, so we're hoping our study will add something useful to that. Are you comfortable?"

Surprisingly, I was, despite the nervousness.

"All right, then," she had told me. "I'll leave you to it. You'll hear some taped suggestions on the headphones first, to help you to relax, and then the pink noise will begin. Just try to verbalize whatever you're experiencing."

My grandfather's warnings had swirled in my thoughts only briefly before I had pushed them aside as I'd settled myself in the chair and deliberately opened my mind to whatever might come.

The image had, in the end, risen as clear as a painting: a view of a bench by a pond in a park, with a pair of swans sailing serenely along in the shallows beneath a great willow whose branches wept down in a gentle cascade of pale green.

I did as instructed, and talked about what I was seeing, describing the park and the swans. When a young boy appeared with a toy boat in hand, I described him as well, and said what he was doing.

This went on for some time. The boy was just setting his sailboat adrift on the pond when a curious thing began happening all round the image's edges. They started to shrink inward, as though I'd taken a step back, and they went on shrinking until I saw not just the image, but the screen it was appearing on, and behind that a wall much like the wall of the room I was now in myself. As my view tilted slightly a few strands of hair blocked the edge of my eye and a hand that was not my own hand brushed them back and a voice—a male voice that I'd never heard—greeted me.

Hi.

I felt his awareness, his trace of amusement, but having never found myself in anybody's head before I wasn't sure of the correct response.

I'm Rob, he said. *You're new here?*

This time I replied, a little hesitant, and told him, *Yes.*

The sailboat was still drifting on the screen, but my view angled sharply down instead, away from it, and I found myself looking the length of a plain black shirt buttoned across a flat male stomach, a simple black belt and, stretched casually out in the chair below that, lean athletic legs covered in snug-fitting denim, and the scuffed and rounded toes of black Doc Martens.

His hands were laced, relaxed, across his stomach, and I saw the gold glint of a signet ring, a small one, on his right hand's little finger. They were nice hands, square and capable. Nice legs, too, come to that.

My view came up again and focused on the little sailboat and the willow and the swans. He told me, *You be sure now to tell Dr. Fulton-Wallace what I'm wearing.*

And with that, he very gently pushed me out again.

I don't know what I looked like when they finished with the test, untaped my eyes, and took the headphones off, but Dr. Fulton-Wallace seemed concerned. "I thought you might have felt unwell," she said, "when you stopped talking."

I reassured her I was fine. A little stunned, perhaps, and strangely tired from such a minor effort, but I dutifully told her, "I'm supposed to tell you what he's wearing."

She paused in the middle of tidily winding the cords of the headphones. "I'm sorry? What who's wearing?"

"Rob. The man in the other room."

Setting the headphones down, she exchanged a quick glance with her assistant before giving me her full attention, warily. "What is he wearing?"

I described the clothes I'd seen and finished with the signet ring. She jotted all the details down, then taking out her mobile dialled a number. "George? It's Keary, here. Who are you using at your end, today? Oh, right. And what's he wearing?" Here she paused, and briefly smiled at her associate's reply. "Yes, that's very funny, but my interest is professional. Just tell me what he's wearing."

As she listened, I could see her smile give way to incredulity. She said, "Do me a favour, take a picture of him, will you? Yes, again, very funny. Just please take the picture? Thanks."

Shaking her head she rang off, but the tone in her voice was admiring. "The devil," she said.

It would be two more weeks before I met Rob face-to-face, both of us in the same room. I'd been heading down south for a weekend at home, and not ten minutes after we'd pulled out of Waverly Station my train unexpectedly stopped.

In the midst of the murmured confusion that followed, the elderly woman who'd taken the window seat next to me glanced out the window and said, "Oh, I do hope there's not been an accident."

I'd reassured her, "It's probably nothing."

"Debris on the line," said the young man just over the aisle from us, his quiet voice certain. "We'll not be here long."

It surprised me that I hadn't noticed him earlier. I usually didn't miss noticing good-looking men. And on top of it all, he'd been reading a book, and a man doing that didn't often escape my attention.

He sent us a friendly look, lifted his book and went on reading. *The Dead Zone* by Stephen King. I felt my mouth curve. The story of a man who has the curse of seeing visions of the future life of anyone he touches. Rather the reverse of my own curse, but I could sympathize.

The young man reading seemed to like it well enough. He looked absorbed, his dark head bent so that one wave of hair fell just beside his eye, his jeans-clad legs stretched out as much as possible in that cramped space, one foot edged slightly out into the aisle. He was wearing black Doc Martens, and on seeing them my first unguarded thought was, *Oh God, wouldn't it be great if* he *was Rob.*

The thought just hung there for a moment, then incredibly he raised his head and looked at me and grinned, and I turned twenty shades of red.

"I'm Rob McMorran," he said, lowering the book again and holding his place with his thumb while he held out his right hand, the hand with the narrow gold signet ring on the last finger.

I slammed my defences in place before braving the handshake, and kept it brief. "Nicola Marter."

And that was the start of it. By the time the train got under way again I'd learned that he was a police constable, coming up on six years in the force, and that he didn't live in Edinburgh but journeyed up from Eyemouth in the Borders; that he drove most times, except his car had broken down two days ago so he'd been forced to use the train, a minor hassle since the train didn't actually stop in Eyemouth. "The nearest stop's Berwick," he'd told me, "in England, and then you get into a taxi, turn round, and come over the border again."

"Well, at least it's not a fortified border," I'd consoled him, "with guards and wire."

"It should be." His tone had been dry, but his eyes had been mischief. "They're nothing but trouble, the English."

"We are not. We're wonderful people."

"Oh, aye? Will you prove it, then? Give us a len of your mobile."

"I'm sorry?"

He'd held out his hand and rephrased. "May I borrow your mobile? Mine isn't working."

"Oh." I'd handed the phone over, and Rob had dialled a number that set off an answering ring tone from one of his own pockets. Calmly ringing off, he'd passed my mobile back across the aisle. "Thanks."

"That's a sneaky way of getting someone's number."

"What?"

"You could have asked."

He'd looked at me, all innocence, and said, "I've no idea what you're on about."

And looking at those eyes I had agreed with Dr. Fulton-Wallace, that he *was* a devil. But I'd missed him when he'd left the train at Berwick.

Ten miles out, my mobile had chimed out the tune that meant a text message had just arrived. "Am safely back in Scotland," it had told me. "Where are you?"

We'd texted back and forth the next three hours, my whole way down to London. I had asked him later why he'd gone to all that trouble, typing all those texts, when he could simply have reached out to me with thoughts. He had the skill.

He'd told me, "You weren't ready for it, then."

I'd slipped my hand in his and said, "I'm ready now."

But I'd been wrong.

I set Rob's wristwatch on the shelf beside the pillow of the bed and curled myself into the blankets, staring dry-eyed at the dark.

I didn't want to think about the rest of what had happened on that evening after I had bought the watch for him, after we'd walked out holding hands into the rain-slicked street, with all the streetlamps coming on. I'd played that evening over in my mind enough times since that I could run it forward like a film at will, and feel that I was back there; feel the dampness of the air, the rising chill that made me glad of Rob's more solid warmth beside me as he held the pub's door open so that I could go ahead of him.

The pub was crowded, but with patience we found two stools at the bar together, and when Dr. Fulton-Wallace turned up a short while later, Rob gave up his seat to her and stood behind us, close against my shoulder, so the three of us could talk.

"Thanks for coming," she said, getting to the point: "I've been looking at both of your scores on this latest psychometry study, and I'd like to have your permission to film you."

"Oh aye?" said Rob.

"I've been doing this twenty years, now, and I've never seen anyone who can do what you can do, Rob. And both of you working together—I think it would really inform the community, if we could properly document it."

I felt a cold flip in my stomach.

Rob said, "Well, I'd have to apply for permission to take part in something like that, we've got rules in the force about public appearances, but if ye send me the details I'll certainly ask."

I kept out of the whole conversation that followed. If Rob even noticed he didn't let on, he was talking enough for the two of us anyway, and Dr. Fulton-Wallace was too focused on the details of her project and the good that it could do to be distracted by my silence.

The big man behind her who only a moment before had been talking and joking along with his mates had gone silent as well, leaning closer as though he were listening. And when she finished her last drink and thanked us and wished us good night and went out, he made some comment thickened with whisky and expletives that made his friends burst out laughing.

"Did ye ever, in your whole life, hear a bigger load of shite?" he asked them, and they all agreed that they had not. Then more loudly, so everyone round us could hear, he announced, "This lad here and his girlfriend, they're reading our minds."

"Freaks," said a lanky young man with a shaved head who stood on the fringe of the group. "Go on then." He stepped forward and faced Rob, belligerent. "Read *my* mind. What am I thinking?"

Rob answered him calmly, ignoring the looks we were drawing. "You're wanting to fight."

The big man prodded Rob like a bear baiter. "And are ye seeing a fight in his future then, laddie?"

Rob said, "I am, aye. But not with me." Tilting his head to one side he looked quietly at the young man with the shaved head a moment, then told him, "Your mother . . ."

"Right, here we go!" someone predicted, to more scattered laughter.

Ignoring them, Rob said, "She'll be home from hospital soon. And you've nothing to fear, it was never her heart."

In the moment of nearly stunned silence that followed, he finished his pint, set the glass down, and looked at me. "Ready to go?"

Feeling colder than ever, I went with him, hearing the talk and the comments beginning again at our backs.

Freaks.

Outside it was starting to rain again, lightly, the streetlights and headlights reflecting and running together the way all the colours had done in a painting I'd once seen deliberately ruined by acid. A beautiful picture destroyed.

And it wasn't Rob's fault, but I turned on him anyway. "How can you not let that get to you?"

"I'm a policeman. That's not the first drunk in a pub I've come up against."

"No, I mean everyone pointing and whispering, saying you're different."

He shrugged. "I am different," he said. "So are you."

"I don't want to be different."

He slanted a thoughtful look down at me. "Aye, but you are. Were you thinking to hide it your whole life?"

I didn't know how to reply to that. But I did know I could never take part in a film of my psychic ability, baring my secret to strangers and skeptics alike who'd be watching me, judging me.

Rob stopped me there on the pavement and turned me to meet his eyes. "Hiding the person you are," he said, "won't make you happy. I never hide who I am. What I am."

Freaks.

I'd nodded. We'd gone out to dinner. He'd walked me home afterwards. And at the door when he'd kissed me good night, he'd done something he'd never done.

Always before when we'd kissed, though there hadn't been that many times, he had kept his thoughts closed to me. This time the wall had been very decidedly down. I'd been slammed by the force of his feelings, a flood of sensations that caught me and tossed me around like a turbulent river and knocked the breath out of me, so when he'd lifted his mouth from my own I had felt like I'd just escaped drowning.

I'd thought at the time he was showing me how things could be with us, if I could get past my own reservations. But now, looking back, I felt certain that Rob, with his gifts, would have already known what was going to happen, which meant that his kiss was intended to say something else, though I didn't know what. Goodbye, maybe.

Aloud, he'd said only, "I'll see you, then."

"See you on Monday," I'd said.

But I hadn't. I'd closed the door after him, run up the stairs, and I'd gone right on running.

"You're quiet this morning," Rob said. He was driving, his eyes on the road as he swung round the first turn at Old Craighall Junction and onto the Edinburgh bypass. It was just after nine and the traffic was easing a little but Rob's car still had to contend with the lorries. He'd been rather quiet, himself.

I replied, "It's taking all my energy, digesting what I ate this morning. Your mother wouldn't let me out the door without a full cooked breakfast."

"Aye, well, that's my mother. Did she give you porridge, too?"

"She did. I likely won't need food again for days." She'd also sent me off with a spare blouse, in case I spilled something on mine, and loaned me a stylishly cut denim jacket, in case I got cold. I was wearing the jacket now. "I like your mother," I said.

Rob agreed she was easy to like.

"And your father is charming."

"Aye, he would agree with you, there." A faint smile, but he wasn't about to be sidetracked. He sent me another look. "Did you not sleep well?"

"I slept. Are there horses," I asked, "in your field?"

"Yes and no." With a twitch of his mouth he explained, "It's the shadowy horses you heard, if you heard them last night. They belong to the field, like the Sentinel."

"Oh." I had never known horses had ghosts. "Can you see them, as well?"

"Sometimes."

I looked out the window and watched the world passing and wondered what Rob saw that I didn't see.

"So," he said to me, "tell me about what you want me to do for you, up in Dundee."

I explained how I'd met Margaret Ross, how I'd handled the Firebird, what I had seen. And I told him, too, what I had seen when I'd held Margaret's scarf. Well, a part of it. Not what I'd seen at her doctor's—that seemed a betrayal of confidence—but what I'd glimpsed of her loneliness, and of the travel brochure. "It just doesn't seem fair," I said. "She's spent her life helping everyone else, you know, putting her own life on hold, and she had her heart set on that cruise." It affected me more than it probably ought to have done. I looked down. "The thing is, she's believed her whole life that the carving was worth something. And so it would be, if someone could prove where it came from."

He glanced over. "Someone like you?"

"I just thought if I held it again, really tried, I might see something useful. I'm going to Russia next week, to St. Petersburg, right where her ancestor lived. I just thought . . ." I broke off, feeling suddenly foolish, and wearily rubbing my forehead I said, "I don't know what I thought, to be honest."

"You wanted to help. I'd have done the same thing, in your place."

"No, if you'd been in my place," I told him, "you would have been able to pick up the Firebird and know its whole history without even trying hard. I'm not that good, Rob. You are."

He gave a nod as though he'd fit a puzzle piece in place. "That's why you stopped here yesterday to go see Dr. Fulton-Wallace, was it? You had doubts."

"And she confirmed them."

We were coming off the bypass now at Glasgow Road and for a moment Rob's attention was diverted by his need to navigate, but I had the impression there were several things he would have liked to say. All he said in the end, though, was, "Right. So what's your plan with Margaret Ross?"

"I'm going to give her the scarf back."

"And she'll think you're mad to have come all this way to deliver it."

"Probably."

"Then what?"

"Then I'll introduce you, and say you're a colleague with specialist knowledge, someone who can maybe tell us more about the Firebird. She'll let you hold the carving, and then afterwards you'll tell me what you saw, and I can go and try to prove it in St. Petersburg."

He ran that sequence through his head in silence for a moment, gave a nod, and said, "Seems fair enough. One question."

"Yes?"

"Well, not to show my ignorance," he said, "but what's a firebird?"

I smiled, and giving it its Russian name explained, "It's the *zhar-ptitsa*, a bird out of folklore, with bright glowing feathers, like flames. One feather would light a whole room, and it's said that whenever a firebird's feather falls, then a new art will spring up in that place." I'd grown up on the old Russian fairy tales told by my mother at bedtime, but Rob clearly wasn't aware of them. So while we drove north I told him of the Firebird who stole the golden apples from the garden of the tsar, and made the tsar so angry that he sent two of his sons to catch the bird and bring it back alive.

"The sons were, of course, both entirely useless," I said, "but their younger brother, Tsarevitch Ivan, waited up on his own in the garden and nearly caught the Firebird's tail. The bird, before it flew off, dropped a single feather. Ivan picked it up and took it to his father, and the tsar was so impressed he gave Ivan permission to follow his brothers and hunt down the Firebird, too. So Ivan set out, and ran into a helpful grey wolf who devoured his horse—"

"How was that helpful?" Rob asked.

"Well, all right, *that* wasn't so helpful, but all Russian folk tales have dark parts. The grey wolf decided that Ivan was brave, so he offered to help him, and let Ivan ride on his back."

Rob pointed out that, if the wolf had been thinking ahead, he would never have eaten the horse to begin with. He glanced at my face and said, "Fine, I'll shut up. Carry on."

"It's a magic wolf, Rob. He runs faster than any horse ever could. Now, the grey wolf carried Ivan away to the land where the Firebird lived in a great golden cage in another tsar's garden. The wolf told him, 'Go get the bird, but whatever you do, don't touch the golden cage.' But Ivan didn't listen, and he touched the cage, and he was caught. This other tsar, the owner of the Firebird, said to Ivan he'd forgive him, even let him keep the bird, if Ivan did him one great favour. In another land," I said, "there was a rare horse with a golden mane. The tsar said, 'If you journey to that land and get that horse for me and bring it here, I'll let you have the Firebird.' So the grey wolf carried Ivan to the other land, and in the stables there they found the horse, and hanging near the horse there was a golden bridle, and the wolf said to Ivan, 'Now go get the horse, but whatever you do, don't touch that bridle.'"

Rob said, "And I'm guessing Ivan didn't listen."

"No, of course he didn't. He was caught again, but the owner of the horse with the golden mane told Ivan he would forgive him and let him keep the horse, if he'd first journey to this other land and bring back the tsarevna there, Yelena the Beautiful . . ."

And on it went, with the patient grey wolf helping Ivan through trial after trial, sometimes by shape-shifting, sometimes by giving advice that more often than not was ignored. After Tsarevitch Ivan sat down on the ground for the third time and wept, Rob pronounced him an idiot. And when Ivan's brothers appeared near the ending to kill him and cut him in pieces, Rob thought it fair justice.

"That isn't the end, though," I told him. "The grey wolf came back, and found Ivan in pieces—"

"And ate him."

"No. He brought Ivan to life again, and Ivan went to his father's court and reclaimed all that his brothers had stolen: the horse with the gold mane, Yelena the Beautiful, even the Firebird."

"And what did the wolf get?" Rob wanted to know.

"Nothing, really. He just went away."

Rob looked sideways at me, and then back at the road again.

Hiding my smile I said, "That's not the only Russian folk tale with a firebird in it, though. There is another one I know . . ."

"Is Ivan in it?"

"No. The hero of the second tale's an archer, with a magic horse, and one day the archer sees a feather on the ground, a gorgeous feather, like a flame. Of course he wants to pick it up, except his horse says—"

"It's a talking horse?"

"I said the horse was magic. Pay attention. So the horse says, 'Leave the feather where it lies, for it will only bring you trouble.'"

"And of course he doesn't listen to his horse," Rob guessed, but gamely he sat back and let me tell the second fairy tale.

This one was rather different from the first. The archer *did* pick up the feather, true, and take it to the tsar, and as with Ivan he was sent to catch the Firebird, but after he had done that he was sent to bring a princess from her home across the sea, and on the way he fell in love with her, and she with him. And even though the archer faced much trouble, as the horse had warned, it ended as it ought to, and the archer got the princess for his bride forever after.

"And to show his thanks," I said to Rob, "the archer built the magic horse a stable made entirely of gold."

Rob said, "I like that story better."

So did I.

Rob drove in thoughtful silence for a few miles longer. "Both those stories are alike, though, really."

"How is that?"

"The firebird drops a feather," was his summary, "and if you're fool enough to pick it up and chase the bird itself, you're in for trouble."

"And adventure."

"Aye." He nodded. "True enough. But what you bring back with you in the end," he said, "might not be what you started out in search of to begin with."

I was thinking of that while we made our approach to Dundee

on the long bridge that crossed the broad estuary where the River Tay swept out to meet the wide sparkling sea.

Rob asked, "What's the time?"

I'd forgotten I still had his watch. Feeling for it in my pocket now, I drew it out. "It's nearly half past ten."

Why did you keep this? I wanted to ask him, but Rob only held out his hand for the timepiece and strapped it back onto his wrist with the ease of long practice, and asked, "D'ye ken where she lives?"

All I knew was the address. We had to stop twice to ask people to give us directions.

Dundee was a lovely town, built up the south-facing side of a hill so it always looked straight at the sunshine, its stone-built historic appeal charged with bright modern energy. But Margaret Ross's street didn't have any of that. Her mid-terraced house sat third up in a drab row of others that looked just the same, with their square staring windows and low-walled front gardens and plain iron gates.

I could hear the high whine of a hoover behind the front door as I rang the bell. At the second ring the hoover stopped and I heard footsteps coming slowly, almost cautiously, as though she wasn't used to having visitors.

She recognized me easily, but clearly hadn't caught my name, so I supplied it once again. "It's Nicola," I told her. "Nicola Marter."

"From London." She sounded perplexed.

"Yes." I held up her scarf, neatly folded. "You left this," I said, "in the office. I thought you'd be missing it."

That only made her look more baffled. "Ye've never come all this way up to Dundee to return it?"

Rob, who'd stayed two paces back, stepped smoothly in to rescue me with, "She was coming to Scotland already, ye ken, and since she didnae wish to trust it to the post we thought we'd stop by and deliver it on our way north the day."

I guessed he'd slipped back into broadened Scots to put her at her ease, and it appeared to work. I introduced them, and she pulled the door more fully open, standing back and saying, "Do come in."

Rob followed me. He wasn't hugely tall, but in the small space of the entry hall I felt his presence keenly and it came as a relief to move away, into the tidy front room with its drab green wallpaper and cold and empty fireplace. This was not the room I'd seen the afternoon I'd held the scarf, but still it had that same dejected feeling, like a girl at a dance with her back to the wall watching everyone else whirling by.

Margaret offered me a stiffly upright chair beside the window as she asked Rob, "D'ye work in art as well?"

He told her, "Aye, from time to time. I started off with archaeologists, identifying artifacts."

I glanced at him, but couldn't see the slightest trace of anything to tell me he was lying. Taking up the reins, I said to Margaret, "Maybe Rob could help you learn a little more about your firebird carving, now I think of it. He's really very knowledgeable." Turning to face Rob as though the thought had just occurred to me, I told him, "Miss Ross has this wooden carving, Rob, that's come down through her family, and she needs to prove its provenance."

Rob said he would be pleased to have a look, but Margaret shook her head.

"It's kind of ye, but there's no need. My neighbour, Archie, fetched me from the station when I came back up from seeing you, Miss Marter, and he said . . ." She looked embarrassed. "Well, he said I shouldn't take one person's word for it. That maybe Mr. St.-Croix was mistaken. Archie kens a man in Inverness who used to live in Russia, and he said he'd take the Firebird up to him, if I was willing. Archie's daughter lives in Inverness, he'd planned to go and stay with her already for a visit," she explained. "He left this morning."

I was trying to digest this. "And he took the carving with him?"

"Aye. He'll have it home in three weeks' time," she said to Rob, "so if you're up this way again I'll gladly let ye see it then."

"I'd like that very much," Rob said.

She made us tea, insisted on it, serving it with scones so light and fresh they barely bore the butter's weight. I pushed my disappointment down, and mindful of the loneliness I'd felt when I had held her scarf,

I tried my best to make the visit stretch a little, making conversation where I could.

Rob helped. "Ye have a taste for crime," he remarked, with a nod at the barrister's bookcase beside his own chair, every shelf crammed with hardbacks whose colourful jacket designs were pure vintage.

She smiled and said, "Those were my father's, aye. Loved a good murder, he did. And his spies. He was mad for James Bond."

"So I see."

While Rob studied the titles I nodded in my turn towards a framed sketch on the opposite wall. "That's a beautiful picture. Are those ruins local?"

"Och, no, that's New Slains Castle, up to the north," she said, "near Cruden Bay, where my mother was born. Her family goes a long way back there, all the way to the Anna who first brought the Firebird over here, ye ken, from Russia."

Standing, Rob crossed over for a close look at the sketch, head tilted. "Cruden Bay? Where's that, exactly?"

"Not far north of Aberdeen. They have a lovely golf course. Do ye play the golf?"

Rob let her lead the conversation off again, politely, but I saw his eyes returning to the sketch from time to time, and though he didn't show it, I could sense him growing restless.

After twenty minutes more I set my empty teacup down and smiled and, thanking Margaret, said, "We really ought to go."

She stood and saw us to the door, and thanked me, too, for bringing back her scarf. "It was always a fancy of mine," she admitted, "to own a designer scarf. Foolish thing, really, to waste so much money."

"Oh, I don't know," I said, and smiled. "We all have to indulge ourselves a little bit, I think."

She stood there in the doorway of her plain mid-terraced house, and smiled back at me, but sadly. "Aye, perhaps we do."

I shouldn't have said anything, I knew, to raise her hopes, but I so desperately wanted to leave something she could hold to, so I told her, "I'll be going to St. Petersburg myself, soon, on a business trip. I'll see what I can learn about the Empress Catherine, shall I? And the British who were living there."

A small light flicked on briefly in her eyes. It satisfied me then, but when I got back in the car with Rob and drove away I felt less sure that what I'd done was kind. I sat and wallowed in my doubts until Rob spoke, his own voice quiet, as though he were thinking, too. "Ye ken she's dying?"

"Yes, I know." I looked away. "And so does she."

"This cruise she planned on taking. When . . . ?"

"It leaves in March," I told him. "Sixty days, the whole way round the world." A world that Margaret Ross had only dreamed of from her prison of a house.

We'd reached the ring road that would take us back onto the Tay Road Bridge, and just ahead the rigged masts of an old tall ship rose up against the waterline. The RSS *Discovery* in its permanent display dock, the same ship that had once carried Scott and Shackleton on their first trip to search for the South Pole, only to spend two years trapped in the ice while the crew on the shore met with failure.

We reached the ship and passed it. Reached the turning for the Tay Road Bridge, and passed that, too. I looked at Rob.

He looked at me. "Nice day," he said, and glanced towards the sky for proof before he brought his gaze back to the road ahead. "We could be up to Cruden Bay by teatime."

"Cruden Bay." So I'd been right about his interest in the sketch, and its effect on him.

"Well, given that your firebird carving's up in Inverness," he said, "I thought we might look elsewhere for those details that you need."

"Oh yes? And what's in Cruden Bay?"

He swung the Ford through one more roundabout and took the turning north before he answered me. "Slains Castle."

chapter
EIGHT

We lost the sunshine as we crossed the River Ythan north of Aberdeen, and minutes later it began to rain. Not hard at first, but steadily. The road we were on hugged the coast but the change in the weather had flattened the light to a dull grey outside and the clouds pressed so low there was little distinction between sea and sky.

Rob was looking ahead with the faintest of frowns, and I knew he was searching for the jagged line of castle ruins we'd seen in the sketch that hung on Margaret's wall.

I asked, "What is it that you feel, about the castle?"

He couldn't put it neatly into words. "It's like . . ." He exhaled hard, his mouth a stubborn line. "It's like I've someone tugging at my sleeve, ye ken, and wanting my attention. I can feel it just like that, like I'm supposed to come and see."

"Well, you'll be lucky to see anything in this." I looked with doubt beyond the thudding wiper blades that seemed to barely pass before the windscreen was awash again. "It's getting worse."

It really was. Rob had to slow his speed because of lack of visibility, and by the time we reached the outer edge of Cruden Bay he'd conceded that, even if we found the castle, we couldn't explore it in this weather. Not that it mattered.

I'd already mentally altered my plan for the day to allow for our coming this far up the coast. There was no way that I would be able to catch the last train down to London tonight, that was obvious. And it was even more obvious there was no way we could ever have driven the whole distance up here, and looked round Slains Castle, *and* driven back down again, all in one go. Rain or no rain, we'd have to find somewhere to stop for the night.

I had known this when we'd headed north from Dundee. I'd accepted the logic. But now it felt suddenly close in the car.

I said, "Rob."

"Aye?"

"I'm sorry for making you do this."

His frown of concentration softened as he watched the road. "Ye've not made me do anything. I volunteered."

"For a trip to Dundee. Not a full weekend excursion." I tried to see beyond the thudding wipers. "Margaret said they had a golf course here, which means there ought to be at least a couple of hotels."

Steering from the road into a little car park sheltered by high hedges on two sides and on the other by the watery dark outline of what looked to be a pub, Rob switched the engine off and stretched his shoulders, leaning back into the seat. "How's this one?"

Peering out my window, I could just make out the sign: THE ST. OLAF HOTEL.

"This looks fine," I said.

Rob held his coat over our heads as we made a run for it over the waterlogged gravel and round to the door on the far side, but with the wind gusting sideways the rain still attacked us, and I was half soaked by the time we blew into the entryway, pushing the door shut behind us.

The narrow entry hall served double duty as the hotel's lobby, warmly elegant with panelled wood and carpets and a small desk. Doors stood open on each side to what appeared to be a breakfast room and, opposite, a dining room, and at the hall's far end a staircase climbed to a half-landing on its way to the first floor.

A woman came to welcome us, dark haired and tall, with friendly eyes.

We were in luck, she said. They had a room.

I asked, "Only the one?"

"Aye." The look she gave me after glancing at Rob seemed to question my sanity for even thinking of sleeping alone. "But it does have two beds."

It was a large room done in burgundy and white and restful green, with a dark mirrored wardrobe that filled one whole wall and a beautiful window that took up one half of another. I dropped my handbag and my borrowed jacket on the smaller bed so Rob would not be moved by chivalry to claim it for himself. He was bigger than I was, and the larger double bed would give him room to sleep more comfortably.

Right now he was standing at the window, looking out. The view was fogged with rain and mist but I could still make out the green expanse of what must be the golf course with a ridge of dunes beyond it, and the fainter smudge of headlands to the north and south.

His gaze had angled north and I could feel again the waves of his impatience and his restlessness.

"You can't go out in that," I said, and nodded at the rain.

He turned as if he had forgotten I was even there, and then I saw the tension leave his shoulders as his mouth curved slightly. "I could try. The castle's only over there."

I couldn't see it. "Where?"

He closed his eyes briefly and sent me the image—a towering ruin of red stone that seemed to rise straight from the sea-battered rocks.

I pushed it aside with a shiver. "Yes, well, I don't want to have to explain to your mother how I lost her son over the cliffs, so forget it."

The curve of his mouth deepened slightly, but he didn't argue, and I took advantage of that to suggest we go down and have dinner.

"The sign downstairs said they served evening meals starting at five," I said, "and I'm starving."

The dining room of the St. Olaf Hotel had a lovely warm feel to it, dark wood and red and gold tones and the brass shining bright on the fireplace below a high ceiling with elegant crown moldings. At one end of the long room stood the bar, with polished bottles in behind, and at the other end a tall bow window jutted out to form a bay just large enough to set a table. Mirrors reflected the soft light of lamps and the walls were a gallery of old framed pictures and prints.

Watching Rob study the specials board, I said, "It's my treat, I'm paying, so order whatever you like."

"Why should you pay? It was me who suggested we come further north."

"I'm paying."

He gave a shrug, letting me choose where to sit. "Well, all right. But I'm not inexpensive. I'm having the sirloin steak, with battered mushrooms to start."

It was wonderful food. I had Brie wedges followed by crisply fried haddock, and white wine that warmed me so thoroughly from the inside that I ceased worrying about the storm still flinging rain against the window.

"It'll pass," our waitress told us, her tone sure. "The forecast calls for sun in the morn." She took our empty plates in hand. "Are you up for the golf?"

I shook my head. "We were hoping to walk up and look round the castle."

She assured us it was worth the walk. "You'll have to get through the fence, but that's not so much bother. It's pulled down in places."

"The fence?" I asked.

"Oh, aye. It's all been fenced off, Slains. It's privately owned, and the plan is to have it converted to holiday flats."

I couldn't remember if I'd seen a fence in the image I'd had from Rob earlier of that great ruin set right at the cliff's edge, but holiday flats at the edge of a precipice sounded a little unsafe.

"It was never a ruin until the last century," our waitress said when I voiced my opinion. "There's a picture there of how it looked afore the Earl of Erroll sold it from the family in 1916, and the later owners stripped it bare and had the roof removed so they'd not have to pay the taxes. That's when Slains began to fall to ruin."

"Oh," was all I could think of to say.

"If you want to learn the history of the castle, we've an author here who wrote a book about it. Ye can buy it in the shops," she told us proudly.

Rob roused himself from wherever his drifting thoughts had taken him to ask her, "What's that picture, there?"

She followed his gaze to a large framed picture hanging just above my head. "That's the Bullers o' Buchan, and well worth the walk, if ye still have a mind to go up on the coast path the morn." It looked like a large sea cave, only without a roof, leaving it open above to the sky.

I saw Rob's gaze return to it a few times while we drank our tea and shared a dish of sticky toffee pudding floating warmly in a sea of cream.

I finally asked, "What is it that you're seeing?"

He glanced up one more time before admitting that he didn't know. "It's fuzzy, like. But I'm not at my best." He fought a yawn. "We should try to go see it the morn, though, if we have the time."

His use of the conditional reminded me Rob's time was not entirely his own. I didn't work weekends, but Rob, between police work and the lifeboat crew, might not have that same luxury.

"I've the day off," he told me, before I could ask, "but unless you'll be taking the sleeper to London, the last train from Edinburgh leaves around suppertime, and we'll be four hours at least, on the road going down."

Which meant we'd only really have the morning here, to tour around. And if we were to have another early start, I thought, we ought to have an early night. I caught the waitress's eye again, but when I asked for the bill she said, "Nae bother. I'll put it to your room. Which room is yours?"

"Room four," I said.

"Oh, aye. You'll see the castle from your window when the sun comes out."

Rob didn't need the sun to see the castle.

Upstairs, he wandered over to the window once again, already wearing that distracted gaze that meant his mind had drifted far away. He seemed well rooted there when I went to take the first turn in the bathroom, but when I came out I discovered he'd shifted my things to the larger bed, and was now stretched out full-length on the single one, eyes closed and quietly breathing.

I'd never been in this position with him; never watched him sleeping in a bed. We hadn't reached that stage in our relationship before I'd run away from it, so even though I tried hard not to stare I couldn't help it. He was even better looking when he slept. My brother looked more boyish to my eyes when he was sleeping, and more vulnerable, but Rob looked every inch a man. The relaxation of his features only emphasized their strength. And when I tugged a blanket from my own bed so that I could cover him, I knew that I was doing it as much in self-defence as from concern he might get cold. It would be easier to sleep, I knew, if I weren't forced to watch the steady rise and fall of Rob's broad chest, or see his hands linked carelessly across the muscled leanness of his stomach.

As it was, I had to turn my back completely when I got in bed myself, and face away from him. But even then, I still could hear the rhythm of his breathing, slow and deep and reassuring, like the waves I knew were rolling to the shore beyond our window, and at length I let them carry me to sleep.

I woke alone in the hotel room.

From the angle of the sunlight spearing in from the east-facing window, it was fairly early in the morning, still, but Rob had neatly made his bed, and when I turned in mine I found the blanket that I'd covered him with tucked round my own shoulders.

He'd been down to breakfast, too, it seemed. He'd left some kind of scone and a banana for me on the bedside table. And a note.

Good morning, read the bold slash of his handwriting. *Come find me when you're ready.*

It sounded more a challenge than an invitation when I read it through the first time, and in some ways I supposed it was, but there was something oddly comforting as well in knowing I could find him anytime I wanted. First, though, there were other practicalities, like eating what he'd left for me, and showering, and going down to settle our account with the hotel.

The same waitress who'd served us last night was on breakfast room duty. She greeted me brightly. "Good morning. Ye've got a fair day for your walk. Have a seat by the window, I won't be a moment," she said. "Will you have tea, or coffee?"

"I'm not having breakfast," I told her, "but thank you. I just need to pay for the room."

"Nae bother, he's already done that. Your man," she said helpfully, as though it needed explaining. "He paid at the front desk afore he went out, said you wanted an early start."

"Yes. Yes, we did." I couldn't honestly be irritated with him, and I should have known he'd be too much a gentleman to let me pay. I smiled and asked her, "Can I change my mind about the coffee?"

When I stepped outside the hotel I had two hot steaming takeaway cups, one of coffee, one of tea, a welcome insulation for my hands against the morning chill. I paused a moment on the gravel, turned my face towards the breeze and closed my eyes, and sent my thoughts out. *Rob?*

The answer came back clearly. *Here.*

I saw the play of white-ridged waves against a wide deserted crescent curve of sand, and gave a nod, not caring that he couldn't see me. He was on the beach.

I likely could have walked across the golf course, but despite the early hour I could already hear the crisp metallic chink of clubs and balls and didn't fancy getting knocked unconscious first thing in the morning by a drive gone wide, and so instead I walked the long way round, along the road and down the gently sloping street of terraced shops and houses with a rushing stream that chased beside the pavement I was walking on, the whole way down to where a white wood footbridge crossed above it to the broad, fawn-coloured beach.

I had to round a ridge of sand dunes that rose high like proper hills, with tufted marram grass that flattened when the wind blew. Rob was sitting halfway up one, with his crossed arms resting on his upraised knees, his steady gaze directed not towards the endless sea and the horizon, but the nearer line of waves that rolled to shore and foamed to nothing on the sand.

I climbed to join him. It was harder than I'd thought, to climb that deeply shifting dune, and I did it ungracefully, but Rob seemed too absorbed to take much notice. He did shift aside, though, in the level spot where he was sitting, to make room for me as I collapsed beside him. We were in a sheltered hollow with the wind-shaped sand and blowing grasses rising gently to each side of us and shielding us behind.

Rob took the cup of now-cooled tea I handed over to him. "Thanks."

"You're welcome." I cradled my coffee and looked to the beach as well. "What are you looking at?"

"Just what you see." When he lifted the takeaway cup for a drink I could see a faint smile touch his mouth at the corners. "But afore you came," he told me, "I was watching Margaret's Anna."

I still found it difficult to tell if he was teasing me. I had to ask, "You're serious?"

"Dead serious. Just there." He gave a nod towards the empty beach. "I'd no idea it was her at first, ye ken. It was the woman I was watching."

He had lost me, now. "What woman?"

"Sorry." I could see the effort that it took for him to organize his thoughts into an order that allowed him to explain.

He started at the moment when he'd woken with the sunrise to a pressing sense of restlessness. Not wanting to disturb my sleep, he'd fought it for a while, but when the urge to get outdoors had overwhelmed him he'd gone down himself, alone.

"I left you breakfast."

"Yes, I ate it. Thanks."

"No problem. I was thinking," he admitted, "I might walk up to the castle, have a look around."

"Without me?"

"Well, I would have gone again, when you had wakened. But the pull that I was feeling was so strong. It didn't take me to the castle, though," he said. "It brought me here."

I looked along the ridge of dunes, deserted but for us. "What did it feel like?"

"I no ken." He sifted sand between his fingers with a shrug. "A kind of longing, like, if that makes any sense."

I felt an edge of it myself, I thought, and found my own gaze drawn far out towards the distant line where sea met sky, as though there might be something there for me to see, that I'd been waiting for. But what, I didn't know.

Rob said, "And then I saw the woman. She came down that hill, just over there." He pointed to the headland by the harbour to our left. "And at the bottom of the hill she stopped a moment, as if she were feart to take another step, but then she finally came across, and passed just underneath here, and I realized what she was."

I had a sense of that, as well. "A ghost?"

He gave a nod.

"And did you speak to her?"

"There'd have been no point, she'd not have heard me."

"But," I said, "your Roman ghost, your Sentinel—you talk to him."

His glance slid sideways to me as he raised his tea to drink again. "The Sentinel's a spirit. All that made him what he was in life, he has that still, it's just that he no longer has a body. But this woman, she was nothing like the Sentinel. She was more of a shadow," he said. "A residual ghost, is the way they're described, I think. Something happens in a place, ye ken, that carries deep emotion, and it leaves such an impression that the shadow of the person keeps repeating it forever. If you have the eyes to see."

She'd been an older woman, so Rob told me, with an almost regal grace that had intrigued him, and her clothes had clearly marked her as a woman of another time, her long gown dragging heavily across the tide-wet sand yet leaving no trace of a trail, just as her feet had left behind no footprints.

And because he'd been intrigued, he'd set his focus on her, trying to see back in time to when she'd been a person, not a shadow.

I still wasn't sure how Rob saw things, when he looked back, but from what he was saying I gathered that, while I could only see a narrow window on the past, he saw the whole of it.

He'd seen the older woman walking past. She'd walked a little farther on before she'd stopped and, looking up, began a conversation with a younger, bright-haired woman sitting partway up the dunes. He might have listened in, had his attention not been stolen at that moment by a burst of childish laughter from the beach.

"There were five children," Rob said. "All one family, from the look of it, though not a one was over ten years old. And the youngest of them, she'd have only been this high." He held his hand above the sand to show me. "Small, ye ken, still walking on her toes, the way they do. But she could run."

He painted me a picture with his words till I could see her, too: the tiny girl with windblown brown curls running with her brothers and her sisters and a giant mastiff dog who seemed to take delight in teasing her to try to take the stick he carried in his mouth. But when she'd run too closely to the waves in her pursuit, both of the women who were playing with the children had gone after her, and one of them— her mother, Rob assumed—had called her: "Anna!"

When the little girl had failed to stop, the woman had put on a burst of speed herself and caught the child and, lifting her, had swung her in a wide and joyful arc of skirts and water spray and in delight the little girl had laughed with such abandon that it made Rob smile himself, though he was watching from a distance of some centuries.

And then he'd unexpectedly been brought back to the present by the nudgings of a small dog and the feeling of a tennis ball pressed wetly to his hand. The dog, a little flop-eared spaniel spotted brown and white, had seemed entirely unrepentant for the interruption. Dropping the wet tennis ball, well caked with sand and slobber, in Rob's lap, it had backed off a step and crouched, tail wagging fiercely in encouragement.

A young man on the beach below had called up an apology. "He's not my dog," he'd told Rob, "he's my brother's. I'd have taught him better manners. Angus, come on now."

But Rob, dog-lover that he was, had reassured the other man it was no bother, and he'd made a fuss of Angus, throwing out the ball along the beach a few times while exchanging comments with the other man about the weather and the quickest way to reach the castle.

"Just mind how you go, after all of this rain," had been the man's advice. "The path will be pure mud, and there are places you'll come too close to the edge to wish to slip."

He'd called the dog back and they'd headed off towards the row of houses waiting on the far side of the footbridge while Rob, left alone once more, had turned his mind again in search of little Anna.

"But," I asked him, playing skeptic, "how can you be sure that it was Margaret's Anna? Anna would have been a common name, in those days, both in Russia and in Scotland. We don't know that she was Scottish."

"True enough." He admitted he hadn't been sure. "But she felt right."

Not really the kind of hard proof we could offer to experts, I thought.

Rob said, "Experts be damned." He glanced round at me. "Surely ye've felt at least once in your life, simply felt it, that something was right?"

It wasn't only that he'd read my thoughts so easily. He was sitting too close, and his eyes were too blue, too distracting. I dragged my gaze free and looked back at the water and asked, "Did you find her again, then?"

"Oh, aye." At the edge of my vision I saw his head angle away once again and I knew he was looking towards the strip of sea-wet sand that glistened in the sun. "Not as she was when I'd left her," he said, "but I found her."

She'd been older by a few years, maybe seven now, he guessed, or eight. But even so he'd known her by her brown curls, blowing wildly in the wind, and by her laughter.

As before, she'd been with other children, only three others this time, the eldest practically a teenager and hanging back to walk beside the woman Rob had taken for their mother, while the youngest boy and Anna ran ahead.

The boy was chasing seagulls, only chasing them at first and charging at them when they sank from flight to settle on the sand, so that they rose again and shrieked and wheeled to ride the wind above the little family.

Anna screamed at him in her turn, "Stop it, Donald! Leave them be!"

The boy had grinned, and being slightly older and a full head taller than the little girl, had kept his distance easily. But when he'd stooped to pick a bit of driftwood from the sand and taken aim at a young seagull that had not been quick enough to fly away, the girl had closed the space between them in a lunge that knocked him over.

Anna, for all her small size, had the best of the brief fight that followed, refusing to be dislodged till Donald's swinging hand caught her a blow on the side of her head.

"Donald!" That was their mother, advancing to put a swift end to the battle. "Stop that! What sort of a mannie are ye, taking your hand off your sister's face?"

"She took her hand offa mine!" Donald, scrambling upright, looked fiercely defiant. "And fit wye are ye allus taking her side of things? I'm your own son! She's not even a Logan."

Anna, still rubbing the side of her head, stopped abruptly. The air had gone suddenly still. The two other children, a few feet away, traded glances as Donald himself seemed to wish the words back, shifting guiltily under his mother's incredulous gaze. Then all eyes swung to Anna.

She rose to her feet in the silence, a little bit shakily, seeking reassurance in her mother's face and finding something else, something that looked more like apology.

Her lower lip began to quiver. "Are you not my mother?"

"Anna."

"Am I not a Logan, truly?"

"Anna," came the pained reply, "I love you as my own, I always have, I—"

"No!" The shout was meant to shut the explanations out, to shield the girl's emotions from a new assault.

The woman reached her hands towards the little girl, a shine of tears beginning in her own kind eyes, but Anna wrestled free and shouted, "No!" again, and ran, as though the devil and his army of dark angels were pursuing her.

Rob paused to drain the last bit of his tea, which must by now have been as cold as ice, and told me, "She ran there."

I looked where he was pointing, to the headland by the harbour, and the line of cliffs beyond it. "To Slains Castle, do you mean?"

"I think so, aye."

I was surprised he hadn't followed her, but when I said as much he only gave an offhand shrug and said, "Well, that was when you called me, so I reckoned I should wait for you."

Always the gentleman, I thought.

If Rob read me that time he didn't respond, he just rolled to his feet like an athlete and stretched out his shoulders before reaching down with his free hand to help me up, too. "Let's go find her," he said.

chapter NINE

I'd never seen a ruin so wildly beautiful as Slains. Rising in places straight up from the edge of the cliffs, with the spray of the North Sea exploding against the dark rocks far beneath it, the castle was a fierce reminder of what could endure against the elements and time.

It would have been a great imposing structure in its day, or so I judged from what was left of it, the jagged sprawl of ruined rooms and arches with the crumbled stairs that led to nowhere now, and hollow windows gazing silently towards the ever-changing sea. The stretch of ruins farthest from me might have been the stables once, and closer still—so close that I was standing in its shadow—one tall, square-walled, roofless tower rose above the rest in what, if it were living and not made of brick and stone, I might have taken for defiance.

Standing there, I tried in my imagination to rebuild the castle as it once had been, to give the walls and tower back their proper form, and set a roof on top to keep the weather out, and glaze the gaping windows with glass panes to block the wind. What I came up with was most likely a fair semblance of Slains Castle in its prime.

I knew that Rob, beside me, probably saw everything more clearly, but he seemed right now to be more focused on the fence that stood between us and the ruins. Built of chain link, it stood higher than his head and had been staked the whole way round to cut off access.

With his head tipped to the side he told me, "Easier to climb it near the posts, it's not so wobbly."

"Can police constables trespass? I'd have thought it was unethical."

"And who's trespassing? I'm only after saving a wee girl who's up here somewhere on her own." His face was admirably straight but for his eyes. "You need a hand with this?"

I could, in fact, climb nearly any fence, of any height. It was a skill I'd learned from following my brother, and I put it to good use now, scrambling up and over easily so that I was already on my feet when Rob dropped catlike at my side.

He grinned. "Can ye do that with trees, as well?"

"Climb them, you mean? Only up," I admitted. "I'm a coward coming down in trees, the branches are too far apart and never where I need them. I got stuck in one for hours, once. My brother Colin had to talk me down again."

"Oh aye? And how'd he manage that?"

"He had me close my eyes, and then he told me where to put my hands and feet, and I just did it." I could still recall his patient voice, instructing me: "Six inches left. Now two feet down, that's it, you've got it, I won't let you fall . . ."

I turned, and caught Rob watching me. He smiled and looked away again, towards the soaring bit of castle wall that stood much closer to us, now, its granite facing stones reflecting tiny scatterings of light.

Rob closed his own eyes, with his head held to the side a little as though he were listening, and then his eyes came open and I had the sense that he was seeing something very different from what I was seeing.

He was still aware of me peripherally, though, because he kept on talking even while he walked along the outer wall, describing as he went: "It's like a garden, here, walled in, with paths and trees." He stopped, inhaling deeply. "There's a lilac tree, just here, that's full in bloom."

Which meant, I thought, that in the place where he was walking it was summertime, but only just—not at the season's end, as it was now, but somewhere nearer its beginning. When would lilacs bloom up here? I wondered. Late in May, perhaps, or early June?

"And there's the kitchen door," he told me. "That's where she went in."

To me it was only a breach in the broken wall, but Rob still ducked his head under the long-vanished lintel as he crossed the threshold, and I felt a curious urge to do likewise. I envied him, envied the things he was seeing, and I think he must have been fully aware of that, too, because he started taking more care with his verbal descriptions, more time with the details, until he was painting the picture so vividly I, too, could see the flagged floors and the broad open hearth and the women who turned from their work in surprise as young Anna ran by with her face streaming tears.

Following Rob as he followed the girl through the twists of the corridors, I wasn't seeing the deep roofless passages open above to the cries of the gulls, where the wind off the sea became suddenly stilled and the shadows fell thickly. Instead, in my mind, I was seeing what Rob was describing, the warm plastered walls and the ceilings and floorboards, and doors leading off into storerooms and sculleries. This was the servants' dominion, this ground level, but Anna didn't stay here.

She ran up, to the rooms that no longer existed because all the beams and the floorboards had long ago fallen away, leaving shells of the walls with their great gaping windows, and even if I'd climbed the crumbling circle of stairs that remained, I could never have followed her.

Rob could, though.

Stopping a moment he looked up as though he were getting his bearings, then with his gaze fixed on a place in mid-air he changed course and walked till he was under it, leaning his shoulders against the high wall that was all that divided the room we were in from a dizzying drop down the cliffs to the sea.

With a nod of his head he said, "She's in the library."

I asked him, "What's she doing?"

And he told me.

Slains was not her home, and yet she knew its corners well, from trailing after her Aunt Kirsty while she did her work. The earl had always treated her with kindness, and she'd always found a comfort in this corner of the library, her hiding place, tucked safely out of sight behind the tallest, broadest armchair that sat angled to the fireplace. There was no fire now, it being summer, yet the corner kept its warmth and sheltering appeal, and Anna curled herself within it, arms wrapped tightly round her knees.

She heard the voices rise and fall downstairs, her mother's voice among them. *No.* She caught the thought and changed it. Not her mother. Donald's mother, but not hers. Not anymore.

Her breath snagged painfully within her chest, and then she held it altogether as she heard firm steps approach along the corridor. A handle turned, the door began to open, and she pressed her face with eyes tight closed against the leather chair back, crouched as quiet as a beetle in her corner.

The door swung shut. She couldn't see the person who'd come in, but she could tell it was a man because his boots made a distinctly heavy sound against the floorboards. He walked straight towards her chair and she shrank smaller still, and when the chair back moved she squeezed her eyes more tightly shut as though that might somehow prevent her being seen, but no discovery came, and no recriminations, and she realized he was merely sitting down.

The armchair shifted as he settled in it. Anna braved a peek beneath the chair and saw his booted feet stretched out towards the unlit hearth. And then she heard a scraping as he pulled the little table closer to him, singing lightly to himself. It was a pleasant tune, although she didn't understand the words as they were in some foreign language, like the strange words of the fishermen from France who sometimes called upon her father in the night.

No, not her father, she corrected herself. She was not a Logan. She was—

"Curse this blasted palsy," said the man all of a sudden, as the sound of something falling interrupted Anna's thoughts.

Peering underneath the chair again, she saw that several painted wooden pieces from the chessboard on the table had been tumbled to the floor to lie there scattered in disorder, and the black-haired king had fallen to his side upon the carpet and was gazing at her mournfully with darkly painted eyes.

"I apologize, my lads," the man said gently to the chessmen as he bent to pick them up, "my hands do shake these days, and show my age." He leaned and moved his foot a fraction and his boot heel caught the black-haired king by what seemed sheerest accident and kicked it farther underneath the chair, much closer now to Anna's hiding place.

The man continued picking up the other scattered pieces, and she heard the clicks as each was set again upon the board. "Where is your king, lads? For of all of you, he is the one I should not like to lose. Where is he?" Shifting in his chair again, the man seemed to be searching. "Gone," he said at last, "and lost. Ah well, that is unfortunate."

From underneath the chair, the painted wooden king looked up at Anna and she looked at him uncertainly.

The man went on, "'Tis likely that the Earl of Erroll will not let me use his hospitality again, if I do so misplace his treasures." And he gave a sigh so sorrowful that Anna could not help but feel an answering regret in her own heart, and reaching out she closed her hand around the errant king and crept out of her corner to return him to the playing-board in silence.

She could see the stranger, now. He was a man much older than her father or her Uncle Rory, older even than the earl who kept this castle, and his hair had greyed to match the whiteness of the close-trimmed beard that edged his lean and kindly looking face. His smile cut crinkles round his eyes.

"I thank ye, lass. 'Tis a great kindness ye have done me."

When she gazed at him, not answering, he gave a nod towards the armchair facing him and asked her, "Will ye sit and keep me company awhile, or will your mother be expecting ye?"

She felt the swell of tears begin to burn again and pushed them back and said, "I have no mother." Bravely sitting in the chair, she watched him set the painted pieces in their places on the board.

He asked her, "Do ye play the chess?"

She shook her head.

"It is the grandest game," he said, "for those who have the patience and the wit to learn it."

Anna saw him set a small piece on a square and frowned as something deep within her memory turned and tugged. "What's that?"

"The pawn? Well, he's the smallest soldier, yet the game would be for naught without his efforts."

In behind the lines of pawns the taller rows of varied chessmen stood—the kings and queens and horses' heads and castle towers, but it was the little pawns who most caught Anna's fancy, and she heard a woman's voice repeating in her memory, "That one is my favourite, too," and felt a sense of sadness that she did not understand, although it mingled with her own and made her ask, "What does he do?"

The man was watching her. He smiled again and said, "Well now, I'll show ye."

She had always had an easy time of learning things, and this game had a structure to it that she found appealing, and a challenge that was made more real by how the stranger chose to introduce the players and their parts, as though they were real men upon a battlefield.

"But fit wye can the . . . ," she began, to be corrected by the man.

"Say 'why.'"

"Fit wye should I say 'why'?" she asked.

"Because it is more ladylike."

She frowned. "Why can the pawn not kill a man who's standing right in front of him?"

"His shield gets in the way," the man explained. "He has to lunge his sword arm to the front and side, like this." He demonstrated, and his skillful motion had a strength that deepened Anna's frown until he asked her, "What?"

She answered with the full directness of her seven years, replying, "You were telling tales, afore. You do not have the palsy."

"Have I not?" The crinkles formed around his eyes again. "Well, neither are ye motherless. In fact," he said as he leaned forwards, giving his attention to the chess pieces, "it seems to me that ye have quite the opposite affliction. Ye've two mothers I can name, and both of them do hold ye dear, and if there is another lass in all the world can make that claim, I've yet to hear it."

Anna eyed him doubtfully. "Two mothers?"

"Aye. The mother who has raised ye as her own, and dried your tears when ye had need of it, and loved ye all your life. That's one. And then there is the mother who gave birth to ye, and loved ye even more, if it were possible, so much so that she would not see ye come to harm, and left ye here at Slains to keep ye safe."

She did not understand, and plainly told him so.

His eyes were patient. "No, I'd not expect ye to. Now," he said, returning to the board between them, "which of these two kings will ye lay claim to?"

Anna chewed her lip and looked from one king to the other.

"White moves first," the man reminded her, and still she felt compelled to choose the black-haired king she'd rescued from beneath the chair.

Still thinking, she began, "Fit wye—?"

"Say 'why.'"

"Why did my mother leave me here at Slains?" she asked him. "Did she die?"

"No, she did not die. Why did ye choose the black king, and deny the other?"

"He's a proper king," was her excuse. "The real king has black hair."

His mouth curved. "And who is the real king?"

"Why, the king over the water." It surprised her that a man of his great age could be so ignorant. "There's a prince in London claims he is a king, but he is not, he's but a prince, and comes from Hanover and cannot speak in either Scots or English. And," she said, "he is a thief, besides."

"A thief?"

She gave a solemn nod. "He stole the crown he wears. The Earl of Erroll said so."

"'Tis a wicked thing to steal," the man agreed. "But to be fair, I would not think the Prince of Hanover a wicked man, so much as a misguided one." He set the white king squarely in the centre of his space, behind his line of white-painted defenders. "'Tis a fact he is no king and wears a crown that is not his, but he was not the first to wear it, nor the one to steal it from the rightful king, James Stewart. That deed was done when James was but a babe," the man revealed, "and 'twas his sisters stole the crown away, to pass it from their own hands to a foreign prince."

"His sisters?" Anna's eyes grew round. "Fit wye . . . why would they do that?"

"Some will tell ye it was purely for religion, for the sisters, they were Protestant, and James was raised a Catholic, and the English and our Scottish Presbyterians can never bide a Catholic on the throne. But 'tis nearer to the truth," he said, "to tell ye it was done for the same reason most men steal, and women, too: for riches, and for power."

"But it wisnae right for them to take the crown," said Anna, "and 'tis wrong the Prince of Hanover should keep it."

"Ye've the heart of a true Jacobite." The man was smiling.

"What's that?"

He said, "A Jacobite is one who would defend King James, our king over the water, as ye say, and fight to bring him safely home again."

She gave a nod. "The Earl of Erroll's one, then."

"Aye, he is. And so am I."

She liked the fact that he conversed with her as though she were his equal and had wit enough to understand, and so she felt secure in asking, "Why are ye called Jacobites? The king is James, not Jacob."

"In the Latin, James is written as *Jacobus*, lass. Have ye not learned the Latin, yet?" He clucked his tongue. "And ye the daughter of one of the noblest families of Scotland."

He was teasing her now, she thought, mocking the fact she'd been raised in a fisherman's cottage, mocking the fact that her father . . . *no*, not her true father, she stopped to remind herself. And that meant it was just possible that he was telling the truth. She asked, "Am I?"

He nodded, his steady hands turning the chessboard round

carefully so the black pieces were nearest to Anna. "Your father's own grandfather was a great soldier—the Black Pate, they called him, for his hair was black as the king's, and he rode with the greatest of heroes of Scotland, the Earl of Montrose. He was brave, the Black Pate. He'd a fire in his eye and a fire in his heart and there's no man could equal his skill with the sword, and the people who saw him ride past kept the memory forever."

"Did you see him ride past?"

"Aye, I did, many times," he admitted, "for he was my father. And *your* father's father did marry my sister, which makes me your uncle."

She gave a slight frown, knowing no other way to accept this strange news of the loss of one family and gain of another within the same morning.

"Your father," he informed her, "came from Perthshire, and his father was the Laird of Abercairney."

She looked down again along the row of silent waiting pawns and something stirred again, but dimly, in her memory. "Was my father a soldier?"

"He was. A colonel in the service of the French king and King James, upon the continent. A Jacobite, as you are." His gaze softened as he said, "Ye have the look of him."

"I do?"

"Oh, aye. He always was a handsome lad, was John. He was a favourite of the queen, King Jamie's mother. Thought the world of John, she did. It was in serving her that he first came to Slains, and met your mother. Her name," he continued, "was Sophia. She was of the Western Shires, a lass so beautiful that when they met, or so your father told me once, the very world stood still in that one moment, just for them."

Anna closed her eyes and tried imagining the soldier and his lady and the whole world standing still around them both, and when her eyes came open once again the older man was watching her with quiet understanding and affection.

"Aye, a rare fair thing it is, a love like that. And so they married, but they married all in secret, for your father was a wanted man. The English and their allies had a price upon his head that made it dangerous for anyone he loved."

She asked, "Why dangerous?"

"Because the English soldiers, had they kent about your mother, might have taken her and threatened her with harm to make your father do their will. The strongest soldier cannot balance long upon the blade that does divide his honour and his heart," the man said, "and whatever way he falls, the cut will kill him."

He had turned the chessboard round without disturbing any of the pieces. Now, with thought, he chose a white pawn from the centre of his row and moved it out two squares into the field of battle.

"So," he said, "your mother kept the secret, when your father's duty called him back again across the sea. You were already growing then within her belly, and she kept that secret, too, from all but those she trusted. But the English had their spies among us, then as well as now. One of the worst of them, a man of wealth and power, learned the truth about your mother and your father, and she feared for ye, and rightly, for she knew the same men who would seek to do her harm to make your father dance their tune, would without conscience also harm his child. She sought to hide ye, and 'twas then your other mother and the father that did raise ye did a brave and loving thing, and said they'd keep ye as their own until your true father returned."

She took this in, and turned the explanation over in her mind till it began to make some sense to her, and slowly eased a little of the hurt within her heart. She moved a pawn in her turn. "Then they will be coming back for me, my mother and my father."

He took so long in answering she thought he had not heard her. Many older men, she knew, were hard of hearing, and in truth when she looked up she found him focused on the chessboard with the fiercest concentration. As he moved another pawn she said, more loudly, "They'll come back for me."

Again he did not answer straight away. He seemed to think a

moment, then he said, "There was a battle, lass, five years ago, when ye were very small. A battle bloodier than any I have ever seen, or hope to see again. It happened in a place called Malplaquet. Your father fell there."

He had said the words so evenly, as though they did not pain him, yet she saw the tightened lines around his mouth and when he looked at her again his eyes were like her Uncle Rory's eyes had been when the old mastiff, Hugo, had slept on one morning in his corner of the stable without waking.

"In a better place now, aren't ye?" she'd heard Uncle Rory tell the sleeping dog, and then she'd seen his shoulders rise and fall and heard his breath catch as though somebody had hit him, till he'd noticed she was standing there. He'd sharply looked away then, and gone out, but not before she'd seen his eyes.

Her father, too, must now be in that better place where Hugo was, she thought, and there would be no coming back from there. She swallowed hard to hide her disappointment. "And my mother?"

"Well, by then ye were so settled in your family, with your brothers and your sisters, she had not the heart to take ye from the place where ye were safe and loved. She said it would have been a selfish thing to do, to risk your comfort for her own, and 'twas a measure of her love for ye that she did find the courage to go off alone and leave ye here, for of the choices that your mother made in life," he said, "that was the hardest of them all."

She saw the flicker in her mind's eye of a woman's face, too pale and framed by brightly curling hair, and of a gentle voice no louder than whisper that had said, "Go to your mother." Feeling once again that pressing sense of sadness, Anna asked, "Can I not go to her?"

"She's living far away, the now. 'Tis not a journey for a child to make. And how then would your other mother feel, to lose your love and so be left behind?" he asked her. "Ye'd not wish to break her heart as well, now would ye?"

"No, but . . ." Anna's voice trailed off, because she couldn't think of how to set things right, to make herself and both her mothers happy.

"See now, nothing that we do in life is easy," said the man. "Your pawn will capture mine in his next move, and yet that move will leave ye open to attack then from my bishop three moves hence. Each choice we make has an effect for good or ill, for all we may not yet perceive it at the time."

Her little chin set stubbornly. "And if I do not take your pawn?"

"Then my pawn will take yours, instead, and it will be my knight who moves to put your king in jeopardy."

She said, "Then I will stop your knight."

He laughed. "I do not doubt it."

They were deep in play when someone knocked upon the door, and Anna's Aunt Kirsty stepped into the room, her worried expression dissolving as she saw the two of them sitting there playing. She said in relief, "Colonel Graeme, ye've found her."

"She found me, in fact," said the older man. "And I've been glad of the company. Faith, I've not faced such a clever opponent since I taught her mother to play this game."

Kirsty asked, "You taught her mother?"

"I did," he said, lifting his gaze very briefly to hers, as though telling her something in silence before adding, "here in this very room, and with these men."

Anna looked at him keenly, intrigued that her aunt had addressed him as "Colonel." She asked, "Were you a soldier, like your father and my own?"

He smiled and admitted, "I'm soldiering still, lass. 'Tis why I am now come to Slains, as it happens. And since ye'll be burdened with me for the rest of the summer at least, ye'll be able to have your revenge on me."

"What for?" she asked him.

"For this." With a move of his aged hand, he moved his white knight to capture her queen. "Checkmate."

Anna indignantly reached out to lift her king out of harm's way.

With the painted piece clear of the chessboard and clutched to her chest so that only the top of his black head showed in her small fist, she said, "No, you'll not have him."

The colonel sat back in his chair for a moment, then traded a look of amusement with Anna's Aunt Kirsty. "Aye, lass," he said warmly to Anna, approval at war with another emotion in his smiling eyes, "ye've the heart of a Jacobite."

chapter
TEN

H e was walking her home.

It felt strange to be following people I couldn't see, but I had faith that Rob, walking behind me, saw clearly enough for the both of us, so when he said Colonel Graeme and Anna were just up ahead, I believed him. They were, from the angle at which he was watching them, slightly more inland and not quite so close to the cliff's edge as we were, but they were three hundred years in the past where no fenced fields impeded them, blocking their access and forcing them onto the coast path.

I saw them as Rob was describing them, Anna on restlessly dancing feet leading the weathered old soldier along.

Rob said, "He's not a tall man. He's not all that old, either, not by our standards. He'd be in his sixties, I'd guess. And he's not walking now like an old man at all, but like someone who's spent his life marching—his back's straight, his head's up except when he bends it to listen to her. He's got grey hair, combed back and tied here," Rob said, putting one hand at the nape of his neck, "into one of those, what d'ye call them? The wee braided tail things."

"A queue?"

"Aye, that's it. It goes well with the cape and the sword."

I glanced over my shoulder. "He's wearing a cape? In the summer?" I couldn't quite picture that.

"Only a short cape," said Rob. "It's attached to his coat at the back, at the shoulders, and hangs to his knees. And his coat's a bit shorter than that again, maybe to here." His one hand brushed his leg at midthigh. "It looks more like a really long waistcoat, without any sleeves, and he's wearing a plain white shirt underneath that, and a plain pair of breeks, and high boots."

"In the summer?"

"I'm not the one dressing him." Rob's voice was dry.

"Is he really her uncle, then?"

"Great-uncle, aye. Anna's father was his sister's son, if ye work it all out."

I was thinking. "If he was a colonel, I wonder if there'd be some record of him somewhere, then? It's a fairly high rank, colonel, isn't it?"

Rob shrugged and said, "He'd have been in the French army, likely, if he was a Jacobite. I no ken what kind of records they kept."

"He said that his father was somebody famous. Black somebody."

"Black Pate," he said. "As in black head, so I'm guessing that his hair was black. And aye, I mind his name getting a mention or two in the history books."

"Maybe the history books mention his sons, as well."

"What would that prove?"

"Well, for one thing," I said, "it would prove Colonel Graeme existed."

Rob countered with logic, "I ken he existed. He's walking right there."

"But no one else can see him, Rob. And knowing something's not the same as proving it. I mean, right now we can't even prove Anna Logan existed," I pointed out. Stumbling over a rock in the path, I stopped walking and sighed. "This is probably hopeless, you know, what we're doing. A fool's errand."

Rob had stopped walking as well, and was standing a half step behind my right shoulder, from where he could easily keep me from tumbling over the cliff if I slipped. "How's that, then?"

"It just is. We can't prove anything, this way. How can we?" With a sigh, I tried explaining. "All I really wanted was for you to hold the Firebird so you could tell me something of its history—who had made it, and how Empress Catherine came by it, and when and why she'd given it to Anna, or at least where Anna lived, there in St. Petersburg, and those would have been things I could investigate. But this . . ." Lifting one hand in the general direction of where Colonel Graeme and Anna had gone, I said, "We're following a little girl, Rob, and you said yourself she can't be more than eight years old, which means it might be ages yet until she gets the Firebird. Besides which, we're in Scotland, not in Russia."

"Well, she obviously got from here to there," said Rob. "If I can find her house, find where she lived, then I can skip ahead so maybe we can see her leaving."

When he stated it like that, so calm and practical, it almost made me think it was that easy. "And just how would we prove *that*, on paper? She's a fisherman's daughter, she's not likely to have left a record of her life behind."

"She's no fisherman's daughter," Rob reminded me. "Her father was the Laird of Abercairney's son, the colonel said. Black Pate was her great-grandfather, and she herself can roam the Earl of Erroll's castle as though she were part of his own family. For a lass so small, I'd say she had connections."

I turned so I could see his face, the faintly stubborn jawline. "Do you always see the positive in everything?"

"I see the possibilities." His eyes were narrowed slightly as he scanned the fields ahead. "They'll soon be out of sight, if we stop here."

I turned again, and went on walking, taking more care with my footing as the path came very close now to the edge.

Rob followed silently at first, then unexpectedly he said, "I was a lad of six, ye ken, when I first saw the Sentinel. Kip saw him, too—my collie Kip—and they'd be walking side by side out in the field, and every time the Sentinel came close to me he'd smile and try to speak, except he'd speak in Latin and in those days I'd no way to understand him. But I saw him. Saw the camp as well, or bits of it. And when the archaeologists came looking for the lost Ninth Legion, I could tell them where a wall had been, or where they ought to dig. They had no proof," he pointed out, "afore they started digging. Even when they found the wall, the camp, they really had no proof the Ninth had been there. Not at first. It came in pieces, so it did, and never where they'd been expecting it. An edge of broken pottery, a coin, all scattered pieces, yet together it was proof enough to satisfy the academics."

I was far too focused on my feet to turn around again. I asked, "Is this your way of saying I should have more faith?"

"I'm saying proof may not be lying in plain sight, all neat and tidy, as ye say. And aye, it may be that we never find a document that helps, but if we dig enough we may just find enough of those small pieces to convince whoever needs convincing."

I felt the warmth of reassurance, less because of what he'd said than from the fact he'd used the pronoun "we" while he was saying it. I found I liked that "we."

"Mind how ye go," said Rob. I felt his hand against my elbow as he guided me a half step farther from the cliff's edge. "There, that's safer."

Up ahead I saw a square of closely pressed small cottages. "Where are we now?"

"At the Bullers of Buchan."

I glanced at the curve of the cliff, and the white spray and foam of the water below, but it didn't look anything like the framed photograph hanging above us at dinner last night. I was going to say so when Rob said, "The actual Bullers, the sea cave, is just a few steps past those cottages, see where the sign is? But we're going this way." His arm brushed my own as he pointed along the short track that connected the cottages to the main road.

"Are you sure?"

"Aye, of course I'm sure. D'ye not trust me?"

"It's only that last night I thought you saw something to do with the Bullers of Buchan."

"I'm not sure of what I saw last night," Rob told me, "but just the now I'm seeing your Anna legging it up the road there. We can stop on the way back," he promised, as I took a final look over my shoulder.

Rob moved to the front when we walked at the side of the road, so that any approaching cars had to go round him first. I tried to look at the scenery. I did. We were close to the sea, still, and watching the changeable clouds chase their shadows towards the horizon should really have been more diverting, but always my gaze was pulled back to the roll of Rob's shoulders, and the dark curl of his hair against his collar, things I had no business noticing.

Of course I found him physically attractive. I had always been attracted to him, but that didn't change the deep divide between our lives. Up here, with nobody around, it was an easy thing for me to talk with Rob about the things he saw and heard, and let him lead me after phantoms from the past, but in public it would be a different story— I'd be too embarrassed, too afraid of everybody judging me and thinking me a fool, or worse. And Rob could never be less than he was, I knew, or hide his gifts. It wasn't in his nature.

It would never work between us, but the logic of that knowledge didn't stop me watching him so closely that time telescoped so when he left the road's edge and turned off towards the cliffs again, it took me by surprise to see how far we'd come.

I could no longer see the jagged shape of Slains behind us, nor the houses at the Bullers, though farther up ahead along the coast I saw what looked to be a large town or small city.

Rob identified it. "Peterhead."

But Anna and the colonel hadn't gone the whole way there. They'd stopped, as we had, at this little sloping hollow near the road. I saw the scattering of granite stones that still stood at right angles to each other in one corner and I guessed before Rob told me that this once had been a cottage.

Rob built the walls again for me with words, their heavy sturdiness topped with a low thatched roof and pierced by little unglazed windows with their shutters left unfastened to the daylight. It was hard to think a family could have lived here, all five children and their parents, in what Rob said was a single open space inside, with swept dirt floors and whitewashed walls, no room at all for privacy. And yet I felt the comfort they had felt here, and the happiness. It resonated round me like a singing voice heard faintly on the wind, from far away, and without meaning to I placed one hand upon the stone beside me and

I closed my eyes and stretched my mind towards that distant feeling. I found nothing. Only silence.

When I opened my eyes I saw Rob with his back to me, shaking his dark head as though he were puzzled. "It's gone."

"I'm sorry?"

"The cottage," he said. "It's not here. I only went a short while forwards, not too far, to see if I could find her as a teenager, but all of this"—he nodded at the cottage walls that he alone could see—"is gone. It's all in ruins."

He turned. His gaze dropped briefly to my hand, still resting on the stone, and with that damnably quick way of adding two and two he asked, "Did you see anything yourself?" Like that, so normally. As though I could.

I felt the small smile twist my mouth, and raised my hand to push the wind-whipped hair back from my eyes again. "Of course I didn't. I don't . . . I *can't* see the way that you do."

Rob's expression grew more thoughtful, as though he'd heard something in my tone I hadn't put there by design. He crossed the ground between us, thinking. Sitting on the stone beside me, he asked, "Would you like to?"

There was no good way to answer that. My envy of Rob's gifts was so at war with my own yearning to be normal and the warnings of my grandfather that I could only shake my head and say, "It doesn't matter. Really. This is working fine, with you describing things."

He gave an absent nod, as though agreeing, and then studied me in silence for a moment before asking, "Can I try something?"

My voice turned wary. "What?"

"Give me your hand."

"Rob."

"You said that you trusted me."

"Yes, but . . ."

"Then give me your hand." His was outstretched, and waiting.

Reluctantly, I slipped my hand into his and then raised my defences as I felt his fingers close warmly round mine.

"D'ye mind that first day at the Emerson," Rob said, "when we did the ganzfeld? Try doing that now."

"Rob . . ."

"It's not so hard. Clear your thoughts, close your eyes, just hear the wind and the waves and the gulls now, and focus."

I tried. "It's not working."

"Relax." A faint squeeze of his fingers. "You've managed to find your way into my mind afore this."

A small warmth spread from his hand to mine and I strove to ignore it, while focusing all my attention on clearing my mind of its whirlwind of thoughts and emotions. At last I felt the calming sense of peace, as though I'd settled in a warm relaxing bath, and from the blackness that surrounded me the little moving images began their cinematic play, a filmstrip running in reverse.

I wasn't in Rob's mind at all, I thought. This was how my own visions started.

I waited for the moment when one image would project itself and grow to blot the others out, when gradually I realized that these images weren't running at the speed I was accustomed to. The filmstrip slowed, and paused, and ran a few frames forward.

In confusion I asked Rob, *Is that you?*

Is what me?

Doing that.

He didn't answer straight away. He'd found the frame he wanted, and already it was growing and expanding as it took us in, but where my visions would have stopped and settled in their boundaries, this one widened far beyond what I had ever seen before, so very swiftly that it flooded all my senses with a dizzying assault of scents and sounds.

I felt, in that first moment, like a seagull hanging on the wind high over sea and shore, and looking down with a perspective only flight could give. I saw the grey horizon and the darkness of the waves, and felt the stab of winter's cold as I looked down upon the little cottage, thatched and shuttered as Rob had described it, drifted deep with snow that showed two lines of dragging footprints leading to the door, which was half-blocked now by the figure of a man.

These things I saw before my line of vision swooped and started lowering and raced across the snow until it reached a level just above the one it would have been at if I'd stood upon the ground. The line of vision of a man about Rob's height, I realized.

God. My voice, yet even I could not have said if I had meant it as a prayer or as a heartfelt exclamation.

Rob responded with, *You're with me now? You're seeing this all right?*

I gave a nod, or thought I did, and we went once around the cottage like a panoramic camera, past the man who stood within the cottage doorway with his back to us, his rough dark cloak of woollen cloth still caked in places from the snow, and smelling thick with smoke that seemed more acrid than a wood fire's.

It was so early in the morning that towards the east the sun still showed as glints of red and spreading gold behind the windborne clouds above the sea, and when that same wind blew, it nearly robbed my lungs of breath.

I couldn't turn from it as quickly as I might have done, because I wasn't in control. Rob was, so if he stood a moment longer looking out towards the sunrise, I could only wait and brave the wind until he turned away to face the cottage.

Rob?

Hang on.

This time the movement didn't feel like flight. It felt like we were running as we swiftly crossed the few feet of remaining ground and slipped straight through the cottage walls as though they had been made of mist, as though we both were ghosts.

We were inside.

chapter ELEVEN

The man behind the colonel filled the doorway of the cottage, with his great dark cloak that blocked the light and dripped with melting snow. His breath had frozen in his beard and left it white and ragged, so to Anna's eyes he looked like some fierce Highlander, like those she'd often heard about in tales but never seen, although this man did not wear Highland dress. Beneath the cloak his legs were tightly cased in breeks and boots, though one was wrapped above the knee in strips of cloth soaked through with brownish stains. He favoured it, that leg, and put his weight upon the other as he waited in the doorway while the colonel talked.

She wasn't meant to hear them. She was meant to still be sleeping, huddled warmly in the long bed with her brothers and her sisters, for in truth it was but first light and the day had not yet properly begun, and it was plain from how her father and her mother and the colonel and his friend were talking, quietly and low, with care, that what they spoke of was not for the children's ears.

Her mother seemed distraught. "So close?"

The colonel nodded. "Half a day behind us, and perhaps by now much less than that."

Her father raked his hair back with one hand, the way he always did when forced to think more rapidly than was his wont. "The king?"

"Is safe," the colonel said. "We saw him off ourselves."

"He'd scarcely landed," was her father's comment, edged with bitterness.

The colonel didn't offer any argument, which made her father bold enough to follow with, "How can he now abandon all who've fought and bled this winter in his cause?"

The colonel's steady gaze held something like a challenge. "Would ye now abandon him?" When he was met by silence, he went on, "The king must play upon a larger board than you and I. Sometimes a piece must fall so that the rest of them survive, but I assure you he does feel such losses keenly, and his leaving of this shore was yet the hardest choice that I have seen him make."

"Aye, 'twill be very hard to watch our ruin from the safety of his ship."

"The sea," the colonel said, "is never safe. Have not ye learnt the truth of that in all these years, lad, that ye've been a fisherman?"

Her father met the colonel's gaze, but grudgingly. "Why did you not go with him?"

"The king has other men to keep him safe, and with that devil Argyll's army in pursuit along this coast mere hours behind us, there are others more in need of my protection."

Anna huddled in the blankets as the sharp wind struck the cottage walls and wailed outside as though it wanted entry. She knew little of the battles that had occupied her parents' talk since harvest-time, except a cousin of her father's had been killed at Sheriffmuir, wherever that might be, and from what Colonel Graeme had just said, it seemed that death had been the devil's doing. Pressing closer to her sleeping brother's side for warmth, she tried to shut her ears to all the shrieks of winter wind; tried blotting out the vivid image of the devil and his army drawing nearer by the minute.

She could hear her mother speaking. "We are grateful to you, Colonel, for the warning. And to you," she told the other man, who'd waited all this time in patient silence, "Mr. . . . ?"

"Jamieson," the colonel gave the answer. "Captain Jamieson."

The man within the doorway gave a brief nod to her mother, and from deep beneath her blankets Anna peered at him more closely. He was younger than the colonel, near to her father's age, but rougher-looking with his bearded face.

Her mother told him, "You are wounded, sir."

His leg above the knee was slowly leaking red into the brown stains of the bandage now, but with a shrug he told her, "I can travel."

"So must you," the colonel told her parents. "Gather up the children, there are French ships waiting just offshore to carry us."

"And English ones to keep them there, no doubt." Her father's voice was grim. He shook his head. "I'll take no ship, nor risk my children to the English guns. I'll take my family overland to Slains. The castle walls are thick enough for safety, and I'll warrant even Argyll will be like to tread with care upon the Earl of Erroll's property."

"A man like Argyll," said the colonel, "cares not where he treads. And when he comes, with his dragoons and all his hired band of foreign soldiers who have never heard the Earl of Erroll's name, what then?"

"You're saying I cannot protect my family?"

"I am saying," said the colonel, "that a fox that goes to ground may be dug out."

Her father stood more straight. "And one that makes a dash across an open field risks just as much."

The two men faced each other down with level stares and stances, neither willing to give ground. At length her father glanced away and finished stubbornly, "My family goes to Slains."

The colonel held his tongue a moment longer, then he gave a nod. "If ye will not be swayed, sir, then that surely is your right. But understand that I must guard *my* family as I will." Her father frowned as though he did not fully understand, and so the colonel spelt it out for him: "Ye take your children where ye must, but Anna comes with me."

When the captain, at his shoulder, shifted slightly on his feet as though to protest, Colonel Graeme said, "She is my nephew's daughter, and her blood is bound to mine, and for the love I bore her father and the love he bore her mother I'll be damned if I will ever let the lassie come to harm. She comes with me."

The captain glanced towards the bed where Anna and the other children lay, and Anna was so fascinated by the hardness of his face she did not look away, but met his eyes. If it surprised him that she was awake and listening, he gave no outward sign of it. He only held her gaze a moment, studied her, and finally said, "Good morning."

All the others turned to look at her as well, and since there was no point in hiding in the blankets any longer Anna sat up fully, straightening her back as her own gaze slipped to the colonel and she asked him, "Is the devil really on his way here?"

Colonel Graeme, as he often did, delayed his answer with a question of his own. "And do ye fear the devil, Anna?"

Anna heard again the wicked wailing of the wind, and was not sure. She looked to where her mother and her father stood, and then towards the door that was still blocked by Captain Jamieson, and guarded by the colonel, and it seemed to her that nothing could so easily get past those two men and their swords, and suddenly she knew that she was not afraid. Not really.

So she said as much. And when she asked the colonel, "Can your ship outrun him?" she felt something stir within her, like the thrill at the beginning of a great adventure.

"Aye." His smile came easily, as though he somehow knew what she was feeling, and he looked to Captain Jamieson. "My nephew's child," he told the captain, and his pride was obvious as he said once again, "She comes with us."

It was decided, then.

Her mother dressed her warmly, in two layers and a wrap, with heavy woollen stockings that felt scratchy on her legs and Donald's old boots that were too large for her small feet. "Mind the colonel, now," her mother said in a brisk tone that sounded nothing like her own. "Do as he tells ye, with no argument."

"I never argue."

"Anna."

Anna held her tongue, but only for an instant while she watched her mother's busy hands. "Will you be coming after, when the devil's gone?"

Her mother's hands fell still. She paused, then, "No, we'll not be coming."

Anna frowned as she absorbed this. "Ever?"

"No." Her mother raised her head and showed a smile that, like her voice, seemed not quite natural. "The colonel's right, the place for ye the now is with your family."

Anna struggled with a swift confusing tangle of emotions, but through all of it she sought to learn the truth. "Do you not want me anymore?"

"Of course I do, of course I want ye. From the first day ye were put into my arms ye've been the best and finest daughter I could wish for, but ye never were my own to keep." Her mother's smile began to tremble slightly, but she steadied it. "And there are other hearts that have a greater right than mine to claim your love." She raised a hand to smooth the hair away from Anna's face and smiled more brightly. "Here now, I've a giftie for ye."

Anna took the little parcel from her mother's outstretched hand and stared at it in wonder. It was just the size of her own palm, and wrapped in cloth so beautiful she'd never seen its like—a bit of silken stuff the colour of the lavender that grew beside the kitchen door at Slains. At first she thought that was the gift itself, and would have thanked her mother for it had she not been gently told to open it.

Inside, a single curl of hair lay bright against the lovely cloth, its cut ends tightly tied together with a soft blue ribbon.

Her mother gently told her, "'Tis Sophia's hair, the mother ye were born to. Ye did ask for that the day she left, and I have kept it for ye since."

With one uncertain finger Anna touched the curl. "My mother's hair?"

"Aye. And where she has gone she has a curl of your hair with her that she took from you that day, tied with that same blue ribbon, so that she may keep your memory close." Her mother watched as Anna touched the curl again. "Is it not beautiful?"

"It is a different colour from my own." That disappointed her.

The colonel had been listening, behind her. "Aye," he said, "ye have the look of your father, the bonny brown hair and the eyes that your mother so loved."

The mother who'd raised her agreed. "She once told your Aunt Kirsty his eyes were the same colour as the winter sea."

The colonel said, "Did she, now?" Looking into Anna's eyes he smiled. "And so they are. Are ye then ready for a voyage on that sea?"

Her mother held them back a moment. "There is one thing more." From underneath her own clothes in the low box in the corner of the cottage, she drew out a folded garment made of finest Holland linen, traced with lovingly embroidered sprays of vines and fading flowers. As she rolled it tightly, wrapping it within a square of rougher homespun cloth, she said to Anna, "This was made by your Aunt Kirsty for your mother, for her wedding night, and 'twas your mother's wish that you should have it. It was made with love and carries love, and that will shield ye better in this life than any armour." She re-bound the bit of silken cloth that held the curl of hair again, as well, and handed both to Colonel Graeme. "Will ye guard these for her?"

"Aye." He took them carefully and found a place of safety for them underneath his coat. As he looked around the small room at the faces that were watching him, he asked her father once again, "Ye're certain that ye will not come?"

Her father shook his head, then asked, "Where are ye bound?"

"To Flanders, if the wind allows. There is a monastery of the Irish nuns at Ypres, where I have many times found shelter in the past. I'll send ye word from there."

"God keep ye safe," her mother told him, and he nodded in return.

"And you." His hand touched Anna's shoulder. "Say goodbye, now."

It was hard. She felt the sting of tears as she embraced her brothers and her sisters, and it worsened when the warm familiar feeling of her mother's arms wrapped round her. "Be a good girl, now," was all the last instruction she received before her mother turned away again to give her father space to crouch in front of Anna.

His eyes were strangely glistening, but when he blinked they cleared again. "Ye'll no forget us, will ye?"

Anna shook her head. "No, Father."

With a twisting of his mouth he quickly leaned to kiss her forehead. "That's my quinie." As he stood he told the colonel, "Best be on yer way, then. We'll be no sae far ahind ye."

Captain Jamieson had turned away himself, as though to give the family privacy, but now he gave a nod and for the first time took a step back from the doorway, letting in a gust of wind and snow that swirled beneath the low-set lintel, breathing cold into the room and making Anna shiver.

All at once she felt uncertain.

Colonel Graeme told her, "Anna, take my hand."

She raised her chin. She had to look a long way up to find his eyes, but they were smiling when she found them. "Come, there is no cause to be afraid."

Anna felt the captain's watchful eyes and let her chin lift higher. "I'm no feart."

For once the colonel didn't make an effort to correct her speech. He only closed his hand around the littler one she offered him, and with a final backwards nod towards her parents, led her through the door.

The sun, if it had risen fully yet this morning, had stayed hidden well behind the clouds. Across the white folds of the cliffs the light fell strangely flat and cold, and where the men and Anna broke the freshly drifted snow they left no shadows.

Anna found it difficult to walk as quickly as the men, although the captain went a step ahead and made a trail for her. Her too-large boots dragged heavily upon her feet, and made her stumble.

When she stumbled for the third time, Captain Jamieson glanced back.

Above her head the colonel raised his voice above the wind to reassure him, "She'll be fine. 'Tis only that the snow is deep."

The captain nodded understanding. Then without a word, he

reached to lift her up and off her feet and swing her round into the
shelter of his chest, and Anna let the colonel's hand go as she wrapped
her arms around the captain's neck instead. His shoulder smelt of
sweat and smoke and sodden wool, and yet she felt the strength of it
and pressed her face against it as her eyes squeezed tightly shut against
the lonely sight behind them of the cottage growing smaller, ever
smaller, at their backs.

Rob had long since let go of my hand, but when I stood two steps
from the brink of the Bullers of Buchan and stared down the deadly
sheer drop of its sides, a small traitorous part of me wished he would
hold it again.

I had never been good with heights. Looking up, going up, that
was no problem, but looking the other way made me feel dizzy and
sick inside, just like I had on the day when my brother had talked me
down out of that tree.

And I'd never looked down upon anything quite like the Bullers of
Buchan.

Long ages ago it had probably started its life as a sea cave, a cleft
in the line of the cliff with a hollow behind where the water poured
through with each wave, with each tide, wearing fiercely away at the
rock till at length there was no more support for the roof of the cave
so that fell, tumbling inward and into the swirling dark water below.

What it left was a deep open shaft, ringed on all sides by cliffs, with
the mouth of the old cave still standing below as a narrow cleft opening out to the sea. There were gulls wheeling under us, wings flashing
white as they chased their own shadows above the seawater that boiled
on the black rocks below.

I eased back a step more from the edge, glancing over at Rob.
"They left from here?" I asked. "You're sure of that?"

He gave a nod. "There was a little sailboat, like a fishing boat,
moored just down there. It took them out to meet the bigger ship."

I didn't look where he was pointing, down among the rocks. My
gaze was drawn up instead, across the wide North Sea that glittered

underneath the August sun, and I tried hard to picture how that same sea would have looked to little Anna in the depth of winter.

Aloud I only said, "Except they didn't go to Russia."

Rob corrected me. "We no ken where they went, we only ken where they were bound."

I searched my memory for the colonel's words. "The monastery of the Irish nuns at Ypres."

"That's right."

"That's Belgium, isn't it?"

"It is." His hands were in his pockets now, his stance relaxed, and yet I didn't need to read his thoughts to sense his restlessness. It radiated from him like a living thing; electrified the air. His sideways glance at me was casual. "When is it that you're meant to head to Russia?"

"Thursday."

"Ah."

I made an effort to be practical. "I can't just go to Belgium."

"Why? It's not so far. You fly or take the Eurostar," he said, "you're there and back."

"And you can't go there, either. You've got work, you've got commitments . . ."

"I'm on holiday," he said. "Did I not tell ye?"

There was no way I could figure out, from that blue dancing gaze alone, if he were telling me the truth. "Well, you've still got the lifeboat."

"I can take time off from that as well. I'd only have to clear it with my coxswain." He was daring me a little, I could feel it. With his head tipped to the side he asked me, "What are you afraid of?"

There was no way I could hold that gaze. I tore my own away and told him, "Nothing."

I'm no feart. I saw the childish face turned upwards to the colonel's in my mind, and I narrowed my own eyes against the brightness of the water.

"Rob, you're sure the little Anna we've been following today is Margaret's ancestor?"

"I'm sure."

"But how? I mean, there could have been a dozen Annas living here . . ."

"I'm sure." His tone was not so stubborn as assertive, with the confidence of someone wholly certain of his facts. He left no room for me to question that, but given it was Rob I didn't need to. His abilities, his instincts, were so far beyond my own that if he felt so sure of something, there was nothing I could do but trust his word.

And if the Anna we'd been watching was, in truth, the one to whom the Empress Catherine had been speaking in my vision, that first flash I'd had the day I'd held the Firebird, then I knew that Anna had once been in Russia, in St. Petersburg. But how she'd come to be there, and with whom, and where she'd lived, and what on earth had brought her into Catherine's orbit—these were questions I still didn't know the answers to, and if I were to truly have a go at pinning down some sort of provenance for Margaret's treasured Firebird while I was in St. Petersburg, my time was running out.

I said, "That thing you did today . . ." That so incredible, amazing thing he'd done that had transported me and let me see another time more vividly than I'd imagined possible. I cleared my throat. "Is that the way you always see? I mean, if we did go to Belgium, could you . . ."

"Aye." He smiled a little. "That's the way I always see."

The stab of envy that I felt was so keen I was sure he would pick up on it, but his attention had been caught by something at my feet.

Distracted, I looked down myself. At the edge of the Bullers of Buchan a single white feather had snagged on a low clump of blowing grass and withered wildflowers, fighting the wind that was trying to tear it away.

It was only a gull's feather, ragged and plain, not a feather of flame from a firebird, but I felt Rob's amusement before I looked up at him.

There were those eyes again, daring me, waiting.

"That's how it begins," he said, "isn't it?"

Hands in his pockets, he patiently watched while I looked down again at the feather. The wind caught its end and it started to lift and on impulse I bent down and reached for it.

As I stood, feather in hand, Rob's smile turned to a grin and his gaze angled out to sea. "Belgium, then."

Letting my gaze follow his I fought back a swift twist in my stomach that might have been dread or excitement, and gave a nod. "Belgium."

chapter TWELVE

Sebastian leant back in his chair. "Belgium?"

"Yes, well, something came up rather suddenly, with an old friend," I said, trying to keep enough truth in the words so that I'd sound convincing. "I know it's a bother, but I only thought since it's quiet this time of the year, and I'm already heading out Thursday, it might be all right."

He studied me as though I'd just done something that intrigued him. "Do you know," he told me in a thoughtful tone, "I don't believe I've ever seen you be quite so spontaneous."

I shrugged, and was about to make excuses when he caught me out with,

"Tell the truth. You've got it all arranged already, haven't you?"

"Sort of." I held out a moment longer before giving in. "Well, yes. I've hired the new receptionist, and she can start tomorrow, so you won't be on your own."

He was smiling. "Who'd you hire?"

"Her name is Gemma. Gemma Richardson. You liked her."

He searched his memory. "Gemma . . . wasn't she the little blonde?"

I shook my head. "Brunette. She'd worked for Sotheby's."

"Ah." Sebastian nodded. "Gemma, yes. Long legs, big . . ." Meeting my dry look, he finished innocently, ". . . eyes."

"Yes, well, she's got a big brain to go with those eyes," I said. "She'll be able to get up to speed quite easily, I think. I've briefed her on your schedule and appointments for the next week, so there shouldn't be a problem while I'm gone. I'll have my mobile, if you need me."

"You seem very sure that I'll say yes."

I faced his teasing look with patience. "Well?"

"Belgium." Steepling his fingers he considered my request. "You'd leave tonight, you said?"

"That's right. And we'd be coming back on Wednesday, so I'll have lots of time to make my flight the next day."

"Two nights in Belgium," was the only thing he took from that. His eyebrows rose in speculation. "When you say 'an old friend,' do you mean 'an *old* friend,', or . . . ?"

"Sebastian."

"Yes, all right." He grinned. "Go on. I can't complain, now can I, since you've gone and got me Gemma. Just be sure to take your mobile."

He'd already rung me twice before we'd even made it onto the M20.

Rob, negotiating traffic, had stayed silent in his undemanding way the first time I'd been speaking to Sebastian, but when I rang off now he sent a glance in my direction and one eyebrow lifted over the hard line of his dark sunglasses as he asked, "Is he aye troubling you like this?"

"Not always. Only when I leave the office."

"He was quiet all the weekend."

"Well, he likely had a woman with him," I explained. "Besides, I don't work weekends."

"And you're not working the now," was Rob's reminder. "Put that thing away."

"Rob . . ."

"Put it down, or switch it off, afore I throw it out the window."

From his tone I knew he wasn't being serious, but nonetheless I humoured him and stuffed the mobile deep into my pocket.

"Thank you. Now," he said, "what were you saying about Colonel Patrick Graeme?"

"Oh. I looked him up. He was the captain of the Edinburgh Town Guard, when he was younger, so a man of some authority, but when King James the Second—"

"Seventh."

"Sorry?"

"To you English," Rob corrected me, "he was the second king named James to rule ye, but in Scotland we'd already had six James's afore him."

"Well, both names would be right, then."

Once again I got the sideways glance. "Whose history are ye learning, at the moment?"

"Scotland's, I suppose."

"Then learn it properly." His tone was lighter than his words, but I still took the dare.

"All right, then. When King James the Seventh left and went to France in exile, Captain Patrick Graeme followed him. He left his wife behind, I think, in Edinburgh. At least at the beginning."

"Children?"

"He had four sons, from what I could find. Two became Capuchin monks, one was trained as a doctor, and one went to sea."

"What, no soldiers?"

"Apparently not." I consulted the papers I'd scribbled on last night when I'd done my Internet searching. "The seagoing one and one monk died as fairly young men, but the other monk seems to have made quite a name for himself. He was called Father Archangel."

Rob said, "Still, from those bloodlines you'd think you would get at least one soldier."

"Maybe that's why Colonel Graeme was close to his nephew," I said. "Anna's father."

"And what did ye learn about him?"

"Colonel Graeme told Anna that her father's name was John, and that *his* father was the Laird of Abercairney, right? Well, there was a John Moray, the third son of Sir Robert Moray of Abercairney, who became a lieutenant-colonel in the Regiment of Lee, one of the Irish regiments that served the king of France."

Rob thought that sounded right.

I said, "John Moray died around 1710."

"That would fit. What we saw at the cottage," he said, "was most likely happening right at the end of the '15."

"The what?"

"The rebellion of 1715." His eyebrow was lifting again. "Do they not teach you any real history at all, here in England?"

"Go on, then. Enlighten me."

"King James the Seventh had three children," Rob told me, patiently. "Two daughters, by his first wife, and a son by his second. The birth of that son was what set off the first revolution, ye ken, against James, in the late 1680s, for James meant to raise his son Catholic, as he was, and that was a problem for those who opposed him. They wanted a Protestant heir to the throne. So they fought against James, and he went into exile, and they set his daughters, whose mother had raised them both Protestant, to rule in his place. The first daughter was Mary, along with her husband—you've heard about William and Mary? And after came Anne. By the time Queen Anne died, James the Seventh was dead as well, and her half brother, whose name was James also, was nearly my age by then. He still lived in his exile in France, and there's some talk," he told me, "that Anne thought to make him her heir, for her own children all died afore her, but none of her English advisors would have that. When she died, in 1714, they went for her closest relation who was a good Protestant, and brought him over from Hanover—Germany," Rob said. "And that's how you end up with King George, the first George, who barely spoke English. The Jacobites, not just in Scotland, ye ken, but in England, too, weren't having *that*. So they started a war, and brought young James, King James the Eighth, over from France to win back his crown."

"But he didn't."

"No. Most of the fighting was over afore he arrived. What we saw at the cottage near Slains," Rob remarked, "was the end of it, all of the Jacobites making a run for it with England's ally, the Earl of Argyll, at their heels."

"Was he Scottish?"

"He was."

I was silent a moment, still sorting out all the alliances and the betrayals of those tangled times, and the cause that had brought a man of Colonel Graeme's great age back from France into Scotland to fight for the man he considered his king.

"It's a shame," I said. "All of the fighting they did, and for nothing."

"Well, they'd not have seen it that way. It was James the Eighth's throne, he'd been born to, and in their view there was no act of parliament could change that fact. They were fighting for honour and justice. Not bad things to fight for."

I smiled at his tone. "And would you have fought, too, with the Jacobites, if you had lived back then?"

"Most likely." Briefly pressing back against his seat, Rob stretched his shoulders as though they were cramping.

He didn't look tired, but I knew he'd driven several hours already down from Scotland, and we had another five at least ahead of us. I'd booked us on the Eurotunnel shuttle, which was faster than the ferry, but it also meant Rob wouldn't have much time to relax and rest while we were crossing over to Calais.

He said, "I'm fine, I like to drive. I'll not need rest."

"Must you do that?"

"Do what?"

"Answer questions I haven't asked."

"But you did ask it."

I said, "Not out loud."

Rob apologized. "Sorry. It all sounds the same, to me." Keeping his eyes on the road he asked, "Is it not that way for you? When my dad was mucking about with ye there, you answered him as though you'd heard his voice."

"I did. I mean, I do. But I'm not used to having somebody else do it to *me*."

"I must have done it all the time afore," he pointed out. "You never mentioned that it bothered you."

"Yes, well, it's been a while."

Rob seemed to find this curious. "Your grandfather must do it, though."

I shook my head, and thought of those few times when, as a child, I'd reached my thoughts to him and with a frown he'd brusquely pushed me out. "He never talks to me that way."

Rob drove in silence for a moment, then he said, "He likely hears you, though."

There was a kind of certainty to how he said the words that made me turn a little in my seat to look at him. I nearly asked him whether he was speaking from experience, but just then I was saved by a demanding ring tone from my pocket.

Rob's eyes rolled. "I hope he pays you well, this guy."

"He pays me very well." I fished my mobile out and answered, "Yes, Sebastian?"

I wasn't awake when we drove into Ypres.

My eyes drifted open to a sudden awareness of silence. Somewhat groggily I realized we were parked, and it was late at night, the softly amber streetlamps casting glittering reflections over cobblestones along a narrow curve of street with old-style houses shouldered tightly to each other.

It had rained. The water pooled and glistened in the low uneven places at the edges of the road, and as I turned my head to look at Rob, a low branch of the tree above us caught the wind and dipped and flung a spattering of drops across the windscreen.

Rob was securing the car with the handbrake. "Heyah."

"When did that happen?" I asked.

"What?"

"When did I fall asleep?"

"Ten minutes out of Calais."

"Oh, no. Rob, I'm so sorry."

"For what?"

It seemed obvious. "Letting you drive all that way without company."

"I had the radio, it was no problem. You did say the Novotel?"

I gave a nod. "On Sint Jacobsstraat."

"Good, because that's where we are." When he opened his car door the cooler night air flooding in brought me fully awake, so when Rob told me, "I'll get the bags from the boot," for the first time I noticed what I hadn't noticed before.

Neither of us was speaking out loud.

I let it pass, because although he didn't look tired I expected he must be, from driving all day, and it seemed likely that he didn't even realize he was doing it. The same way he'd reached out his thoughts to mine last Thursday morning, when he'd still been half asleep. Could that have only been four days ago? It seemed much longer.

"Here," I said, using my proper voice this time as I got out, too. "Let me carry mine."

"I've got it." His spoken voice was sure.

"Yes, well, chivalry is very nice, but you don't have to—"

"I've got it." He stubbornly tightened his grip on the handle, and steered me towards the hotel entrance, just a few steps up the street, its facade a warmly backlit line of modern glass and metal that stood out against its older-world surroundings. I couldn't even hold the doors for Rob, the glass slid open automatically, inviting us to step inside an open-plan interior with lounge and restaurant shadowed for the night.

Rob waited by the elevators while I sorted out our reservation at the long wood curve of the reception desk, and took his key card from me while we rode the elevator upwards. When we had reached our floor he followed me, still carrying the luggage, and he only set my bag down when he'd had a quick look in my room to satisfy himself that it was safe.

His room was next along the corridor. I heard the deadbolt lock of his door click just after I'd turned mine, and heard the water running as he washed and brushed his teeth, and heard the creaking of the bed as he lay down. I half-imagined, hours later, I could hear his quiet breathing as I watched the play of shadows on the ceiling overhead. He might as well have been beside me.

Still, I much preferred to put my restless, fitful sleeping down to having slept those hours in the car while we were driving, and at first light I gave up the effort altogether. Through the gauzy curtains at my window I could see the Gothic tower of an old church rising close against the red-tiled rooftops of the houses next to the hotel, its pointed spire set off by smaller pinnacles.

The sky looked flat and uninspired, a wash of watercolour grey that dulled the courtyard grass below me and the deep green tops of trees that showed beyond those same tiled roofs, in front of where the church was, but just as Rob had gone out on his own at Cruden Bay in search of Anna, so I reasoned it was only fair if I went first this time to find the convent.

If the research that I'd done on Sunday night when I got back from Scotland was to be believed, it wouldn't take me long. The convent of the Irish nuns had been on this same street.

The air felt cool when I went out, and once again I seemed to have just missed the rain, for on the narrow pavement all the bricks were freshly wet and when I crossed the street I had to place my feet with care to keep from slipping on the cobblestones. Rob's car was where we'd left it, parked with others at the little low-hedged square of trees and greenery in front of the old church—St. James's Church, my printed map informed me.

Like the better part of Ypres, it had been levelled in the First World War and reconstructed afterwards. They'd done a brilliant job. From where I stood, the church appeared to be its proper age and looked authentically medieval.

The street, too, had the look of illustrations from my childhood book of fairy tales: the crowded curving line of old brick houses with their distinctively stepped gables and their chimney pots. On top of one, a lonely-looking mourning dove had settled and was calling rather plaintively across the steep tiled roofs.

Apart from me, the only creature that appeared to take an interest in the bird's repeated crying was a little black-and-white cat that had stopped right at the pavement's edge to prick up her ears and listen.

When she saw me, she arched herself up and came forwards on dainty white paws to investigate, while I looked at my map again.

There was no mark to tell me where the convent of the Irish nuns had stood. It, too, had fallen victim to the guns of the Great War and been reduced to rubble. I had found a faded photograph online that had been taken shortly after that, and it had shown a section of the ruined facade still standing, starkly black and white against the tumbled mounds of scorched and broken stones and bricks and tiles. I'd printed that as well, but looking at it now I could see nothing in the photograph, no landmark, that could give me any clue as to the spot where the photographer had stood to take that picture, so I couldn't try to replicate the angle.

At least, I thought, my reading had assured me there would be a plaque.

It wasn't till I'd walked the whole length of the street to the small tidy roundabout at the far end, then turned around and come back up on the opposite side, all the way past the hotel and up the short distance to where the street opened out into the main square of Ypres, that I realized I might have a problem.

I tried again. Winding up at the green square in front of the church for the second time, I faced the black-and-white cat, who had climbed to the roof of the car beside Rob's and was watching me idly, as though I was giving her some entertainment. I told her, "Well, that's odd."

She blinked at me.

"What's odd?"

The voice wasn't female—or feline—but that didn't keep me from jumping a little as I spun to find Rob a few steps behind me, with two cups of takeaway coffee held warm in his hands. He had clearly been out and about. Wedged between his chest and bicep was a crinkled paper bag that smelt like heaven in a way that only came from proper bakeries, and my stomach did a rumble in response. "Are those croissants?"

"I got a wee assortment," he said, passing me my coffee so he'd have a hand free to hold out the bag. "I go all shoogly in a pastry shop, I just take one of everything."

I chose a chocolate-covered something, and was halfway through it when he asked again, "What's odd?"

"What? Oh. There's meant to be a plaque that says exactly where the convent was, but I've been up and down the whole street twice and I can't find it." Looking at him hopefully I asked, "You don't see any ghostly Benedictine nuns about, I take it?"

He grinned and glanced round. "Sorry, no."

"Well, then. Maybe there's a library in town that has old maps."

Rob's glance flicked to me, then, in that briefly shuttered way that made me think he knew something I didn't. I asked him, "What?"

He shrugged his broad shoulders and made a great show of selecting a pastry. The cat, little traitor, had gracefully moved one car closer to Rob and was watching the bag with a great deal of interest.

"We'll not need a map," he remarked.

"You can find it without one?"

His eyes said the answer was obvious. "I wasn't thinking of me."

"Rob, I can't. I can't just . . . see things."

"You've no need to see it, you'll feel where it is. It's like dowsing."

"Yes, well, I can't dowse, either."

"You'll never ken half of the things ye can do," was his reasoning, "if you won't try." He was stating a fact, not reproaching me. Nor was it really a dare, though I couldn't not take it as one.

I felt torn. On the one hand, I wasn't like Rob; wasn't nearly as gifted as he was, I knew that, and really, it suited me fine. I had no great desire to step out of my safety zone.

But on the other hand, I truly *did* want to help Margaret Ross. And in two days I'd be in St. Petersburg, all on my own, and I might have no choice but to use my gifts then, or else I might never find what I was hoping to find. I'd have wasted my one shot at chasing her Firebird.

Practicing now, with Rob's guidance, seemed logical.

Still, I couldn't decide. "What if somebody sees us?"

"And what will they see? Were ye planning to spin around widdershins, chanting or something?"

"Rob."

"Well, then. You're only walking on the pavement, aren't ye? Surely they'll recover from the shock." I caught the teasing glint in his blue eyes, and this time I could not mistake the dare.

"All right," I said.

He held the paper bag towards me so that I could take the last croissant before he folded it and put it in his pocket. "Fine then, lead the way."

I looked in both directions, not quite certain whether I should go towards the central square or back towards the roundabout. The mourning dove was calling once again, and Rob was watching me.

"You're ower thinking," he said. "Trust your feelings."

So, because I didn't want him knowing that I wasn't feeling any-thing, I gave a nod and headed for the roundabout.

The narrow road curved gently past the Albion Hotel, an older building on the corner with red doors underneath a brightly hanging Union Jack, and tidy topiary trees that flanked its entrance. As we passed, a woman came out with a broom and started sweeping down the steps and gave a smiling nod to Rob, who shot a smile back and said, "Good morning." Then to me, a few feet farther on, he said, "You see? It's not so difficult."

I wanted to believe him. I tried stretching out my feelings. Just like dowsing, he had told me. "Do you dowse, Rob?"

"Aye, from time to time. You want a well dug, I'm your man. Quit sidetracking, and concentrate."

It wasn't any use, I thought. I wasn't getting anything. I led him all the way down to the roundabout in silence. When we stopped, he told me, "That's all right. Go back again, but slowly, and you'll find it."

I heard the tone of certainty behind his words and turned on him. "You know exactly where it is. You see it, don't you?"

Rob ignored me. "Back again, but slowly," he repeated.

I sighed, and started back up on the other side, past all the ancient-looking doors of all the old brick houses. There were cars parked in a tight line all along the street on this side, leaving less room on the pavement. Rob fell into step behind me, uncomplaining, while I tried to persuade him to give me some sort of a hint.

"It's a big building."

"Thanks very much," I said drily.

"You asked."

"We'll be doing this all day, you know, if you don't—" Suddenly I faltered and stopped walking. We hadn't come very far up from the roundabout, just to the point where a lane angled off to the right between houses whose only remarkable feature was that they looked modern. The next few houses up along Sint Jacobsstraat were modern, too, their high flat fronts and staring windows livened only by a burst of unexpected colour in the one house at the centre of the row whose stuccoed walls were painted an alarming shade of orange, with a deep pink trim.

I wasn't even sure why I'd stopped walking, till the breeze blew and I felt it for a second time: the tiny mental tug, like someone tapping on my shoulder.

Turning, I saw Rob too far behind me to have touched me, and I asked him, "Was it here?"

The slight curve of his mouth was all the answer that I needed, and I felt a rush of sudden childish pride. I tamped it down with practicality. "I still can't see it, though."

"Well, I can help with that." He took a thoughtful look around us. Ypres was waking up—the sound of traffic could be clearly heard now, and a car came speeding down the narrow curving street beside us, closely followed by another one. Rob nodded at the lane. "Let's try down here."

The lane was short, and offered little shelter. At its other end, the smooth brick paving changed to rougher cobblestone with moss and puddles in between, and opened to another narrow street with houses on only one side, and a green tangled mass of trees all down the other, like the edge of some great park.

From my map I guessed it was, in fact, the park along the river walk that marked the margins of the old town walls. A line of cars was parked here, too, and yet it was a quiet place, and peaceful.

Rob found a spot where we could sit on sloping grass beneath an overhanging tree, and shrugged his jacket off to spread it out so we'd have something dry that we could sit on, and he asked me, "Are ye ready?"

"I don't have to do this by myself, too, do I?"

With a flash of his warm smile he held his hand out, and I gave him mine.

I said, "You do realize that, assuming Margaret's Anna even made it here to Ypres, and that you find her, it's long odds we'll find anything to tell us why she went to Russia."

Once again I got the slanting, shuttered look. "I like long odds," he said.

And closed his fingers over mine.

chapter
THIRTEEN

She was cold, as much from nervousness as from the wind that chased along the dark length of the street, lit only by the lantern that the boy who led them carried. The wind chased that as well, and when the flame dipped to evade the gusts it threw black, grasping shadows on the brick walls of the houses and made Anna hold more closely to the coat of Captain Jamieson. He'd carried her the whole way from the riverside and had not set her down until the colonel made him do it. Even then, he'd said in protest, "She is tired."

"She is not wounded, and you are," had been the answer Colonel Graeme gave. "And if ye lose that leg, ye'll be no help to her at all."

She did not like to see them arguing. She'd told the captain, "I can walk, sir," and obligingly he'd put her down, but she could tell he had not liked to do it.

She had once asked Colonel Graeme, in their crossing on the ship, why Captain Jamieson refused to let her play about the decks without him being at her side. "I'm no a bairn," she had complained.

"Nor does he think ye one." The colonel had been tucking her beneath the quilts that lined her narrow berth, set near his own, and for a moment he had seemed to think in silence. Then he'd said, "He had a wee girl once, about your own age."

Anna had frowned. "Does he not have her now?"

"He lost her."

That was all the explanation she'd received from Colonel Graeme, and she had not dared ask Captain Jamieson himself. But that was probably, thought Anna, why he carried her as often as he did, because he'd lost his own girl once and did not want to lose another, not when

Colonel Graeme would have held him fiercely to account for being careless.

Even now, when she was walking at his side, he kept his one hand on her shoulder and he did not seem to care that she was holding to a rough fold of his coat to borrow courage.

It was just as well that he was walking slowly. He'd been walking with more effort for the past few days, and often had to stop and rest, but Anna didn't mind. Nor did she mind that this dark street seemed longer every step they took, because in truth she did not wish to go where they were being led.

The colonel had explained to her, repeatedly and kindly, why the convent was the place where she must stay while he and Jamieson went on to Paris. Paris, he had told her, was too dangerous.

"The nuns are loving women, they will care for ye and keep ye safe from harm. And they will teach ye."

"Teach me what?"

"To read and write," he'd said, "and how to be a lady."

"I've nae wish to be a lady."

Captain Jamieson, who'd sat nearby, had turned his head at that and she had watched the corners of his eyes grow slightly crinkled, as they did when he was trying not to show a smile. "No? What would ye wish to be, then?"

"I'm a Jacobite," she'd told him, "just as you are. When I'm grown I'll be a soldier, like my father was, and kill the men who killed him."

Captain Jamieson had raised his eyebrows then and looked to Colonel Graeme who had said, "Did I not tell ye she was John's own lassie, through and through?"

"Ye did, aye." Captain Jamieson had settled in his corner. "And in more than just the look of him, it seems. So tell me, Anna, when ye've killed the men that killed your daddie, and their children come to hunt for *you*, what will ye do then?"

Anna had thought solemnly, and said, "I'll kill them, too."

"Ye'll have the fighting never end, then, taking one eye for another. Do ye think your daddie's soul will rest the better if ye do avenge it?

I can tell ye it will not." His gaze had found hers almost gently. "I've killed many men, and aye, a few of those were killed for vengeance, but I'm just as plagued by ghosts now as I ever was," he'd told her. "Maybe more so."

"But you fight men still."

"I do."

She'd been about to ask him why when Colonel Graeme interrupted with, "A soldier has no choice. And nor do you," he'd said to Anna. "Only lads and men can go for soldiers, never women."

"Why?" she'd asked.

"Because that is the law. Which ye can read yourself," he'd finished neatly, "when the nuns have taught ye how."

And that had been the end of the discussion, for a while.

When they had finally, after many days, made landfall, Colonel Graeme had again begun to talk about the nuns. They were from Ireland, he'd told her, and had chosen to become God's brides instead of any man's, to serve him better and to help the poor and weak.

Anna had said, "My Aunt Kirsty is married, and she helps the poor. She takes food from the kitchens of Slains every day to the village, to those who have need of it."

"Aye, your Aunt Kirsty has aye been a generous woman," the colonel had said.

"But then why can the nuns not be married to men?" had been Anna's next question.

The colonel had glanced at the captain, who'd grinned and remarked, "Are ye sure that her daddie was John, and not Robin?"

The colonel had laughed out loud, and when she'd glared at him, wanting to share the joke, he'd said, "Your father had brothers, and one of them, Robert—or Robin, as we call him—trained as a lawyer. 'Tis certainly true ye've a rare gift for argument."

Anna had looked at the captain and said in a clear voice, "My father was Colonel John Moray."

He'd looked at her small upturned face, so indignant, and he'd smothered his smile then and reached down to brush one hand over her dark tumbled curls. "Aye, I ken who your father was."

Walking behind, and still keenly amused, Colonel Graeme had said, "He was aye asking questions as well, was your father, when he was a laddie. I tell ye now what ye should do, Anna. When we are come to the convent at Ypres, ye should ask the nuns there why they cannot be married to men."

That had set him off laughing again, and had made Captain Jamieson's eyes crinkle up at the edges once more, though his face had been carefully sober when Anna had glanced at it.

Now, as the captain stopped walking for the fourth time in the dim shadowed street of the old town, she studied his face and was troubled to see his mouth set in a hard, painful line.

"It is nothing," he said, when he noticed her looking. "'Tis only an ache in my leg from the damp, it will pass."

The boy with the lantern stopped walking as well, at a narrow arched door, and said something briefly that Anna could not understand. On the ship coming over she'd heard foreign languages spoken, and had learned a few words of Spanish and Swedish from some of the crew, but what the boy spoke wasn't either of those. Colonel Graeme understood it, though, and even gave a short reply before the boy departed with the lantern in his hand, a swaying light that swiftly shrank to nothing in the darkness and took all the shadows with it as the night closed in around them.

As she huddled at the captain's side, the colonel rang a bell hung in the entryway, and all at once the door was opened to them in a wash of warmly yellow light, and Anna shut her eyes against the unknown and the brightness as she passed across the threshold with the men. When she dared open them again, she saw the three of them were standing in a neatly austere parlour with a screen of wooden bars fixed down its centre to divide the room in two.

It had nothing of the grandness of the Earl of Erroll's drawing-room at Slains, nor of the comfort of the main room of the cottage that had been her home till lately, but from how it had been furnished, with its carved wood chairs and paintings and the polished silver sconces with their candles, something told her this was meant to be the finest of the convent's rooms. A place for guests.

Beyond the bars she saw the painted Christ upon his cross and felt his eyes upon her, neither suffering nor joyful, only steady, as though he could somehow see within her soul and know how much she did not wish to stay here.

She was bothered by those bars. The colonel had explained to her, in detail, what a cloister was, and how the nuns had chosen to live separate from the larger world, and how they did not freely mix with those from the outside, but she had not imagined bars.

And when the farther door swung open and two figures robed in black with veils drawn down over their faces entered into that barred section of the parlour, Anna shrank from them as though they had been creatures in a cage.

She pressed more closely to the side of Captain Jamieson, and felt the weight of his hand settle warmly on her shoulder, reassuring.

"Colonel Graeme, may I say how pleased I am that Providence has spared you," said the foremost nun. Her pleasant voice had something of a song in it that sounded only slightly foreign, Anna thought, remembering the nuns had come from Ireland into Flanders, and so kept their Irish way of speech.

The colonel made a show of great respect, and yet his eyes were smiling. "Were ye praying for me, Abbess?"

"I was praying for the king, and trusted you'd be standing close enough beside him that God's shield would guard you also." Her head turned slightly to the side as she said, "Sister Xaveria, would you kindly bring those two chairs forwards so that we may sit, for neither of these gentlemen will take a seat till we ourselves have done so, and the colonel looks incapable of standing any longer." With her veiled face angled now to Captain Jamieson, she asked him, "Are you wounded?"

"It is nothing," said the captain for a second time, but Anna noticed he seemed grateful for the chance to sit, his injured leg stretched out before him as though it had grown too stiff for him to bend. She took the smaller armless rush-backed chair between his own and Colonel Graeme's, and sat waiting with her fingers tightly clasped together in her lap.

The nuns appeared not to have seen her while the captain had been standing, but she felt the gaze of both of them upon her now. The nearer one, the abbess, said, "And, Colonel, surely this must be your daughter or your niece, she is so like yourself to look at."

Anna hadn't yet been told she looked like Colonel Graeme, but he gave a proud nod now and told the abbess, "Anna is my nephew's lass, my nephew John, who lies at rest within your abbey here. He was a friend to you, as I recall, and you to him, and it seemed only right to bring his daughter here to let ye have the care of her, with him no longer able to protect her, and myself and Captain Jamieson away to serve the king."

The captain shifted slightly at the mention of his name and drew the veiled nun's steady gaze a second time before she gave her full attention back to Colonel Graeme. With a nod she said, in tones more quiet, "Aye, I well recall your nephew, and he was indeed a loyal friend to all of us. We'll guard his daughter well."

"Her name is Anna," said the colonel. "Anna Mary. She has sheltered with a family north of Slains these past eight years, and for her safety she has used their name of Logan as her own. I'd think it best if she were entered in your records by that name as well, for even with her father dead his living brothers risk much for the king, and 'twould be safer for the lass and them if none else ever learns she is a Moray."

The abbess gave a nod of understanding and agreed that these were troubled days. "The Lord knows best, and yet it sorely grieves me that His plan so often brings our young king such keen disappointment, and costs many other men their lives and liberty."

The colonel asked her, "Have ye news of any that were taken these past months in Scotland?"

"No." The black veil rustled slightly as she shook her head. "Your son will doubtless have heard much, for where he is there are men daily passing through as refugees. But we ourselves," she said, "have had few visitors of late. The Duke of Ormonde, my great-cousin, may have brought an end to Queen Anne's war in Flanders, but the treaty that he wrought has seen us traded since from France to Austria, and so we see no more the loyal regiments of Irishmen who served the King of France to serve King James, and who were wont to give us presents and their company when e'er they passed. Nor do we any more receive the pension that the King of France did grant us. You will find us much reduced," she told the colonel. "Poor and friendless."

Colonel Graeme smiled, and told her, "Never that." He slipped a hand within the lining of his coat and drew out a worn purse that clinked with shifting coins. "Here, this will be some solace to ye, and will pay the costs of Anna's keep and education till I come again."

The abbess, as she took the money from him through the bars, raised one hand from the folds of her dark robes to make the sign to bless him, and she called those blessings down in words as well. "But you are weary, Colonel, and must rest. Come, let us lodge you with our neighbour, for he is a good and kindly man and will, I'm sure, have room for you."

The wave of desolation Anna felt then, when she knew the men were leaving her tonight with these strange women, was as forceful as the one she'd felt when she had glimpsed her last blurred view of her home on the snowy cliffs of Scotland; even more so, because then at least she'd had the colonel walking at her side, and Captain Jamieson to carry her, and now she would have neither.

When she looked at Colonel Graeme she discovered he was watching her, and wanting to be brave for him, she bit her lower lip to stop its trembling and blinked hard against the rising sting of tears.

His gaze grew softer. "Shall we keep ye one more night with us?" he asked her, and she nodded, and he turned to tell the abbess, "If your neighbour will allow it, then, we'll have the wee lass with us one night longer. It will give ye time to make a proper place for her, and we can take our leave of her the morn."

The abbess nodded, and the adults bade good night to one another, and an older woman who was not a nun appeared and led them out again and saw them safely to the neighbour's, but of all this action Anna only had a faint awareness. Her emotions had been raised to such a pitch that this reprieve, so unexpected, had left all of her exhausted. And yet, when they had been admitted to the neighbour's house and met the man himself, a cheerful man the same age as the colonel with a lively, smiling wife to keep him company, and Anna had been washed and settled in beneath a mound of woven blankets on a palette by the kitchen hearth she did not want to close her eyes, because she knew that if she slept and woke it would be morning and the stay of execution would be over.

The colonel and the captain and their temporary landlord and his wife were sitting round the kitchen table not far off from her, all speaking in that same strange foreign language that she could not understand, but Anna focused on the sound of it to keep herself from drifting.

They were drinking wine from earthen cups, and talking. Sometimes one would laugh, and sometimes all, and other times the four of them grew sober and a pause would stretch as though they had mislaid the words they sought. It was in such a pause that Colonel Graeme glanced towards the hearth and saw that Anna was not sleeping, and instead of being angry he instead turned to their host and made a comment with a nod towards a corner of the room that Anna could not see, and with a slow smile and another nod to answer him, their temporary landlord rose and fetched a fiddle and a bow, and sat down heavily again beside the colonel, and began to play.

The music had a longing sound, a weeping sort of wildness to it that made Anna think about her cottage and the sea and all the gulls that wheeled and cried above the waves along the cliffs, but still she would not close her eyes.

She watched as Colonel Graeme leaned in closer to their host and hummed a tune that danced its way on to the fiddle's strings, a lively ballad that the colonel gave the words to in his richly rumbling voice, to sing the praises of the "worthy, gallant Grahams" and their fight against the Campbells in defence of old King Charles. The verses followed one another in their rousing way, till Anna's feet were all but dancing underneath the blankets, keeping time as Colonel Graeme sang:

> *"'Cheer up your hearts, brave Cavaliers,*
> *For the Grahams are gone to Germany . . . '"*

"Aye," said Captain Jamieson, "and she'll be marching there as well, if ye keep on with that. She needs a cradle song."

The colonel grinned. "For one with Graeme blood, my lad, that *is* a cradle song. What did your mother sing to you?"

"I scarce remember."

Anna, watching him, was trying to imagine Captain Jamieson a tiny bairn whose mother rocked and sang to him, but her imagination could not conjure it.

The colonel, leaning back, said, "When we met this past November marching down to Sheriffmuir, did not ye tell me that ye'd lived a settled life afore this winter, with your own bairns and your lady?"

Picking up his cup of wine, the captain eyed him warily and made no answer as the colonel carried on, "Well, surely now, your lady kens a cradle song or two."

"She does. And she's the one to sing them."

"Did ye never sing a song to your own sons, or to your daughter?"

Captain Jamieson looked down at that, and Anna thought it cruel of Colonel Graeme to remind him of the little girl he'd lost, and yet she saw the colonel's eyes were anything but cruel. In fact, as he sat waiting through the silence that fellin between the two men, the expression on his face was understanding, even kind. And finally Captain Jamieson took one long drink and set his wine cup down again and shifted in his chair, his injured leg stretched out before him.

Looking to their host he asked a question and received a shrug and a shaking of the head in answer, so he started singing on his own, his voice as low as Colonel Graeme's had been, yet more quiet, like the evening wind in summertime that calmed the waves along the shore and brought the seabirds home.

The song was slow, as were the words, and touched with something close to weariness that made them seem to hang a moment in the room's hushed air:

> "'O'er hills and high mountains,
> long time have I gone,
> And down by the fountains,
> by myself all alone:
> Through bushes and briars,
> I walk without care,
> Through perils and dangers,
> for the loss of my dear.'"

He sang the last four lines again, the way the tune demanded, and the fiddle joined him for the final line and carried on with him through all the many verses that came after, till its pure and clear lament was interwoven with the captain's voice that wrapped round Anna like the dark and soothing night.

He sang about a maiden who passed all her days in wandering and loneliness because she had been driven from the side of her true love, and wanted only to be near him once again.

Anna felt her eyelids growing heavy as she listened, and at length she let them close, but still she kept awake to hear yet more about the maiden, always wandering, in hopelessness and tears.

And when the maiden's lost love finally heard her weeping and returned to bring her comfort, Anna smiled against the roughness of her blankets as the captain in his deep voice sang the man's vow to the maiden:

> "'My love, cease thy weeping,
> now listen to me,
> For waking and sleeping,

my heart is with thee;
Love, let nothing grieve thee,
and do not complain,
For I never will leave thee,
while life doth remain.'"

Both voice and the fiddle repeated the last loving lines of that promise, but Anna was already drifting in slumber and heard nothing after "I never will leave thee" because she could feel herself being pulled down like a weight, into darkness.

Her dreams were a confusion of bright images and darker sounds, and once she felt that she herself was lost amid the hills and did not know the way to turn to find the path to lead her homeward, and she panicked for a moment till she heard the captain's voice, not far off, saying quietly, "Ye'd salt the wound."

"'Tis past time someone healed it," Colonel Graeme said, as low, and then the hills were gone and Anna was behind the sturdy convent bars surrounded by the black-veiled forms of women, and they closed around her till she could not see beyond the blackness, and she pushed against it.

Something crashed.

It startled her to wakefulness.

She heard the murmured voices from the far side of the room, the captain saying he was fine, he'd only fallen, and the colonel asking questions, and the captain saying he should leave it be. "Ye'll waken Anna."

"She's asleep yet," said the colonel. "Let me look at it."

"I've telt ye there's no need."

But Colonel Graeme had already risen from his chair, a looming shadow in the room, made larger by the faint glow of the firelight. Stepping past Anna he borrowed a flame from the hearth with a candle and carried it back to the place where the captain half-sat and half-lay on the floor by the table.

"Let me look at it," the colonel said again, and this time though the words were hardly louder than a whisper they still sounded like an order.

Anna's eyes were mostly shut, but through the curtain of her lashes she could see the captain gingerly unwind the length of bandage from his leg, and Colonel Graeme took the candlestick more firmly in his hand and bent to look, and then he said a word she'd only ever heard her Uncle Rory say when he'd been pushed beyond his limits, for it was an ugly word.

"How long," the colonel asked the captain, "has it been like this?"

When stubborn silence met him he glanced up and asked more forcefully, "How long?"

"A week. A little longer, maybe."

This time Anna did not know the word the colonel used, but Captain Jamieson said warningly, "Mind what you say. The lass—"

"—is sleeping," Colonel Graeme said, and spoke the word again, with feeling. "How the devil did ye walk on that?"

"I had no choice."

"On top of it, ye're burning with a fever, lad. We need to fetch a surgeon."

"I thank ye, no," the captain said. "I have been bled enough. I'll heal." He pushed the colonel's hand aside and, reaching for the toppled chair behind him, used its sturdy side as leverage while he laboured to his feet. "I've always healed."

"Some wounds," the colonel told him, "are more complicated."

Or at least that was what Anna thought she heard him say . . . she wasn't paying full attention, because suddenly the captain seemed to sway and lose his balance, and his shadow on the wall collapsed to nothing as he fell.

chapter
FOURTEEN

R ob was rubbing his own leg, to work out the stiffness.
I asked, "Are you all right?"

"I'm fine. I'm just not used to sitting so long." He was standing now, flexing his knee to restore circulation. He asked, with a nod at my mobile, "What did he want this time?"

"He needed a letter I'd written to one of our clients." Ordinarily I wasn't all that bothered by Sebastian's constant calling when I wasn't in the office, but this morning I'd been less pleased by the interruption.

Rob had heard the mobile ringing first, and he had smoothly switched the focus of his concentration back into the present from the past, and brought me with him. I had found the change more difficult. A part of me, a large part, wanted only to be back there in the dark warmth of that kitchen, to find out why Captain Jamieson had fallen, and what Anna had done next.

Rob stretched his shoulders too, and while he rubbed his neck he shot a quick glance skywards. "Well, it's likely just as well he rang. We're going to get rained on, from the look of it."

I looked as well, and saw the massing darker clouds that had come slowly creeping underneath the sunless stretch of grey, pushed into place by that cool breeze that now had risen so it bordered on becoming a light wind. I knew that if it rained, we couldn't sit here any longer. There were thick leaves on the branches of the tree that arched above us, but the breeze itself was blowing from the side, we'd have no shelter. I tried hard to hide my disappointment.

Rob turned. "Are you hungry?"

"Sorry?"

Patiently he said, "It's nearly lunchtime. Are you hungry?"

There was no way it could be so late, I thought. We'd only just got done with breakfast, we'd had coffee, and . . .

"It's half-past twelve." He turned his wrist to let me see his watch, as proof. "We could have lunch, and wait till this blows over, try again a little later."

It took too much effort, thinking, so I told him, "Fine."

Rob looked at me a moment, then he smiled and said, "Come on, then," and he walked with me across the narrow street and back along the little alley leading to Sint Jacobsstraat.

The first fat drops of rain began to fall as we came round that corner. By the time we reached the pink-and-orange-painted house a few doors up, the clouds let loose with vengeance and Rob laughed and turned his collar up as best he could against it, and he caught my hand in his and pulled me after him into a private covered driveway cut into the ground floor of the nearest house, just wide enough to let a car pass through into the little courtyard I could glimpse behind.

With dark brick walls, their bottom edges green with moss, and a low, wood-planked ceiling that muffled the noise of the rain, the space had a secluded feel, safely confined.

Rob shook aside the strands of dark hair dripping water in his eyes and said, "So much for lunch."

"I wasn't hungry."

"Were ye not?" The brick walls cast his voice back in an echo, deepened with good humour. "Well," he said, "I've got a bar of chocolate, here." I heard the rustling as he rummaged for it in his pocket. "If we split that, and you promise that you'll feed me well tonight, I'm game to have another go."

"Right now?" I looked at him with hope. "You're sure?"

He answered me by snapping off a section of the chocolate bar and passing it across while he took stock of our surroundings with a practiced eye. "We're right within the convent walls, ye ken. It should be easier to see things."

"Was it harder, looking in from the outside?"

He shrugged. "I'd not say harder, not exactly, but it takes a bit more energy." He'd found the place he wanted, and he moved the few steps over to it, pressing back against the rough brick wall. He held his hand out. "Ready?"

For a single moment I considered what it was that I was doing, and how silly it would look to someone passing, and how dangerous it might be if the owners of the house came home and drove in with their car, and the hundred other ways that it was crazy.

Then I pushed it all aside, and took my mobile out, and turned it off, deliberately, and went across and took Rob's hand and told him, "Ready."

And I closed my eyes.

She wasn't meant to hear.

She'd heard them say so, when they'd carried Captain Jamieson into the other room. She'd heard them say that it would frighten her to hear, that it would give the captain more pain if he thought that she could hear, so they had kept their voices quiet, and she'd kept her own eyes shut so they would not know she was listening, because she did not wish to cause the captain yet more pain.

He'd only groaned the once. She'd heard him through the wall, and she'd curled deeper in her bed and closed her eyes more resolutely, till his restlessness had seemed to pass.

The colonel had been in the kitchen talking to the surgeon, then— a younger man whose voice and accent marked him as an Englishman, and who had come so hastily in answer to their call that he had taken several minutes to restore his breath.

He said, "For all they scarified the wound when he received it, there remains only one opening, and that is at the highest point, so matter may not drain. The wound must slough and grow inflamed before it heals, and this it has not done, and so you have this problem of the discharge and the fever."

"Is there any of the musket ball remaining in the wound?"

"I cannot say. The only remedy," the surgeon told the colonel, "is to make a second opening below the first, and probe it well, and then to draw a seton through the whole length of the wound."

She did not know then what a "seton" was. It would not be till morning when she saw the large, broad, evil-looking needle with its knifelike tip, and saw the strip of silk with which they'd threaded it, as wide as her own thumb, that she would understand why Colonel Graeme had exhaled so heavily.

His footsteps had been heavy, too, as he had crossed the floor to where the table stood, and lifting something from it that had clinked and sloshed like wine within a bottle, he had said, "Then he'll have need of this."

The sounds that she'd heard after that had been the worse because she'd known the captain did not mean to make them; that whatever they were doing to him tore the noises from him through clenched teeth, and that he strangled any sound he made before it could be fully formed.

"Brave lad." The colonel's voice came very gently through the wall. "Brave lad. 'Tis nearly done."

But still the sounds went on and on till Anna pressed her hands against her ears to block them out, and squeezed her eyes more tightly shut so God Himself would see she was not listening and let the captain know she could not hear him, for she knew that he had pain enough and could not suffer more.

At length the house descended once more into silence, and she slept, and when she woke, the little room was filled with sunlight and the colonel was beside her, sitting comfortably and reading the small book he always carried in the pocket of his coat.

She pushed herself up till she sat among the tangled blankets, and was rubbing at her eyes when Colonel Graeme set his book down on his knee and said, "You're up, then. Good. I was becoming bored with my own company."

The details of the night before began to trickle through her memory and she looked towards the empty chair behind the colonel, at the table, as she asked him, "Captain Jamieson?"

"Is sleeping still."

She frowned. "Are ye done hurting him?"

The colonel's smile was faint. "Ye heard that, did ye?"

Anna shook her head, and Colonel Graeme let it pass. He only said, "The captain's leg was very badly hurt while we were fighting, lass, in Scotland, but the surgeon's set it right again. Now up," he said, "and get ye dressed. There's water in that basin by the hearth, that ye can wash with."

The air outside the blankets had a bite to it, and Anna quickly washed and tugged her outer clothing on again while Colonel Graeme read his book.

She'd often seen him reading it before. The leather cover was well worn and gleaming smooth from all the hours spent in his hand, but still it did not have the rich look of the books that lined the high shelves of the Earl of Erroll's library at Slains. It looked more like the only book she'd ever seen in her own cottage, so she asked, "Is that a Bible?"

That amused him. "Bless ye, no. 'Tis nothing so improving. No, this book is an account of Mr. Lawson's daring voyage to the colony of Carolina, and his own adventures with the Indians and settlers there. When I was but a lad I dreamt of making such a journey for myself," he said, "but now I've grown too old for it."

"Is it so far?"

"America? It is, aye. Clear across the world. My eldest son, my Jamie, went to settle in the colony of Darien around the same time Mr. Lawson first set foot in Carolina," said the colonel, with a nod towards his book, "but I lost him afore he could tell me any of his own tales."

Anna thought it odd that both the colonel and the captain should be careless with their children, for they both seemed to be careful men. She asked, "Where did you lose him?"

Colonel Graeme looked confounded by the question for a moment, but her meaning must have penetrated, for his eyes showed understanding. "He was sailing for the Company of Scotland when he died." He dropped his gaze again and took a keener interest in the pages of his book. "It happened years ago. I've lost two sons, for all that, but the two that I have living are a comfort to me."

Anna hadn't known that "lost" meant "dead." She was absorbing this when something struck the colonel, and he said, "Ye may meet one of them, in fact, while ye are here, for he's a monk and though he's not of the same order as the nuns, he's yet been known to pay a visit to the Lady Abbess now and then. They call him Père Archange," he told her, "meaning 'Father Archangel,' though some will simply call him Father Graeme. Ye may ken him by his face, he looks like me. He was a soldier once, as I am."

Anna frowned. "But if he was a soldier, why did he become a monk?" If she could live a soldier's life, she thought, with all of its adventure and its travel, she would never give it up to pass her days in dull and silent prayer.

The colonel closed his book. "He had a friend, a good friend, in his regiment. As close as brothers, so they were, but they fell out and quarrelled and they fought a duel, and Patrick won the contest. But in winning, he had killed his friend, and that was something he could not atone for in his mind, nor in his heart, except by laying down his weapons altogether. There are times," he said to Anna, "when our victories have a cost that we did not foresee; when winning brings us loss." His gaze fell kindly on her face. "You are too young to understand that, lass, but hold it in your memory so ye'll mind it if ye ever do have need of it, so ye'll not make my son's mistakes."

She nodded. "But I could not be a monk," she told him. "Only men are monks."

"Aye." He was smiling. "And I reckon with your father's blood and all the Graeme in ye that ye'll never make a nun."

Her heart rose hopefully. "So then ye'll take me with you, and not leave me here?"

His smile faded. "Anna."

She had finished dressing and was standing close enough to him that he could take her shoulders in his hands, and draw her to him in a comforting embrace. "I cannot take ye where I'm going, lass. The dangers are too great, the now."

She told the laces of his shirt, "I'm no feart of the danger."

Colonel Graeme lightly kissed her hair. "I ken well ye're no feart. But it is not yourself alone who'd be in danger if I took ye into Paris." He sighed the way he did when he was trying to explain something, and did not have the words to hand. "Ye mind the day we met?" he asked her, finally. "When we sat there in the Earl of Erroll's library and played the chess, and spoke about your mother and your father, and I telt ye why it was they had to keep their marriage secret?"

Anna nodded, and she felt the roughness of his shirt against her cheek. "Because the people hunting for my father might have used my mother ill to make him do the things they wanted."

"Aye. And when your father was away and fighting and ye were a bairn, why did your mother hide ye with another family?"

"So the bad men widnae find me," Anna said.

"Exactly." Colonel Graeme's voice was a deep rumble in his chest that offered comfort. "They were very brave, your parents. If the agents of Queen Anne had ever chanced to catch your father, he'd have stood through any torture they'd have tried to use upon him, and he never would betray his king. But if they'd learnt ye were his daughter, if they'd ever taken ye or threatened ye with harm . . . well, then." The colonel did not specify what Anna's father might have done then. All he said was, "Men can bear most hurts, lass, but there's few of us can bear to see the ones we love best made to suffer for our sake."

"But Queen Anne's dead," said Anna, "and my father, too. So who is left to do me harm?"

"Your father still has brothers, lass, and they still serve the king. And so do I." His hand felt heavy on her hair. "Those men who sought your father would be happy to lay hold of any one of us and turn us to their cause, and they'd use any means to do it." Still more plainly, "They'd use any*one* to do it, any person we did love. They'd try their best to capture ye, to hold ye hostage. Maybe worse. And that is why," he said, "I cannot take ye with me."

She was not persuaded. "You're a soldier, you could guard me."

"No, ye will be safer here. But I would never leave ye undefended. Here." He set her slightly back from him so he could tuck his book back in his pocket and exchange it for another, smaller item. "This," he told her, "was your father's."

Anna did not try to hide her curiosity. She reached to take the necklace Colonel Graeme held towards her, and she stared. "It is a stone."

A little black stone with a hole worn in its middle, through which somebody had strung a leather cord.

The colonel said, "My grandmother would tell us children always, if we chanced to find a wee stone with a hole in it, we ought to wear it round our neck to keep away all evils. And *your* grandmother, my sister Anna, telt the same tale to your daddie when he was a lad himself, and all his life he kept his eye out for a stone like that, until . . ."

"He found it?"

"No." The colonel smiled the smile that warmed his eyes. "Your mother found that stone for him, one day while they were walking out together on the long beach close by Slains."

The same beach, Anna thought, where she herself had run so freely and so fast that sometimes she had felt she might take flight and leave the ground to hang upon the sea wind, like the wheeling gulls whose shadows raced across the sand. She touched the stone with one small finger, wonderingly, and felt its smoothness, warm from Colonel Graeme's pocket.

"When your father went away from Slains, to come back here to fight," the colonel said, "your mother gave that stone to him to wear around his neck, to keep him safe."

The corners of her mouth drooped, just a little. "Then it does not work. Not truly."

"Ye'll believe what ye believe," said Colonel Graeme, with a fatalistic shrug. "But Malplaquet was not the only battle that your father fought, and I did see him many times afore that day walk clear through cannon fire that would have made an end of any other man. So *he* believed it, and I daresay I believe it, too."

He watched her while she gazed down at the stone, with faith and reason tumbling over one another in her heart, until she finally closed her fingers round the gift and held it tightly, and remembering her manners thanked the colonel.

"You're most welcome. As I said, I would not leave ye undefended. Anyway, ye'll have the nuns to see ye do not come to harm."

If Anna made no answer it was only because, privately, she did not think the Irish nuns of Ypres could be a match for Colonel Graeme and the captain when it came to taking care of her.

As if he'd read her mind, the colonel added, "And of course ye'll still have Captain Jamieson awhile, for he'll be biding in this house until his leg has healed to satisfy the surgeon."

That cheered her. "Can I visit him?"

The colonel, with affection, brushed a curling strand of hair back from her eyes and shook his head and said, "He would not have ye see him lie abed. It makes him surly and ill tempered. But one day, when he is better, he'll come visit ye himself."

Two weeks had come and gone since Colonel Graeme had left Anna at the convent, and had handed to the abbess the small parcel that he'd carried out of Scotland, with the nightdress and the lock of hair wrapped carefully inside it. "That is all the lass has left of her own mother," said the colonel, "and I pray ye guard it well for her."

He'd bent to Anna then and said farewell and kissed her for a final time, and then he had been gone. The Abbess Butler had turned back her veil.

She'd looked much older and yet not as frightening as Anna had imagined, with a long face and plain features that were dominated by her nose and forceful chin. Her eyelids sagged, but Anna thought her hands were truly beautiful.

"My child, come," she'd said, and held those lovely hands towards her, "let us show you how we live, and see you settled."

By the time that Captain Jamieson was well enough to visit, Anna nearly had adapted to the convent's hours, and learnt to sleep and wake in keeping with the pattern of the prayers. She'd started at her daily lessons, too, but on this morning now, when she was shown into the parlour by her teacher and she saw the captain sitting close beside the bars, she instantly forgot what she'd been taught and rushed towards him with a happy cry.

He looked a bit surprised, but still he stood and held the hands she thrust towards him through the bars, and when her teacher, Sister Xaveria, tried reminding Anna of the bounds of ladylike behaviour, Captain Jamieson assured the nun he did not mind.

"It has," he told her, "been a long time since I've had so fair a welcome."

Sister Xaveria nodded, and took a step back. She was one of the nuns Anna liked best. Beneath her black veil she had light-coloured eyes and a pleasant soft face with a mouth that, while frequently serious, had not forgotten how to smile, and Anna fancied that the nun was smiling now as she replied, "She has been hoping for your visit for some time. She's talked of little else."

"Indeed." That seemed to please him. Keeping hold of both of Anna's hands, he asked, "And what have ye been learning?"

Anna found she could not answer him, for suddenly she felt the clutch of something in her throat, and felt the heat rise in her face as unshed tears pressed stinging just behind her eyes. She had no voice.

The captain bent, and looked more closely, and his voice turned gentle. "Anna."

And that gentleness undid her. Two great tears squeezed out and trickled down her burning cheeks, and Anna's vision blurred with more as she looked up at Captain Jamieson, and still she could not speak.

His brow was furrowed with concern. "Are ye unwell?"

She shook her head.

"Are they unkind to you?"

She thought of saying yes, because he might then take her with him, but the nun and Christ upon His cross were watching her, and so she told the truth. She shook her head again, and this time managed words: "No, they are kind."

His one hand let hers go so he could smooth the hair back from her cheek, and with his thumb he brushed a tear away, his own eyes growing shadowed. "D'ye miss your home? Did we do wrong to take ye from it?"

"No." The word surprised her when she said it, for she realized that she meant it, but the misery welled up from somewhere deeper still inside her till the captain asked her, "What, then?"

Anna could not put a name to it. She could not find the way to tell him how she felt inside, the way a bird must feel, she thought, when it was caged; that she was weeping because she could no more walk where she might wish to walk, or say what she might wish to say, and that there was no beach where she could run.

The captain looked at her, and looked to where she held his hand, and in his eyes there grew a quiet light of understanding.

Silently he raised his gaze from Anna's face to that of the veiled nun who stood behind her. "Is there anyplace where we can walk together," he asked Sister Xaveria, "where there are no bars?"

chapter FIFTEEN

The convent church had bars as well, that ran the whole width of the altar, severing the space into the part within the cloister and the part where public worshippers could come and pray in peace. Until this morning, Anna had remained behind that screen and joined the nuns in their devotions at the designated hours. She and the other students were not roused within the night for matins, but they shared the sunrise prayers of lauds, the "little" prayers throughout the day, and best of all the peaceful evening vespers.

But as lovely as the prayers were, her attention had been commonly distracted by the flags hung in the choir, the captured colours of the enemy once taken in a nearby battle by a regiment of exiled Irish soldiers who'd stayed loyal to King James, and who had carried those flags here to be preserved as an example of their victory.

Quite often, while the nuns were at their prayers and Anna should have been as well, she found her gaze diverted upwards to those banners, while she, dreamy-eyed, imagined them a-flutter on the battlefield above the clash of men, her father in amongst them, and in her mind it was his own hands that tore the banners down . . .

There was less room, here in this austere space outside the choir, to harbour Anna's daydreams, but she did not mind this morning, for she had the captain here to keep her company.

He seemed to limp more heavily upon his wounded leg, she thought. Or else perhaps she noticed it more keenly now. She tried to keep her own steps slow, and used as an excuse the nuns' own teaching that she should not walk too quickly.

"We are not to run," she said, "or make much noise."

"So you've companions then?" he asked her. "Other students?"

"There are four of us." The other girls were older, she explained to him—her sister Mary's age, and while she'd seen them at their lessons, she had never really spoken to them. "Sister Xaveria says we should try to be silent."

"Oh aye? Why is that?"

"I think so we can better hear God talk to us," said Anna. "But I've never heard him yet. I'm no sae good at keeping silent."

"No?" His mouth curved slightly.

"We are allowed to sing," she told him, "and the nuns sing often at their prayers, although their songs are not so lovely as the cradle song ye sang about the maiden and her love."

"Ye liked that, did ye?"

"Aye. Will ye sing it to me once again, so I can learn the words?"

"Here?" Glancing round he said, "'Tis hardly proper for a church. When I have pen and paper I will write the verses down for ye."

She told him, "But I cannot read."

"Then ye will have to learn." He raised his head in thoughtful study of the window nearest them, its small panes letting light pass through to mark the floor they walked upon. "The world becomes a wider place, with but a little learning."

"Were you sent to school, when you were my age?"

"Aye."

"And were ye made to hold your tongue?"

His mouth curved yet more broadly as he bent his head as though in contemplation of her problem. "'Tis a habit worth acquiring, keeping silent when ye can. 'Tis by their words that men betray themselves, and often by the smallest of their actions, which ye'll rarely see unless ye hold your tongue and use your eyes instead. Ye'll learn more of a man if ye look at his face when he's looking at somebody else than ye'll learn any other way, but," he advised her, "ye have to keep silent to do it."

She put this in practice by watching the captain's face, seeing the way his mouth tightened whenever his left foot came down. But she could only keep silent a moment.

She said, "There's a man who comes sometimes to Slains who was hurt in the same leg as you, only his surgeon took the leg clean off so now it just ends at his knee."

"Well, I've a mind to keep my own leg," he replied, "since the surgeon here shows no desire to have it."

"I do not like the surgeon," Anna said, and he looked down at her.

"He is a good man." Then he faintly frowned and asked, "When did ye meet him?"

Anna frowned herself. "Why did he run that needle through your leg?"

He raised an eyebrow. "What, the seton needle? How did ye . . . ?"

"I saw it. They were cleaning it."

The captain gave a nod, and looked away, and told her, "When a wound is festering and will not heal, it helps to use a seton. That's the cloth. Ye saw that, too? This wide, and like a ribbon? So the surgeon threads his needle with the seton, and he pulls it through, and leaves a length of seton in the wound, with both its ends outside and hanging."

Anna looked to where the barest outline of the bandaging around the captain's thigh stretched out the fabric of his breeches. "Is it in there now?"

"It is."

"Why?"

"It acts like a wick in a lamp," he explained, "so the surgeon can introduce medicines, and so the festering matter can drain from the wound."

Anna liked that he spoke to her as Colonel Graeme did, using the grown-up terms, as though he fully expected that she'd understand.

She asked, "Will ye have it there always?"

He shook his head. "No, when the surgeon decides, he will draw it back out."

"Will it hurt when they do that?"

He didn't reply straight away. Then he angled his gaze down to hers. "I've had worse hurts," he promised her. "They heal."

Still, she worried for his health between the times he came to visit her, and when two days had come and gone together with no sign of him, her worry grew to such a level that she could not concentrate upon her lessons or her meals. The Abbess Butler came herself to learn what had made Anna so distressed, and when she heard the cause, she sent a message to their neighbour's wife, and made arrangements for that woman to take Anna from the convent for an hour to pay a visit to the captain.

He was sitting on the bed but fully dressed, his injured leg stretched out in front of him. "And what is this I hear?" he asked her. "Pining for the likes of me? Ye want to have more sense." But he was smiling when he said it, and she thought that he looked privately as pleased to see her as she was to be there.

He looked paler than he should have been, more shadowed round his eyes, and she regarded the new bandage round his leg with some suspicion. "Did they take the seton out?"

"They did. And straight away my leg became so melancholy from the loss," he said, "that it refused to carry me. 'Tis why I could not come to see ye these past days."

His straight face did not fool her, and she told him so. "A leg can never tell ye what to do."

"Ye think not? Wait till you are my age, lass."

That didn't fool her, either, because he was not so old. His hair was brown, still, and had not begun to whiten. When he saw how she was watching him, he flashed a sudden smile that made his face look even younger. "If ye want the perfect truth," he said, "the day they took the seton out I fell into a fever, and the surgeon would not let me leave my bed. But you can see he kept me occupied."

Her own gaze followed his to where a small round table had been pulled up close beside the bed, a chessboard and its pieces set in waiting at its centre.

Captain Jamieson was watching her. "The colonel said it was a game ye like to play," he said, "and so I thought it best to practice."

It was such a lovely chessboard that she could not take her eyes from it.

The captain told her, "Come," and with an effort moved his leg aside to make a place for Anna to sit on the edge of the bed, within reach of the table. "Will ye be white or black?"

She chose the black, because the black king was her favourite still, and this king was more beautiful and detailed than the one she'd learned to play with in the Earl of Erroll's library. His beard was curled, his crown made gold with gilt, and she could see the ermine cuffs upon his robe. The other pieces were as finely made, with one exception. "Why," she asked, "did no one paint the pawns?"

"They are small men."

That made her rise to their defence. "But they are brave. They are the first to march to battle."

"And the first to fall." His glance was difficult to read. "I only meant the pieces here are small in size, and would be difficult to paint. 'Tis likely why they were left plain."

"Oh."

"What mark would ye give them, then?"

She frowned, and thought, and was not sure.

The captain said, "Perhaps it is their brave hearts that would mark them, like the Bruce."

She knew the story of King Robert, called the Bruce, that ancient Scottish king who after his own death had sent his heart upon Crusade to keep his promise made to God and to his men, and so had earned the name of Braveheart.

"But our hearts," said Captain Jamieson, "we carry close inside us, as do these wee soldiers here, and none will ever know our worth but by our actions."

Anna watched him move his first pawn out into the wooden field of inlaid squares, and without knowing why, she said, "I've always liked the pawns the best."

The captain paused, and looked at her, and seemed about to make reply when suddenly she realized, "But the Abbess Butler says that games are idle pastimes that do not please God."

He took this in without a word, the corners of his mouth turned slightly upward in a smile that held no humour. Then he said, "The Abbess Butler is a very wise and loving woman, and I do not doubt she would allow this one transgression, though I'd argue God is more accomplished in the game of chess than either of us, having played so long with living pieces. And, like you, he seems to like his pawns."

She heard the bitterness, but did not understand it, so she simply said, "Is that because He sees into their hearts, and sees their braveness?"

Captain Jamieson glanced up at that, and when he spoke the edge had left his voice. "Aye, let us hope He does."

And satisfied, she moved her own pawn forward then, a small courageous soldier on that field of dark and light.

May came, with all its brightness, and the sound of birdsong filled the convent's garden every morning, and the sun fell warm on Anna's shoulders as she helped the nuns in cheerful silence do their work.

She liked to feel the earth between her fingers, and the crushed green scent of herbs, and best of all she liked the task of pulling out the stealthy, spreading weeds that always sought to bind and smother the more useful plants and flowers.

Her efforts pleased the abbess, who while watching her one morning said, "Now do that with your thoughts as well, pluck out the needless vanities and worries, and you'll find you grow the straighter for it."

Anna liked the abbess. She liked all the nuns, in fact. They could be stern when it was warranted, but mostly they were kind and smiled often, and they had a peace about them that she knew she'd never have herself. There were but half a dozen each of lay sisters and choir nuns who, together with the abbess, formed the whole of that community, and Anna by this time had learned their faces and their names, and some few details of their lives before the convent.

On the rainy afternoon when Captain Jamieson next came to visit for their walk within the church, she shared what she had learnt about one of her favourite nuns. ". . . and she was born in Scotland, too, and speaks the same as you and I do, and her true name is Maclean,"

she told him. "Mary Louisa Maclean. Is that not a bonny name? Her
mother's father was an earl, the earl of Kilmar . . ." Here she faltered in
her memory, and the captain guessed.

"Kilmarnock?"

"Aye. He died, though, and her uncle died as well, and so her
cousin is the earl now. But he fights against the king." And with those
few words she dismissed him from her thoughts. "Her father, though,
does serve King James. His name is Alexander. Have ye met him?"

"If he's Sir Alexander Maclean," said the captain, "then yes, I have
met him."

"She says he's a good man. He left her in Scotland," said Anna, "the
same way my own father left me when he came to follow the king.
But," she added, "he fetched her across at last, for he did not wish to
leave her with those who thought wrongly and served the wrong faith."

Captain Jamieson glanced round the quiet interior of the small
church, with its silver lamp burning a light in the dimness. "And what
is the right faith?"

"The nuns say there is but one true faith to follow."

"And what do you say?"

He was asking a serious question, she knew, so she answered him
with honesty. "Colonel Graeme is a Catholic, but he says he loves my
mother and my mother is a Protestant, so I think God must surely love
as broadly as the colonel does, and see the good in all men."

"See the brave hearts of his pawns, ye mean?" The captain's smile
showed faintly. "Are they teaching ye philosophy, the nuns?"

She wasn't sure. "But I am glad there is a Scottish nun."

"She makes ye feel at home, then, does she?"

"Aye. She's very bonny, and she sometimes tells me tales about the
queen at St. Germain. I think she would have liked to stay there best
of all, and not become a nun, but by the time she came across from
Scotland," Anna said, "her father had another wife and daughter, so
there wisnae any place for her with them."

She sobered for a moment, and she wondered if her mother, since
her father's death, had found another husband, and borne any other

children. She would have to ask the colonel when she saw him next, for he seemed to know much about her mother.

Captain Jamieson was watching her, but he did not intrude upon her thoughts. He only strolled along in silence for a while, and then he said, "That is an interesting tale, and I am glad ye've found a country-woman here to keep ye company, but I am not so certain she'd have wished for ye to tell me all she said to ye."

"Why not? It is no secret."

"Perhaps not, but it is not your tale to tell." His sidelong glance held not reproach, but patience. "My mother, when I was a lad, liked to say 'all that's heard in the kitchen should never be told in the hall.'"

"What does that mean?"

"It means what ye hear among family and friends, ye should never repeat among strangers."

"But you're not a stranger," she told him, as though that were obvious.

"Am I not?"

"Of course not." Impulse made her slip her hand into his larger one as she said, "Did ye ken my father's buried in this church? He has a stone, the abbess says."

They found it on the inner wall, a monument very elaborately carved of white stone, with stone flowers that spilled to each side, and below them a central rectangular frame held the words that she couldn't make sense of, for all the nuns' teachings.

"'Tis nothing but your father's name in Latin," said the captain, and he read: "'*Ioannis Moray D'Abercarni*.' These initials here, above the name, they mean: 'To God, the Best, the Greatest.' *Deo, Optimo, Maximo*."

It came as no surprise to her that he could read in Latin, for truthfully it seemed to her the captain could do anything.

More words were woven with the other carvings round the frame that offered images of life and death. From either side a human skull grinned down, one sprouting what appeared to be an eagle's wings, the other with the soft wings of an angel.

Anna stared with wide eyes at the skulls, and the densely carved flowers beneath that appeared to be living on one side and dead on the other. Two words were set right at their centre, and shivering slightly she tried to pronounce them herself, minding what she had learnt of her letters: "Mem . . . memen . . ."

The captain said, "'*Memento mori.*'"

She asked, "What does that mean?"

He slanted a quiet look down at her, letting his gaze rest a moment on her troubled face, then his hand tightened warmly on hers, reassuring. "'Tis nothing ye need to be thinking of. Look, see those unicorns up there?"

She liked the unicorns. Reared up on their hind legs and facing one another, they seemed to be dancing.

"They're the unicorns of Scotland," said the captain. "And that oval piece between them shows your father's shield, as differenced from his father's and his brothers', with the chevron there between three stars."

"Are those words Latin, too, beneath the unicorns?"

He nodded. "'*Sine Labe.*' 'Tis the motto of your grandfather, and all of Abercairney."

"So it is my motto, too."

"Aye."

"What does seen-ay lah-bay mean?" she asked him.

"Without stain." Again his mouth curved slightly in the way it sometimes did, into what might have been a smile had it not been so tight and fleeting. "A noble motto, to be sure, though few men ever can achieve it."

From looking at his face she could not tell if he were speaking of himself or of her father. From the things she'd heard him say to Colonel Graeme in their travels, it was plain he'd known her father well. She fancied they'd been friends.

She asked him, "Captain, did ye fight in the same battles as my father?"

His head turned as he looked down at her and answered, "Aye."

"And did he ever mention me?"

"He did not know he had a bairn at all, while he was fighting here in Flanders. And 'twas likely just as well. It would have made his falling harder, if he'd known that he was leaving ye behind without a father to defend ye."

"Did my mother never tell him?" It was worse, somehow, to think that he had died not even knowing she existed.

Captain Jamieson said gently, "There was hardly time. Your mother did the best for ye she could. She kept ye safe."

She looked at him, and suddenly she realized something else. "You kent my mother, too?"

He nodded. "Aye."

Her breath caught, and so many questions tumbled over one another in her mind that she could scarce make sense of them, but one above all others needed asking. It was difficult. She held his gaze for courage. "Do ye think she'll ever come for me?"

She knew he would not lie to her. It was not in his nature. He exhaled as he shifted once again to ease his injured leg, and said, "A woman cannot travel with the freedom of a man."

"Does she live far away, then?"

"Far enough." His eyes were cast in shadow, but she thought he must have seen her disappointment, for he gave her hand a gentle squeeze again and looked away. A moment's silence fell between them.

He said, "Anna, when my leg is healed I must go to the king, and do what he would have me do, and for this next while, till the king has found a place where he may settle and be safe, my own life, too, must be unsettled." His quiet voice cast back a hollow echo from the wall of ancient stone with all its marble monuments. "But this much I can promise ye: When I am done my duty to the king," he said, "I'll take ye to your mother."

Anna hardly dared to hope. She had to tell herself again the captain did not lie, and still she asked him, "Truly?"

He was looking at her father's stone, the oval shield and motto. "Truly. But it may yet be a while afore I can come back for ye. Both Colonel Graeme and myself have paid the nuns to keep ye for the year, if it proves necessary."

Anna sagged inside. A year seemed far too long to wait.

He turned again, and seeing her expression said, "It may not come to that. I will not leave ye caged here any longer than I must."

So he *did* understand about the bars. She sought to balance things by telling him again, "The nuns are kind."

"Aye, so they are, and they'll take care of ye. But while I am away ye do your part, and guard your health. 'Tis one advantage of the cloister, that it keeps much illness out, but in the winter months ye must dress warm and not fall ill," he said, with such insistence that it made her think again about the little girl he'd had himself once, and had lost.

She did not feel it would be right to ask him how his daughter died, because it might call details to his mind that brought him pain. She only paused, and thought, and then asked, "Captain Jamieson?"

"Aye?"

"Is your daughter . . . is she in the same place as my daddie?"

For the painful space of several heartbeats she thought he might never speak, but finally he said, "Aye."

"And do ye think he's taking care of her, as you are taking care of me?"

This time as he looked down at her his mouth curved not at all, and yet she thought his eyes looked as they did when he was wont to smile. "I'm sure of it."

"Well then," she told him, wrapping her small fingers still more tightly round his own, "she will be fine, I think."

And so they stood awhile, with Anna gazing upward at the unicorns of Scotland held forever frozen in their dance, the three stars fixed in stone between them, and she prayed a very selfish prayer: She prayed the captain's leg would take a long, long time to heal.

chapter
SIXTEEN

She knew the day when it arrived, because he would not look at her. He took her hand as always while they walked, but he was holding it more closely and she'd chattered on some minutes before realizing his gaze had not yet lifted from the floor.

He limped, still, but his jaw no longer tightened with each step of the offending leg, and when she looked to where the bandage just above his knee had always been, she only saw the fabric of his breeks now lying smooth.

She stopped, and made him stop as well, and said, "Your leg is healed."

"It is."

"And you will go now to the king."

He gave a nod. "Aye. 'Tis my duty."

She had practiced for this moment, for she'd wanted him to see her being brave. The small betraying tremor of her lower lip was overridden when she raised her chin. "When will ye go?"

"This afternoon."

Too soon, she thought. It was not fair.

He seemed to read her thoughts. His voice was gently understanding when he asked, "And would ye wish to be a soldier still, and always be in duty bound to leave the people ye hold dear, as I must?"

Did he hold her dear? Her heart swelled proudly as she nodded. "If I were a soldier, I could follow you."

"Brave lass." His gaze fell warm upon her upturned face. "Ye'll follow me already, with your feet or no." And seeing that she did not understand, he tapped the left side of his chest with his free hand and said, "I have ye here now, in my heart, and where I go I'll have ye with me there, to keep me company."

His gesture had reminded him of something, for he reached inside his jacket now and drew from it a long and folded piece of paper. "I have something for ye."

Anna had to let go of his hand to take the paper, for she needed her two hands to hold it properly. She eased the stiff folds open and saw lines of words in bold black ink. The letter "T" she recognized, and here and there the letter "M," but all of it was written as a grown-up wrote, the slanted letters joined to one another, and she could not understand the words for all she'd never wanted more to know the trick of reading. Feeling frustrated, she asked, "What does it say?"

"It is your song," he said. "The cradle song I sang ye, of the maiden and her wandering. The music's there as well—ye see these notes across the top? When ye have learnt to read the words, ye can apply yourself to learning those as well, and then ye'll know the way to sing it."

Anna held the treasured paper with one hand while with the other she reached up to let her fingers skim the little blots of ink with stems that danced across the top part of the page, above the words, to make the music. It had been so many days since they had spoken of this song, she'd thought for sure he had forgotten. "You remembered."

"Aye. Did I not promise ye I'd write those verses down?"

She nodded solemnly.

"Well, then." He crouched before her so that he could be on her own level, though it caused him pain to do it. She could see the sudden tightening along his jaw that showed for but a moment and in that same moment was dismissed. "I've never made a promise yet," he said, "that I've not kept. Ye hear?" He waited till she gave another nod before continuing, "So bide ye yet a while, till I come back for ye."

"And take me to my mother?"

"Aye."

She looked him in the eyes, then. "Will I please her? Will she love me?"

"Do ye doubt it?"

Anna did not want to show him doubts. She wanted very badly to believe. Instead she asked, "Has she a husband?"

He was slow to answer, as though weighing what he ought to tell her, but at length he answered honestly, as she had known he would. "She does."

"And other children?"

"Aye," the captain said, "but I believe your mother's heart has long since had a hole in it the size and shape of you, and it will take yourself to fill it, for none else can do that for her."

He was watching her and willing her, she thought, to trust his words, but still she doubted. "Captain Jamieson?"

"Aye?"

"If my mother disnae want me, will ye take me home with you?"

His leg, she thought, must still be hurting dreadfully because he closed his eyes a moment, and again she saw his jawline tighten, and again she saw it pass. He said, "Your mother has been wanting ye these eight years, Anna, since she had to give ye to another. She's been wanting ye and waiting, and ye never need to fear her heart will change."

"But she might die. My father died."

He reached a tender hand to tuck a straggling curl behind her ear. "Ye worry overmuch," he said, "for one who will be staying in this convent with the nuns and all their comforts. 'Tis myself ye want to pity, for I must now find a way to pass the days upon the open road without a lass to talk with me, and make me look a fool at playing chess."

He'd meant to make her smile, to tease her, but it only turned her thoughts towards his journey and the unknown service he might have to do the king.

"Will there be battles where you're going? Will ye have to fight?" she asked him.

"Och, I doubt there will be battles for a while."

"But there are still bad men," she reasoned, "like the ones who tried to catch my father."

"There will always be bad men. But Colonel Graeme and myself will never let them do ye harm. Nor will the nuns."

She could not tell him it was not her own safety she worried for, because she found it suddenly was taking all her effort just to hold her brave mask in its place. Her gaze slid to the shadowed corner of the church that held her father's monument, and then she realized what she had to do.

The song sheet folded neatly on its creases as she thanked him for it, and with care she tucked it through the opening that gave her access to the linen pocket tied beneath her skirts. In the corner of that pocket she could feel the small black stone strung on its leather cord, the stone that had the hole in it, and taking it with care into her hand she held it out to show the captain, on her open palm.

"This was my father's," Anna said, and told him all that Colonel Graeme had explained to her about the little stone and what it meant within her family, their belief that it would keep away all evils. "Will ye take it, please, and wear it?"

Captain Jamieson looked down at Anna's hand, and at the stone, and for a long while it appeared he had no words. He cleared his throat, and said with roughness in his voice, "I think your daddie would have wanted ye to have that, and not give it to another."

She was not supposed to argue with her elders, so the nuns each day reminded her, but how else could she let the captain know that he had come to fill the hole left by the father she had never known, and that she'd miss him even more than she now missed the family that had raised her? How could she let him know that when he'd gone away and left her, she would carry in her heart a hole the size and shape of *him*?

If she tried to tell him outright, she would shame herself by weeping. She could only match his stubborn nature with her own, and say, "But I am safe already. And the stone is mine to give." Her upraised hand shook only slightly as she held it nearer to him. "Please."

He looked a moment longer at the stone, and then at her, and then in silence he reached out and closed his calloused fingers round the gift, and still in silence with great care he slipped the cord around his neck so that the stone lay underneath his shirt, below the hollow of his throat. He took a breath as though to speak, and then without a word he reached again and drew her to him.

There was fierceness in his hard embrace, and yet his hand was gentle on her hair as though he feared to break her, holding her so tightly.

Anna held him back. It was like being wrapped in warmth, she thought. The hard wall of his chest beneath the worn wool jacket felt like a protective shield through which no harm could penetrate, and while she nestled there within his arms the world seemed very far away, and unimportant.

She could not have said how long he crouched there holding her, the roughness of his cheek against her forehead, but at length he kissed her hair and gently set her from him and prepared to stand.

She tugged once at his jacket so he'd stop just long enough that she could kiss his cheek. When grown-ups kissed and said farewell, she knew they often wished each other health and a safe journey, and she had practiced words herself for this, the worst of all her partings. But the words would not be called to mind, and so she could but stand and tell him nothing.

He had straightened to his full height, now. His eyes looked strangely bright, she thought, and red around their rims, and he said nothing, either, only gave a kind of nod and glanced away. She saw his eyelashes were wet, and that seemed strange to her as well, and yet it could not be from weeping because everybody knew a soldier never wept.

She managed not to weep herself, although she found it very hard.

The Abbess Butler let her watch him through the window while he left. He was on horseback, looking tall and strong and wonderful. He saw her at the window and he raised his hand as he went by, and at the far end of the street he slowed his horse and brought its head around enough that he could look the long way back at her. She saw his arm lift one more time—one final wave, one last salute, and then he turned the horse and they rode on.

The world beyond the window blurred.

She had a vague awareness of the Abbess Butler standing there behind her, of the soothing words, the sympathetic hand upon her shoulder, and the fact that she had not been left alone, and yet already she could feel the hole beginning in her heart.

And when the first tear fell, she knew she'd never be a soldier.

chapter
SEVENTEEN

R ob wasn't feeling up to conversation yet. He hadn't said as much,
but I could sense it when I looked at him, and so while he was
finishing his dinner I sat back and watched the people passing by us on
the pavement.

We had picked a restaurant fronting on the town's impressive
market square, ringed round with buildings reconstructed from the
rubble left by the bombardment of the First World War, the darkly
Gothic Cloth Hall with its high clock tower at the western end, its tall
spire shadowed by the church spire rising close behind it, and the long
tall line of ancient-looking buildings, with stepped gables and steep
roofs that looked too perfectly medieval to be real. The courthouse
at the eastern end of the long open square looked like a palace, built
of golden stone with carving round its windows and a curious round
metal tower rising from the centre of its high roof.

It was busy in the square. Cars stood angle-parked all down the
great expanse of it, while round the streets that ringed it other cars
sped past or crawled along according to the temper of their drivers,
and the pavements were alive with tourists.

And at our side of the square a little funfair had been set up, neon
lights around its side stalls with their games of skill and luck, and a
small dragon-headed roller coaster that lurched round its corners with
a rush and rattle, making all the children that it carried shriek and
hold their arms up bravely.

When we'd first been seated it had been a little quieter because
it had been coming up on eight o'clock—the time, our waitress told
us, of the ceremony held each evening here in Ypres to honour those

who'd fallen in the First World War, and had no graves. The ceremony took place at the Menin Gate, just visible beyond the square, an arch of pale stone built above the bridge that crossed the moat. The traffic would be stopped, our waitress said, and music played, and words recited, with each night a different honour guard of soldiers from one of the many countries that had lost men in that unforgotten war. "It's very beautiful," she'd told us. "Many tourists come to see it. It is something to remember."

We didn't go ourselves. I heard the playing of the Last Post, and the bugle's call to Reveille, but given the emotional intensity of what I'd just been witnessing, I didn't really want to face more sadness, and I doubted Rob did, either.

It had taken something out of him this time, our going back. I hadn't noticed it at Slains, or at the cottage, but this time when we had surfaced from our visions of the past there in that shadowed covered driveway, Rob had leaned a moment longer up against the hard brick wall, and closed his eyes.

"Are you all right?" I'd asked him.

"Aye, I'm fine."

He looked fine, now. We'd been here for an hour, and he'd polished off his steak and Flemish beer. I'd ordered fish, myself—small rolls of sole in the Normandy style in a mushroom sauce enlivened by bits of red apple, with piped mashed potatoes and salad, but most of it still sat untouched on my plate.

Rob had glanced at it once. When he did it again now I nudged the plate over the table towards him. "Go on then."

I watched him eat, looking for any sign he might be tired, but he looked the same as he always did.

We'd stayed partly outdoors, not going right into the restaurant but taking a table instead on the front covered patio where the glass walls at each end blocked a lot of the breeze, and the raised wooden floor lightly bounced with the steps of the servers. Rob might have preferred somewhere softer to sit than the black metal mesh of these chairs, but the restaurant's interior had looked too intimate, too softly lit, and I'd thought I would find it more comfortable here in fresh air and bustle. I'd thought that our meal would feel less like a date.

But it hadn't worked out that way. For starters, the table—a small, square grey table dressed up with a grey linen cloth draped across it—was *so* small there wasn't a way we could sit at it without our knees touching. Ever the gentleman, Rob had made room for me, shifting his feet a bit farther apart, but that hadn't helped. Now my knees were between his, and that only made me a lot more aware of him.

And for another thing, I hadn't counted on just how seductive this mental connection would be, that we'd shared today following Anna. Breaking that connection had been difficult, like stepping from a warm room to the wintry world beyond. It had been harder because Rob's mind had stayed open to me, fully open, as though . . .

That was it, I realized. He'd had no defences up at all, as though he hadn't had the energy to raise them.

He'd finished my dinner. The cutlery clanked as he set it on top of his stacked empty plates and slid everything off to one side to make room for his elbows. He didn't exactly lean closer, but in that confined space it felt like he did as he lifted his gaze so it levelled on mine.

"I'm fine," he assured me. "I've done this afore, and with less cause. Truth is, I enjoy it. So stop feeling guilty."

"I'm not. I just—"

"Nick."

No one else ever called me that. And if they had, it would never have hit me with all the effect of that one little syllable rolled in his deep Scottish voice. I'd forgotten the sound of it. Now it brought back a whole rush of remembered scenes I wasn't ready to face, so instead I said, "I'm just concerned."

"No need for that." His tone was light, but it was meant to make a point. "I've got a mother."

"And you don't need two?"

"Exactly."

"Sorry. But you look—"

"Like hell?" he guessed.

"No." *Hardly that*, I thought, then quickly closed my mind before he heard me.

"Like what, then?"

The rain spared me from answering. It came on unexpectedly, and pattered hard against the bright red awning overhead and made the people who'd been standing round outside scoop up their parcels and their cameras and dash in to find a place to sit.

An older couple took the table nearest ours, and Rob was forced to move his leg again to give them space, while to our other side a family with young children dragged another chair across and squeezed themselves into the corner.

We were well surrounded, now. Their conversations, private as they were, flowed round and over us and I knew anything I said to Rob they'd hear as well, so I said nothing for a while.

The waitress came and took our empty plates, and brought another beer for Rob, and for myself a cup of coffee garnished with a tiny biscuit and a little square of Belgian chocolate. I drank it while the older couple tried to choose which battlefield to visit the next morning, and the children on the other side decided on their meals, with much negotiating, and I couldn't help but wonder what they'd think if I asked Rob the question forming in my mind.

No doubt they'd all react the same way as that big man and his mates had in the pub that night in Edinburgh two years ago. They'd think us freaks.

I carefully unwrapped my chocolate, thinking. Then I let down my defences. *Rob?*

He looked at me expectantly, not giving any sign that he had noticed how I'd spoken. Not surprising, since he'd told me it all sounded just the same to him.

I took a breath, and went on, *Can I ask you something?*

Watching him, I saw the moment's lapse before the realization

struck him; saw his gaze dip down to touch my mouth before returning to my own, a dawning light of pleasure in the depths of his blue
eyes, as though he'd just received an unexpected gift. He answered
with his own thoughts: *Ask me anything you like.*

There was a freedom, I thought, talking to him like this, while the
people seated round us carried on their conversations unaware. *How do
you stop and skip ahead like that?*

I'm sorry?

Well, when we were watching Anna in the convent . . .

Aye?

*We didn't stay and watch her all the time that she was sleeping, for ex-
ample. You just stopped, and skipped ahead and found her somewhere else,
and then went on from there. How did you do that?*

Practice. He leaned back and looked away from me, relaxed. *I
stumbled on the way to do it when I was at school, by chance, and found it
saved a lot of time when doing things like this. And so I practiced. I could
teach you, if you like.*

My skepticism must have carried clearly in my thoughts without
my having to express it, because Rob, still looking out towards the
square, half-smiled while making his reply. *You underestimate yourself,
I think.*

Yes, well. I haven't got your skills.

*Most skills are learnt. Or at the very least, developed. If I handed you
a cello, would ye ken the way to play it? No. But given time and practice,
ye could learn.*

You're an optimist. It came out as an accusation. *Anyway, it's not a
good analogy. You're working with a cello, I've just got a ukulele.*

His gaze slid back to mine, amused. *You finished with that coffee, yet?*

Almost. Why, do you want to leave?

You read my mind. A wave of warmth rode with those words, and
then his thoughts withdrew. He hailed the waitress, paid our bill, and
pushed his chair back as though he'd been sitting long enough. Aloud
he said, "Let's take a walk."

It was dark now, after ten o'clock according to the clock face on the tower of the Cloth Hall, which at every quarter hour let loose a beautifully melodic peal of bells, a proper carillon that lingered in the fresh night air. The rain had stopped, and left a fairyland of bright reflections on the street outside and in the square—the glimmer of the funfair's flashing lights and coloured neon, and the even wilder colours of the prizes hung in clusters from the ceilings of the side stalls.

Couples sauntered past with strollers bearing tired toddlers, fighting sleep and watching fascinated as the dragon roller coaster rattled round its loops to the delighted screams of those inside it.

"Want to ride the roller coaster?" Rob asked, teasing.

"No thanks. I'm not good with thrills," I told him. "I get sick."

"I'll make a note of that."

We passed a stall hung thickly with assorted cuddly toys, including two huge purple unicorns, and looking up I thought of Anna's father's grave and of the dancing unicorns that graced his stone memorial within the convent's church. The showman in the stall, misunderstanding my interest, called a challenge out to Rob that needed no translation.

Pausing, hands in pockets, Rob looked down at me and grinned. "Are you wishing for one of the unicorns, then? Shall I win you one?"

It wasn't a ball-in-the-bucket or hoopla game, but a full-size shooting gallery with tethered air rifles set in a row, watched by large mural paintings of James Bond and Wild West gunslingers.

Doubtful, I asked, "*Could* you win me one?"

"Aye, I'm a decent shot."

Of course he would be, I thought, given his profession. Policemen might not go around shooting their guns all the time, but they had to be trained how to use them.

He handed his coins to the showman and shouldered a rifle and started to pick off the targets.

"You're showing off," I said.

"I might be. Why?" he asked me, sighting down the barrel of the gun. "Are ye concerned?"

He said it lightly, but I knew then that this wasn't about winning me a prize, because my brother did the same thing, sometimes, when he felt the need to prove himself. He went all manly and competitive.

I must have stung Rob's pride, I thought, implying that the day had taken more from him than he could handle, so in penance I stood by and let him demonstrate how wrong I'd been. He did it so decisively that in the end the showman finally stopped him, made a gesture of defeat, and with a long pole hooked one giant purple unicorn down from the ceiling.

Rob handed it on to me, looking decidedly pleased with himself. "There you go, that'll mind ye of Scotland."

It would remind me of much more than that, I knew. "Thanks," I told him. "But what on earth am I supposed to do with it?"

"Anything you want to. That's the point," he said, "of having one."

It proved, if nothing else, to be a brilliant conversation starter. On our way back down towards Sint Jacobsstraat we met a half a dozen strangers who felt moved to stop and chat and comment on my unicorn, and it drew a lot of interest from the knot of men who'd spilled out from the Old Bill Pub across from our hotel, to stand and drink their pints there on the pavement near a little chalkboard sign that read: LIVE FOOTBALL.

Rob got talking with them, friendly as he was, and learned they'd come from Belfast just this morning, and done duty as the honour guard this evening at the Last Post ceremony at the Menin Gate. And so of course he bought them all another round, but when they tried to urge him to stay longer, have a drink with them, he shook his head and told them thanks, but no.

"You've better things to do, eh?" one man joked as we were leaving.

"Aye." Rob smiled in reply, but there was nothing in his tone or face to match their own suggestive laughter as we started off again along the pavement, and he didn't sling his arm around my shoulders as he'd done when we were dating. Both his hands stayed in his pockets as he matched his steps to mine. It was like walking with my brother.

The hotel's front facade was a bright blaze of light, the glass doors sliding open as we neared them, but instead of heading through them Rob walked on and led me farther down to where the car sat parked along the quiet square of green before the looming shadow of the church.

The street was darker, here, although the sulphur-yellow streetlamps fixed along the gabled rooflines of the huddled houses made the rain-washed cobbles glitter gold in places.

Rob said, "Let's put your wee friend, there, in the boot."

He travelled well-prepared. I watched him shift a first-aid kit, a toolbox, and a duffle bag to make room for my unicorn, and then from underneath a folded tarp he took a heavy woollen tartan blanket. And another.

"What are those for?"

"Well, it's like I said." He slammed the boot securely closed and locked it, turning back to me, his eyebrow lifting, "I have better things to do."

The covered passageway of brick beneath the houses where we'd stood that afternoon was now closed up, great wooden garage doors securely locked against intruders, but there still remained the sheltered spot beneath the trees where we'd first sat this morning. The narrow street here, with the banks and trees all down the one side and the few dark shuttered houses on the other, was so quiet I could hear the murmur of the moat that ran unseen behind us.

As Rob spread one of the blankets down I said, "You're mad. We'll freeze to death out here."

We wouldn't, I knew. It was only that sitting with Rob in the daylight was different from sitting with him in the dark.

"Have ye no faith at all?" He was waiting for me to sit down, so I did, with reluctance. "Tomorrow," he said, "we'll be off back to London, and Anna's still well stuck in Ypres."

"She could be here awhile," I said.

"Aye, so she could." He sat too, close beside me but giving me space. "But we won't be." The heavy warm weight of the second wool blanket shut out the night's chill as Rob tucked it around me. "We've only the one night left." Holding his hand out, he looked at me. "Let's make it count."

chapter
EIGHTEEN

Anna knew that she was not the only one within the convent's walls who felt alone. Sometimes at night she heard a woman weeping, softly distant, and the melancholy sound stole down the corridor and seemed to wrap around her own small body lying silent in her bed, and give a voice to her own misery.

She'd thought that it might be Dame Clare. She'd heard the story from the older girls, about the young and tragic lady who had loved a soldier from the Regiment of Clare, that gallant regiment that charged a nearby battlefield ten years before and captured the enemy's colours for their bravery, those colours that now hung within the choir here at the convent. But the lady's soldier fell in that same charge, and grief had brought her here to live and be a pensioner and daily make her peace with that same God who'd cruelly taken all her dreams.

Dame Clare, thought Anna, had cause to spend her nights lamenting, but the other students told her it was not Dame Clare she'd heard. The weeping woman was, they said, a new arrival to the convent, neither nun nor pupil.

"I was told," one of the older girls said, hushed and speaking slowly so they'd not be overheard at dinner, "that her lover was an English spy, who wooed her for the simple fact her family lived at St. Germain and had connections to King James. But finding she could tell him nothing useful, he abandoned her, and now he's gone to Paris and her shame has been discovered so her family sent her here."

The older girls thought this was wildly romantic, and one of the younger girls thought it a scandal, but Anna just thought it unfair.

After all, it hadn't been the sad young woman's fault that she had caught the eye of someone so deceitful, and had trusted him, and Anna thought it very wrong the spy was still at liberty while the young woman had now been disgraced and shut away.

When she said so to Sister Xaveria after their prayers the next morning, and asked her how God could allow such injustice, the nun asked, "And how did you hear of this?"

Anna explained, ending with, ". . . and so she telt me that it could-nae be Dame Clare."

They were still standing in the choir of the convent church, and Anna cast a quick look upwards at the captured flags that hung above them, swaying slightly to the unseen movement of the air.

"She telt me," Anna added as an afterthought, "that Dame Clare disnae weep."

"'Tis true." Sister Xaveria looked up, as well. "She does not weep. She prays."

"Ye've seen her, then."

"Of course. She's lived here with us ten years now, of course I've seen her. So have you, I should imagine."

"I have not."

"We rarely see the things we don't expect to see."

Anna, not understanding, asked, "And did she lose her lover in that battle, truly? Is that why she shut herself up here?"

Sister Xaveria smiled. "We are not shut off from the world, my child. Not even here. We merely seek to live more fully in the world, without distraction, so we may more clearly hear God's voice and do his bidding."

Which did not answer Anna's question, but she'd learned that Sister Xaveria often preferred to ask questions rather than answer them, so it was not a surprise when the nun asked, "And where have you heard this sad tale of Dame Clare? Not from any of us, surely?"

"No. From the other girls. Some of their parents, at court, heard the story, but I reckoned you'd ken the truth of it better than anyone."

"Oh yes? And why me, particularly?"

"Because," said Anna, "your own sister married a man of that regiment."

Sister Xaveria's eyebrows rose up till they touched the smooth edge of her wimple. "And where did you learn of that? No," she said, raising a hand, "do not tell me. I can see I ought to teach tomorrow's lesson from the Proverbs, starting with: '*Qui ambulat fraudulenter revelat arcana qui autem fidelis est animi celat commissum.*'" She translated, for Anna's sake: "'A tale-bearer revealeth secrets: but he who is of faithful spirit concealeth the matter.' Do you know what that means, Anna?"

"Aye." Anna nodded.

"And what does it mean, then?"

"It means that what's heard in the kitchen," said Anna, "should never be said in the hall."

The nun's mouth twitched. "Exactly."

She might have said more, but at that moment Anna saw something that made her stop listening. Near the far wall of the chapel, beyond the dark bars of the grille, stood a man looking up at her father's stone monument. A man with brown hair tied back over his collar, his hands clasped at a soldier's ease behind him. With his back to her, he looked like . . .

"Captain Jamieson!" she called out in delight, and leaving Sister Xaveria's side made a rush to the bars. "Captain!"

"Anna," the nun warned, rebuking her for calling out so loudly in the sanctity of church, perhaps, or simply for behaving in a manner unbecoming to young ladies, but the shout had served its purpose.

Anna watched the man turn round, and with a stab of disappointment she saw it was not the captain, but a slightly younger man who peered towards her through the shadows of the church.

Unclasping his hands he strode forwards, relaxed at first, then as though being compelled, his gaze fixing on Anna's small face with increasing amazement. His eyes lifted once, to the nun standing just behind Anna.

"Sir." The nun veiled her face as she greeted him. "You are most welcome."

"Sister Xaveria." Dropping his gaze back to Anna, he asked in a low voice, "Whose child is this?"

Anna stared at him, not understanding the flash of emotion that twisted his features as though something pained him. "Her eyes . . . and her hair . . . she's the image of . . ." Pausing a moment, he gathered himself and then asked again, hoarsely, "Whose child is this?"

Anna felt Sister Xaveria's hand on her shoulder, a gentle and steadying hold, reassuring. The nun told her, "Anna, this is Mr. Maurice Moray, youngest brother to the Laird of Abercairney. And your uncle."

Sitting in the parlour with the Abbess Butler and Sister Xaveria together with her on the one side of the grille, and looking at her Uncle Maurice sitting on the other, with the full grace of a gentleman, his back straight and his head up, proudly, Anna wondered whether her own father had once looked like that.

But no, she thought. Her uncle's eyes were blue, and Colonel Graeme had been firm in saying that her own eyes were the colour of her father's, like the sea in winter, mingled grey and green. The colour that her mother had so loved.

And her father's face had surely been more handsome.

He was trying not to stare at her. "I did not know."

The Abbess Butler gently said, "Nor did your brother. I believe his wife decided it was safer to conceal the child."

"His wife?" Reacting as though from a blow, he sat back in his chair. "Where is she now, this wife? Is she well cared for? Is she—?"

Gently interrupting him, the Abbess Butler said, "Your Uncle Graeme will, I have no doubt, tell all to you when next you see him."

"God," he said, then caught himself, and rubbing one hand on his brow apologized for uttering profanity in such a holy place. "'Tis only that . . . I did not know." His gaze fell warm on Anna's face and searched for something there, but what it was she could not fathom. "She does have his features, does she not? It is as if he were not . . . were not . . ." Cutting off the final part of what he might have said, he sharply turned his head towards the window and developed a fierce interest in the plain unchanging view of tiled rooftops that it offered. Quietly he said, "He was the best of us."

The room sank into silence for a moment, as though all the adults' thoughts had merged in one sad place.

The Abbess Butler finally asked, "How fare your other brothers? Did you leave them well in Scotland, or have they come over with you?"

"No, and no," was his reply. "They are not with me, and I did not leave them well." He exhaled, heavily. "My brother Robin has again been taken captive, and there's none will give me word of how he does, though I do fear that, having entertained him now so many times, the English will be keen to see him suffer when he comes to trial. As for my brother Abercairney, he was with us all the time at Perth until the king came, but he sickened and became too ill to come away when we made our retreat. It was his wife who found us passage finally, in a ship sent from the South Firth."

"Us?" the Abbess Butler asked. "Then you do have companions?"

"Aye, Sir Thomas Higgons came, as did Sir William Keith and his son George, and Mr. Graeme, Newton's son. We had designed for Gottenburg, but found the winds too contrary, and then a Danish frigate did detain us several days at Copenhagen, but at length," he said, "we made Danzig, and there we took to land. The roads are wearying, but safer than the sea."

"Will not you let us host you here in lodgings for the night?"

He shook his head. "I thank you, no. I could not pass so near to Ypres without a visit to your church, to see John's grave, but I did not intend to stop for long. The others have but gone to find a meal and fresher horses, and will soon return to fetch me. Then we must continue on to Paris," he explained, "for I am carrying a goodly sum of money for the king, and will not rest until I put it in the safe hands of his agents there." He seemed to think of something, then, and focusing on Anna, asked the nuns, "Have you sufficient funds to care for her? I have not much that is my own, but what I have is yours, and I could surely borrow from the funds I carry if—"

The abbess raised her hand. "Your Uncle Graeme has already generously supplied her needs."

He gave a nod of understanding, and what might have been regret. "And were it peacetime, she would surely find a home at Abercairney, and a cheerful playmate in her cousin James, my nephew. Or with Robin and his family—he has several sons and daughters now." His smile was thin, and hardened against memory. "But these times are far from peaceful, and my family, for its honourable history, has no place where it can stand with any safety."

"We will keep her safe." The Abbess Butler did not look so old, thought Anna, when she spoke like that, in such a bold, determined tone. "And to that end, it would be better, sir, if you did not inform your other brothers of her being here, nor mention her to anyone in Paris."

He agreed. "You may rely on my discretion. For my part, it is enough to know that something yet remains of John." His gaze searched Anna's face a moment longer, then he looked her squarely in the eye. "Your father was the best of us," he said again, but with more force this time, as though he wanted to be very sure she understood. "He was a good friend, and a better brother, and a man of honour. Mind that, now."

She raised her chin and said, "I ken fine who my father was." There was no trace of insolence in how she spoke the words, nor yet a tone of argument, but simply an assertion of the fact.

Her Uncle Maurice stared a moment, then the corners of his mouth turned upwards slightly. "I perceive you do not have his looks alone," he told her, "but also his temperament, God help ye." Softening, he said more gently, "God help ye," and rose to his feet.

"I shall write," he told Sister Xaveria, "if you'll permit it."

"Of course."

And they blessed him and wished him Godspeed.

His first letter arrived three weeks later, addressed not to Anna herself but to Sister Xaveria, and saying nothing of any importance, but Sister Xaveria read it out loud to her anyway. "Tell my niece," he'd written, "that her father loved to read, and I do hope she will apply herself most diligently to her studies, that she may do likewise."

Anna tried.

She had a gifted ear for languages, and soon could understand and follow much of what the Flemish-speaking lay sisters were saying while they worked, but printed words were something altogether different. Through the long heat of the summer and the early autumn she applied herself as diligently as she could, and still each time a letter came to Sister Xaveria from Uncle Maurice in Paris, the nun without asking would read it aloud, as though knowing the effort would bring Anna frustration.

Perhaps, Anna thought, that was why Captain Jamieson had never written a letter yet to her, from where he had gone. He was waiting until she could read them.

The thought made her try all the harder, until her hand ached in the evening from copying out the full alphabet, over and over, and she slept too soundly to hear the mysterious woman who wept still, but rarely.

And then, at the start of November, she took out the song sheet the captain had given her, as she did every day, and traced the bold slanted handwriting, and for the first time the lines and the loops formed themselves into shapes with a meaning.

She held her breath, not daring to believe it as her eyes raced downwards . . . there it was, her favourite of the verses, and she read— she truly *read*—the words the wandering maiden's steadfast lover sang:

"'. . . *cease thy weeping,*
now listen to me,
For waking and sleeping,
my heart is with thee.'"

Anna's tight chest could scarcely contain all her fullness of joy and of pride, and so eager was she to reveal her discovery to Sister Xaveria that she was practically running when she reached the classroom.

The nun turned from the window. "Anna! You are very early."

Anna caught her breath. "Aye, Sister Xaveria. I—"

"You must try to say 'yes,' Anna."

"Yes, Sister Xaveria. I—"

"It is just as well that you are here, for we've received another letter from your uncle." As the nun withdrew the letter from her habit, she asked, smiling, "Shall I read it to you?"

Anna would have said that she could read it for herself, but she knew well how rude it was to interrupt an elder, and Sister Xaveria had already begun to read aloud. As with each letter that had come from Uncle Maurice, there were several references to Anna and her studies, and to facets of her father's life, as though her uncle sought to piece together for her sake a whole and rounded image of his brother by revealing him in parts, in minor words and deeds and preferences that only someone close within their family would have known.

She'd learnt so far that, like herself, her father had not liked to sit for long without a useful occupation; that he'd valued honesty; that books had been his solace, and that he could charm a wild bird into his hand—a rare accomplishment, in Anna's view, and one she had been trying since, without success, to copy.

In this latest letter, Uncle Maurice wrote: ". . . if Anna seeks to calm her temper, she might use her father's trick of counting backwards from one hundred, all in silence, which he claimed had never failed him."

Anna smiled at that, as did Sister Xaveria, who set the letter down a moment as Sister Scholastica came in to ask a question of her. While the two nuns spoke within the doorway of the classroom, Anna picked her uncle's letter up and gloried in the fact that she could read it for herself.

And then she frowned. She was still frowning when Sister Xaveria came back to finish the letter. "Why, Anna, whatever is wrong?"

Anna's glance was a deep accusation. "My name is not in there," she said to the nun. "I have learnt how to read, and my name is not written at all in that letter."

A light of astonishment mingled with something like pride brightened Sister Xaveria's eyes. "You have learnt how to read?"

"Aye, and what you have read me is not what my uncle has written."

The nun asked, "Would you then believe I could tell you a falsehood?" She looked down at Anna and thought for a moment, and then she went on, "Do you know what a cipher is, Anna? No? Well, read through this again, if you would. And then tell me what name he does mention, more often than others."

Obedient, Anna read slowly once more through the letter, and said, "Mrs. Avery."

"Correct. Mrs. Avery is you, my dear. And where it speaks of your foxhound, that means of your father."

"But why would he not use the proper words?"

"Well," said the nun, "when a person writes something they wish to keep secret, they sometimes make use of a cipher that alters the meaning of words, as your uncle has."

"So the bad men cannae read it?" guessed Anna. She studied the letter a third time, with new eyes, and slowly came to realize, "He does mention me so many times."

"He does. And what does that reveal?" Sister Xaveria was speaking like a teacher, now. "It is as I once told you, Anna: That which we do not expect to see, we rarely notice."

Anna thought about this afterwards. It was the same thing that the nun had said when they'd been speaking of Dame Clare, and how although the lady lived within the convent as a pensioner, and surely ate and went to prayers, she went about unseen and unremarked by those who did not think to look for her.

At mealtimes Anna looked for her, and when she joined the nuns at prayers she raised her bowed head now and then to peer into the shadowed corners of the choir and chapel, but she did not see Dame Clare.

And then one morning near November's end she *did* see a new face among the more familiar ones—not someone old enough to have lost her true love ten years ago upon the bloody fields of Ramillies, because ten years ago this woman would have been a child herself, as

Anna was—but someone whom she had not seen before: a pale young woman, with a face so very beautiful that Anna found it difficult to keep from staring.

Christiane, they called her, and it soon became apparent she was neither nun nor student. With a growing sense of wonder, Anna realized she was looking at the woman she'd heard weeping in the night, the one who'd loved an English spy and been cast off by him, and sent here to do penance.

She was mesmerizing. Anna watched her praying, and she wished that she herself could be as elegant and poised. While doing daily chores she hoped to be assigned to do her work where Christiane was working, and she copied with great care the other's graceful movements. As the days wore on, the nuns and Christiane herself became aware of Anna's hero-worship, and began indulging it—the nuns because they thought it good to give the sad young woman someone else to focus on besides herself, and Christiane because she seemed to find it cheering to have Anna working close to her.

One morning while the two were cleaning windows in the church, where winter's frost had delicately traced its feathered patterns on the leaded glass, the Scottish nun who was still one of Anna's favourites stopped to wish them both good afternoon, and praised their efforts, and moved on.

"She's Scottish, too, like you and I," said Anna proudly.

Christiane was well aware of it. "My father knows her own, at St. Germain. 'Tis why he sent me here, because Sir Alexander had sent his own daughter to this place, and had assured him that the nuns were kind. And it was well away from Paris."

"Is it such an awful place," asked Anna, "Paris?"

"It is wonderful." And Christiane, who'd been there many times, began to paint a picture for her of the bustling streets, and parks as green as Paradise, and ancient churches ringing bells across the lovely river winding through it all. "It is like nothing you have ever seen," she promised Anna. "Maybe one day you'll be fortunate enough to go there."

"Maybe," Anna said. "My Uncle Maurice lives in Paris."

"Oh, yes?" The window Christiane was cleaning had a stubborn curve, and she was concentrating.

"Aye, he carries money for the king."

"The King of France?"

"No, our king," Anna said, for surely having lived so long at St. Germain before this, Christiane would know which king one ought to serve. "All of my uncles serve King James, as did my father."

"All? How many uncles have you, then?"

She had to think of that, and finally answered, "Three. One is in prison, now, and one is yet in Scotland. He's the Laird of Abercairney."

Christiane looked round in some surprise. "Would that be Sir William Moray?"

Anna nodded. "Do you know him?"

"I have heard my father speak of him, most highly." She appeared to be impressed, and Anna swelled inside with pride and pleasure that she had so gained her new friend's interest.

"Tell me, where in Paris does your Uncle Maurice live?" asked Christiane. "Mayhap I know the place, and can describe it to you."

So the winter carried on, through Christmas and Epiphany and Candlemas, and then in the first week of March word came from St. Germain that Christiane was to return there for the wedding of her brother.

"I shall soon be back," she promised Anna, but the days that followed her departure stretched with boredom for the girl, whose thoughts were brightened only by her sudden realization that it was now nearly spring, when Captain Jamieson would surely be returning for her.

She had nearly memorized the wandering maiden's song, now, and hoped to learn the music, too, so that when he did come for her she could reveal how studious she'd been, in keeping with his wishes.

When she heard the clatter of a single horseman riding down the street, she always paused to listen in the hope the sound might stop outside the convent's doors, and even though it never did she felt the growing pleasure of anticipation, for she knew the captain would not soon forget his word. He'd told her plain: "I've never made a promise yet that I've not kept," and truly she believed him.

But the man who came to fetch her, in the end, was not the captain.

The stranger turned up suddenly one morning, when the sun had not yet risen. Anna had not yet been wakened for the day. The Abbess Butler roused her urgently but gently, and with swift hands helped her dress, and guided Anna, half asleep and in a daze, into the parlour, where the lamps were lit.

There a man stood like no man she had ever met. He wore a long brown robe that brushed the floor and had a long hood hanging down behind, and at his waist his belt was made of simple rope. His beard was brown and long as well, though speckled through with grey, and he had cut his hair most strangely, with a short fringe all around and on the top no hair at all.

The Abbess Butler told her, "This is Father Archangel, and you must go with him, my child." There was a gate within the grille that Anna had not noticed ever, but the Abbess Butler swung it open now and herded Anna through it, careful not to leave the cloistered side herself. She pressed a parcel wrapped in rough cloth into Anna's hands and told the brown-robed man, "'Tis all of her belongings, pray they are not lost to her."

He gave a nod to show he understood, then came more close and bent to Anna's level, taking her small shoulders in a warm and kindly hold. His beard and hair were strange and frightening to Anna, but his voice, when he did speak to her, was Scottish. "Anna, I am not a stranger, lass. Your father was my cousin."

Anna blinked to clear the blurriness of sleep, and looked more keenly at his eyes. They were familiar to her.

Father Archangel. The name stirred something faintly in her memory. "Are ye Colonel Graeme's son?" she asked. "The one who was a soldier, once?"

"The very same. I'm sent to bring you to a place of greater safety."

Anna did not move. "But Colonel Graeme and the captain said the nuns would keep me safe."

Above her head the monk exchanged a silent glance with Abbess Butler, but he only said to Anna, "So they would, but for the danger that is coming there is little they can do. It is my father's own instruction that you come with me."

He smiled encouragement, and lightly squeezed her shoulder as he straightened with his hand outstretched, and told her, "Come. We must be on the road without delay."

And still she did not move. "But Captain Jamieson is coming for me soon," she told them both, and to her own young ears her voice was small and powerless. "He'll not ken how to find me if I leave."

The monk looked once more to the abbess. "Captain Jamieson?"

"A travelling companion of your father's," she replied. "The child was fond of him."

"He telt me I should bide here till he came," she said.

The Abbess Butler touched her hair. "I will be sure to tell the captain where to find you, child. Now go, and God be with you both."

But Anna did not wish to leave. She looked again to Father Archangel, and tried to make him understand. "But I am safe right here," she told him. "I am safe."

He looked at her with sympathy, and turning up his hood he took her hand. "Not anymore."

chapter
NINETEEN

R ob told me, "You're getting attached to her."
"Why would you say that?"

He looked at me sideways. "Because you are."

"Yes, well." I turned from his too-knowing eyes as he opened the car door so I could slide in on the passenger side. "She's a likeable child."

"Aye, no argument there." Shutting my door, he came round to his side and lowered himself to the seat a bit creakily, as though his legs were still stiff from the cold of the night before. He'd had only half a night's sleep, and had not shaved this morning, but he was still easy to look at, the day's growth of beard lending even more strength to his near-perfect features. It just wasn't fair, I thought.

Rob looked a question at me, and I realized I'd sighed, so I covered it now with a half yawn and asked, "Are you certain they went to Calais?"

"Aye. Not all of us fell asleep after the monk left with Anna." His glance was dry. "I heard the nuns talking. I ken where he took her."

Calais wasn't really an obvious choice, and I said as much. "I would have thought, in the wake of the 1715 rebellion, with all of those Jacobites coming across to escape persecution, it would have been crawling with spies."

"Very likely."

"Not really the safest of places to take her, then."

"I'm sure the monk had a plan. She could hardly have stayed here."

He'd seen what I'd missed last night, after I'd fallen asleep on his shoulder. He'd stayed awake, sitting there on the grass, and he'd seen the arrival of two men in priests' robes, with letters they'd claimed had come straight from Queen Mary in Paris.

"She had a great fondness," the one priest had said, "for the child's father, and she would have her kept safe at Chaillot."

Abbess Butler had taken her time while she'd read through the letters. "I was not aware that the queen knew the child was here with us."

To which the priest had replied, "The child's uncle did mention the fact, I believe, and the queen at once ordered us here to escort her back safely."

The abbess had nodded, and read through the letters again while the priests stood and waited. And then she had said, "I regret you have wasted a journey."

"How so?"

"Well, the child has already left us."

The first of the priests had displayed a decidedly unpriestly show of frustration before he'd regained his composure. "With whom did she leave?"

When the abbess pretended uncertainty, he'd asked more pointedly, "Girls of her age do not travel alone. Who did come to collect her?"

"Ah. One of her other relations," she'd said. "I asked not his name, but she knew who he was."

Which, I thought, to give her credit, was a truthful answer. She had not asked Father Archangel his name, for she'd already known it, and the little girl herself had recognized that he was Colonel Graeme's son. My admiration of the Abbess Butler had grown even stronger when I'd realized how she'd managed to hold off the "priests" without having to compromise her honesty.

I was still thinking of this when Rob started the car and reversed neatly out of the parking spot.

I asked, "Were they really priests, do you think?"

"Oh, I doubt it. They probably worked for, or with, that girl's English spy."

"Christiane's boyfriend." I frowned.

"Aye. She finally found something useful to tell him," he said with a shrug.

"Well, I hope it was worth it." My voice came out darkened with sarcasm. "Using a child like that."

"Anna got careless. She made a mistake. She'd been warned not to share all the things she'd been told."

"She was only a child," I defended her. "And she'd been promised the convent was safe. She thought all the bad people, the 'bad men,' were English, and came from outside. Christiane was like her—she was Scottish, a girl, and she lived in the convent, so why wouldn't Anna have thought it was all right to talk to her? Honestly."

Rob's sidelong glance made a point. "See? You're getting attached to her."

"It was a rotten thing Christiane did," I said, "taking the trust of a child and betraying it."

Rob, more forgiving, or possibly just more pragmatic, said, "Aye, well, she did it for love. Love can make people do mad things, sometimes."

As we crossed over the next road the pale Menin Gate rose beside us on Rob's side, but through my own window I caught a swift glimpse of the old market square where we'd eaten last night. Just a glimpse, but enough to make note of how different it looked in the grey early morning, the funfair shut up and forgotten, the lights and the sound and the magic extinguished by daylight.

I thought of my unicorn, riding along in the boot, and a part of me—only a part, mind—forgave Christiane just a little, for wanting so badly to win back the love of her Englishman. Maybe she had.

It was not a long drive to Calais.

I'd been through it a dozen times, mostly by train, but I'd never once stopped to look round, or to think of the town being anything more than the end of the Chunnel—a touristy transport hub crowded with ferries and coaches.

"And refugees," Rob added, as we approached from the south, up a boulevard edged with young trees and mansard-roofed buildings with bright red-brick walls. "People wanting to get clear of all the wars in their own countries pay the traffickers and wind up here in migrant camps or worse, in hopes they'll find a way to get across the channel into England."

A hard life, to be sure, and I was silent for a moment while I thought about the desperation that drove people to abandon their own country, their own home. I said, "It's sort of the reverse of what the Jacobites were doing, then, in Anna's time. I mean, there would have been a lot of people coming over from the Scottish side . . ."

"And England," Rob put in. "Some travelled south, and came through England in disguise. Wherever they could find a boat to bring them over."

"But they were just refugees as well, escaping war."

"The aftermath of war, more like," he said. "The persecution. When the 1715 went wrong, the English got their own back. Anyone who'd had a hand in it was hunted, fined, imprisoned, stripped of what they owned and loved. A lot were hanged."

I thought of Anna's Uncle Maurice, and his worry for his brothers left behind in Scotland, one imprisoned, one too ill to flee, and wondered whether they'd survived that time of treachery.

"The English," Rob said, "would have had their own spies in Calais, and paid informers with the Jacobites, reporting back who came and went, and why. No doubt the colonel's son, the monk, was doing much the same thing for King James."

"Wouldn't that be against his vows, or whatever?"

"He was a soldier first." Ignoring the grand impressive town hall building we were passing on his side, Rob glanced across and out my window at a tall stone column that appeared to be some kind of war memorial, carved round with sculpted images of sacrifice and valour. "Whatever vows he took, I doubt he could stand by and not take sides."

A little farther on we crossed a broad canal and at the far side of the bridge Rob slowed, and swung us through the roundabout, and in a sudden moment of decision made a right turn at the corner of a park onto a very narrow street that ran along the park's north edge.

On my side of the car, a rather uninspiring row of flats stood solidly in line along the pinkish pavement, some with weathered balconies that overlooked the trees and greenery stretching to the right of us. The flats gave way to a low red-brick building, and Rob reverse-parked at the curb just across from it.

I looked at the sign on the building, and then at Rob. "The Musée des Beaux Arts? Are we going in?"

He shook his head.

Glancing past him to the park, I guessed again. "We're having a picnic."

"No." He grinned, and opening his door got out and stretched his shoulders. We'd been on the road for just under two hours—not that long, by Rob's own reckoning—so I assumed the stiffness he was showing came from having sat outside for half the night, with me asleep against his shoulder, more than from this morning's driving. He recovered quickly, though, and by the time I got my own door open he was there to hold it for me.

Of all the men I'd dated, he remained the only one who'd ever done that.

"Well," he said, when I remarked on it, "you've led a sheltered life. As I recall, you said you'd only had two boyfriends afore me. Unless you've had a couple since . . ."

I turned to look at him, expecting that his blue eyes would be teasing, and instead found they were nonchalantly guarded, and a bit too unconcerned.

I said, "I haven't."

And then, because I couldn't hold his gaze, I looked away. There had been moments when I'd wondered whether Rob was seeing anyone, because it seemed a bit too unbelievable that after these two years he'd still be unattached, but when he'd come to Ypres with me I'd known without a doubt he wasn't seeing anybody at the moment. He was far too much a gentleman to spend this kind of time with me alone, if he already had a girlfriend. He'd have counted it as being disrespectful to both of us.

He swung my door closed and walked round to lean against the car and although the sun was too high now to catch him in the eyes, he took the dark sunglasses from his pocket, put them on, and settled back to look more keenly at . . . well, at whatever he was looking at.

I couldn't tell, from watching him, if he was seeing things as they were now or as they had been, but I had the sense that he was standing with one foot in each reality, a bridge between the present and the past.

I let a moment pass in silence before prompting him with, "Well?"

"Well, it's a fair-sized town, Calais. We're in the old part of it, now, the part that stood within the town walls, with the moat all round it, back in Anna's day. But even so, there were a lot of streets and houses then, and it was busy all the time with people, so there's not much point in wandering round," he said, "to look for her. Like looking for a needle in a haystack."

I had no doubt, having seen him work, that he could have found one of those, if he had set his mind to it. But clearly he had settled on a plan.

I prompted, "So?"

"So, Calais was a guarded town. With walls. If Anna had been coming from the channel side, by boat, with Father Graeme, they'd have had to use the harbour to the north. But when they left the convent, back in Ypres," he told me, "they were on the road. And if they travelled overland, as we did, they'd have come straight through that gate."

I came around to lean beside him on the car, and looked. "Where is it?"

"You tell me."

"Rob, I can't—"

"You're away off to Russia the morn," he reminded me. "When were you planning to practice?" He had me there. Fully aware of it, he said, "I ken that you do things by touch. I'm not thinking you'll see it the same way that I do, but you should be able at least to sense where the gate *was*, like you did with the convent."

I gave it my best shot.

It took a few minutes. It wasn't a small mental tug at my sleeve this time, as it had been in Ypres; more like a settling sensation of certainty, knowing without knowing why. "There." I pointed. "I think it was there. Am I right?"

For an answer, he draped an arm over my shoulders. "Let's see."

It threw me off balance, that casual touch. I'd grown used to the hand-holding, even though that on its own was an intimate contact, but this—with Rob's arm a warm weight at the back of my neck and his hand resting loosely just over my sleeve—was the sensory equivalent of being hit by something like a brick, and it took all my concentration not to physically react.

But then I had to let that concentration lapse, to join my thoughts with Rob's and see what he was trying now to show me. And that, too, was overwhelming.

I could see the old walls of Calais take shape, just there in front of us: tall heavy walls of yellow stone, with crenellated battlements that rose above our heads and cast a deep and chilling shadow on the place where we were standing. And the gate was where I'd thought it would be, large and flanked by square protective towers, a great portal and portcullis with the carvings of what probably were royal coats of arms cut in the stone blocks set above the massive archway of its opening.

The size and scale and strength of those old walls was truly breathtaking, but that was not the thing that overwhelmed me. It was seeing all the people—soldiers walking round in blue coats with their swords and muskets, people dressed more plainly hauling merchandise of every kind, the chaos and the rolling wheels of carts and constant shouting doing battle with the sounds of clopping hooves and barking dogs and crying gulls. It was a full-on, no-holds-barred assault that left me reeling, and I had to pull away from it and come back to the present.

"How on earth," I asked Rob, "are we going to find her in all that?"

"With patience." When he took his arm away I found I missed the warmth of it. Perhaps he felt a little colder, too, because he folded both his arms across his chest and said, "She's going to be moving, though, when we do find her, so the biggest challenge will be keeping up."

"You mean we'll have to walk?" I hadn't thought of that. I looked around. "But Rob, these streets won't all be in the same place, surely. Wasn't Calais flattened in the war, and then rebuilt?"

"Aye. But there were some bits still left standing, I can navigate by those."

"It's not your navigational abilities I'm questioning. It's . . ."

"What?"

"Well, what's to stop us walking straight into a wall, or something? Or into the middle of a busy street?"

I couldn't see his eyes behind the sunglasses, but I could feel the touch of faint amusement in the downward glance he sent me. "I'm not, ye ken, walking about in a trance. Did we go off the coast path and over the cliff up by Cruden Bay?"

"No, but—"

"Well, then. Have some faith." He turned his head away again and focused on the unseen gate. "I've been doing this awhile," he reassured me. "I'll no walk ye into traffic."

There was something in the way he said that, something sure and confident that made me feel protected. Valued. *Safe*.

So when he straightened from the car and told me, "There she is," and held his hand to me and said, "Come on," I took his hand without a thought, and followed where he led.

chapter
TWENTY

Her head was aching. They'd arrived too late last night and found the great gates of the town already shut and locked and guarded, so the farmer who had carried them the last part of their journey in his wagon had found room for them within his own house in the lower town, and they had waited there till daylight and the bells that would ring out across the walls to say the gates would soon be opening.

She had not slept well, there in that strange house, nor had she slept well since they'd come away from Ypres, feeling the constant sense of something evil riding close behind them. Father Graeme had said nothing of the danger they were trying to outdistance, and he'd done his best to cheer her through the days with conversation, and he'd told her Colonel Graeme would be waiting for them when they reached Calais.

That last had cheered her most of all, so she'd been sorely disappointed when they'd found themselves shut out by those great walls last night.

She'd wished then for the patience and good temper she had seen in Father Graeme. She'd never heard him once complain, and somehow he had brought them all this way without her ever seeing coins exchanged, relying on his robes and his resourcefulness. "A Capuchin," he'd told her as he'd set her on the final wagon, "gives away the things he owns, and lives but by the charity of others, as our Lord did when he lived upon this earth."

It seemed a most uncertain way to live, and she had told him so.

"I disagree. There may be many things uncertain in this life, but 'tis for certain we were made in God's own image, and I've not yet met a woman nor a man who does not carry God's capacity for charity, however deep it hides. I seek the good within men's hearts, and give them means by which they may express it."

"Why?"

"Because it is in giving of ourselves and our possessions that we best please God; by actions, not by words. And all men do deserve a chance to earn God's grace."

"Even the men who do bad things?"

He'd tucked a blanket fold around her and said, "Aye. Sometimes especially the men who do bad things."

She'd remembered Colonel Graeme saying that his son had killed his best friend in a duel, and had then left his life of soldiering and so become a monk to serve his penance. She could not imagine Father Graeme killing someone.

Nor, this morning, did it seem he could have been a soldier.

He was walking, not with the bold rolling strides of Captain Jamieson, but with his head bent humbly as he guided Anna through the morning bustle of Calais. The town made Anna think of Scotland, of the market day in Peterhead, for many of the tall and close-packed houses they were passing here were built of brick and in the Scottish style, with tiled roofs and windows set with glass. And of the women she could see a number of them wore a green shawl like a plaid wrapped round their heads and shoulders, looking not unlike the women of the village close by Slains.

But the sense of familiarity was shattered when a raucous group of Englishmen pressed past them. Father Graeme gathered Anna closer to his side and urged her through a narrow archway in the nearest building, which delivered them into a little courtyard paved unevenly with stones that made her slip while trying to keep up. He slowed his steps to make her effort easier, and turning, led her carefully across a threshold.

Only once before had Anna been inside an inn, and that had been a year ago with Colonel Graeme and the captain, on their first night after being landed from the ship that had just carried them from Scotland. She'd been too exhausted then from all her travels to be much impressed with anything she saw, but now, despite her aching head, she looked around with interest at the low-beamed ceiling and the roughened walls and trestle tables pushed beneath discreetly shuttered windows. The inn's landlord, with his apron strings tied sturdily around his ample middle, was settling an account with two men standing at the bar, but when he turned and saw the monk he gave a nod of welcome and said something briefly in a language Anna recognized as French, but did not understand.

The two men turned as well, and looked at Father Graeme with distaste.

The nearest of them said, in cultured English, "Faith, another begging Capuchin. Get out your purse, Ralph, for we'll have no peace from him until he's had a coin."

If Anna had been larger, she'd have struck them for their insolence, but Father Graeme took it in his stride. His face and voice stayed calm. "God's blessings on you both," was all he said, "and it is certain that your charity will find a like reward, but if ye seek to give, give not that coin to me, but to our landlord here, that he may bring some broth and bread to feed this child."

The man's companion looked disgusted also as he said, "A begging child as well. May God preserve me from a Papist."

Anna's blood ran warm with anger as the first man tossed a few coins on the bar before the landlord, but the monk laid a calm hand upon her shoulder, and the landlord, without changing his expression, pushed the coins back to the man and told him, "No payment is required for me to serve a man who serves the Lord."

The Englishman appeared prepared to argue till a woman's voice— a Scottish voice—said lightly, from the dimness behind Anna, "Come now, gentlemen, do not so soon forget your manners."

Everybody gave the woman coming down the staircase from the floor above their full attention. She was somewhere in her middle years, yet pretty in her face and movements, and her gown, while simply cut, was meant to catch the eye. She showed a daring flash of ankle as she raised her skirts a fraction so as not to trip as she came down the final steps, and looking at the Englishmen she fixed them with a bright fair smile that gave her unlined face a youthful aspect. "Father Graeme is a good man, and besides, he's not a man to trifle with. Before he wore those robes, he fought alongside my good husband in the wars in Catalonia, where I'm told his sword arm was the strongest in his regiment, and so it would be wise," she said, "to speak to him respectfully."

She let her dark eyes twinkle at the monk, and held her hands to him in greeting. "Father Graeme. 'Tis a happy turn of fate to meet you here."

He smiled back. "Mrs. Ogilvie. Were you not lately in London?"

"I was. And my stomach does wish I had stayed there, and not crossed the channel at all," she said, putting a hand on the front of her bodice with feeling. "I have never been so tossed about as I was in that packet boat. Only our own light heads, I do believe, could have kept us from drowning, sir, in so prodigious a storm." With a laugh quite as bright as the rest of her, she said, "It seems drowning is not the way God has ordained for my exit."

The nearest of the Englishmen was staring at the monk, now, with bold eyes that sought to measure him. "And *you* were once a swordsman?"

Father Graeme smoothed his beard against his robe as he looked down. "Well, Mrs. Ogilvie mistakes her facts a little." As he raised his eyes again he met the other's look of satisfaction and, to Anna's joy, extinguished it. "I carried a musket in all my campaigns, not a sword."

"In Catalonia," the Englishman repeated, as though disbelieving that fact, also.

"Aye."

"And on whose side, sir, did you fight?"

For a moment Anna thought she glimpsed a flash of Colonel Graeme's mischief-loving nature in the monk's mild eyes, but it was gone before he answered, "On the side that God did choose to favour." With a humble nod he asked them, "Do excuse me," and releasing Anna's shoulder moved alone along the bar to where the landlord now stood.

Anna held her place with the invisibility accorded children in such gatherings, and watched the woman and the men with open interest, noting how the men had straightened in their stances and appeared to be competing in their efforts to appear their very best for Mrs. Ogilvie.

The woman, if aware of it, pretended not to be, and merely asked them, "Are you both recovered from your passage over, also?"

"More or less," the one man answered, looking round. "Where is your other fellow countryman and friend this day?"

"If you do refer to Captain Thomas Gordon," she said lightly, with a roll of her expressive eyes, "he is no friend of mine. In fact, 'twas his fault I was nearly drowned in crossing, for he was in such a haste he would not wait, but did insist upon us going halves to hire that wretched packet boat."

"And Captain Gordon is his name?" the nearest of the Englishmen enquired. "Another soldier?"

Mrs. Ogilvie corrected him, "A sea captain, till lately. Yet remove him from his wooden world, and truthfully he knows no more of travelling than does a child of six. "'Twas a relief," she said, "to get him off my hands."

"He left this morning?"

"Yes. He is in a prodigious hurry to be at Dunkirk," she told the men, "by Saturday. I wish to God he may be so soon wanted."

Anna's gaze had narrowed thoughtfully upon the men, suspicious of their questions, and she might have pointed out to Mrs. Ogilvie that Englishmen were never to be trusted, and that telling information to them was not overwise, but she knew well that it was not her place to speak till she was spoken to, and no one seemed inclined to even notice her, much less deign to speak to her. And so she watched, and held tight to the parcel of her things that she had carried out of Ypres, and waited.

Father Graeme soon returned. "I wonder, Mrs. Ogilvie," he said, "if you would join myself and Anna in our meal."

She looked at Anna then, and smiled in her bright way, and said, "Of course," and taking leave of the two Englishmen crossed over with the monk and Anna to a table set in the far corner of the room.

Once out of earshot of the others, Father Graeme told her, low, "I wish to ask a favour of you, if I may."

"You've but to ask. You know that I could not deny you anything," she teased him to begin with, but in glancing at his face again she cast aside the light demeanour and grew thoughtful. "What is it you need?"

"It is a favour I can only ask of one I trust," he said. "My father wrote that he would meet us here, but either he has not yet come, or else he is mistaken in our meeting place. I need you to stay here and guard the child, while I go to make sure my father is not waiting for us at my house."

The woman's eyes touched Anna's face. "Does she need guarding?"

"Aye, she does. 'Tis why my father makes this journey, for he is intensely fond of Anna."

Mrs. Ogilvie remarked, "Your father's good regard is not an easy thing to win." She seemed impressed, the fine arch of her eyebrows growing more pronounced as her regard of Anna grew more keen. "Good morrow, child. How are you?"

Anna's head still ached, and she was hungry, but she knew that it was not polite to make complaints. "I am quite well, I thank you, madam."

Mrs. Ogilvie contained a smile. "Such lovely manners, Father Graeme."

"Aye, she was but lately with the Irish Dames at Ypres."

"The Abbess Butler?"

Father Graeme gave a nod. "And she would be there still, had I not received a summons from my father to go fetch her hence without delay, and bring her out of danger."

"Danger? What could . . . ?" Breaking off, she fixed the smile again upon her face and sat back as the landlord came to bring them bread, a jug of wine, and broth that smelt of cabbages and onions. Mrs. Ogilvie was generous with her thanks, and waited till he'd gone again before she leaned in, speaking quietly herself. "What danger could there be at Ypres for such a child?"

It was a question Anna had been wondering herself, for Father

Graeme had said nothing to her of why he had taken her away, apart from saying that the convent was not safe. She broke her bread with care, and listened.

Quietly the monk said, "This is Anna Moray, only daughter of my cousin John. My father took great pains to hide her safely, but there was an . . . indiscretion at the convent. A young woman who'd been staying there did somehow learn of Anna's true identity, and passed that information to an English spy at Paris with whom she'd been keeping company."

The jolt that Anna felt within her chest was so great she felt sure her heart had stopped its beating for that moment. It began again, but painfully, and sent a surge of warm blood upwards, pounding in her ears.

It was not possible, she thought, that Christiane could have betrayed her trust. Not Christiane. Her eyes began to sting.

"My cousin Maurice Moray, Anna's uncle," said the monk, "is now at Paris also, and has long been trusted by Queen Mary and the king. So when my father learnt, by secret channels, that the agents of the Prince of Hanover had set a plan in place to seize the child and use her as the means to turn her uncle's loyalties, he sent to me at once."

Across the table, Mrs. Ogilvie agreed that Colonel Graeme had done wisely. "But where will she go from here?"

"I've not been told," the monk admitted, "but my father never moves without a plan." He'd only eaten several bites of bread, and chased them down with a small tumblerful of wine, but now he added, "And he always minds a schedule once he's set it, which is why I am surprised that he did not arrive ahead of us, and why I do suspect he may be waiting in some other place."

He looked to Mrs. Ogilvie, who nodded and assured him, "I shall stay with her, till you return."

He thanked her, and with one hand gave a lightly reassuring stroke of Anna's bent head as he promised her, "I'll not be long."

She kept her head down, so that no one else would see her misery. Her guilt. In memory she heard Colonel Graeme saying how, if

English agents had been sly enough to catch her father, he'd have stood through any torture without talking; and that clearly was a trait of all the men of Abercairney, for her Uncle Robert had now been in prison twice, they'd said, and neither time had he been broken. So the English would expect her Uncle Maurice to be just as strong.

Unless . . . unless the English captured *her*, and let her uncle know it.

"Men can bear most hurts," the colonel had confided, "but there's few of us can bear to see the ones we love best made to suffer for our sake."

It went both ways, she thought, for nor could she bear to allow her Uncle Maurice to be turned against his conscience and his honour as a consequence of her mistake in trusting Christiane.

They'd warned her, they'd all warned her to be careful, but she simply had not thought that Christiane would ever . . .

"So," said Mrs. Ogilvie.

Remembering the nuns' instruction that it was polite to give her full attention to an adult who was speaking, Anna clutched the little parcel of belongings on her lap with both her hands and raised her chin.

"It has been a good while since I have dined with a young lady." Mrs. Ogilvie was smiling. "You'll forgive me if my manners do not equal those of Abbess Butler and her nuns at Ypres, for I fear I have been far too long in London, these past months. They do not share our Scottish ways, in London." While she scooped a spoonful of the broth her light gaze took in Anna's features, and again the eyebrows arched. "I must confess I am astonished I did not mark the resemblance before now. You are the image of your father, may God rest his soul. Has anybody told you this?"

"Yes, madam." Anna's voice was flat.

"I met him several times at St. Germain, although my husband would have known him rather better," Mrs. Ogilvie remarked. "I did not know that he had married." She said nothing for a moment, while she ate, and then her thoughts changed course. "And is your Uncle Maurice well?"

She did not know. She hoped he was. But she could say no more than, "He was well last time he wrote to me."

"I'm glad to hear it. Shall we have more bread?"

It seemed a little odd to Anna that the woman did not simply raise her hand to call the landlord over, but excused herself and went across to speak to him. Odd, too, that having done that, Mrs. Ogilvie should stop again to speak to the two Englishmen, who'd taken their own table near the bar.

Something fluttered deep in Anna's stomach, making her uneasy. She ignored it to begin with, because Father Graeme trusted Mrs. Ogilvie. He'd said so. And he'd not have left her alone with someone who did not deserve his trust. She told herself that several times, and yet the fluttering continued, the uneasiness not helped when both the men turned round to look at her, then looked away again.

The landlord brought the extra bread, and Anna thanked him in a small voice, and when he enquired if there were something else she needed, she replied, on impulse, "Yes, I need to use the privy, please, sir."

"Use the . . . ? Ah." His face cleared, and he gestured to another doorway at the back. "It is just there."

She thanked him once again, and sidled from the bench with care, her bundle of belongings clasped like armour to her chest. Across the room she saw the landlord pass by Mrs. Ogilvie and tell her something, and then Mrs. Ogilvie looked over with a nod and smiled at Anna in an understanding way. One of the Englishmen rose slowly from the table and began to walk towards the other door. But no one came to follow Anna.

Just outside the inn's back door she found the privy standing close beside the building, and she crouched within the foul-smelling dimness of its confines for a moment while she tried to calm the thoughts that whirled in tempo with the racing of her heart.

She ought to stay, as she'd been told, and wait for Father Graeme here. And yet . . . the awful feeling would not leave her. She tried arguing against it. She was only being silly. Mrs. Ogilvie was kind, she was a friend, and she was Scottish . . .

So was Christiane, a small cold voice within her pointed out.

She screwed her eyes up tightly in that moment of decision, and then calling on each scrap of courage she could claim, she pushed against the privy door and fled into the courtyard as though every English spy upon the continent were at her back.

She had no destination in her mind but finding Father Graeme, and for that, the church spire soaring high above the tiled rooftops of the huddled, leaning houses seemed a beacon to her. Monks were men of God, she reasoned. God was in the church. So Father Graeme would be there, as well.

Except, when she had finally pressed her way through all the people in the alleys and the streets to reach the relatively open space surrounding the great church, she saw no sign of him. And when she tried to enter in the church itself an old man chased her out again, reproving her in French.

She said, in English, "Please, I need to find my friend, the monk."

The old man answered in her language, with a frown, "No monks live here," and waved her off towards the south. Which only brought her back to where they'd entered in that morning, by the great gate in the high stone wall.

The gate, as it had been then, was still busy with the streams of people moving round and through it, while the soldiers standing near the heavy chains of the portcullis gave approval to the passports and the papers, and the Searchers opened portmanteaus and trunks. The Searchers now seemed very busy with the portmanteaus belonging to a gentleman who stood beside a carriage while the driver tried to hold the four impatient horses dancing on the cobblestones.

The gentleman, to Anna's eyes, appeared to be the same age as the monk—not yet as old as Colonel Graeme, nor as young as Captain Jamieson, but somewhere in between, though Anna never found it such an easy thing to tell the age of any man who wore a wig. His shaven face was very handsome, and his clothes were very fine, and he stood tall and straight and calm, so that the hard set of his jaw alone betrayed his own impatience.

A heavier-set man with no baggage strolled past the carriage and, tipping his hat, said, "Good morrow, Captain Gordon. I had thought you'd be away by now."

"Aye, so had I," the handsome man replied, "but these men have developed quite an interest in my breeks and hose, and seem most disinclined to let me leave till they have counted every pair."

He was a Scotsman, Anna realized, and a day ago his voice alone would have been cause enough for her to trust him. But today she only stood and stared, and did not dare approach him.

With a laugh the other man asked, "Have you paid them, sir?"

"I have."

"Well, pay them more, and they will cease."

"I've paid already for my passage through this gate," said Captain Gordon, "and paid more again to get a pass to go to Dunkirk."

"Pay them more," the other man repeated, "else you'll never get to Dunkirk, sir. It is the custom of this country."

"'Tis no less than robbery," the captain said, but taking out his purse he offered new coins to the Searchers, who immediately stopped what they were doing and became more friendly, closing up his portmanteaus.

The captain grinned, and thanked the other man for his advice. "Will not ye share the carriage with me?"

"I thank you, no. I go but to the lower town, and as you see, I have a need for exercise." He slapped his ample belly, tipped his hat again, and said, "A pleasant journey, Captain Gordon."

Captain Gordon. Anna suddenly remembered where she'd heard that name before. The man who'd come across with Mrs. Ogilvie just yesterday had been a Captain Gordon. Mrs. Ogilvie had been complaining to the Englishmen about the captain's being in a hurry, and the trouble he had been to her. "He is no friend of mine," she'd said.

Which was, in Anna's view, a very large point in his favour.

She moved closer to him, wondering if she could trust him just enough to ask him where the monks lived in Calais, when someone called out, "Anna!"

Without thinking, she turned round. She'd hoped it might be Father Graeme, but she did not see him, and her gaze began to dart around in panic as she looked for the two Englishmen, who must by now, along with Mrs. Ogilvie, have noticed she was missing from the inn. She did not see them, either; but she did see the old man who had just chased her from the church, and with him two priests dressed exactly like the priest who'd been the nuns' confessor at the convent.

The old man studied Anna, gave a nod, and made a comment to the priests before he shuffled off again, and wearing smiles the priests approached her.

"Anna Moray!" called the tallest one again. "We have been looking for you. God be thanked, we've found you safe."

She saw his eyes, and she did not believe him. And apart from that, he'd called her "Anna Moray." No one seeking her who had been sent by anyone she trusted would have ever used that name.

She backed away a step, and then another, looking round one final time in hopes she might glimpse Father Graeme or his father in the vast confusing ebb and flow of unfamiliar faces.

One more backward step and she had bumped against the side of Captain Gordon, who said, "Steady," in a voice that, while surprised, was not unkind. It was that hint of kindness, she thought afterwards, that gave her the idea, and the courage.

As the two priests drew yet nearer, Anna spoke up in a clear voice, with the ladylike and proper words that she'd been taught: "I do not know these men." And then she turned and tilted up her head to look at Captain Gordon. "Do you know them, Father?"

He said nothing, staring down at her, and Anna held her breath.

If he denied her, if he did not play along, then she was lost. No one would stop two priests from taking charge of any child, no matter how that child might scream and weep.

She saw the smallest flicker of what might have been astonishment disturb the blue depths of the captain's eyes. It seemed to Anna that he stood and looked at her a long time, as though he were seeing something he had not expected and could not believe.

She raised her chin a trifle higher, and allowed her eyes to mutely ask him, *Please*.

He told her, "No." And then, his eyes still on her upturned face, he said, "I do not know them, either."

Then he raised his head and told the priests, "Good fathers, I'm afraid you do mistake my child for someone else, for my name is not Moray." With a firm hand he laid claim to her, and turned her so her back was to the strength of him, his one arm laid with fatherly possession on her shoulder.

Neither priest could stand against the calm ice of the captain's gaze. The bolder one said, "Do excuse us, sir, we meant no harm."

"No, I am sure that you did not. Come, child," the captain said, "get you in the carriage, for we must be on our way."

She let him lift her, numb, onto the seat, and there she sat, her little cloth-wrapped bundle clasped against her, while the priests bowed to the captain and backed off a step.

The Searcher standing nearest to the captain drew a paper from his coat and read it over with a frown, and told the captain, "But this pass is for—"

"My daughter and myself," the captain told him, in a sure tone that left no room for an argument, and drawing out his purse again he paid the Searcher two more silver coins before he climbed into the carriage, too, and settled on the long seat beside Anna.

She was shaking as they rode out through the gate.

He angled in his seat to look at her. "Are you all right?"

She'd thought to get a lecture. She had not expected gentleness, and coming on the heels of so much turbulence it made her eyes begin to fill with tears she had no wish to shed.

He asked, "Where are your parents?"

"Dead." A half lie only, she consoled herself.

"Where do you live? How came you to Calais?"

She did not answer him, because she could not think of any way to twist the truth, and when a moment had gone by in silence, Captain Gordon tried again.

"Well, have you any family left?"

Her eyes stung as she thought of Colonel Graeme and his son, and of her uncles, and the mother she would never know, because she could do nothing but endanger them. No matter what she did, or where she went, she knew now she could never let the truth of who she was be known to anyone, or else the people she loved most would suffer for it.

Fighting back the tears, she shook her head. "No. I have no one."

She could feel his gaze upon her face, as though he, too, were making a decision. He asked quietly, "Is your name truly Anna?"

Anna thought, and then decided that much of herself was safe to keep, and so she nodded.

"Anna Moray?"

"No." She could not ever claim that name, she knew. Nor could she any longer be the Anna Logan who had lived at Ypres, and been betrayed by Christiane, and who was being searched for now by those who meant to hurt her uncle. She must evermore be no one's child.

And yet, if all her dreams were thus to shatter, Anna thought, she could at least pick up the brightest shard of them, and cling to it, however much it cut, and take it with her into the unknown.

She drew a breath, and said, "My name is Anna Jamieson."

chapter
TWENTY-ONE

It had seemed a good idea at the time.

I hadn't wanted Rob to drive the whole way back to Scotland in the dark, not after all he'd done to help me. And I knew his nature well enough to know he would have pushed on and not taken a hotel room here in London for the night. And while I didn't have an extra bedroom in my flat, I had a sofa that converted to a bed that both my brother and his girlfriend had assured me was quite comfortable.

So it had seemed a natural extension of our travelling together that, when Rob had found a spot to park along my road, I should invite him up to have a meal and stay the night to rest before he headed home to Eyemouth.

When I'd asked him, it had all seemed very reasonable. But . . .

"The trouble," so my brother had once told me, "is you never really stop to think things through."

And he was right. I hadn't stopped to think how small the flat would feel, when Rob walked in. Or how a simple, stupid thing like watching Rob eat steak-and-onion pie with salad at my cluttered table would so traitorously push all my domestic buttons, sending my mind wandering to thoughts of sitting down to dinner with him every night. I found the easygoing comfort of his company seductive, like a lazy current drawing me downstream, and every now and then I'd lose my grip upon the shore and float a little farther down before remembering I ought to swim against it.

When Rob half-rose from his chair after dinner, intending to help with the washing-up, I made him sit again.

"You cooked the meal," was his reasoning.

"Hardly. I warmed up a frozen pie. Somehow I doubt that will get me on *MasterChef.* Give me that plate, will you? Thanks." There was no way, I thought, I was going to let him help out in my kitchen, a room so incredibly small that I couldn't take two steps in any direction without bumping into the worktop. I said, "The TV remote's there by the sofa, if you want to watch something."

I took my time with the washing-up, although there weren't many dishes to deal with. But when I came out again into the sitting room, Rob wasn't watching TV. He had sat himself down at my desk in the corner, where earlier I had switched on my computer, and with his head propped on one hand he was reading what looked like a digital scan of an old book.

"What's that?" I asked.

"*The Old Scots Navy*, by James Grant," he told me. "I'm getting to know Captain Gordon."

"The man Anna left with? You found him?"

'I did. Mrs. Ogilvie said that his first name was Thomas."

"When did she say that?"

"When she was talking to those English guys," he told me, "at the bar."

I took his word for it. "And?"

"Captain Thomas Gordon," he said, clicking back to open up the screen for Wikipedia. "Or Admiral Thomas Gordon, as he later was. That's him, right?"

I leaned closer in, to look over Rob's shoulder at the image of a painted portrait on the screen. It showed an older man than we had seen, white-wigged and softer round the chin than I remembered, but the eyes were still the same, and he was standing with the same square-shouldered confidence. "That's him."

"He used to be a captain in the Old Scots Navy," Rob said, "and it seems he was acquainted with our friend the Earl of Erroll up at Slains. But after Scotland lost its independence in the Union, there was no Scots Navy anymore. They took the Saltire down and flew the Union Jack instead, and after that Queen Anne died and the military men like Captain Gordon had to swear an oath to say they'd only serve King George. I guess his conscience wouldn't let him swear that, not when in his heart he thought James Stewart was the rightful king, and so he quit." Rob turned his head so I could see the crinkles of good humour at the corners of his own eyes. "Guess where he became an admiral?"

"Where?"

To answer me, he scrolled down to show me a subheading: "Later Career—Russian Navy."

"You're joking."

"The tsar himself, Peter the Great, hired him on as a captain, and brought him to Russia."

I read through the article. "Yes, but it doesn't say where . . . ?"

Rob switched screens again to the page of another scanned history book, this one about Scottish soldiers in Russia. He pointed the paragraph out. "To St. Petersburg."

"Wow." It was more than I'd let myself hope for—the link that not only tied Anna to Russia, but to St. Petersburg. And if the tsar himself had hired Captain Thomas Gordon, and had known him, it was possible that Anna could have met the tsar's wife: Catherine.

I looked at the long row of reference tabs open across the top of the computer screen, showing the trail of his search. "You've been busy," I said. "Thanks for doing all this."

"Aye, well, I'm only a constable, not a detective, but I can still find the occasional suspect. If you tell me where the paper is for that," he nodded briefly at my printer, "I can print you off the whole of it, so you can take it with you."

I'd have much rather taken him with me, instead. How on earth was I going to manage to find Anna all on my own, without Rob?

While he printed the pages, he opened a new search window, saying, "It might help to find a few maps, as well, showing the place as it would have looked then . . ."

I was glad I was standing behind him, so he couldn't see me, or know from my face how uncertain I suddenly felt. "Rob, I wish—"

The imperative ring of my mobile cut in as Rob angled his head to look over his shoulder, his eyes waiting patiently for me to finish my sentence. Except that those eyes were a part of my problem, I thought. When they watched me like that it was hard to remember what I'd meant to say.

The mobile rang a second time. I dragged my gaze from Rob's and told him, "That'll be Sebastian."

And it was. "You're back." Sebastian sounded pleased. "And how was Belgium?"

"Lovely, thanks."

"And how's your . . . friend?"

"Stop fishing."

When I glanced at Rob I caught the glint of something in his eyes I took to be amusement, though in hindsight I decided it was mischief. Rising from the chair, he stretched to his full height and crossed the floor behind me, with a light touch on my back as he went past. He said, "I'm going to take a shower."

There was silence on my phone line for a moment, then Sebastian's voice said, "Well, well, *well*."

I sighed. "You wanted something?"

"Only to go over your instructions for St. Petersburg."

"That sounds very formal." I smiled. "Is this *Mission: Impossible*, then? Will my phone self-destruct when you finish?"

"Let's hope not. How else will I talk to you while you're in Russia? Now listen," he said. "Here's your schedule."

I jotted it down while he spoke. It was simple enough. My plane landed in mid-afternoon in St. Petersburg. After that I had only to go to the hotel and rest. Then on Friday, I'd meet with Sebastian's friend Yuri, who worked at the Hermitage. He would be able to update me on the exhibit, and Wendy Van Hoek. Wendy herself was due to arrive in St. Petersburg Friday evening.

"There's supposedly an opening reception on Sunday," said Sebastian, "but I'm hoping Yuri can find some more private place to introduce you. Either way, you have till Monday morning to convince her she should sell the Surikov to us, for Vasily. Monday afternoon, you fly back here to share a victory drink."

"You have a lot of faith."

"In you? Of course. I trained you, after all."

That made me smile against the phone. "How are you getting on with Gemma?"

"She's very good."

"You're being nice?"

"You have to ask?"

"With you? Of course."

He laughed and let me score the point, then smoothly hit the ball back to me. "Shouldn't you be showering?"

"Good night, Sebastian."

"Seriously, Nicola," he asked me. "Is this somebody whose name I should remember?"

"He's a friend," I said. "That's all." And ringing off, I went to pack my suitcase for St. Petersburg. It didn't take me long. I had my suitcase zipped and standing ready in the entry hall before Rob reappeared. He smelt of soap, his hair still damply curled against his forehead from the shower, and he'd changed into a plain clean T-shirt and a pair of track pants that were evidently what he meant to sleep in.

"Will ye help me with the bed?"

"What? Oh. Sure." I felt as tangled up inside as if I'd been an adolescent, and purposely I kept my eyes away from his the whole time we were pulling off the cushions of the sofa bed and swinging out the mattress. I fetched sheets and blankets and an extra pillow from the airing cupboard, and we made the bed together, one of us on either side. And then I said, a bit too cheerfully, "Good night, then."

"Nick?"

Again too brightly, "Yes?"

"What do you wish?"

My gaze did lift to his, then, startled. "Sorry?"

He sat nonchalantly on the bed's edge, barefoot. "Earlier, afore your boss called, you were saying that you wished for something."

"Oh. Right." It seemed harmless to say it, since there was no way it could actually happen. "I wish you could come to St. Petersburg with me, that's all. But you can't. You need a visa to get into Russia," I said. "I've already got mine, it's for business and lasts a full year, so I just come and go as I please, but you'd need one for tourists, and even a rushed one takes time. I'd have been there and back before you ever got one." I forced a smile. "Anyhow. I've got a lot more to go on now, haven't I? Thanks to you."

"Anytime." He stretched out full length on the bed, settling back with his hands linked behind his head, closing his eyes. "You'll do fine."

I didn't argue that. I only said, "Good night," again and crossed to my own room, and closed the door.

He was holding me.

I surfaced in the darkness of my bedroom to the feeling of his head close by my own, his warmth beside me, one leg nudging mine beneath the blankets, and his arm a settled weight across my stomach.

"Rob."

He didn't move. I lay there for a moment, coming fully into consciousness, and then I let my eyes close while I let myself relax into the strange and unexpected situation. I had never shared a bed with him before. And though I knew he shouldn't be here with me now, I somehow lacked the will to wake him right away and make him leave.

He was too warm, his hold too strong and too possessive to be easily dislodged, and I had never felt so perfectly protected, and at peace.

I wasn't sure when he'd come in. I hadn't been aware of it, nor had I thought he'd make a move like this when he'd been acting all this time as though he were no longer interested. But clearly there'd be complications if I let him stay and didn't wake him; if we both woke up together in the morning, in my bed. I knew I'd have to make a move.

It would be easier, I thought, for me to simply go and sleep out in the sitting room myself. That way I wouldn't have to shift him. Taking care, I slowly reached across to lift his arm from where it lay across my stomach.

Then I stopped, because there wasn't any arm there.

My own fingers brushed the fabric of my top, confusingly. My hand moved farther, to where I could feel the warmth of him . . . and touched the empty blanket. Even more confused, I turned my head against the pillow.

I was in the bed alone.

But still I felt the hold of his embrace. I felt it even when I sat up, pushed the blanket off, and stood. I felt it while I eased my bedroom door open and, careful not to make a sound, went tiptoeing across the silent sitting room to see with my own eyes what seemed impossible.

He lay sleeping as I'd felt him—on his side, with one arm resting on the rumpled sheets, protectively. And looking at his face I felt a swift, insistent tug beneath my heart, as though someone had tied a string around my ribs and pulled it sharply.

Breathing in, I focused, with my gaze still steady on his sleeping features, and I very, very gently pushed his mind from mine. He didn't wake.

I felt the cold, without him. Even after I'd returned to my own bed and burrowed deep within the blankets, I felt cold. And worse was yet to come, I knew. It wasn't such a hard thing to make Rob let go of *me*, I thought, but how in heaven, after this, could I let go of him?

chapter TWENTY-TWO

Rob glanced down at his watch, then scanned the traffic just ahead of us. "Your flight's at half-past nine, ye've no got time."

"It's barely six o'clock. Besides, it's on our way. And trust me, it will only take five minutes." I was ready for his sidelong glance, and met it with full innocence.

"Five minutes?" he repeated, to be sure.

I gave a nod. "He said he'd have it ready for me."

"When did he say that?"

"I rang him earlier."

"Earlier?" Rob raised an eyebrow. "What is he, nocturnal?"

"Very nearly. Here," I said. "Turn left here, and then right just where that other car is turning."

I'd grown up here, in this little terraced house in Acton, with its 1920s pseudo-Tudor timbers trying hard to make it look distinguished in a slightly dodgy neighbourhood.

My grandfather answered the door fully dressed, freshly shaven, his thickly white hair brushed back neatly. He always took pride in his clothes and appearance, and even at his age he looked rather dashing. He shot a suspicious look over my shoulder to where Rob stood leaning against the parked car at the curbside. "Who is that boy?"

Rob had shuttered his thoughts, I knew, at my request. "If he knows what you are," I'd told Rob, "then he'll give me a lecture. And that will take more than five minutes."

I kept my reply simple. "That's Rob, Granddad."

"Your fancy boss gave you a driver?"

"He isn't my driver."

"He opened the door for you."

"Yes, he's got very good manners," I said. "But he's only a friend."

With a final hard stare beneath lowering eyebrows, my grandfather switched his attention from Rob back to me when I asked, "Did you manage to find it?"

"The book? Yes, yes, I know where it is."

I could sense the faintest cautionary nudge about the time from Rob, as I went in the house behind my grandfather, but after all, it had been Rob who'd said last night that it would be a help to me to have an old map I could use for reference.

And I'd suddenly remembered, just this morning, where I'd find old maps.

The book was on the table by the fireplace in the sitting room, beside the half-drunk cup of tea and partly finished crossword that was evidence my grandfather had been awake awhile, and on his own. "Is Mum at work?"

He gave a nod. "The hospital was busy place at three o'clock this morning. Was an accident. They telephoned to call your mother in to the laboratory."

As a biomedical scientist, my mother was frequently working odd hours. I was sorry I'd missed her, and said so.

My grandfather shrugged. "She would only have been curious," he said, "about your driver. She'd ask questions. Is as well that you have only me." He handed me the book. "Here, take it. Keep it. I don't want."

It was a history of St. Petersburg, in photographs, old drawings, maps, and paintings, with small passages of text. A proper coffee table book. I could remember when my father had come home with it, excited to have found it in the bookshop round the corner from the school where he was teaching, and he'd given it so proudly to my grandfather. "That's where you came from, isn't it? St. Petersburg."

My grandfather, accepting the gift graciously, had set it on the table, where it stayed at least a year before he'd put it in the cupboard in the corner. I had never seen him open it.

My father, loving all things Russian as he did, had never fully noticed that my grandfather had done his best to cut away all ties that might have bound him to his homeland, and the city where he'd suffered the experiments that had forever changed him and embittered him and left him so distrustful.

I'd never learned the full story of how they'd got out of the Soviet Union—my mother had been ten, and could only remember an overland journey through Finland, she thought, and my grandfather wouldn't give details—but I knew it hadn't been easy, though he'd always counted it well worth the cost. He had changed his name, after arriving in London, from Ivan Kirilovich Birkin to John Birkin, which to his ears sounded practically English. A good English name, for a man who was finished with being a Russian.

He looked at the book in my hands, and said, "I would have got rid of that long ago, but it would have made your mother sad. Is good you need it now. You keep it, Nicola."

I thanked him. "It will come in handy."

"Why do you want to go back to that place? I don't know. You should go to Miami. Is warm in Miami."

"I'm going for work."

"Work." His face told me just what he thought of my job, but we'd had that discussion enough times he didn't seem keen to revisit it now. All he asked was, "Are you staying long in St. Petersburg?"

"Only till Tuesday."

"You don't drink the water."

"I won't."

"You don't forget. It makes you sick, that water."

"I promise," I said. "I won't drink it. But speaking of drink, shall I bring you back vodka?" The one thing he hadn't renounced, of his heritage. "What flavour, this time?"

He shrugged. "Maybe if you can find the blackcurrant. And one without flavour."

"All right."

When he walked me back out, he again looked at Rob with suspicion. "He looks," he said, "like a policeman."

"He is a policeman."

My grandfather frowned. "Then you don't bring him back again, Nicola. Is not good, to have a policeman out there where my neighbours can see." He glared at Rob, who raised his head and met the glare with perfect calm.

For one unsettling moment, I imagined that I saw a flash of recognition play across my grandfather's stern features, and thought perhaps that he and Rob were speaking to each other with their thoughts, but then I realized how ridiculous that was.

"He never talks to me that way," I'd said to Rob, when we were driving down to Ypres.

"He likely hears you, though," had been Rob's comment.

I kissed my grandfather goodbye, and tried. *Goodbye, Granddad.*

I could feel his mind shove mine back, even as his arms embraced me. "Be well, Nicola. Come home safe."

And then, as it had always been, the door was closed between us.

I was quiet on the drive to Heathrow. I wanted to think it was only because I was tired and a little distracted, and not because Rob would be dropping me off and then leaving, and I wasn't sure how I felt about that.

I had thought of and discarded several speeches by the time I realized Rob had parked the car, and since I hadn't been expecting that, it threw me momentarily off balance so that I could only come around and stand beside him while he took my suitcase from the boot, my mind still searching for the proper words to say.

I started with, "You didn't have to park, you know. It costs too much."

He set my suitcase on its wheels and reached back into the boot as I carried on, "And anyway, this is the long-stay car park, Rob. It's not—" I broke off when he hefted out a duffle bag and slung it on his shoulder before slamming shut the boot. And then I asked, "What *are* you doing?"

"Coming with you."

"Rob, you can't."

He took my suitcase in his other hand and motioned me to go ahead. "Try walking and arguing at the same time, or the courtesy coach will be leaving us here."

I stayed right where I was. "But you can't come."

His broad shoulders lifted and fell again in what I took for a brief, resigned sigh as he faced me with patience. "You did say you wished I would come to St. Petersburg, did ye not?"

"Yes, but—"

He started to walk while I tried to keep up with him.

Tried to explain. "But it isn't that easy to travel to Russia, Rob. Even if you somehow managed to get a seat on the flight, you'd still need a visa. I told you last night."

"Aye, you did." Unconcerned, he slowed slightly to keep between me and a car that was passing. I caught at his arm.

"Rob, you can't get a visa the same day you travel."

"Well then, it's a good thing I got mine a month ago."

"What?" Letting go of his arm, I stared after him as he walked on with our luggage. "What?"

He was already several steps farther ahead, and he didn't turn back to explain. But when we were riding the courtesy coach to the terminal, he slid a hand in his pocket and pulled out his passport and handed it to me, as proof.

It was actually there, pasted in. A real visa.

"But how did you . . . ?" I didn't bother to finish the question, because there was only one possible answer. "You knew." There were people around us, we weren't on our own, so I gathered my thoughts with an effort, and told him, *You knew I would come up to Eyemouth to find you.*

Rob didn't reply. With his head angled slightly away, he appeared to be watching something through the window.

Rob.

A wall of static blocked me out, which might have made me irritated if I hadn't noticed that he looked a bit uncomfortable, as though this weren't a conversation he was keen to have.

He didn't ask to have his passport back. I waited until we were in the terminal, and standing in the queue to get our boarding passes. Then I held his passport up and open to the visa page, and said, "The thing is, you have to know the dates to get a tourist visa."

"Really." He was fishing in the zippered outside pocket of his duffle bag for something.

"Yes. You also have to know—at least, you *used* to have to know— where you'd be staying. And not just the town or city, but the actual hotel."

"Is that a fact?"

I wasn't wrong, I thought. The glance he shot me was defensive.

"When," I asked him, "did you know?"

I half-expected him to use his standard line, to smile at me and say, "I've no idea what you're on about." Instead, he gave an odd, self-conscious shrug. "The end of May."

"More than three months ago?" I didn't have a right to be upset, I knew. It wasn't Rob's fault he could see the things he saw, but even so, the knowledge that my life was such an open book to him, that he could know what I would do before I knew it for myself, was still unsettling.

He'd found his airline ticket, and seemed grateful to have something else to focus on, but as the minutes stretched, my silence brought his gaze in search of mine. I met it with a frown.

"Just how much *do* you see?" I asked. "How far ahead?" I'd been so busy making use of his ability to see the past, I'd overlooked his other gifts.

He thought a moment. Then he said, "It all depends."

"On what?"

"On who I'm looking at." His tone held the frustration of a person trying to explain in words a thing for which the language was inadequate. "Some people are more difficult. My father. You."

"But you still see my future."

"I see bits of it." He took a deeper interest in the writing on his airline ticket. "Bits of what it could be."

I was tempted to explore what he might know about that future.

What it could be. What it would be. Whether he was in it, anywhere. But part of me was too much of a coward to go down that road. The past, I thought, was safer.

There was one thing I'd been wondering for two years. So I asked him. "Did you know that I would leave, that night in Edinburgh?"

He didn't answer straight away. I might have missed the nod, except he followed it with, "I was never sure, ye ken, on when. I'd only seen the part where we were walking in the rain, I'd no idea what the day would be."

I struggled to adjust to this; to how it changed the meaning of my memories of our time together. "But," I asked him, "if you knew that I was going to leave, why did you stay with me so long?"

He raised his head and looked me in the eyes. "Because I wanted to. Because it was my choice."

The chaos of the terminal around us shifted out of focus, blurring into one receding whirl of noise and colour, and the only person who looked clear and real to me was Rob.

"And this is your choice, now," he told me. "If you'd rather that I didn't come along, just say so."

I could see that he was serious. He'd walk away if that was what I wanted, what I asked of him. He wouldn't try to change my mind.

My choice, I thought. My firebird to follow.

I stood a little straighter, cleared my throat, and asked him, "Rob, would you come with me to St. Petersburg?"

His smile, though it came slowly, nearly stopped my heart.

"It's all a bit last minute, like," he said, and dodged the smack that I'd have landed on his arm, "but aye, I think I can. There's just one problem."

"What?" I waited for it, then relaxed as Rob held out his hand, the glint of humour in his eyes restoring balance to my world.

"They'll never let me through security," he said, "without my passport."

chapter
TWENTY-THREE

M y efforts to teach Rob a few words of Russian were drawing some decidedly amused attention from the flight attendant and an older woman sitting just across the aisle.

We'd started with the basic phrases: How are you? Good morning, thank you, things like that, and now I was writing the Cyrillic alphabet down for him on the paper napkin from my lunch tray.

Rob, while waiting, practiced his new phrases on the flight attendant. When she cleared away his own tray, he smiled brilliantly and thanked her with, "Spa-CEE-ba."

Smiling back, she said, "Pah-ZHAL-sta," which was one of those great multipurpose words that meant "you're welcome" in one context, "please" or "here, this is for you" in others.

Rob, encouraged, told the flight attendant, "Min-YA Za-VOOT Rob."

I smiled myself, not looking up, and said, "That's good pronunciation, but you're telling her they call you 'slave.' That's what 'rob' means."

The older woman sitting on the aisle tossed out a dry remark in Russian about women having fantasies, which made the flight attendant laugh and bend to pat my arm. "With such a man," the flight attendant said to me, in Russian also, "so good looking, you be sure to teach him how to say 'I have a girlfriend.'"

Rob, who didn't understand a word of this, sat patiently and waited till the flight attendant moved away before he asked, "So what's my Russian name, then?"

"It's still Robert, just pronounced a little differently." I wrote it down for him: "Роберт. RO-byeert. You see?"

"So the 'P' is an 'R.'"

"That's right."

Picking up the paper-napkin alphabet, he pointed out, "But there's a perfectly good 'R' down here. Well, it's backwards, but—"

"That makes a 'yuh' sound," I told him. "Like 'yard.'" See, I've put all the sounds of the letters beside them."

He studied the list with a small frown of fixed concentration.

"It's not the world's easiest language to learn," I said. "And Superman you might be, but I don't think even you could become fluent in one plane flight."

Rob glanced over, with the crinkles showing at the edges of his eyes. "You think I'm Superman?"

"The point is," I said, "you don't need to be able to understand Russian. I'll be there to translate." I knew from the warmth of my cheeks I was blushing, but Rob had already turned back to his alphabet.

Shrugging, he said, "I like learning things."

Watching him working to master the letters and sounds on that napkin, I felt once again that small tug at my rib cage, that small wash of tenderness, and just as quickly I shielded my feelings and thoughts. But I *was* glad he'd come.

I'd been privately dreading the challenge of doing this leg of the journey without him. I'd told myself it was because he was just so much better than I was at seeing the past, and without him I didn't stand much of a chance of accomplishing anything useful. Assuming I even found Anna, the limits of my own skills meant that I most likely wouldn't be able to tie her to Catherine the First and find tangible proof that would help Margaret Ross sell her firebird carving for what it was worth.

If I'd had a month in St. Petersburg, maybe. But in just a handful of days, I could never have done it. With Rob, now . . . with Rob, it was possible.

That was the reason, I'd told myself firmly, why I was so glad he had come. Only that. Not because of the way that I felt when he smiled, or the fact that I felt more completely alive in his company than I had felt for a very long time.

And as for that traitorous inner voice trying to get my attention, to point out that this couldn't possibly last, that like holiday romances it only worked in the moment and wouldn't survive a return to the real world—I buried that little voice deep down inside, and ignored it.

The real world, I knew, would intrude soon enough. But for now, just for now, I was here on a plane next to Rob, with his elbow and mine touching, warm, on the armrest between us, and I didn't want to think further ahead.

He had picked up my pen and was carefully copying "Роберт"—his name—on the alphabet napkin. "How's that?"

"Perfect. But it should really be this, if you want to be properly Russian." I borrowed the pen back and wrote down a second name under the first, and then watched as Rob worked it out, letter by letter.

He said, "Brianovich? What's that?"

"Your patronymic. Unless you're on really close, intimate terms with people in Russia, you don't use their first name alone, you use their first name and their patronymic. All you do for that is take their father's first name, and then add the proper ending for a man or woman. You're Robert Brianovich, for example, because you're a man, but if we had the same father my patronymic would be Brianova, or Brianovna."

"What is it really?" he asked.

"Philipovna."

He gave the brief nod that I knew meant he'd got it all sorted. "So if I had two kids," he said, "Jean and Jack, they'd be Jean Robertovna and Jack Robertovich."

"You've got it. Except little Jean would be 'Yana' in Russian, and Jack would be 'Ivan.'" I said it the proper way: "EE-vahn."

Rob smiled. "So what's 'Nicola,' then?"

"Well, there isn't a Russian equivalent, really. My parents, I think, really wanted to call me Natalya, but nobody wanted to upset my grandfather, so they picked something more English."

"Your granddad's not so keen on Russian names?" Rob asked.

"My grandfather doesn't like any reminders of Russia."

"I see." His smile turned briefly private. "He's not ower fond of me, either."

"What makes you say that?" I cast my mind back to this morning, when I had been leaving my grandfather's house and he'd stood in the doorway and glared out at Rob, and I'd thought that the two of them might have been— "Rob," I began, "did you . . . ?"

"No." His tone held a hint of amusement. "But he did."

That floored me. "He *spoke* to you? What did he say?"

"I'm not sure. What does this mean?" he asked, before speaking a short and succinct Russian phrase that made people in nearby seats turn their heads, scandalized.

Even the older woman on the aisle leaned over and told me, in Russian, "You should not be teaching him such things."

Rob leaned back, all innocence, closing his eyes as I sent him a look.

"Aye," he said, "I've a feeling your grandfather's not ower fond of me."

The drive in from the airport took us past the modern factories and industrial monstrosities and bleakly structured Stalinist apartment blocks and buildings that belonged more to the stoic past, when the city had been known as Leningrad, than to the brighter history of pre-Communist St. Petersburg.

My mother had been born here, and my grandfather. He'd been a little boy when Hitler's armies had come overland and cut off the supply lines of the city, and like everyone in Leningrad he'd starved and suffered through more than two years of that relentless siege, those endless bitter winters while the people all around, including many of his family, sickened, died, or disappeared.

And yet the city had survived, as it had always done; endured the changes of its name and government, stood fast through war and siege and revolution, and through all of that had managed still to shelter and encourage art and dance and life and beauty.

It was what my mother always told my brother and myself that she missed most of all about St. Petersburg—the beauty that lay everywhere, in unexpected places, if you only had the eyes to see it.

That was why, the minute we had got into this taxi, I had taken out the book that I had borrowed from my grandfather and given Rob a different sort of introduction to the city than he would have had from simply looking out the windows.

"So there was nothing here at all," he summed up, flipping through the maps, "until Peter the Great started building."

"Well, there was a small Swedish fort just up here," I said, and pointed it out. "But you're right, it's a very young city. He wanted a port, you see. Russia was virtually landlocked in those days, except for this smaller port all the way up on the White Sea, at Archangel, only the ice froze that solid for half the year, and Peter wanted a proper port, and a real navy, like everyone else had." I turned back a page to the earliest map. "Sweden's navy controlled all this here, all the Baltic, but Peter came up and just took this. He captured their fort, and he surveyed the land, and he started to build. It was technically Sweden's, I think, when he founded St. Petersburg, and I'd imagine they thought they could just take it back. But they didn't count on Peter's bloody-mindedness. He wanted what he wanted."

"So he got his seaport."

"Yes. It was a swamp, this, when he started building. Lots of islands and canals, a lot like Venice. It still floods," I told him, "when the winds are blowing the wrong way."

"Like in Amsterdam," said Rob.

Which might, I told him, have been part of the attraction. "Peter loved Amsterdam. He'd spent some time there, when he was a young man, learning to build ships and things, and he loved it. He wanted St. Petersburg to look like Amsterdam, modern and Western, with lovely wide streets and canals."

He hadn't missed by much. The older section of the city, nearest to the Neva River, had a rather Amsterdam-like feeling to its architecture. Our hotel, the Nevsky Grand, was on a shaded boulevard just off the

Nevsky Prospekt, in behind the great Cathedral on Spilled Blood, and just a short walk from the river and the Hermitage.

Sebastian never stayed here. It was in an older building, and the rooms, though clean, were very small. Sebastian liked his space, and wanted luxury when travelling. I wanted friendly service and a comfortable bed in a hotel that had at least a bit of character, and everything about the Nevsky Grand Hotel, from its old stone facade with the wrought-iron vine work and old-fashioned lanterns hung over the door, to the elegant sconces hung high on the walls of the narrow but welcoming entry hall, gave me the sort of a feeling I liked.

I was less sure, though, what Rob would think. I warned him, as we jostled through the entry hall and into the reception room, its floor tiled boldly black and white beneath a high beamed ceiling with a chandelier, "Just so you know, the rooms are very small."

"Because I'm so manly and huge, d'ye mean?" He kept his face serious. "Well, that might be a problem, but I'll try to cope." He grinned when I elbowed his arm. "Will ye stop that? You're aye hitting me with something."

"I am not."

"Are sot," he shot back, looking like a boy of ten as he turned that half-laughing smile full force upon the clerk at the reception desk.

I saw her blink, and then respond. She was pretty and dark haired and I felt a stabbing of something that I was ashamed to admit felt like jealousy. I had no right to feel jealous, I told myself. I'd had him once, but I'd left him and now he was no longer mine. He could smile at whomever he liked. And to prove it, I smiled myself at the clerk, if a little too brightly.

She took our passports, which was standard procedure in Russian—they'd be given back to us in a few days—and she used them to read our names. "Mr. McMorran," she said, "and *Miss* Marter." I gathered that Rob's reservation had been made some time before my own, but she managed to find us both in her records. "And it is two rooms, yes?"

She sounded almost hopeful, and this time the stab went deep enough to make me almost want to tell her no, we'd just have one room, thank you. But remembering in time how complicated that might get, I caught myself and took a breath before I answered, "Yes, that's right."

Rob's innocent expression didn't really reach his eyes. He winked and told the clerk, "I cannae trust her to behave herself."

I let him score the point. I waited till we'd signed the forms and got our keys and climbed the several steps to the first floor to take the lift before I told him, "You're impossible."

"I'm not. I'm fairly easy."

I said lightly, "You can tell the desk clerk that, you'll make her day."

Rob looked at me a moment, and although I kept my own gaze firmly to the front I caught the slight tilt of his head and saw his smile flash briefly. "Not my type," he said.

"Is that a fact?"

"It is." Flexing one arm as he shifted his grip on my suitcase a little, he said, "I'd be yours for the price of a coffee, the now."

I smiled myself, and pressed the button for the lift. "I have something better on offer," I told him, "than coffee."

chapter
TWENTY-FOUR

The wind had an edge that was chilling my ears. It had ruffled the river's wide surface and raised little waves that had splintered the afternoon sunlight's reflection until the broad river was sparkling.

I unwrapped my ice lolly, watching while Rob chose his own from the freezer of the ice-cream vendor's little sidewalk stall beneath its small square awning. "You say this is a ritual of yours?" he asked.

"It is."

I'd found this spot when I had done my term of study here, and it had quickly grown to be my favourite place in all St. Petersburg. The ice cream, I'd decided, was a bonus.

St. Petersburg had been constructed, not just on the mainland, but across a group of islands where the river here divided into several branches on its journey to the Gulf of Finland and the Baltic Sea. The main branch of the Neva River flowed between the south bank and the largest island in the delta. Rob and I were on that island—Vasilievsky Island—now, right at its farthest eastern point, known as the *Strelka*, or quite literally, the arrow, where a rounded spit of parkland speared the river and divided it, and offered an unequalled view of all the land-mark buildings on the waterfront.

The traffic passed behind us in a steady blur, with brightly coloured coaches stopping in a constant rhythm, letting off a stream of tourists who were instantly besieged by men with strings of amber beads, and sets of little painted nesting dolls, and "real fur" hats to sell as souvenirs.

Behind the row of coaches, just across the street, the Old Stock Ex-change—now the Naval Museum—commanded attention from high on its flight of steps, white in the sun, like an old Grecian temple, with

columns along the full length of its portico. Framing the view from
our side of the street were the two massive pillars of deep earthen red
that were still lit as beacons on special occasions, and stood like great
sentinels at either end of the half-circle park. We were standing just
now at the base of one pillar.

Ordinarily, I'd have been sitting on one of the white-painted
benches set all round the manicured lawn, where beds of lovely coral-
red impatiens made a cheerful show against the green. But I was keen
today to show Rob the whole view of the Embankment just across
from us, to help him get his bearings before we began our proper
search for Anna.

The wind struck even colder and I turned from it, and from the
pillar, but instead of heading for a bench, I led Rob round onto the
curving stone-paved path that rimmed the park, edged on its inside by
a tidy row of trees that had been planted in behind the benches, and
protected at its outer edge by a grey waist-height granite wall. From
here we had a panoramic view of many older landmark buildings of
St. Petersburg, the south shore in particular, with its impressive line of
what had once been princely residences and grand royal palaces, like
long and gilded wedding cakes of pastel greens and yellows edged with
white, their rows of windows catching sunlight as it danced across the
river that was wider than the Thames.

Rob turned his collar up against the wind and took a bite of ice
cream. "You might want to get a warmer sort of ritual. With cocoa,
like."

"I thought you Scots were hardy."

"Hardy, hell. I'm from the Borders. St. Petersburg would be at
the same latitude as Thurso, on the northern tip of Scotland. It's all
Hielanmen up there, they like the cold."

He didn't fool me. With his face towards the water he looked perfectly contented and at ease, as I imagined all seafaring men would
look with such a view. Ignoring the Embankment for a moment, he
gave a nod towards the golden spire rising just across the river to our
left, a narrow spike of brilliant splendour soaring from the shining

gold-domed rooftop of a steeple, that in turn rose from a jumble of red rooftops in behind high bastioned walls. "And what would that be?"

"That," I said, "is where the city of St. Petersburg began: The Peter and Paul Fortress. You can't really tell from this angle, but it's on an island as well, just a little one." I knew this part of the history by heart. "After Peter the Great kicked the Swedes out of their fortress, further upriver, he came here and started to build his own. Legend has it he marked the spot with a cross of sod he cut himself, using the bayonet of one of his soldier's muskets, and from what I know of Peter the Great I wouldn't put it past him. He was a very hands-on sort of ruler."

"When was all this, then?" asked Rob.

"Well, they started the fortress in 1703, and about ten years later they started to build the cathedral, that one with the gold spire. Trezzini designed that," I said, "Domenico Trezzini, an architect brought here by Peter the Great. He designed some of the greatest buildings here, at that time—not only the fortress and cathedral, but the Twelve Colleges, here on this island, and the Summer Palace, over there," I said, directing Rob's attention to the south bank of the river, further upstream. "You see where that big clump of trees is, beyond the bridge? Just there. It's a beautiful place. Gorgeous gardens. It's not a grand palace at all, really. Peter the Great wasn't fond of extravagant homes. He liked comfort. He lowered the ceilings, supposedly, in his own houses, to make them more cozy."

Rob let his gaze drift back down to the great Winter Palace—the Hermitage—splendid in sea green and white with gold trim, holding court on the south bank across from us like some majestic grand lady.

"So that," he said, "wasn't his doing, I'm thinking."

"No, that was built half a century later. It wouldn't have been here," I told him, "when our Anna came to St. Petersburg." Then, when his mouth curved, I prompted him, "What?"

"She's 'our' Anna, now, is she? And you ask me what makes me think that you're getting attached to her?"

I tried not to make my small shrug too defensive. "I told you," I said. "She's a likeable child."

"She might not be a child when we find her," he pointed out. "Did ye not say that when you first saw Anna she was a young woman?"

"Oh." I hadn't thought of that. Frowning a moment, I conjured the image of Anna as I had first seen her, her head bent before Empress Catherine. It seemed such an age ago . . . could it have honestly only been last week? "So how will we know her, then?"

Rob didn't make a reply. He was watching the river with eyes narrowed slightly as though against the wind, but I knew better.

"Rob."

I saw his eyes change focus. "Aye?"

My exhaled breath wasn't exactly a sigh. Not exactly. "You see it all, don't you? You don't need me telling you which buildings were here and which weren't, you see the whole thing." It was not a real question, and Rob didn't treat it as one, didn't bother to answer, because we both knew what the answer would be.

"I was watching the ship," he said, "just over there. It's a galley, I think."

All I saw were the long and low sightseeing tourist boats, like glassed-in barges, that nosed their way upstream and under the bridge on their way to a leisurely glide through the city's canals. And far down in the other direction, a cruise ship lay moored where the water was deeper; but that, I knew, wasn't the ship Rob was seeing.

I must have sighed again, a proper sigh, because he glanced at me and looked away, amused, and said, "For someone so reluctant to let on you have the Sight, or use your gifts, you seem fair envious of mine. I wonder why that is?"

"Are you to be my therapist, as well?"

He turned his head, and met my eyes. "As well as what?"

It was a good thing, I thought later, that I'd caught the lightness of his tone and known that he was teasing, or I might have found it difficult to drag my gaze from his, and turn my fierce attention to the river's passing current. "As my overworked and underpaid assistant."

I had always liked the way he laughed, so deep and genuine. "Well, time I did my job, then."

I was ready for the arm around my shoulders, this time. Ready for the feelings that went with it, as I closed my eyes and let my own thoughts drift and blend with his. And through Rob's eyes I saw the river and the city as it had been in its infancy.

I'd known that it had risen quickly from the barren, unforgiving land that had, till then, been nothing more than swamp and scrub ringed round by thin birch forests where the wolves had prowled and waited. Peter the Great, being tsar, had commanded this city be built to his plan, all its waterfront houses and palaces kept the same height, their grandness a testament to his own vision of Russia as part of a wider world, looking to Europe and not to the insular past.

He had made this his capital, ordered his court here, "invited" the best of his subjects—the merchants, the tradesmen, the wealthy—to come and build homes here, along with the peasants, the slaves, and the workmen he'd needed to carry out all that construction. They, too, had built homes, and the city had taken its shape in a decade, though what Rob was showing me now was, I gathered, a decade beyond even that, in the 1720s.

I knew this because, on the opposite shore, I could see what must certainly be Peter the Great's old Winter Palace—not the first one he'd had built, but the second one that had replaced it in 1721, and been rebuilt in its turn six years later. I recognized its homage to Palladian design, the ground floor faced with rough stone in a feature architects termed "rustication," and two more storeys rising over that one, with a pediment and columns, looking just as I remembered from the old engraving in the book my grandfather had given me this morning.

The Hermitage, across from where we stood, had not been built yet. In its place were other houses, built of stone and very grand, in that same Flemish baroque style the tsar had been so very fond of, having happy memories of his time in Holland.

And there were no bridges, either. Peter had been adamant about not wanting bridges on his river; he had wanted all his citizens to share his love of boats, and learn to use them. From the river I was seeing, it appeared to me the people of St. Petersburg were giving it their best shot, for the Neva was alive with boats and vessels of all sizes, from what looked to be a ferry barge midway between the left bank and the right, to the great galley Rob had seen further downstream, with its line of oars lifted and clear of the water.

I'd always thought of galleys as a feature of the ancient world, of Greece and Rome, with slaves chained to their oars like in *Ben-Hur*. I hadn't thought to see one here, in Russia, in the eighteenth century, but galleys, to be honest, weren't the chief of my concerns.

Just looking at the south bank of the city, at the size and breadth and scope of it, the movement on the river and the chaos of activity beyond, I felt a sinking sense of hopelessness. My concentration faltered, and my mind slipped clear of Rob's. I felt his arm shift on my shoulder, and his keen gaze angled down to mine.

"What is it?"

"How," I asked him, "are we ever going to find her, in the middle of all that?"

"You asked me the very same thing in Calais," was his patient reminder, "and we found her there."

"Yes, well," I said, "in Calais, we could stand by the gate, there was no other way she could come in by land. But here . . ." I shook my head. "Did you see all those houses, Rob? Even back then. We'll be walking around all weekend. It's impossible."

"Challenging," was his correction. "But hardly impossible." Looking downstream once again, to the spot where the galley had been and where now there was only a bridge with the cruise ship behind it, he let his keen gaze wander back up along the Embankment. "That big compound there, with the spire in behind like the one on the church in the Peter and Paul Fortress—what is that place?"

"That's the Admiralty." It, too, had been built in the very first years of St. Petersburg. "Peter," I told him, "was all about boats. Like the Rat in *The Wind in the Willows*. They were his great passion. Besides, if he wanted to stand up to Sweden and England, he needed a navy, and so he created one here—he brought in the best men he could find to build ships, and the best foreign captains to sail them, experienced men who could train his own sailors."

"Like Captain Gordon," Rob said.

"Exactly like Captain Gordon. He had experience in both the Scots and Royal navies, didn't he?"

"Aye." Rob was thinking. "And considering his long career in Russia, and how high he rose, I'm guessing he'd have done a lot of business at the Admiralty."

I saw where he was going with his logic. "So, you think that if we look for Captain Gordon, he might lead us back to Anna?"

"That's the plan. Okay with you?"

I thought it rather brilliant, but if truth be told, I wasn't in a hurry to go anywhere. I found I liked the pleasure of just standing here— within the shelter of Rob's arm, his chest a solid wind block, in my very favourite spot in all St. Petersburg. I didn't want to leave to follow anyone, not even Captain Gordon.

But I knew from how the shadows of the trees were falling round us that we only had a few more hours of daylight left, and time was never patient, so I gave a nod and said, "Okay with me."

He walked behind me as we crossed the lovely bridge that joined Vasilievsky Island to the south bank. There was traffic here as well, a steady stream of it, and people passing by us on the pavement, and a few less hurried tourists who had paused against the intricately wrought green-painted iron railings of the bridge to take their photos of the grand Embankment as the afternoon slipped on into the golden glow of evening.

The Admiralty looked like a palace itself, with its deep yellow walls and its row of white pillars. Behind it, a garden of tall trees and quiet green shade made an island of sorts in the midst of the cars whizzing round it. This was the Alexander Garden, and if one believed the history books, through all the siege of Leningrad there hadn't been a single tree from here chopped down for firewood, no matter how the people froze and suffered. It was typical, I thought, that even in a time of ugliness and deprivation, people here had done their best to shield a thing of beauty.

I found a bench and sat beneath the trees, while Rob walked back and forth along the wide red gravel pathway, with his head up and his eyes alert, as though in search of someone. Which he was.

When half an hour had passed, I purposely stopped looking at the time and watched the trees instead, the dancing play of light between the leaves. And when the leaves began to blur I let my eyes drift closed because they wanted to, and after all I hadn't had much sleep last night . . .

"Nick."

Rob was standing next to me, his hand outstretched.

I surfaced with an effort and a smile. "You found him?"

"Not exactly." With my hand in his, he told me, "Come on. We'll be walking."

chapter
TWENTY-FIVE

H er laugh turned the head of the sentinel standing on guard at the house of Lord Admiral Apraxin, across from the Admiralty, and from the long look he gave both herself and the man walking with her, she guessed he had no love of foreigners. Many still didn't, although there were certainly many more foreigners living here now than there had been when she'd first arrived, and the young Duke of Holstein, now pressing his suit for the hand of the tsar's daughter, had brought a whole host of new faces with him, his courtiers and cavaliers, testing the patience of men like this sentinel.

As she herself did, no doubt. But she couldn't have held in the laughter.

"You're only inventing this," she told the man at her side.

He denied it. "You give me too much credit if you think I could invent a speech like that one."

Anna stepped aside to let a sledge go past, the horses' breath a fog around their frosted muzzles as the sledge's runners sliced the hard-packed snow. "And so what did Sir Harry say then, in reply?"

"Sir Harry has wit of his own, as you know, and he told Mr. Elm-sall that should he desire such another display, he'd be happy to lighten the barrels beforehand."

She laughed again. "Do you merchants do no work at all, at the Factory?"

"'Tis winter," he said, "and the trade has been slow."

Someone called to her: "Anna!," and turning she saw a tall soldier approaching across the great open space teeming with people and horses. Charles always walked like that, she thought—in a straight line, with full confidence everyone else would get out of his way. Which they usually did. She lifted her cheek for the cold but affectionate brush of his kiss, and said, "Charles, do you know Mr. Taylor?"

The two men assessed one another in that vaguely measuring way that men did when they met, that all the centuries of civilizing influence had not yet managed to erase from male behaviour. Charles was several inches taller than her own companion, and a shade more sturdy, and secure in his advantage he remarked politely, "No, I've not had the pleasure."

"Mr. Taylor is a member of the Factory," Anna told him. "Mr. Taylor, may I introduce Lieutenant Gordon."

"Sir." Charles inclined his head in that distinctive blend of Russian and Scots mannerisms that, together with his accent, marked him as a member of the second generation, born in Moscow to a father who had come across to Russia at the turn of the last century. "Allow me to congratulate you."

Mr. Taylor looked perplexed. "That's very kind, I'm sure, but—?"

"And my cousin. I was not aware she had become betrothed."

Anna rolled her eyes and looked at Charles in a way that let him know she knew what he was doing, and was unimpressed.

Beside her Mr. Taylor said, "Lieutenant, I assure you we . . . we are not . . . Mistress Jamieson has done me no such honour."

"No? You will forgive me, but with you escorting her in public, I assumed that was the case."

She came to Mr. Taylor's rescue, saying smoothly, "I was lately on an errand to fetch letters that had come for the vice-admiral," she said, showing him the packet she was holding, "but the servant who went with me felt unwell, and Mr. Taylor kindly offered to accompany me home." She did not bother saying that the servant felt unwell because he had stepped into Trescott's tavern for a half-hour, nor that Mr. Taylor's offer had been more of an insistence, but it hardly mattered now, for Charles ignored her.

With a sympathetic look at Mr. Taylor, he said, "Shall I now relieve you, sir, that no one else should make the same mistake?"

His solicitous expression could not hold. When Mr. Taylor, with a reddened face, had quickly taken leave of them, Charles broke into a grin and Anna glanced at him reprovingly.

She said, "You've embarrassed him."

"Nay, I have flattered him." Falling into step beside her as she started walking once again, he said, "No doubt he has designs of it. You see the way he looks at you."

She saw. But still she asked, "What way is that?"

"The way a boy looks at a newly shining sword he must not play with, yet desires with all his heart."

"Only a soldier," she said, smiling, "would imagine any girl would find it pleasing to be thought of in the same way as a weapon."

"'Tis in truth the highest compliment." He steered her round a knot of huddled men. "But I did not intend to please you, I was merely stating facts." He cast a keen glance at her face. "You do not fancy him, I take it?"

"Mr. Taylor is a good man, and a kind one."

"Damning words." Charles grinned again. "You do not fancy him."

"I've little time," she said, "to fancy anyone. My days are full."

"Ah yes. How is my uncle?"

"Must you say it in that tone?"

"What tone?"

She sighed. "As though the term were illegitimate."

His short laugh had no humour in it as he said, "Your choice of terms is . . . interesting."

Anna said, with little patience, "Play your games of words with men like Mr. Taylor, not with me. You know I did not mean it in that sense."

"No, it was the proper term, I do believe. My grandmother did lie with the vice-admiral's father, and without the benefit of marriage bore his child, which makes our claim upon the Gordon name most illegitimate."

She turned on him, not caring they were standing in the middle of the street. "When has he ever made you feel so? When, in truth, were any of your family made to feel so? Was your grandmother cast out? No. She was cared for. Was your father, as a blameless infant, sent to be concealed? No. He was educated well," she said, reminding him of what they both knew was the truth, "and sent here with good prospects by the vice-admiral's arrangement. That his sons now think themselves ill-used would doubtless have astonished him."

She wheeled at that and walked on without bothering to look behind to see if he was following.

He was. His long strides caught her up before she'd reached the tall gates of the Admiralty, and for the whole length of its walls they ventured on in silence. Then he cleared his throat. "Am I to then assume," he said, "my mother has been by, to pay a visit?"

"Aye, this morning. With her usual complaints."

"She asked for money?"

"She returned what the vice-admiral tried to give her, for the purchase of your regimentals." Glancing sideways at his new brushed army uniform, its gold braid all intact, she told him, "And in truth they do look very dashing."

"Thank you." With his head bent, he allowed the briefest flash of the old smile that had endeared him to her years ago. He thought a moment then, and added soberly, "My mother's bitterness is not my own."

"Your mother is a bitter woman." She was judging, and she knew it, but she'd seen Vice-Admiral Gordon's face this morning after Charles's mother had stormed from his chamber, and she was in no mood yet to forgive. "When I first came here, as a child, and you and I were introduced, did he not say, 'This is my nephew'?"

"Yes, he did. And he has never called me less, I will admit it. But my father was no more than his half-brother, and my blood is more diluted still."

"I do not share his blood at all," said Anna, "yet he treats me on a level with his daughters, and has always done so."

"Does he?" Charles said the words so rashly that he seemed to want them back, because he paused before he asked, "Did he send Nan to fetch his letters from the Custom House? Or Mary?"

It was obvious he hadn't, so she didn't bother answering.

"Of course he didn't." Charles's tone implied that was the end of the discussion.

They had reached the western limits of the Admiralty and crossed together into the tight maze of streets where many of the British lived. Already the November afternoon was growing dark, and soon the watchmen would be coming out to start their long patrols and climb their towers, ever vigilant against the sliding shadow of a thief, or the bright flicker of a flame that might again engulf the houses that were springing up so quickly all around, their wooden walls daubed thick with plaster to present a fine appearance that, in spite of every effort, could not yet withstand the frost and every spring gave way to cracks and imperfections.

Like the families who lived in them, Anna thought. She said to Charles, "You know him not at all."

"I know that blood is blood, and I am certain that, for all the love the vice-admiral might bear me, I am yet one more unsought responsibility he well could do without."

She thought on this so deeply that she did not realize they had reached the front door of her house until Charles stopped and placed a hand upon her shoulder, keeping her from walking on. She roused herself, and looked at him. "Will not you come inside?"

"No." To her disappointed face, he added, "I have somewhere I must be."

She nodded, if a little wistfully. "I'll tell him that I met you."

"Yes, you do that." He looked at her a moment with what might have been regret. Or even pity. Then he added, "You may give him my affection." His kiss warmed her cheek as he bent down. "And mind that you tell him how dashing I looked in my new regimentals."

Inside, the lobby of the house was in near darkness, and she had to stand a moment till her vision had adjusted. It was early yet, she knew, to light the candles, but she saw the warm glow spilling through the partly opened door of the vice-admiral's room, beyond the antechamber, and she gladly shed her cold wool wraps and went to give his letters to him.

Nan and Mary were upstairs. She heard their cheerful voices rise and fall in conversation like a song, and knew that if she were to join them she'd be happily included, but she wanted Gordon's company, just now.

He was in bed, as he had been these past two days, yet she was pleased to see that he was sitting up and reading, with his pipe in hand, and there was nothing of that whistle in his breathing that there could be when these bouts of asthma laid him low.

"I have your letters," she announced, and leaning in exchanged them for a kiss that landed just where Charles had kissed her, so she added, "I met Charles near the Admiralty. He walked me back. He would have come inside, but he did not have leave to be so long away from duty, though he said to give you his affection."

"Did he?" The vice-admiral, looking pleased, set his book and his pipe down and started to open his letters.

"He looked very well," she remarked. "And quite dashing, in his regimentals."

"No doubt." He'd unfolded the first letter, and with his eyes on it, asked in an offhand way, "Why did you need Charles to walk you back? Where was Gregor?"

"Gregor fell ill at the Custom House." Anna schooled her face to look convincing. "Mr. Taylor very kindly walked me back across the river, and Charles saw me the rest of the way."

That earned her a brief glance above the letter's edge. "Mr. Taylor of the Factory?"

"Yes."

Returning to his reading, he said, "Ah."

She might have felt exasperation at his obvious amusement had she not been quite so pleased to see his sense of humour surfacing again, after what had been, in her view, too long an absence.

He'd had more to bear these past few years than many lesser men could have endured, and that he'd borne it strongly and with minimal complaint had been a model others facing so much loss might aim to follow, but she'd seen his grief in private and she knew that the events had left their mark.

The first had been the foolish, needless death of his son, William, in a youthful drunken brawl in faraway Gibraltar, cruel news that had reached them in the first cold winter they had spent here. Then had come the even crueler death of his beloved wife, who'd fallen ill not long after she'd come across to join them in St. Petersburg. And this past spring she'd been followed by her daughter Jane, the vice-admiral's stepdaughter, whose decline and death had also been a bitter loss to Anna, who had nursed Jane in her lodgings for those final wrenching months.

They had shared much in common, she and Jane—both loving the vice-admiral and belonging to him in a way, yet neither one his own.

I know that blood is blood. So Charles had said, and Anna in her heart knew he was right.

"What troubles you?" asked Gordon. "Usually you do not keep so quiet."

Anna saw no need to weigh her words. "Am I a burden to you?"

Setting down his second letter, partly opened, he gave her his full attention. "No, of course not. Why should you imagine that you are?" His mind was quick. "Did Charles say something to upset you?"

"No."

His eyes were on her face, now. "No?"

She had been but a child when she had first locked gazes with him in Calais, and in two months she would be seventeen, but in the time between she had not learnt the trick of telling lies to him without revealing it. She looked away. "He only said he felt himself a burden to you sometimes, and I wondered whether I . . ."

"No." In his voice there was no hesitation. "You have never been a burden." Looking down again, he seemed to fix his concentration on the wax seal of the letter he was opening, and told her, low, "You've been a blessing."

Anna blinked the grateful wetness from her eyes, because she knew he would not thank her for a show of strong emotion. He was softer than he seemed, inside, and did not like to show it. "It is only that you have this house," she said, "and the expense of it, and Nan and Mary and the servants."

"I shall have one servant less, if Gregor does not make it home by nightfall," was his dry remark. "And if you think I'm eager to be rid of you, then I suggest you go ask General Lacy his opinion on the matter, and he'll set you straight."

"General Lacy?" She frowned as she sat on the edge of the bed.

"Aye." This letter was stiffer and more tightly folded than the first. He had to open it with care. "He met me in the street the other day and asked me would I think of sending you to live with him awhile."

She couldn't think why General Lacy, whom she'd only rarely seen, would ask a thing like that, but Gordon knew the reason, and enlightened her.

"He saw how kindly you took care of Jane," he said, the rough edge to his voice a slight betrayal of his sentiment, "and thought you'd be good company for his own wife, who has been ill herself and is in need of some assistance."

"General Lacy has more servants in his house than we do."

"Aye, but he wants a girl of rank to be his wife's companion," Gordon said. "I told him no, he could not have you, and he seemed to take it well, which if I know him means he plans to make a new attempt to sway me in a few days' time. And I shall tell him no again."

She took this in, and turned it over in her mind while Gordon read his letter. It might not be such a bad thing, she considered, to go live with General Lacy for a while. His house was grand, and he himself by reputation was a kind and generous person. And besides, by her employment with so powerful a man she could not help but earn the vice-admiral more favour with those men who could advance him.

"You should tell him yes," she said, "if he has need of me."

When Gordon did not answer, she glanced round and saw him bowed above the letter with his handsome face set deep in lines of sorrow. She had seen those lines before.

"Someone has died?"

His nod was brief. "A friend." He passed a hand across his eyes. "I am a fool to weep, for it was hardly unexpected. He was old, and I have neither seen nor heard from him for years, but still," he told her, in a voice that rasped a little, "it is hard to lose a friend."

He took a moment to compose himself, then setting down the letter showed the shadow of a smile and told her, "We had some adventures in the old days, back in Scotland. Colonel Graeme was the very best of men."

The fire on the hearth was suddenly too far away, and Anna felt a cold hand wrap around her heart and squeeze until she could not draw a breath that would be deep enough to let her speak. She turned her face away, before her brimming eyes betrayed her, and she stood and took a not quite steady step towards the fireplace, in search of warmth.

There was a chance, she thought, that it was not *her* colonel. Not the man whose laughing eyes and Highland voice still came to her in dreams sometimes; who'd told her of her parents and their love for one another, and who'd risked his life to fetch her safely out of Scotland for no other reason than that she was his own nephew's child, and blood was blood . . .

She felt the memory of his arms wrapped strongly round her, that last morning that she'd seen him, when he'd left to go to Paris and she'd wanted to go with him. She could hear his voice, regretful even now: "I cannot take ye where I'm going, lass." And her own childish answer: "I'm no feart."

She watched the flames dance on the hearth and saw them blur and wished him back again to hold her as he'd held her then; to kiss her hair and tell her he forgave her for the lie, for feeling fear, for being so afraid of bringing harm and danger to him that she'd run away, that she'd left *him*, to keep him safe.

Vice-Admiral Gordon, from the bed behind, was asking, "Did you know him? Colonel Patrick Graeme was his name. He lately lived in Paris."

"No." She had not known if she would have a voice, yet there it was, if not entirely her own. "I did not know him." In her mind she saw the chessmen in the Earl of Erroll's library at play upon the board, and smiling eyes that watched them move. She asked, "How did he die?"

"In his own bed, at peace." The pause that followed afterwards seemed overlong, and yet she felt the trail of wetness on her cheeks and knew she could not turn around. At long last Gordon's voice said gently, "Anna. I have never pressed you for the details of your upbringing, but if—"

She interrupted, "They are dull. And for my part, I have forgotten them." And taking up a piece of wood she bent to tend the fire.

A minute later, when she straightened, she'd recovered her control, and when she turned back to the bed her face was nearly as it had been, and the flush upon her cheeks was just as likely to have come from standing too close to the flames as from her misery.

She bore the thoughtful gaze of the vice-admiral till at length he looked away and set that second letter to the side while he attended to the third. The words of this one changed his features yet again, but this time in a way she'd never seen: a sort of pride, edged with excitement.

"Anna, do forgive me, but I find that I must send you out again upon another errand, if you have the strength for it."

"Of course."

"And take Dmitri with you, this time. He is not so prone to falling ill."

Dmitri, from the kitchens, was a sturdy-shouldered man who held his drink with more efficiency than Gregor. Anna nodded, and when asked she fetched the pen and ink and paper from the writing desk and waited while Vice-Admiral Gordon neatly wrote a letter of his own, enclosed the other one within it, and sealed everything with care.

The fact he had not used his letter book to first compose the letter told her this was something private. And his next instructions told her why.

"Now listen very carefully. Take this," he put the letter in her hand, "and these," two silver coins drawn from the bag beneath his bolster.

"Give the first rouble to the guard outside the palace of the tsar, and let him know you come from me. He'll take you to another man, to whom you pay the second rouble, and he in his turn will put that letter safely in the tsar's own hands."

She stared down at the letter and the coins, amazed he'd ask her to do something so important.

"I apologize," he said, "for I can see that you are tired. Were there another way to see that note delivered, I would do it, but I am myself in no condition yet to walk so long out in the cold, and there is no one else to ask."

She paused, remembering her earlier exchange with Charles about her own position in this house. "You could ask Nan," she said, "or Mary."

Gordon studied her a moment, and she knew his eyes were seeing more than she would have them see, because his voice again grew gentle. "Do you think I hold them dearer than yourself, because I do not send them out to be my messengers? The plain truth is, my dear, that while I love my daughters, neither would be capable of taking on a task like this. The plain truth is," he said again, and held her gaze with his so she would know it, "there is no one I can trust, as I trust you."

Her heart, still aching from the news of Colonel Graeme, warmed a little and she closed her fingers tightly round the things that he had given her. "Then I will do my best," she gave her promise, "to be worthy of it."

And with that, she went to find Dmitri.

I said to Rob, "You're such a bloke, sometimes."

"How's that?"

"Well, look at you. Give you a fish pie and a beer and you're perfectly happy."

I'd known he would like this place. The Stolle restaurants were a small chain with several locations strung all through the city, and served what one might call traditional Russian "fast food": homemade pie. This was my favourite Stolle site, just round the corner from our hotel and not far behind the Hermitage, cleanly attractive both outside and in, and designed like an old-fashioned coffee house, painted in warm hues of gold, terracotta, and rich weathered green. Rectangular pies of all kinds with their lattice-work crusts baked to flaking perfection were laid out still warm on the butcher-block counter, where aproned servers sliced off appropriate sections as ordered.

I would have been happy to order for both of us, but Rob had stubbornly wanted to choose for himself, using very bad Russian and sign language and that incredible swift smile that instantly made the poor server forgive him for making her work harder.

"This is no ordinary pie," he excused himself now, in reply to my comment, and shifted his chair at our small corner table to open a little more space between him and the very large man at the boisterous table behind. "It's exceptional."

"What is that, salmon?"

"I think so, aye. And this is hardly an ordinary lager."

I said, "It's a strong lager, that's why. That's eight percent alcohol."

"That would explain it."

"Explain what?"

He looked at me, cheerfully innocent. "Nothing." He ordered another, and drank it while finishing what I had left of my own square of apricot pie.

As always, he'd surfaced from seeing the past looking spent and exhausted, but still rather pleased with himself.

"How on earth," I had asked him a half-hour ago as we'd made our way back past the Admiralty gate, "did you manage that?"

"Manage what?"

"Finding Anna. With all of those people."

"Blind luck. She walked past me."

"But how did you know her?"

He'd shrugged then, and told me, "She laughed."

I supposed, when I thought of it now, that the way someone laughed was the one thing that didn't much change as a person aged. Certainly Anna, in some ways, was unrecognizable from the young girl she had been when I'd seen her in Calais, just yesterday.

This afternoon she'd been more a young woman, already now entering into her late teens with all the mature poise that girls of that long-ago time had most probably needed to gain, unlike girls of my own generation. My own teenage years had been freer, but from the way Anna had set her slim shoulders I'd guessed she had already learned how to balance the weight of responsible burdens.

But still, she'd seemed loved, and her clothes, if not fancy, had looked to be well-made and fine. She'd been wearing a long cloak and hood when we'd first seen her, walking in the snow of the great space beside the Admiralty.

The hood, falling forward, had covered her hair and a part of her face, so it hadn't been till she had entered the house and had hung up her cloak in the lobby that I had been able to see what she actually looked like.

She wasn't a stunningly beautiful girl, but her features were even, and lively enough to be pretty. Her eyes were still lovely, that softly grey-green colour, under arched eyebrows that matched the dark brown of her lashes. Her hair had stayed dark brown as well, and it still fell in curls round her forehead and cheeks.

She stood close to my height, neither tiny nor tall, with a slim build that gave her a natural, tomboyish grace, and she seemed—as she had when a child—to be always in motion, if not in her body, then in her intelligent mind, which revealed itself plainly whenever one looked at her eyes.

Rob was following my train of thought. "Does she look as she did when you saw her the first time?" he asked.

"I'm not sure. Maybe." I'd only had a brief glimpse of her then, and I couldn't be certain.

Rob shrugged. "We'll ken more," he said, "after tonight."

It was already nine in the evening. The sun had just set and the light from inside the warm restaurant reflected back now in the darkening windows. "Tonight?"

"Aye, it's early yet. We've only got . . . what? Three days?"

"Nearly four."

"You'll be working for some of that," Rob pointed out. He had finished my pie and was draining the last of his lager, his eyes shining more brightly blue than they ought to have. Two strong lagers, I thought, drunk as quickly as he had downed those, would have an effect.

I tried the tactful approach. "Are you sure that you're up to it?"

Rob grinned. "You mean, am I blootered?"

"Your accent is thicker."

"I've no got an accent." His arch look accused me of being delusional. "But if you have doubts, maybe you should do some of the driving."

I said, "We're on foot."

"So we are."

"So that doesn't make sense."

Unconcerned, he stood smoothly and shrugged on his coat before gallantly helping me into mine. "Where," he asked, "was the tsar's palace? The one Gordon sent Anna to?"

I remembered the snow, and the sledges; the bite of the wind. "That would have been the Winter Palace. It's not far."

It was, in point of fact, a short walk away in the gathering darkness. We crossed one canal by its bridge and strolled down on its opposite side, with the lights from the buildings all round making shimmering points of bright colour that danced in the black water.

Rob took my hand in his own, and I didn't object. I suspected he'd done it without really thinking, his full senses occupied elsewhere, but I liked the feel and the warmth of it; and when we turned onto the darker canal that led up to the Neva, I was grateful for that contact to assure me I was safe, because at this hour of the evening, even with the few old-fashioned lamps spaced out along the buildings, this was not the kind of place where I'd have come to walk alone.

Our footsteps fell with echoes on the tilting granite paving stones, and echoed still more wildly from the high walls of the buildings to each side of the canal that made the passage feel like some deserted alley streaked with strange distorted shadows. At the farther end, beyond the small arched bridge that marked the edge of the Embankment, cars chased back and forth along the street that ran beside the river, in a constant swishing pulse of tires that faded to the distance, but that noise was muted here beneath the constant slap of water on the cold and slippery walls of the canal itself, its restless surface several feet below the weathered iron railings running at my side.

This was the Winter Canal, spanned up ahead by two bridges—the small one at ground level, and above that the old gallery that ran high over it, a graceful curve built to connect the upper storeys of the Hermitage Theatre on our side of the canal and the even older building on the other, all enclosed with rows of windows that looked lovely in the daylight but at night gave me the feeling I was being watched.

"The Winter Palace used to stand right there," I said, and pointed up ahead to the pale walls we were approaching. "There are drawings of it in my grandfather's book . . . well, drawings of all the Winter Palaces built on this site, actually. The second one, the one Peter the Great died in, was just sort of absorbed into the next, then eventually all that was torn down to put up this theatre." I gave him a short history of how the theatre had come into being in the late eighteenth century, and how it had fallen into disuse in the Stalinist years, and how it had recently been lovingly restored. "And while they were restoring it, they found bits of Peter the Great's Winter Palace preserved underneath where the stage is, and all along here. There was part of the original courtyard, and several rooms, and all that's been restored as well, inside," I said. "And here, just here, is a bit of the palace's old facade. See how this section of wall is a different design?"

The piece of the old facade was maybe four feet wide, rising two storeys and painted a colour that would, in the daylight, be rich butter yellow in place of the pale green that plastered the rest of the theatre. The windows here were old and framed in oak, with metal sills that sloped to shed the rain, and all the simple moldings had been painted white. In at least two places I could see, the architects had left a bit of brickwork bare, to show the structure underneath. And at the pavement level was a deep well, like a cellar entrance, running the full width of that old section of facade and covered by a low, protective, sloping box of Plexiglas set in a metal frame.

Rob stopped, and gave my hand a squeeze. "All right then, go to it."

"I'm sorry?"

"I'm letting you drive for a change. Like I said." Not put off by the look on my face, he went on, "You've been watching me do it for days now. Just give it a go."

"You *are* drunk. I can't do what you do."

"But you've not truly practiced, now, have ye?" His gaze touched my face in the shadows. "Are you not the slightest bit curious to learn the limits of what you can do?"

I looked away. "I know my limits."

"Is that a fact? Well, I've ten pounds says you might just surprise yourself."

"Rob."

"What?" He let go of my hand. "You were willing to come on your own to St. Petersburg. Willing to try to do *this* on your own."

"Yes, well. Willing and able are two different things, aren't they?" I said that lightly, but he wasn't having it.

Whether because of the lager or some more inscrutable reason, he'd turned serious. "When you first got on that train to Dundee," he reminded me, "when you first made the decision to go help your Margaret by holding the Firebird, surely you thought, deep inside, that you could?"

"But I didn't. I couldn't." My voice had dropped low. There was no one around us to hear, but I did it instinctively, faintly surprised at the fierceness with which I defended my actions. "I knew that I couldn't. That's why I got off that train, Rob." I looked at him. "That's why I came to find you."

"Aye, I ken why you did it. But using my gift's not the same thing as using your own, is it?" He, too, had lowered his voice; maybe even stepped closer, I wasn't completely sure. "I think," he said to me slowly, "this makes you feel safer, just being a bystander. Coasting along letting me do the work, as though we were on holiday someplace ye no ken the language." His mouth curved so briefly it might have itself been a shadow. "Like me here in Russia. I no ken the language here, either," he said, "but I'll not let it stop me from ordering meals for myself. I can learn. So can you."

I shared none of his certainty. "Rob."

"Aye?"

I shook my head, breaking away from the steady blue hold of his gaze, because there was no way I could hope to explain.

"Would it really be so terrible," he asked me, very quietly, "to be like me?"

I paused before I said, "That isn't it."

"Then why are ye so feart of what you are?"

I'm no feart. The words in Anna's voice, a memory at my shoulder, made me lift my own chin higher and reply, "I'm not afraid. I just . . . I can't, that's all." And when he would have argued, I explained, "I can't just start a vision cold, like you. It's not the way it happens, for me. I need to be touching something."

Rob considered this, and gave a nod towards the wall. "So that should do. You said yourself it's the original facade of the old Winter Palace that was here when Anna was."

"Well, yes, but it's been plastered over since, and painted. I don't think—"

"The bricks are there." His tone, while quiet, held a challenge. "Will you try?"

I measured his resolve against my own with a long look, and sighed. "And if I can't?"

"You want to have some faith."

The problem wasn't faith, I thought, so much as finding someplace I could stand where I could reach that section of the wall. The wide glass box, like a low greenhouse, that covered the well in the pavement in front of the wall jutted out for a least a full metre, and rose past the height of my knees at its highest point. Climbing on top of it, or even sitting, was out of the question—I wasn't about to trust glass, even Plexiglas, to hold my weight. It was too deep to lean across, also, which meant that I'd have to position myself to one side of that section of wall, and reach over to touch it.

And that was a problem as well, since to one side, the theatre's wall jutted out sharply and made it a tricky affair to reach round it. The other side wasn't much better. It had a great drainpipe that ran from the gutters above and left only a tight space for me to squeeze into. It wasn't a comfortable spot.

But I tried.

With my hand pressed against the cold plaster, I tried. Closed my eyes and reached out with my thoughts. Something flashed very briefly, but I couldn't hold it. The images simply refused to take shape, floating past me and through me and into the darkness.

My arm started aching from being held out at that angle and finally I let it fall, backing away in frustration. "You see?" I told Rob. "I can't do it."

He'd stood back through all of this, giving me room, but I saw him take stock of the wall now, his chin tilting up as he followed the course of the drainpipe before moving in himself. Turning, he leaned back and settled his shoulders so one rested firmly against the long wall where the newer part met the facade of the old Winter Palace. The drainpipe pushed him outward at an angle, yet he looked at ease, relaxed against it with the air of someone who could stay like that all night.

"Come here," he said.

I eyed his outstretched arms warily. "Why?"

"Just come here."

I might have been crossing a chasm, I went so reluctantly; but of the things that I might have forgotten, I hadn't forgotten the feel of his long body pressed against mine when he held me—the solidly shelter-ing warmth of his chest and the weight of his arms round my waist. Loosely linking his hands in the small of my back, he said, "You need support, that's all." Shifting again so his thighs were braced strongly round mine, his boots firm on the pavement, he told me, "I'll not let ye fall. It'll be like that time that you telt me about, when your brother was talking you down from that tree."

This didn't feel *anything* like that, I wanted to tell him, but I went for humour instead. "What, you'll boss me around, will you? Tell me where to put my hands and feet?"

Rob gathered me closer, and I felt the quick laugh that lifted his chest. "Well, your hands, anyway." He nudged my left arm. "Put your arm," he said, "over my shoulder."

His shoulders were muscled and hard like his chest, but his jacket provided a padding that cushioned my wrist as the back of my hand came to rest on the wall just behind him. The wall of the old Winter Palace, that I had been trying to touch in the first place.

He said, "There. How's that, then?"

"It's good," I admitted. My arm and my hand were supported and comfortable, and with Rob holding me there was no way I could fall. In fact, if I just leaned in a little . . .

"Relax," he said. "Put your head down on my shoulder, and con-centrate."

Easy for him to say, I thought. But strangely, it did make it easier, having him hold me. I rested my cheek on the weave of his jacket and let his strong heartbeat compete with the echoing sounds of the night and the quiet canal as my eyes closed.

The noises began to recede, and his heartbeat grew muted, and out of the blackness the filmstrip of images flickered and grew and began to run backwards. I watched the blur, waiting as I always did, until Rob's voice within my mind gently advised me, *You've gone too far back. Stop, and make it run forward.*

I can't do that. You need to—

Concentrate, was all the help he would give me. *Just will it to stop.*

It resisted my will with astonishing ease for the first several seconds, but finally, when I applied all of my effort, the images started to slow.

Rob? Is that me or you?

It's all you. Good, he said when it stopped. *Now, you want to come forwards, but slowly. One frame at a time, almost.*

That was no easier. It took a few tries before I could manage it, and even then I whizzed past where I should have been and had to roll the frames back with an effort. My attempts were as unlike Rob's smooth way of scrolling through time as an elephant's moves were unlike a ballet dancer's, but he was patient.

You're close, now, he told me.

But how will I know . . . ?

You'll ken the right place, when you've found it.

I slowed the frames further, not wanting to pass it again, drawing strength from this newfound control over what I was seeing. Then one of the images, black as the night, seemed to pulsate a little, the smallest vibration. It drew my attention, my focus, and started expanding until it had grown to the size of a cinema screen. I saw Anna, and somebody walking beside her approaching what must be this very canal, looking more dark and lonely than it did tonight, even.

Why are you keeping back? Rob asked.

I'm not. This is just how I see. From the outside, the way I saw everything. From a safe distance. No more than a . . . what had he called me? A bystander.

Go closer.

Rob.

He was deep in my mind now, and nudging me forwards. I felt it as surely as though he were pushing me. Wanting to show him I wasn't the same, I deliberately tried to move nearer the image. It broadened. I tried again. And then again, till I stood at the brink of it, hesitant.

Not ready yet to believe.

Go. He nudged me again, and I gathered my focus and pushed through the image itself, and then I was inside it, incredibly, soaring above what I saw, rising wildly and spinning with little control, till I suddenly felt him right there with me, catching me, holding me steady, and bringing me down to the ground again, safely, as Anna passed by.

chapter
TWENTY-SEVEN

Dmitri was grumbling. He usually grumbled, and being called out of the warmth of the kitchen to walk in the dark and the cold to the palace had blackened his mood even more. He was a Siberian, one of the great brigade of peasant labourers who had been forced by decree to come help build St. Petersburg, spending his days hauling timber and stones for the houses and churches and wharves that had risen by sheer force of will from the marshes. The men who'd been dragged here from all over Russia had been given freedom to leave once their term of hard labour was done, but Dmitri, with no means to make his way back to Siberia, had like so many stayed on as a servant, his old life forever discarded.

What that life had been, and what loved ones it might have contained, Anna hadn't been able to learn, for he never would speak of it, but Anna sometimes suspected that, like Captain Jamieson, he'd had a daughter once, for there had always been something decidedly fatherly in his attachment to her.

Even now, as they made their way carefully over the small wooden bridge of the Winter Canal, the Siberian kept a firm hold of her elbow, as though she were still the young girl she had been when she'd first come to live here, when he and the cook had helped care for her during the vice-admiral's sojourns at sea.

"Fool idea," Dmitri was saying, "to send you so late in the day, in the darkness. You ought to be home getting warm, eating food. Does he want you to end up as ill as himself?"

"I feel fine."

"You feel fine." He dismissed that idea, and said, "You feel frozen. These clothes, they are not made for warmth."

Anna knew that Dmitri, like many traditional Russians, still deeply resented the loss of the old way of dressing, the robes and the boots and the great hanging sleeves that had now given way to the more Western styles that the tsar himself favoured, and that he'd decreed all his subjects should wear. The waistcoats and close-fitting breeches and stockings that men of rank now wore were things that Dmitri despised. "In Siberia, men would not last through the winter in such clothes," he'd often complain, "and the women would freeze in their homes." But he stopped short of actually saying he wished the old ways would return, for the tsar was the tsar, after all, and in Russia the tsar was as near a divine being as one could be without angering God.

Anna hugged her cloak more closely round her bodice, wishing she were able to wear breeches like a man, because the wind now swirling round her woollen-stockinged legs beneath her skirts was sharp as knives of ice.

She had her head tucked down, and so she did not see the dark bulk of the man who waited for them at the bottom of the bridge, until he spoke.

"What is your business here?"

Dmitri, at her shoulder, looked the stranger up and down. "You are no guard," he threw the challenge back. "Our business can be none of your concern. Now stand aside."

"I am the watchman. And whoever passes here becomes my business." The voice was hard, as were the eyes that glittered darkly in the light cast upwards by the lantern that he carried. "Where is your light?" he asked. "You are required to carry one, when you are walking in the night."

Dmitri said, "It is the evening, not the night. It was not even dark when we came out, and we'll be home again by suppertime if you but step aside and let us do what we've been sent to do."

"And what is that exactly?"

The Siberian was trying to contain his temper. "That," he said, "would be between my master and His Majesty, and I assure you both of them will see to it that this becomes *their* business if you interfere."

The wind bit deep, and on the bridge the air grew colder.

Men, so Anna had observed, replied to threats in one of two ways, much like bears. They either dropped and turned and scuttled off, or else they stood their ground and bellowed back and tried to make themselves look larger.

The watchman was standing his ground. "Your insolence demands I interfere! I could lay hold of you for daring to come out without a lanthorn, at this hour," he said.

Dmitri laid his hand upon the long old-fashioned knife he carried, and since Anna knew that knives like that were also not permitted, by the tsar's decree, she stepped in smoothly with, "Good sir, I do apologize. My servant has been drinking, he is not himself this evening. Pray, take no offence at what he says."

Dmitri frowned, but from respect he did not contradict her as the watchman weighed her words. Her accent, when she spoke in Russian, was not perfect, but in this case Anna hoped that fact might help. Bravely moving forwards, she offered him one of the two silver roubles she carried, the ones the vice-admiral had given her to pay the guards at the palace. "Here, take this for your troubles."

He was wary. "In such a time, a man would be a fool to take a bribe."

She did not need him to explain what "such a time" was. Scarcely a week had gone by since the tsar had ordered the arrest of the empress's favourite, the dashing Willem Mons, for his corrupt ways that had made it near impossible for anyone to speak to Empress Catherine without paying him a fee or favour. All of this—so it was said—was done without the knowledge of the empress or the tsar, and not two days ago a crier had gone through the town to spread the proclamation of the tsar that any person who had ever paid a fee to Mons step forward to give evidence against him.

No one truly thought that Mons would suffer death for his offence, for after all his elder sister had once been the tsar's own mistress, in the time before the tsar had met and married Empress Catherine, and Willem Mons himself was such a handsome, charming fellow, of the sort that often knew the way to talk themselves out of the greatest difficulty. But the fact remained that, at the moment, he was fallen from his post and locked in prison, and most likely would stand trial for taking bribes.

Anna summoned a smile, and said, "This is no bribe. I do but seek to pay the fine."

The hard eyes grew more wary still. "What fine?"

"Why, sir, the fine for coming out without a lanthorn." She offered him the coin again. "It is a rouble, is it not?"

A rouble would be more than two days' pay, she knew, for many men. The watchman seemed to think a moment, then he nodded curtly, once, and pocketed the coin. "Be on your way, then."

As the watchman stepped aside to let them leave the bridge, Dmitri took her elbow in a fierce protective grip, his own eyes fixed upon the grand front of the palace as they made their way towards its steps.

"And what," he asked her, "did you go and do a thing like that for?"

Anna was not truly sure, because now she had only one rouble remaining and two more guards yet to be paid, but she replied, "He would have seen your knife."

"He'd not have seen it very long, for I'd have buried it within his thieving heart."

"Dmitri, please." Her glance implored him to be sensible. "I lost one escort earlier today to Mr. Trescott's tavern, and if I lost another to the gallows the vice-admiral would not easily forgive me."

The normally fearsome Siberian softened a little, and despite his pride he showed a grudging sort of gratitude by guiding her around a patch of roughened ice. But still he felt the need to point out that the watchmen of today had lost their manners altogether. And the palace guards were little better.

Anna shushed him as they neared the closest of the two stone flights of steps that climbed the porticoed facade of the great Winter Palace. Near the base of those steps stood not one but four guardsmen, and since she had no idea which one of them she was supposed to approach, she addressed them all, clearing her throat with a small, cautious cough.

"I am come from the Vice-Admiral Gordon," she said, "on a matter of business."

All four guardsmen looked at her, and she'd begun to think that maybe none of them was the right guard, the one whom she'd been told to pay, until at last one of the younger guardsmen stirred and came across so that he stood quite close to her, his back blocking the view of the others as he held his open hand between them. "Let me see your business, then," he said.

When Anna put the one remaining rouble in his palm, he closed his fingers round it with a nod and told her, "Come this way. But only you, alone. Your man must wait."

Dmitri frowned, but both of them knew better than to argue or to try to make demands, so he stayed back while Anna climbed the curving stairs behind the guard, who asked her, low, "There is a letter?"

"Yes."

He nodded for a second time, and led her through the shadowed, torch-lit portico and past another guard into the palace. It was not as grand a place as she'd imagined it would be, although she realized she should not have been surprised by that, for Gordon had so often said the tsar did not feel comfortable with grandeur. And she'd seen with her own eyes how much at ease the tsar looked when he strode the streets himself, so tall above the men around him and with so much energy, yet dressed in nothing grander than his dark green regimentals, with no wig nor fancy trappings and adornments to reveal his rank.

His palace, she decided, was much like the man—constructed with an eye to practicality and comfort, not to fashion. This reception room she stood in was not so unlike the rooms she walked through every day at the vice-admiral's house, save for the icon set high in the far-facing corner to serve as a focus of humble devotion. The doors, with their draught-blocking curtains drawn back at each side, stood wide open to other rooms leading beyond, and they, too, looked as unpretentious.

Where she had expected to be dazzled, she instead felt welcomed, and the feeling gave her courage.

"Wait here," said the guard, "and I will find the man you need."

The man who would deliver the vice-admiral's letter to the tsar. The man who would expect a silver rouble as his payment, when she had none left to give. She tried to think of what to do, of what to tell him, but her thoughts were interrupted by the male voice rising angrily within the room that opened to her right.

Through the door that stood ajar she could just glimpse a tall man's figure entering the chamber from the room that lay beyond it, and when next his voice erupted Anna recognized it as the tsar's.

He raged, "You dare to ask for such a thing? For him? It is beneath you."

The Empress Catherine—for, thought Anna, no one but the empress would be brave enough to stand against the tsar in such a temper—made reply more calmly, but as clear: "I have forgiven him. Why cannot you?"

"You ask too much."

"You used to be forgiving."

They were speaking, Anna thought, of Willem Mons; they must be. She had never lived with men so volatile, who gave vent to their anger at this volume, and it made her feel uncomfortable, uncertain whether she should cross to close the door and try to give them privacy.

The tsar fired back, "How can you think that such a man is worthy of forgiveness? He has spat on all I stand for. All I've built. Do you not understand the damage he has done? My Russia, all that I have made, my whole life's work—it stands as all here in St. Petersburg must balance, on the thin supports we drive into the swamp, and let but one of those foundations fail," he warned, "and everything will fall, and then the swamp will rise and swallow it again, you understand? And *my* supports, my pillars, these have been obedience and honesty. Above all, I would give my people honesty!"

"I know."

"He smiled. He *smiled* while he betrayed my trust. While he betrayed you."

Empress Catherine started to say something, but the tsar was not yet finished.

"No! I will not have you ask for mercy. Not for him."

"For her, then. For Matrena." Willem Mons's other sister, who'd been fool enough to join him in his scheming and was also now in prison and awaiting trial. The empress told her husband, "She is young still, and so beautiful."

"You think I value beauty? Do you?" Suddenly a great resounding crash made Anna jump, as though the tsar had smashed a window with his fist. He shouted, "Thus I can destroy the thing of greatest beauty in my palace!"

Anna thought that, had she stood in front of him herself, such violence would have stunned her into timid silence, but the Empress Catherine only said, with admirable calm, "And have you made the palace any the more beautiful, in doing so?"

The tsar, confronted with that gentle challenge, did fall silent. Then he asked, in pure frustration, "What am I to do with such a woman?" And his booted feet stomped heavily across the floor before a door slammed, hard.

A male voice close to Anna's shoulder said, "Good evening," and she jumped again, and wheeled to face the man who'd so surprised her. He was not a guard. His clothes were richly made, embroidered heavily with silver, and he wore a long grey wig in the French fashion. "I am told you have a letter you would like to give me."

Anna tried recovering her earlier composure. "Yes," she answered him in Russian, as he had addressed her. "From Vice-Admiral Gordon, for the tsar."

She took the letter from her pocket and, her ears still ringing with the tsar's impassioned speech on honesty, she said, "He sent me with a payment I should give you for your trouble, but the watchman would not let me pass unless I paid him also, so I fear that I have nothing I can give you."

He considered this.

Still holding out the letter, Anna added, "I am sure Vice-Admiral Gordon will be pleased to send you payment by another means tomorrow. I will come again myself, sir, to deliver it, I promise you. But he did say this letter is most urgent."

"Many things are urgent." He assessed her with a gaze that lingered too long for her comfort. "I suppose you are a maiden, still? A pity, for that might have made a more diverting payment. Very well. That is a charming ring you wear. I daresay that will do."

"My ring?"

"Yes. It was not expensive, surely? And I have a daughter of my own who would admire a ring like that."

The ring, a simple gold band with a tiny pearl, had been a final gift to her from Jane, Vice-Admiral Gordon's luckless stepdaughter, before she died. It was a token of affection, not a thing that she could lightly part with. Even as she clenched her fingers in a small show of protection, she was saved from answering by the approach of footsteps and a swish of skirts behind her.

"Then perhaps," the Empress Catherine said, "this girl will share with you the jeweller's name, so that you may commission such a ring for your own daughter, for that is a lovely thought, Sergei Ivanovich."

Anna had never before been so close to the empress. A part of her wanted to stand there and gape, but she quickly dropped into a low curtsy, bending her head in respect, her heart beating.

The man she'd been speaking to bowed as well, deeply and gracefully.

"Sergei Ivanovich," said Empress Catherine, "I thank you for greeting our young guest so kindly. Now, if you would please fetch a maid with a broom, that would be very useful. A mirror has broken."

She sounded so calm and composed, as though having the tsar shout and rage had in no way affected her, that Anna could not help but marvel at her self-containment.

"Yes, of course," said the man.

As the sound of his sharp heels receded, a hand lightly brushed Anna's head. "You may stand, child."

She straightened, still keeping her eyes lowered. The fine silken brocade of the empress's gown filled her vision, a woven enchantment of branches and birds on a field of pale blue speckled richly with pearls that were larger by half than the one in the ring Anna wore. That the empress had helped her to keep.

Since the empress had already spoken to her, Anna reasoned it could be no breach of good manners to say in reply, "I do owe you my thanks, Your Imperial Majesty. You are most kind."

"You are Vice-Admiral Gordon's young ward, are you not?"

In amazement that someone so high should have noticed someone like herself, Anna nodded. "I am, Your Imperial Majesty."

"And you are here on his business, I gather?"

Again Anna nodded, and held out the letter still clutched in her hand. "I was sent to deliver this."

"Ah. For my husband, I'll warrant. I'll see he receives it," the empress said, taking it into her own softly elegant hand.

Anna thanked her, and waited, aware that she could not depart without being dismissed. The pause seemed to stretch overlong; then the empress remarked, "The vice-admiral speaks beautiful Dutch, but he stumbles in Russian. You seem not to have the same trouble, you speak Russian beautifully."

Anna accepted the compliment with proper thanks, but in Gordon's defence added, "But the vice-admiral speaks French also, fluently, and I cannot."

"You are loyal." The words held the trace of a smile, and approval. The hand of the empress touched Anna again, this time under her chin, and she lifted her head in obedience, raising her gaze.

It was commonly known that the empress had not been born royal, nor yet even noble; that she'd begun life as a peasant. A servant. Some dared even gossip that she had consorted with other men before she'd captured the heart of the tsar, and they spoke of her bloodline with open disdain, and dismissed her as common and plain.

Yet to Anna, there seemed nothing plain in the face she was looking at now, with its soft rounded features and warmly intelligent eyes
and the arching black eyebrows that echoed the black of the empress's
artfully curled and massed hair, which was dressed with small pearls
like the ones on her gown.

And the smile of those bowed lips was full of the kindness that
Anna had seen in the smiles of the blessed Madonna, on icons.

The empress asked, "What are you called, child?"

"I'm Anna," she said. "Anna Jamieson."

"But here in Russia, you must use your father's name also, like Sergei Ivanovich. What was your father's name?"

Anna was going to answer the truth, and say "John," till she real-
ized that even so small a thing, seemingly harmless, might somehow
endanger the uncles and family that she still had living, the family
she'd sought to protect when she'd run from Calais in the first place.
The world, she had learned, was not always as large as it seemed, and if
Vice-Admiral Gordon had known Colonel Graeme when they were in
Scotland, he might also once have known Colonel Graeme's nephews.
She could still remember how he'd asked her in Calais if she were truly
Anna Moray, as the priests had called her, and she'd always fancied
there had been a sense of recognition in his eyes, as though the name
were known to him. For her family's sake, and for his own, she could
not let him draw connections between her and her true father.

So she told the empress only, "I do fear I could not say." Which,
she thought, so phrased, was not entirely dishonest. And she added
more truth: "I am sometimes called Anna Niktova by the people of
our street."

The Empress Catherine looked at her, and echoed, "Anna
Niktova?" She gave it the pronunciation Anna had: NEEKtova, from
the word NEEKtoh, for "nobody." Nobody's Anna. No one's child.

"They mean no offence, Your Imperial Majesty," Anna explained.
"The other children whom I played with called me that, when I first
came to live here, and they did it more because I am so headstrong and
would take no one's advice, than from the fact I have no father living."

She was chattering. The empress could not possibly be interested in how the other children had regarded her, thought Anna, but because she could not call the foolish words back she could only drop her eyes again, her cheeks now warmly flushing.

Empress Catherine told her kindly, "It is not always a bad thing to be headstrong, Anna Niktova." Her lovely skirts were moving, rustling lightly on the floor as she began to turn away. "But pray that you do never tell His Majesty the tsar I have so counselled you; for men," she said, "are always to be managed."

And with that, she made a graceful exit through the room where, somewhere out of Anna's line of vision, a fine mirror lay in shattered bits, and was no longer beautiful.

chapter
TWENTY-EIGHT

Rob looked well rested, at least, when he opened the door of his room to my knock the next morning. He had showered and shaved but was still shrugging into his shirt when he stepped to one side to invite me in. "I'm nearly ready," he told me, then noticed my outfit and said, "You look smart. Am I underdressed?"

Adjusting the weight of my necklace against the bright folds of the top that had cost rather more than I cared to admit, I said, "No. It's only that I have my meeting at eleven, and I wasn't so sure I'd have time to come back here and change clothes beforehand."

"That's very prepared of you." He said that straight faced, but when he met my eyes he seemed unable to keep back the smile. "No, really. I admire your ability to plan ahead."

"Says the man who's had his Russian visa since last May."

He let that pass, and asked, "So what's the plan this morning?"

"Well." I had in fact been giving this a lot of thought. "I think it's fairly obvious, from what we saw last night, that Anna hadn't ever met the Empress Catherine till that moment, so I—" Suddenly distracted, I broke off to stare. "Is that a Jacuzzi?"

He turned, too, to follow the line of my gaze to the tub sitting plainly in view in the room. "Aye, it is. I've a sauna as well."

"How do you rate?"

He finished buttoning his shirt. "You have to smile at the management a certain way," was his advice.

"I guess so. Anyway," I pulled my thoughts back on their former track, "I thought, since we know Anna's only just met Empress Catherine, then it stands to reason she won't have the Firebird yet, will she?

So our best bet is to follow her around a bit from this point on—not day to day, of course, but in a general sense, because if Catherine did give her the Firebird, it's going to have to happen in the next two and a half years."

"How d'ye figure that?"

"Catherine," I said, "died in May of 1727. And what we witnessed last night must have happened in November of 1724, because that argument between the tsar and Catherine was about Willem Mons, wasn't it? I mean, they never mentioned him by name, but didn't you get that impression?"

His indulgent glance told me I was missing something.

"What?" I asked.

"I got no impression at all," he said, as though I ought to have figured that out for myself. "They were speaking in Russian."

"Oh." Feeling embarrassed that I hadn't thought of that, I offered Rob an apology and filled him in on what everyone last night had said to each other, so far as my memory allowed. "And Mons," I said, "according to the Internet, was thrown in prison on November eighth, and executed eight days later, so if Peter and Catherine *were* arguing about Mons last night, then what we were saw must have been happening sometime between those two dates."

He agreed that sounded logical, then added, "So it had no real effect then, when the empress asked for mercy. The tsar had Mons killed anyway."

I nodded. "But in fairness, I don't see he had much choice. Peter the Great had worked so hard to bring Russia out of the Dark Ages, but there were so many people opposed to him that he just couldn't afford to be seen to be soft on corruption, and Mons was corrupt." And then, with all the reading I'd done last night on the Internet still fresh within my mind, I said, "He spared the sister, though. He only had her whipped, and sent off into exile. It's a very Russian punishment," I told him. "Exile."

"Aye, we Scots have some experience with that as well." He turned as he tucked his shirt into his waistband, then walked the few steps to the bathroom and turned on the taps, intercepting my next comment with, "And afore you say anything, I'm only washing my hands. I've been minding your lecture. I've got bottled water for brushing my teeth."

"Yes, well, see you remember. The last person who ignored my advice wound up with a nasty parasitical infection."

"Giardiasis," he said, showing off his knowledge. "Caused by *Giardia lamblia*, a single-celled intestinal parasite. I looked it up."

"You couldn't take my word for it?"

He turned the taps off, dried his hands, and sauntered out to join me, reaching for his jacket where it lay across the bed. "Of course I took your word. I only like to ken the details," he explained. "I looked up 'Factory,' too, in the old sense that Anna uses it. I guessed she didn't mean the same thing we do, by the term."

"No," I said. "A Factory was a group of merchants authorized to set up trade abroad."

"I ken that, now. I even ken the place they had their warehouses. Which minds me . . . did you have a chance to sketch a copy of that old map from your granddad's book? The one that showed the streets west of the Admiralty?"

I took the folded paper from my pocket. "This map?"

"Aye. That's perfect, thanks." He flipped it open, scanned it briefly, gave a nod and said, "All right, then. Let's go see what's going on this morning at the Gordon house."

Mary and Nan had been helping her pack.

They were near her own age, and she held them as dear as if they had been truly her sisters, yet always she felt an awareness that they stood a little apart, being Vice-Admiral Gordon's true daughters while she herself was but his ward. To her eyes they were prettier, though Mary was less pretty when she frowned as she was frowning now.

"I do not see," Mary complained, "why they wish you to live in their house. Surely it would not be such an inconvenience for them if you simply went to them each morning and came home each night."

Anna said, "It is not for the days alone that General Lacy and his wife have need of me. I'm meant to be there also in the evenings, for the general's wife may then require companionship or care."

"She is no longer ill."

Nan, neatly rolling Anna's stockings, said, "She is with child."

Her sister straightened. "Is she really? Where did you hear that?"

"Sir Harry told me." Nan's cheeks tinged becomingly with pink although she seemed to try to keep her tone uncaring as she spoke Sir Harry's name. Sir Harry Stirling was a leading figure of the English Factory, and a friend of the vice-admiral, and although he must be surely nearing forty his good looks and clever ways had caught the eye of Nan some time ago, and lately it appeared that she had caught his eye, as well. It would, thought Anna, come as no surprise to see a match made there in future, and that pleased her, not for Nan alone, but for the fact that having someone like Sir Harry Stirling as a son-in-law could only raise Vice-Admiral Gordon's status.

Mary asked, a little saucily, "How would Sir Harry know this?"

Nan's blush deepened. "Why, he dines with General Lacy on occasion."

Anna said, "The question ought not to be how he does know it, but whether he should have repeated it."

Nan looked at Anna, curious. "Did *you* know, Anna?"

Anna gave a shrug, and Mary pounced on it.

"You did know!" Mary said with glee. "You knew the general's lady was with child, and yet you did not tell us."

Anna answered patiently, "The news was not my own to tell."

The sigh that Mary gave was thick with feeling. "I could never keep so great a secret."

From the doorway of the room, Vice-Admiral Gordon's voice remarked, "'Tis well at least one of my girls is discreet." He was dressed to go out, in the finely cut mourning coat that he had worn for these past weeks since the tsar's death, all through the bitter month of February and now into March. With a doubtful glance round he asked, "Is it now safe for a man to come into the room? Are the frilly things all packed away?"

Mary laughed. "Anna owns nothing frilly," she said to her father. "Nor frivolous. And if she did, she would hardly be taking it with her, for she could not wear it. Not now."

The vice-admiral accepted the sense of this, nodding with almost convincing solemnity. "No, I suppose not." He entered the room then, and Anna could see that he carried both hands clasped behind him, the way that he had when he'd brought her a gift when he'd come home from being at sea. "Still," he said, "now that the funeral is past, I daresay there'll be times when the mourning is lifted for various parties and pleasures, and then a young lass may have need of her frills."

With a flourish he drew from behind his back something that looked like a cushion, all oblong and soft. It was only when Anna had taken it into her own hands that she realized it was a bolt of new fabric—a lovely, brocaded silk woven with white leaves and softly blue flowers and small sprays of berry-red blossoms surrounded by curving gold fern fronds that ran like a delicate lace in the background, and all on a pale field of frosted sea green that looked quietly grey in some places when caught by the light.

Anna caught her breath. Something so beautiful could only come from France, and she knew well enough from helping to balance the household accounts how expensive such a fabric must have been. Eyes full, she looked at him. "I cannot take this."

Mary, reaching out to stroke the silk, said, "Nonsense, Anna. Surely it was meant for no one else, it is the very colour of your eyes. Wherever did you find it, Father?"

Gordon shrugged. "It was gathering dust at the Custom House. One of the merchants who came in last autumn had brought several like it from Paris, but had to depart before all of his goods were released, so they've now come to Mr. Wayte, and he suggested that, since I had daughters who liked pretty things, I might do well to choose a few pieces to please them." He smiled down at Mary. "There's silk for you also, and Nan, in your chamber. I chose blue for Nan, since Sir Harry does favour that colour, I hear."

Nan was used to his teasing and only blushed lightly before she, like Mary, rose up on her tiptoes to kiss his cheek, thanking him warmly before dancing off with her sister to see what their own French silks looked like.

Still smiling, the vice-admiral looked down at Anna and said, "I did think you could make a fine gown of that."

Anna shook her head. "You are too generous. I have gowns already. And as Mary said, I can wear nothing else but mourning for a while yet."

"Then you will have ample time to sew your gown." His tone, she knew from past experience, was not about to yield an inch of ground to any argument. "The mourning will not last forever, and the general is more sociable than I am. He does keep a lively dinner table, and who knows but you may meet a young man there more suited to your temperament," he said, "than Mr. Taylor."

Anna sighed, and told him, "Mr. Taylor is a good man."

"That he is." His eyes held fatherly affection. "But not good enough for you. I would have all my girls make matches that are worthy of their rank."

She found it endearing he worried so much about finding them husbands. He'd worried more when they'd first come here, so much so that on his wife's death he had briefly thought of sending poor Jane back to Scotland to her mother's own relations, for he'd feared she'd have no future in St. Petersburg. But Jane had begged him not to, had implored him, in a letter Anna knew Vice-Admiral Gordon still kept tucked within his letter book, to let her stay close by him and not send her back to live with those who had been so unkind to her own mother, and from whom she could expect naught but neglect. And so he'd let her stay, and seen her cared for, as he cared for Nan and Mary, and for Anna, and for Charles and Charles's mother, and his older daughters living still in Scotland—reckless Jean, with her unhappy marriage and her brood of bairns, and gentler Betty, both of whom he yet supported with the payments he sent over. Jane had once remarked that the vice-admiral likely viewed them all much as he viewed the crews of his own ships, and having spent so many years a captain and commander could do nothing less than feel himself responsible for how they fared.

Anna smiled at Gordon now and said, "You need not worry for my match. I have no rank that is my own."

"Then you may borrow mine and raise yourself above what you might otherwise have been. This is a country in which such things may be possible, if one presents oneself in the proper way. And wears the proper clothes." With that, he reached to take the silk from her and placed it with precision on top of the plain items she had packed into the trunk. "What of your treasures? Will they go in here as well?"

He gave a nod towards the parcel that lay lonely on the bed—the same small parcel she had carried from Calais, and from the convent before that. He'd never asked to look inside it. Anna wondered what conclusions he would draw were he to see the Holland nightgown her Aunt Kirsty had embroidered long ago to give her mother, and the lock of bright hair tied with the blue ribbon that had once been hers, and with them both the sheet of paper softened now by frequent reading, bearing words that once had seemed to her a promise, in the writing of a man whose name she'd taken for her own to ease the heartache of her giving up the life she had once dreamt of. If Captain Jamieson in truth had ever returned to the convent, he'd have found that she had gone, and if the nuns had sent him onward to Calais, he would have lost her there as well and gone no farther, for she'd left no trail behind to let him follow her to Russia. But at least he would be safe, she thought. She hoped that he was safe.

She could feel Vice-Admiral Gordon's keen eyes watching her, and waiting for her answer.

Anna shook her head, and picking up the parcel said, "I'll carry these myself."

"Are you then done with this? Good." Lowering the hinged lid of the trunk he latched it firmly. "I will have Dmitri take this over on his sledge, and after dinner I shall walk you to the general's house myself."

Their dinner was a quiet meal, with little said, and afterwards both Nan and Mary saw them to the door, with Mary hugging hard, as though the general's house were in another country altogether, and not only in another street.

Anna told her, "It will be no different from when I was taking care of Jane, when she was in her lodgings. I will see you all the time."

It was Dmitri, though, who seemed most wary of her prospects in her new, if temporary, home. He'd been frowning since returning from the task of taking Anna's trunk by sledge to General Lacy's house, and now as she was telling him goodbye he frowned more blackly and remarked, "You should be careful there. There was a bird perched on their window ledge, an ugly black bird, tapping at the glass. It is not good, to have a bird do such a thing outside your window. Always it means something bad will come. A death, perhaps. An illness. Something bad." His eyes held Anna's so intently she could see the deep concern beneath their darkness as he told her, with more feeling, "You be careful in that house."

chapter

TWENTY-NINE

The general's house was grander than their own. The dark floors gleamed, and smelt of polish, and although it was yet afternoon the candles in the sconces in the entry hall had all been lit to chase away the wintry shadows, sending bright reflections dancing in the shields of brass behind them, raising sparkles from the cut-glass edges of the mirror on the wall.

The walls themselves were half-tiled in the elegant Dutch fashion that the tsar had so admired, and Anna felt distinctly plain surrounded by such richness; plainer still when she and the vice-admiral were escorted by the servant who'd admitted them into the general's drawing-room, where long, heavy curtains of green draped the elegant windows, and glimmers of silver and porcelain adorned every table, and portraits in gilded wood frames hung serenely by tapestried chairs.

There was no icon hung in the corner, as there would have been in a Russian home, but on the wall nearest Anna a silver-tipped wooden cross bore a carved figure of Christ in pale ivory, His face neither joyful nor suffering. That watching face stirred her memory, and just for a moment she felt as she'd felt all those years ago, when she had stood in the nuns' parlour on her arrival at Ypres, so uncertain. Afraid.

Then, she'd had Captain Jamieson close by her side. For a moment, she could have imagined him still, and call to mind the talk they'd had about how God preferred to use His pawns above all other pieces when He played at chess with living men. "Is that because He sees into their hearts, and sees their braveness?" she had asked the captain then, in all her innocence, and he had said he hoped so. With the memory of his reassuring hand upon her shoulder, Anna tried to draw herself up bravely now, in hopes the eyes of Christ upon the crucifix might see within her heart and judge her worthy of this challenge.

When a real hand settled on her shoulder, Anna turned to meet Vice-Admiral Gordon's knowing gaze. He said, "You need not do this, if your mind has changed. You've but to say the word, and I will take you home again."

She shook her head. "I have not changed my mind." And then, because that sounded rather too determined, like a soldier setting out to face the worst, she found a smile that looked half natural, and said, "You need not worry. I am sure I will be happy here."

A man's voice added cheerfully, "If she is not, I'll know the reason why, and see it settled."

General Lacy was a tall man, and his high wig made him duck his head as he came through the doorway from the room beyond to greet them. "A good day to you, Vice-Admiral."

"General."

As the men shook hands, Anna was given her first close view of the general. She had seen him in the street, from time to time, but from a distance, and she never had been close enough to notice that his eyes were blue, like Gordon's, with the same deep creases at their corners, showing that he likely smiled more often than he frowned. He was handsome, though not quite as handsome as Vice-Admiral Gordon, to her eyes. His nose was slightly overlong, his eyes a trifle heavy lidded, but his charming smile and dimple chin would doubtless turn the heads of many women, nonetheless.

And there was something else about him, some rare force of personality that drew the eye and held it. Anna was not certain whether General Lacy had gained this from being in command, or whether it was this unspoken quality that made him such an excellent commander in the first place, for she knew that even Charles, who had small patience with the officers who ordered him about, considered General Lacy the best general in all Russia.

She had heard about his exploits in the recent war with Sweden, how he'd led his men in lightning raids all up and down that country's coast with devastating thoroughness, relying on the galleys that could row him close to shore and speed him off again before the Swedes could move their troops to stop him.

Vice-Admiral Gordon had kept busy in that war as well, and now both men were highly ranked and sitting daily in the colleges the late tsar had established for the running of the government—Gordon in the Admiralty, and Lacy in the College of War.

On any other day the men might easily have turned their talk to business, but today the general kept his handshake brief, and turned to Anna. "Mistress Jamieson, you honour us indeed. I am so pleased you did decide to come and be companion to my wife and children, for I fear I am myself poor company."

She doubted that. His eyes betrayed the quickness of his wit, and his good humour came through in the voice that yet retained the accent of his Irish homeland. She curtsied to him when he took her hand, and she addressed him with the proper title for his rank: "Your Excellency."

Lacy smiled. "It sounds a bit grand, does it not, for such a one as me? Let's not have that, within the house. You have my leave to simply call me 'General', as does this man here." He gave a nod to Gordon, and then looking Anna up and down more closely asked, "And do you never feed her, sir? 'Tis well for her she's landed in my household, for when Lent is done in two weeks' time she'll find our table generous, and she does appear to want a little fattening."

"She grows like that," said Gordon drily. "Feed her as you like, she'll eat it all and more besides and stay as slender as a reed. It will be books you must supply her with, for truly she reads more than any lass I've ever known."

The general's eyebrows lifted as he asked, "Indeed?"

Vice-Admiral Gordon answered with affection, "Aye, she fills her mind as she does fill her stomach, with whatever is to hand. I have found her as deeply engrossed in accounts of the methods for training good soldiers and seamen as in any lighter diversion."

The general turned to Anna. "So you have an interest in our military ways?"

It was not ladylike, she knew, to wish to learn about such things, but she did not feel judged by General Lacy's gaze, and so she answered him, "I find such things of interest, General, yes."

"Then I shall very much enjoy your stay with us," he said.

A woman's bright laugh sounded from the doorway just behind him. "You must not encourage him," she said to Anna, "for he has been known to lay the dinner table out as a great field of battle, so that he can illustrate his tactics."

The general's wife was pretty for her age, which must have been approaching forty. Even in her mourning dress she made a lively figure, and her tone and dancing eyes were just as friendly as her husband's. As she offered her small hand to Anna, she remarked in Russian, "You will doubtless think us very odd, and wish to reconsider your decision when you've been with us a few days."

Anna doubted it, and said as much aloud, in Russian also, adding, "Truly, I am honoured by your invitation, and I'm very pleased to help in any way I can."

The general's wife glanced upwards at her husband, and they shared a private smile before she told him, still in Russian, "You were right."

"Did I not tell you?" Switching smoothly into English, he advised his wife, "Sir Harry does not praise without good cause." And then to Anna, he explained, "Sir Harry Stirling told us yesterday at dinner that your Russian was as clear as any Muscovite's." The general looked at Gordon as he added, "He did also bring us news from his associates in London's Russia Company. It seems our friend's suspicions were correct, and we may yet receive a less than welcome visitor."

Vice-Admiral Gordon's frown appeared more thoughtful than displeased. "Do we know when?"

The general shook his head. "It is but in the wind, at present. But we can continue to prepare. Have you the time to sit awhile, and smoke a pipe? Then come, my friend. No doubt the ladies will be happy to be rid of us."

With that he bowed and took his leave, and Gordon brushed a kiss on Anna's cheek and warmly squeezed her hands, and searched her eyes a final time as though to reassure himself that she was fine with the arrangement. "Send word if you have need of me," he told her, in the brusque voice that she knew was how he masked his deep emotions. "I will call on you a few days hence to see that you are settled."

And with that he turned and left the room, discussing something in low tones with General Lacy while the general's wife regarded Anna with an understanding smile. In a gentle voice she said, "It is a hard thing, is it not, to leave one's home and come to live with strangers?"

Anna thought of all the times she'd done exactly that: The first time that was lost to her, obscured within her earliest of memories, when her mother had released her to the care of others who could guard her safety . . . and the time when she'd been swept up in the arms of Captain Jamieson, and carried from her cottage in the snow, along the cliffs above the Scottish sea . . . and when those same strong arms had last embraced her as he passed her to the sole care of the Irish nuns at Ypres . . . and when she'd journeyed to Calais in Father Graeme's care . . . and when she'd climbed aboard the carriage heading from that town, with Gordon sitting at her side, and half a year of gruelling travel yet ahead of her. So many homes, she thought. So many strangers. And yet all of them had brought her something she would not have missed for all the world, nor yet exchanged for idle comfort and security.

She gathered up her bundle of small treasured things more closely and replied with perfect honesty, "'Tis not so hard, with people who are kind."

The general's wife seemed pleased by that. She gently laid her hand on Anna's arm and said, "Come then, and let me show you to your room."

She felt faintly confused when she woke. Not because she was in a new room, with the windows and furnishings in unfamiliar positions, but because she had the certain sense that she was not alone.

She rolled against the blankets, looking warily around, and met a pair of large blue eyes that peered with curiosity from just above the level of the mattress.

When her heart had leaped and settled once again within her chest, she drew a breath and smiled. "Hello."

She had not yet met any of the children. Or at least, she had not yet been introduced to them. She'd heard them last night, certainly, but they had supped in private with the servant who was charged with taking care of them. "My dear," the general's wife had said, when Anna had enquired about the children, "it would never do to have them all descend on you at once, for though I love my children dearly, they are rather overwhelming."

Anna had returned the smile.

The general's wife, she'd learned, was from Livonia, and of high birth, and owned her own estate there that she'd shared with General Lacy since their marriage. She had lived there until lately with the children while the general led his army on campaigns, but since he'd now been two years in St. Petersburg and it appeared his duties would require him to be here awhile longer, she'd decided that the family should come join him. "Children need to have their father near," she'd said, and it was clear that General Lacy loved his children, for he'd spent much time in speaking of them, with so much enthusiasm Anna could now scarce recall the blur of names and ages and accomplishments.

She looked now at the wide blue eyes that watched her from beside the bed, and said again, "Hello."

The little girl did not smile back, but asked her in a hopeful tone, "Can you catch a bird without hurting it?"

Anna was fully awake now. She raised herself up on her elbows and focused more fully on the child who stood beside her bed—a pretty little girl with white-blond hair still tightly plaited down her back, and in her night-shift. She could have been no more than five or six.

Anna said, "I have never attempted it. Why?"

"There's a bird in our room."

Anna blinked. "Is there?"

"Yes. It flew in through the window and it won't go out," she said. "None of the servants will help, only Ned, and we can't fetch Mama because she's lying down. She lies down in the mornings, she doesn't feel well in the mornings because of the baby inside her, so Michael and Ned have been chasing the bird, but they're going to hurt it."

Anna sat up. "You say none of the servants is helping?"

"Just Ned. Da's already gone out, and the rest said that having a bird in the house was bad luck."

"Nonsense. Rather worse luck for the bird," Anna said, as she rose and shrugged into her coloured silk morning gown, wrapping it closely around her long night-shift and tying the sash before holding her hand to the child. "Show me where."

The child led her down the empty corridor. The general and his wife had bedchambers downstairs, and Anna was grateful for that, since the noise spilling out from the children's room could not have helped but disturb Mrs. Lacy if she had been trying to rest closer by. There were scuffling sounds and a high girlish shriek and the clatter and thud of an overturned chair, and a man's voice cursed lightly in words that should not have been said before children.

She opened the door on a scene that she might have thought comic if not for the worry that showed on the varied young faces all fixed on the grey-and-black crow flapping panicked from window to wall. There were four other children besides the one holding her hand, and all still in their nightclothes. The eldest, a boy, was already quite gangly and tall, on the brink of abandoning childhood, and clearly his father's son down to the feature; the next eldest would have been either the girl with the ringlets of gold or the boy at her side, who both looked to be nine or ten years of age, although the boy was a little bit smaller, all elbows and knees and continual motion. The youngest child, younger than even the girl who had come to fetch Anna, sat huddled on one of the beds with the blankets drawn tightly around her head, not looking up as the bird swooped and fluttered.

"Now, drive it to me, Michael, just like before," said the man who could only be Ned, the one servant who'd come to the aid of the children. Anna hadn't expected that he would be Irish, although she supposed it was not such an odd thing for men such as Lacy to want to employ their own countrymen. Vice-Admiral Gordon had once had a Scottish valet, and a coachman from Scotland besides, but they'd both been much older than this man.

She judged him to be not yet thirty, a lean man but broad-shouldered, with dark brown hair fastened back at the nape of his neck and his jaw darkly roughened with the morning's beard that he had not yet shaved. He wore neither waistcoat nor coat, only his unlaced shirt half-tucked into his breeches, and from the rapid rhythm of his breathing and his look of set determination Anna guessed that he'd been at this for some time.

The bird swooped once more and he dove for it, swearing again.

Anna said, "Will you please mind the use of your language in front of the children?"

He looked at her then, for the first time, his dark eyebrows lifting a little before he turned back to the task at hand, keeping his eyes on the bird in its flight.

The small girl at her side urged her into the chamber and shut the door firmly behind them before she announced, "I have brought Mistress Jamieson."

Not looking round, the man said, "Aye, she'll be a grand help, I can see that."

Anna, stung by his sarcasm, found herself in the uncommon position of not knowing how to reply. The servants of her own house, and Dmitri in particular, had sometimes given voice to their opinions, but they'd never shown her open disrespect.

She felt her temper rise, and when the man had tried and failed twice more to grab the crow as it flapped past, she told him archly, "You will never catch it that way."

"Will I not?" His last great lunge had winded him. He stood now half bent over with his hands braced just above his knees, and turned his head to look at her. His face was not unpleasant, and might even have seemed handsome to some women, but she only saw the challenge in it.

"No," she said. "It is too badly frightened."

At her side the little girl looked up and let out a small cry. "It's hurt! It has a hurt leg, look!"

The crow was trying now to perch and settle, but no matter where it came to rest it could not seem to grasp the surface and its one leg dragged so awkwardly it threw the bird off balance, sent it flapping to the ceiling once again.

In calm tones Anna told the child, "Go to your little sister, now, and tell her not to be afraid. 'Tis but a bird, and does not mean you harm."

It was, in fact, a hooded crow, with black wings and a vest of ashen grey, and had she shared the superstitions of the servants she might well have shared their fears as well, for hooded crows were widely seen as heralds of ill fortune. But she did not hold to superstitions, and she only saw a wounded and exhausted creature, losing strength.

She told the children, "Will you all sit down, please. Be as quiet as you can."

The boys, as boys would do, looked first to Ned to see his own reaction, and a moment passed before he gave a silent sort of laugh and settled in a nearby chair to watch her with the certain eyes of one who thinks to see another fail.

When all were seated, Anna stood alone and waited for the crow to calm.

Ned murmured, "Well, what now? Will you then charm it with a song, to fly down to your hand?"

Again his tone amazed her, and she briefly dropped her gaze to him, and told him, "You are insolent."

"Aye, frequently." His eyes were laughing at her now, and too familiar.

Anna looked away, refusing to allow him satisfaction. For a minute more, the crow flapped round the ceiling in confusion, and then all at once it dropped down with a flutter to the floor, and hopped and limped and dragged its leg in ever smaller circles, till at length it came to rest not ten feet from where Anna stood, collapsing there in weariness.

She tugged once at the loose end of the sash of her silk morning gown, and slipped it from her shoulders as she took a cautious step towards the bird, and then another. It flapped once, and shuffled farther off, and might have taken once more to the wing if she had not, in one swift motion, tossed the morning gown on top of it and knelt to wrap the fabric round and gather up the crow with care, while speaking soothing words to it.

"There now," she said. "There now, you will be well, there is no need to be afraid." Securely swaddled in the folds of coloured silk, the bird tipped its head sharply up to look at her with one bright eye, its long beak moving silently as though it sought to speak.

The room was silent, too, until at once the children started speaking all together, and pressed round her for a close look at the captive crow. This was not at all, thought Anna, how she'd planned to meet the general's children, yet she likely could have done no better for a first impression, since it was soon obvious that all of them, from half-grown Michael to the smallest of the girls, now brave enough to venture from her blankets, thought what Anna had accomplished was no ordinary feat.

The oldest girl said, "But we cannot put it out of doors again, not in the snow, not till its leg has healed."

The brother closest to her age was in agreement. "Can you fix it, Ned?"

The children parted for the man as he came forward. Close, he seemed much taller. Anna did not wish to meet his gaze and so encourage any further insolence, nor was there any safer place to focus her attention, for his chest was covered only by a holland shirt and that unlaced. Instead she looked down as his hands reached, not to take the bird away from her, but simply, and with unexpected gentleness, to turn the wrappings slightly so that he could peel a fold of cloth away to see the injured leg.

His hands were browned as though from being in the sun, and

strongly shaped, and in a line across the knuckles of his left hand rose a narrow ridge of scarring that she could not seem to look away from.

"Yes," he told the children finally. "I can fix this."

Arrogance again, she thought. And yet she felt relief as well, and gladly passed the crow to him, still wrapped within her morning gown. And then, in an attempt to re-establish proper boundaries, she instructed him, "Then go and do so, please. And send a housemaid, if you would, to help us set the room to rights before the children's mother wakes."

He did not answer straight away, and glancing up she noticed that his eyes once more appeared to be amused, and had a light in them that made her feel aware that she was standing there in no more than a night-shift, with her hair undone in curls about her shoulders. Though she felt her colour rising she returned his gaze with coolness, and he gave a nod that managed to both honour her and mock her as he said, "Yes, Mistress Jamieson."

And with the bird held safely to his chest he turned and left, and Anna had the strangest feeling that, although she'd seemed to score the point, she'd somehow lost the game.

chapter
THIRTY

I wasn't sure why Rob had stopped, until he gave his watch a tap and told me, "You'll be late for your appointment."

I'd forgotten. It was not a long walk back, but I was glad I'd worn flat shoes and not the high heels I'd been contemplating earlier this morning. As it was, we reached the entrance to the Hermitage with a full fifteen minutes to spare.

The wind off the Neva was sharp, but at least it had scattered the dull bank of clouds and the sun had come out, shining brightly against a great wedge of blue sky. In the sunlight, the Hermitage glittered like something straight out of a fairy tale, one of the loveliest palaces left in the world with its green and white walls and the gilded trim and those innumerable windows that looked to the river.

Its grand front steps were, as usual, clogged with a great queue of tourists and visitors waiting in groups for admission. Rob hung back.

"You'll be working," he told me. "I'd just be a bother. I'll wander about, I'll be fine."

"Are you sure?"

"Aye, I'm sure. You can just come and find me," he said, "when you're finished."

I nodded, and went on ahead.

I'd met Yuri, Sebastian's friend, twice before this. A senior research associate in the museum's Department of Russian Culture, Yuri had helped me to authenticate the portrait by Makovsky that now hung above my desk, and he'd taken us to dinner once. He was a friendly man, with earnest eyes behind his gold-rimmed glasses, and a wild shock of thick black hair that stubbornly refused to settle into any style. Greeting me with the traditional kiss, he drew back and asked, in Russian, "Will we speak Russian or English today?"

"Russian, Yuri Stepanovich." Smiling, I said, "I'm in need of the practice."

"Then I will give you practice. Come up to the office, it will be better to speak there. More comfortable, and much more private."

Privacy was something that the main rooms of the Winter Palace couldn't offer. Built during the reigns of later eighteenth-century empresses, some years after the time in which Rob and I had just "found" Anna, this was the largest of the six buildings that made up the State Museum of the Hermitage, and inside, it held all the grandeur of a Windsor or Versailles. The ceilings soared, the windows turned the light to something magical, and every surface seemed to be in competition with the next—the painted murals gazing down, the polished columns, malachite and marble and rare woods and gold leaf everywhere. The whole effect was dazzling.

But it also drew enormous crowds each day, with tour groups jostling one another as they shuffled after their official guides, all giving scripted talks in a cacophony of languages while leading their own charges through the warren of the galleries beneath the watchful gazes of the women who sat hour after hour at the doorways of each room to see that no one broke the rules.

The Hermitage owned some three million artifacts and artworks, and even though the items on display were maybe only 5 percent of that, I'd figured from my own past visits here that it would take me years to see them all, but every tourist I could see appeared to be making a brave effort to do just that. Some, who were clearly mid-tour, looked exhausted. The noise and the heat and the bustle exhausted me more than anything else, and Yuri's small office, tucked back in a non-public corridor, felt like a welcome retreat.

It had absorbed a little of his personality, and had a pleasant, rumpled and relaxed feel that invited me to simply shift the papers from a chair and take a seat.

"Here." He passed me a catalog for the exhibit itself, newly printed and smelling of freshly cut paper and ink. "I have sent one of these to Sebastian already, but this can be your copy. You'll find your Surikov in there, on page thirty-three."

I was still studying the cover. "This is beautiful. It's by Polenov, isn't it?"

"Yes. From the time that he lived in his house in the forest, with Repin, in Normandy. He painted several like this, with the road through the trees."

The detail they had chosen for the cover showed a solitary peasant, seen from behind, strolling off along that road, with sunlight breaking through the rain-grey clouds ahead of him. I'd seen another painting by this artist, with a peasant and a donkey on the same road, but the solitary man did seem a perfect fit for the exhibit's title: "Wandering Still: the works of the Peredvizhniki beyond Russia's borders."

As I started to search through the catalog's pages for page thirty-three, Yuri said, "We have put the exhibit itself in the Menshikov Palace. The official opening is not until Tuesday, so the big ceremony will be then, with the two curators from Paris and New York, and our director, but on Sunday there will also be a small preview reception for some of our International Friends of the Hermitage, you should come to that."

"There's no way I could meet Wendy Van Hoek before then, is there?"

Yuri smiled. "She does not arrive until later tonight. But tomorrow we're hanging the final few paintings, your Surikov among them, and she's asked to watch. It would be a good time for you to meet her. I'll arrange it, if you like."

"That would be perfect. Thank you." I glanced at him over the catalog. "What is she like?"

"Miss Van Hoek? Like her father," he said. "Did you meet him? No? Well, he was passionate, very obsessed with his paintings. He viewed them as part of his family. And she has this passion as well. But," he added, as he swivelled back in his own chair, "she also loves living well, travelling, and this needs money."

"So you think she might be willing to sell this one painting, then?"

"To the right buyer, I think that she might be persuaded, yes." Yuri half-smiled. "Only not to Sebastian."

"I gathered that."

"Ah, so he told you?"

"He didn't give details," I said. "All he said was that Wendy Van Hoek didn't like him much."

"Not much, no." Yuri's smile was so broad now that I couldn't help but be curious.

"What did Sebastian do?"

"He didn't tell me, either. I was hoping you would know. From the first time I met them, they've been on the knives," he said, using the Russian expression for people who shared a dislike for each other. "It can happen with people, sometimes. Anyway, it was a wise thing he did, sending you."

I wasn't sure "wise" was the word that applied here, so much as "convenient" or even "self-serving," but I never questioned my boss's decisions in public. Instead, I replied with a vague nod and flipped the last catalog pages to see, close up, what I was meant to be buying for Vasily.

It wasn't an actual painting, a full composition, but rather a "study" of one of the faces the artist intended to paint in a larger work, rendered with great care in oil on canvas the size of a magazine cover.

Yuri, watching my face, knew that I'd found the Surikov. "It is incredibly beautiful, isn't it?"

"Yes. Yes, it is." My gaze didn't lift from the face of the old bearded man on the page, his eyes downcast with dignity, and just the top edge of what I assumed was a scroll of some kind showing down at the bottom, as though he were reading from something. I said, "This is one of the bishops, then? From the mural he did of the . . . what was it, the First or Second Ecumenical Council?"

"That one's from the second, in the year 381," Yuri told me. "I'm impressed. You've done your homework."

"I do try." I smiled. "I like to know the history of a piece."

I knew there'd been four murals painted by Surikov, back in the late 1870s, one for each of the four ancient councils at which the rules and creeds and shape of Christianity itself had been debated and decided by the Church's leading clerics. Those murals had graced Moscow's Cathedral of Christ the Saviour for over half a century, until on Stalin's orders the cathedral had been dynamited, totally destroyed.

There'd been no room in Stalin's Russia for religion, or the art that was a part of it.

Only one mural had managed somehow to escape the destruction, along with the sketches in pencil on paper that Surikov had made to show those who'd hired him what he planned to paint.

From those sketches, we knew what the murals had probably looked like. Two of the sketches had come up at auction a few years ago. Yuri showed me a picture of one of them now, from a file he'd set out on his desk. "You can see here," he said, "this one bishop who's standing and reading the scroll to the others, this is clearly the same man we see in the study in oils. I believe that it's Gregory, Bishop of Constantinople, perhaps even reading his famous speech."

There, he had lost me. I asked, "Famous speech?"

"Yes, you don't know this story? He made many enemies, Gregory did, and a lot of the bishops opposed him, and so he resigned, saying he was like Jonah the prophet, who brought the great storm because he did not wish to deliver the bad news God sent him to carry, and that he was willing, like Jonah, to be cast out, sacrificed, if it was needed. But first, he delivered his finest oration. I think," Yuri said, "this is what we see here, in this mural."

I studied the print of the sketch, and compared it again to the face in the work in the catalog. "I think you're right."

"He has good taste, this client of yours."

I agreed. But it went beyond that, for Vasily, I knew. He had personal reasons for wanting this painting, and when I explained them to Yuri he nodded with new understanding.

"Then I think you may have an excellent chance of convincing Miss Van Hoek to sell you this piece. She is also very sentimental."

"We can hope." I didn't want to overstay my welcome. Yuri was polite enough to sit here talking with me half the day, but I knew that he kept a busy schedule, so I closed my catalog and stood. "This was so kind of you, Yuri Stepanovich. I really do appreciate it."

With a very Russian shrug he said, "It was my pleasure. Have you somewhere you must go at once, or would you like to visit your young man?"

I know I stared at him a moment, wondering how on earth he knew I'd come with Rob, and why he'd mention it. And then the penny dropped, and I remembered who he meant.

I grinned. "Yes, please. I'd love to."

My "young man" was not a person but a painting of a person, hanging on a wall below us in a room on the first floor. It was my favourite of the Russian paintings here, not as important as the larger and more celebrated canvases that easily commanded their own walls and had been lighted so that people could admire them, but this modest portrait did for me what all the best art did: It drew me in, and held me captivated.

Yuri said, "It's too bad we don't have a copy of this in our gift shop, since you're fond of it."

Flattered he'd remembered just how fond of it I was, from my last trip here, I replied, "I really don't mind coming here to visit him. And anyway, it wouldn't be the same. A print would never have this kind of depth." Even though I was with Yuri, I could feel the keen eyes of the woman supervisor seated in the corner settle on me out of habit as I leant a little closer to the portrait. "I always wonder," I told Yuri, "who he was, and how he lived, and what it was about him that caught Briullov's eye."

"You see, for me it is the people who have owned the painting," Yuri said, "that always make me wonder. What their lives were like, and how they came to have this. Why they let it go." As though inspired by my own fascination with the portrait, he looked closer, too. "A painting like this would have witnessed a great many things. It's a pity we can't see what it has seen, over the years."

I could tell him, I knew. I could touch it and tell him who'd owned it, and give him a glimpse of their lives. What surprised me was not that I realized the fact, but how much I was actually tempted to do it. My hand almost lifted and I had to catch myself, not wanting to alarm the woman supervisor.

Even after Yuri had excused himself and gone back to his work, I lingered awhile longer in my study of the portrait, and the urge to touch it was a thing that took some effort to control.

Only a week ago, I'd been half-dreading holding the Firebird carving a second time, and it rattled me now that the wanting to touch and to learn was becoming a kind of compulsion.

That feeling didn't lessen when I left the painting and the room and wound my way back through the crowded galleries. *Come find me*, Rob had said, and yet my mind was too distracted to allow for focused searching, so I didn't try.

I slowed my steps in the Pavillion Hall, a soaring bright space with a high open gallery running around it, supported by rows of white columns and graceful vaults patterned with gleaming gold leaf. From the intricate pale parquet floors to the light-coloured marble and elegant high-arched French windows that looked out across the broad Neva, this was a space that spoke to me of privilege and of royalty. I felt the pull of other voices speaking, too, and trying to be heard.

The other tourists here were mostly clustered round the great gold clock shaped like a peacock, housed in its own cage of glass, or standing to admire the large mosaic set into the floor.

Beneath a giant crystal chandelier, I knelt as though to readjust the heel strap of my shoe, rested one hand on the parquet floor to brace myself, and for a moment, closed my eyes.

The images began to rise, to form into their filmstrip, running backwards in a blur. I tried remembering what Rob had taught me—concentrating hard, I stopped the film and tried to run it forwards, frame by frame. It nearly worked, but then I lost it and the images began to blur again, and . . .

"Miss?" A man's voice interrupted; wrenched me back. "Are you okay?" He was American, an older man, his face and voice concerned. "Do you need help?"

A woman I assumed must be his wife had stopped as well, and others from their group had turned to look. Flushed with embarrassment, I shook my head and stood, assuring him that I was fine. "My shoe . . . ," I offered, as an explanation, and he gave a friendly nod and, when I'd thanked him once again, moved on, allowing me a clear view of the doorway at the far end of the hall, and of the man who stood within it.

Rob, in contrast to the other tourists here, looked fully capable of walking round all day. If he was bothered by the heat, he didn't show it. But I caught his edge of restlessness.

You ready?

With a nod, I went to meet him.

How'd your meeting go?

Fine.

As we walked down the great Jordan staircase, he watched me instead of admiring the opulence. *Are you okay?*

Yes, I'm fine. Why is everyone asking me that?

He responded with silence, and striving for something more normal I asked him aloud, "What did you find to look at, while I was away?"

"Oh, a lot of things. I spent most of my time coveting Nicholas the Second's library. Have you seen it?"

I had. An English Gothic haven, rich with walnut shelves and leather, with a staircase and a fireplace, it appealed to me as well.

Rob carried on, "And there were rooms not far from that with some of Peter the Great's own things in them. I found those fair interesting. Not only his swords, but a few of his nautical instruments, tools for his woodworking, and his old lathes. I had no idea," he said, "that he was such a regular guy."

"That he liked making things with his own hands, you mean? Oh yes, Peter was famous for that. He'd go down to the shipyards and roll up his sleeves and start building the ships right along with the workmen. And it wasn't only big things. Did you see the ivory chande-lier he partly carved himself from walrus tusks? It's really something."

"Next time," was his promise. He fell quiet for a minute more, and then, as we were passing by the gift shop on our way towards the exit, he asked, "Was it something interesting you saw?" To my deliberately blank face, he said, to clarify, "Upstairs. Just now."

I couldn't lie. "I couldn't do it properly. I didn't have you there to help."

"You did it fine last night."

Last night I'd touched the wall myself, perhaps, but Rob had still been holding me, and amplifying what I did. "Last night you helped as well."

"Not much."

"That's your opinion. Anyway, it hardly matters, does it?"

Rob, not fooled, returned the question. "Does it?"

Not at all, I wanted to reply. Because it shouldn't have. For all that I might envy Rob the things that he could do, they had no place in my own life. My normal life.

I sidestepped round it. "Not for what we're doing now. There's nothing left of General Lacy's house that I can touch, is there? It's all on your shoulders."

"For now." With a shrug of those shoulders he followed me out through the exit and into the bustle and flow of the Neva Embank-ment. His hands in his pockets, he looked to the west, past the dome of the Admiralty. I sensed he was keen to go back, to pick up where we'd left Anna earlier, but as though he had tapped into my own vague frustrations and wanted to give me some time to recover myself, to find balance, he brought his gaze patiently back to mine, lifting an eyebrow. "What time does the pie shop start serving lunch?"

chapter
THIRTY-ONE

Anna felt more like herself when she came down for dinner at noon. More composed. She had tamed her hair under its small black lace pinner and wore the black paduasoy gown and petticoat that had been given to her by the vice-admiral's late wife. "It no longer fits me as well as it did," Mrs. Gordon had told her while running her hand down the black corded silk, "but the paduasoy is from Spain and will last a good while yet. A black gown can be of a great many uses."

Her words had been sadly prophetic, for not three months later the vice-admiral's wife had been dead of her illness and Anna had worn the black paduasoy gown while standing with Jane at the funeral. She'd worn it while mourning, and worn it for Jane's funeral, too, but the gown, far from carrying sadness, instead gave her comfort, as if she'd been given not only the gown but the kindness and grace of the woman who'd worn it.

And now, as she entered the dining room, she tried to show that same grace as she greeted the Lacys. The general escorted her round to her chair at the table, then saw his wife seated and took his own chair at the opposite end. Mrs. Lacy looked paler than she had the night before. Anna had seen women suffer the first months of being with child, and she knew that the suffering lasted sometimes till the child had quickened. She hoped it would not be that way for the general's wife.

As if aware of her thoughts, Mrs. Lacy smiled. "I have endured this a great many times, Mistress Jamieson. 'Tis but a small price to pay for so rich a reward," she remarked in her beautifully accented English. "I gather you did meet my children, earlier this morning?"

"Yes, I did. They were most charming."

"And most secretive," she said, "about the details of your meeting, but I see you have emerged unscathed."

The general asked, "You met them all at once? Brave girl."

"She seems to have impressed them," Mrs. Lacy told her husband. "Katie asked if we could keep her."

"Well, then." General Lacy, in amusement, said, "Perhaps we shall."

There were two other places set at table—one across from Anna, and one to her left, to show that more guests were expected. One arrived a minute later.

"Father Dominic," the general introduced the middle-aged Franciscan friar, whose brown robe and tonsured head evoked a stir of memories. The Franciscans were not Capuchins, though Capuchins did count themselves as members of that order, having splintered from the main Franciscan body some two centuries ago. There had been Capuchins here in St. Petersburg till lately, and the sight of their long hoods and beards had always raised the thought of Father Graeme in her mind, but there'd been quarrels between them and the Franciscans and the tsar had, in an edict that had been one of his last, ordered the Capuchins to leave, just this past January.

That left only the Franciscans now to serve the small community of Catholics in St. Petersburg, some preaching at the Catholic church in Greek Street and the chapel for the French on Vasilievsky Island, while others could be found, like Father Dominic, with private families, serving there as tutors for the children, and as chaplains.

Father Dominic, like all his order, was clean-shaven, and his eyes, though not unkind, held none of Father Graeme's humour.

When they'd waited some few minutes longer for the final guest, the general gave the nod of one accustomed to decision making. "Father, will you say the blessing, please?"

"Of course."

The blessing was a lengthy one, but Anna kept her head discreetly bent, as did the others. When the floorboards creaked behind her she thought little of it, until a man's leg came suddenly into the edge of her vision—a strong-looking leg clad in black woolen breeches, a black stocking rolled up and over the knee band, the fall of a black coat pushed out of the way as the man slid with stealth onto the chair beside her own.

Not wanting to put a foot wrong on her first day, she kept her gaze downcast until Father Dominic said his "Amen." Only then did she give rein to her curiosity, glancing sideways and up at the newcomer, who with his own head respectfully bent was just finishing crossing himself.

His head lifted. His eyes briefly angled to hers, and he winked before looking away as the general's wife brightly said,

"Edmund, I thought you had forgotten us."

The general smiled. "No kin of mine," he told his wife, "would think to miss his dinner."

"No indeed." The man at Anna's side spoke easily, without a hint of deference in his tone. "And never during Lent. If you'll forgive me, Father."

Father Dominic asked lightly, "Have you been committing some new sin?"

"I have not, as it happens. I've been caring for a bird, and surely even your St. Francis would approve of that? He preached to the birds, did he not?"

Mrs. Lacy replied, "Yes, he certainly did. Mistress Jamieson, may I present Mr. Edmund O'Connor, my husband's relation, who lately has journeyed from Spain."

Anna somehow remembered her manners, and nodded her head and said, "Mr. O'Connor."

His dark eyes were not disrespectful, exactly, but neither were they like the eyes of a gentleman. More like the eyes of a rogue. "Mistress Jamieson," he said. "Your servant." The stress on that final word, meant just for her ears, was clearly intentional.

Not paying heed to the charge in the air, Mrs. Lacy asked, "What sort of bird was it, Edmund?"

Anna thought he paused before replying, and she wondered whether that was because Mrs. Lacy, being from Livonia, might share the superstitions of the Russians when it came to hooded crows.

The pause was not a long one. Smoothly he replied, "An injured one. It took a while to find a place to keep it, where it would be safe."

"And what," Mrs. Lacy went on, "did you use for a cage?"

"The same cage that we used for the rabbits."

The general reminded him, "We ate the rabbits."

"Aye, that's why I've hidden the bird," came the dry answer.

Wine was poured. Father Domenic, keeping to water and bread for his Lenten meals, would not take any, but Anna was glad of it, passing her cup out of habit across the small glass bowl of water set out at her side before taking her first sip, a gesture that did not escape General Lacy's keen eye.

"Mistress Jamieson, I see you drink to the health of the king who lives over the water," he said.

Anna lowered her cup. "General, I drink the health of the only true king."

"Ah." The general looked down the long table as he passed his own wine cup over his water bowl. "One more for our side," he said to his wife.

Beside Anna, the dark eyes of Edmund O'Connor held innocent as he remarked, "Aye, if ever the king is in need of a bird catcher, your Mistress Jamieson here will do well for him."

Anna, refusing to let him embarrass her, answered him calmly, "At least I did catch the bird."

"And I'd have caught it as well, had I used your technique, but I thought that removing my shirt, and in front of the children, might just be improper."

She coloured a little beneath the raised eyebrows, although she perceived that the eyebrows were raised as much by the plain fact they were arguing as by the argument's content.

The general's wife, trying to hide her astonishment, looked at her husband. "Well."

"Quite." Exchanging a glance with her, he settled back like a spectator at an amusement, and said, "Shall we have some more wine?"

"He delights in provoking me," Anna complained three days later when Mary, the vice-admiral's daughter, stopped in for an afternoon visit. Stabbing the seam of the sleeve she was piecing together with needle and thread, Anna said, "I can hardly request to sit elsewhere at dinner, for then he would triumph. And sitting across from him would prove no better than sitting beside him, and might be still worse, for I'd then have to look at him."

Mary said, "I know of some who would claim 'tis no hardship to look at him."

Anna's eyes rolled. "He himself would be first to claim that, I've no doubt."

"He's certainly more handsome than your Mr. Taylor."

"Mr. Taylor is not mine," said Anna, with great patience, as she drew the needle through the lovely grey-green silk. "And I should imagine whatever good looks God gave Mr. O'Connor were merely to compensate for what he lacks in his nature."

They were sitting in the small blue chamber next to Mrs. Lacy's, with the shutters of its windows fully open to the light. The door stood open, too, and Mary looked at it with meaning, before Anna said, "There's no one who can hear me. Mrs. Lacy is asleep now, and the boys are at their lessons, and the girls are with their dancing master."

"Not the same one who instructed us, I hope?"

"No. This one comes from Holstein."

"Not the Terror from Vienna, then. It is a wonder that we learnt to dance at all," said Mary, with a shudder of remembrance. Picking up the dropped thread of their conversation, she asked, "What of Mr. O'Connor, then? Is he not at home?"

"He does not live here," Anna said. "He lives in lodgings, near Sir Harry's house."

"Ah. That would then explain it."

"Explain what?"

"Why he is suddenly become a favourite subject of the gossip of the merchants' wives. They must observe him every day, if he does live so close to them."

The next stitch wanted care, and Anna bent her head to concentrate. "And what is it they say?"

"Well," Mary, always loving gossip, told her, "I did hear it rumoured he had little choice in leaving Spain; his friends there cast him out."

"And why was that?"

"Some say he used a woman ill, and left her sadly ruined."

"Oh? And what do others say?"

"That he did kill a man."

She had no time for rumours. "With his sword, or with his tongue?" she quipped. "They are both sharp enough."

That drew a smile from Mary. "I confess I do not know. I'll ask them."

"No, I pray you do not bother. You should keep clear of the merchants' wives, at any rate," was Anna's firm advice. "I wish that any man who views us as the gentler sex could spend an hour with Mrs. Hewitt and her friends. He'd soon reform his views."

"If he survived," said Mary, with a laugh. "But I cannot, in all good conscience, speak ill of the merchants' wives, when I may one day join their number."

Anna glanced up. "Why? What merchant now has caught your eye?"

Mary had already furrowed her brow into one of her small but becoming frowns, and now deflected the question by musing, "So then Mr. O'Connor has lodgings of his own, and yet he dines here every day? I wonder why?"

"I should have said from laziness, except I now believe it is the sport of baiting me that he enjoys." She pricked her finger with an overzealous stitch, and rested both hands for a moment, asking Mary, "Am I truly so amusing to annoy?"

"Well," Mary said, "in perfect honesty, you *do* rise rather well to any argument."

"'Tis hardly the accomplishment I wished to show the general and his wife."

"They must not mind," was Mary's reasoning. "They've kept you this entire week without the least complaint. And General Lacy told Papa two days ago how very taken with you Mrs. Lacy was, and that you'd been—and I do quote his words exactly, now—'a welcome light around the house.'"

She felt a wash of pride. "Then," she told Mary, "I shall bite my tongue more firmly, and endure Mr. O'Connor."

"Put him in his place, more like. You are still ranked above him, after all."

With a shrug, Anna bent her head over her work again, saying, "I've no rank at all. I am Anna Niktova, and if I tried putting on airs there are those who would swiftly remind me of that. But," she said, "if I have no rank and he has no manners, then we are evenly matched."

chapter THIRTY-TWO

S he had his queen.

The chessboard lay between them like a battlefield, its armies stripped and decimated, some reduced to standing at the edge and watching helplessly. She'd played the black men, as she always did. Edmund O'Connor, clearly thinking that by playing the white pieces he'd be gaining the advantage, had advised her in his condescending way to choose again, but having spent these several years defending her own black-haired king she would not be persuaded now to change. And now her king stood proud behind the safety of his castle, with a bishop and a knight to guard him well.

Edmund O'Connor frowned, and leaning forward rested both his elbows on the table's edge as he surveyed the board. He'd shed his coat when she had captured his last knight, and sat now in his plain black woolen waistcoat and his shirtsleeves, with the cuffs rolled up his forearms in the manner of a working man.

The general, who had pulled his own chair round and brought it close to better watch the game, smiled faintly but said nothing. There were only the three of them left in the drawing-room, now. Father Dominic commonly took to his bed early, and Mrs. Lacy had gone up herself not long afterwards, and now the candles had burned an inch lower in all of the great round brass sconces that hung on the walls of the room, like gold mirrors reflecting the warmth of the light.

That same light caught the angle of Edmund O'Connor's black eyelashes and slanted shadows across the hard line of his cheek as he looked for an opening . . . looked for it . . .

There, Anna thought. He had seen it.

He lifted the one pawn he hadn't yet moved from its starting position and set it with confidence two spaces forward, so that it came level with her own black pawn on the next square.

She smiled. Her own pawn slid forward and on the diagonal, taking the empty square his pawn had crossed as she captured his piece with a satisfied hand.

He objected. "Now, see, you can't do that. My pawn can go two spaces on its first move, so it didn't set foot on that square."

"I assure you it did, sir. It may not have stopped on that square, but the rules do assume that it crossed it, and so my own pawn is permitted to capture it as it goes by. It is called," she said, "capturing *en passant*, and is a fair move."

"Is it, now?" He sat back, and his dark gaze fell somewhere between irritation and grudging respect. "And you'd know about fair, would you?"

Smiling more broadly, the general said, "She drew you in, my boy. She knew you'd want your queen back, so she cleared you a path and you took it. Mind you, 'twas a greater mistake when you gave her your queen to begin with."

"She only got my queen because I thought she meant to take my knight."

"She did that very neatly, I did notice. It can be a useful military tactic in the field, to misdirect the enemy."

"Is that a fact?"

"It is," the general said. "We did the same thing at Poltava."

The younger man gave a mock groan. "Oh, it's never Poltava again, is it?"

"It was a great battle. One of my greatest, in fact. I was wounded. That gives me the right to repeat the tale daily, should I have a mind to." His voice and his eyes were both rich with the sly humour Anna was growing accustomed to. "I do feel sure Mistress Jamieson, with her fine martial mind, would not find my tale dull."

"Mistress Jamieson," Edmund O'Connor remarked, "could most likely relate it herself, if she's lived here in Russia since she was a child.

I myself have been here but a handful of months, and already I know more than any man needs to about that one battle."

That battle, as Anna knew well, had been Russia's own Battle of Bannockburn—a turning point many believed would long echo in history, the better to savour because the invading Swedes had been defeated on Russia's own soil.

Anna told the general, "I was but a babe in Scotland then. And I have never heard the story but from men who simply did as they were ordered, not from anyone who had a larger part in it. Pray, tell me all you like about Poltava."

Smiling, he decided, "Well, perhaps not all. But how you captured Edmund's queen was not unlike the way we got our men across the Vorskla. Here, I'll show you." Reaching forward, General Lacy started rearranging pieces on the chessboard, over Edmund's dry objection.

"We were not yet done with that."

"Of course you were. Surrender was your only option, lad, there is no honour in denying it. I'm saving you embarrassment." He made a neat square of the rooks, directly in the centre of the board. "We'll say this is the village of Poltava, under siege," he said, and set the white king with a small force just below it. "Charles, the Swedish king, was here, encamped with all his troops. Our armies had assembled on the far shore of the Vorskla River, opposite the Swedes." A tight line of black chessmen gathered down the board's one edge. "We had to get across, but they outnumbered us, and in the water all our men and horses would be vulnerable. So what to do?" He looked from Anna's face to Edmund's, waiting for an answer.

Edmund said, "You cross at night, and choose a place where they won't see you."

"But they knew we had to cross, and so they always watched us. They were waiting for it. We could not surprise them."

He had looked again to Anna, and she tried, but in the end confessed, "I know you said this has to do with how I took the queen, but I cannot connect the two events."

"I'll help you, then. If you did seek to capture Edmund's queen," the general asked, "why did you send your bishop to the far side of the board?"

"Because I wanted his attention to be there, and not upon his queen."

"Precisely."

She began to see his purpose. "Did you draw the Swedish sentries off, then, with a ruse?"

'We did exactly that. We feigned a crossing of the river here, downstream, below the village, and that brought the Swedes out in response, as we had hoped it would, to fire at us and hold us back. Or so they thought. Because while they were shooting at a small part of our forces here," he said, "the whole remainder of our army secretly swung north, and crossed the Vorskla all unnoticed." As he moved the black chess pieces in an illustration of the tactic, something else occurred to him. "And furthermore, the King of Sweden, who was also fooled by our false crossing and had ridden south himself to hold us back, was shot so badly in his foot that day he could not lead his troops upon the final field of battle." With a movement of his hand, he toppled Edmund's white king. "There are many who will say he lost Poltava, and the Northern War, because of it."

"And all because they had no eyes to see what you were really doing," Edmund said.

"Oh, they had eyes." The general settled back into his chair. "That's how we managed to deceive them. They expected us to try to cross that river, in the same way you expected Mistress Jamieson to try to take your knight." He asked, as an aside to Anna, "Why was he expecting you to take his knight, do you think, Mistress Jamieson?"

She knew full well, from looking at the general's face, that he had seen the purpose of each move of every piece upon the board, and so she did not bother, as she sometimes did with other men, to mask her own intelligence. "Mr. O'Connor was trying to capture my own queen," she told him, "by setting his knight out as bait."

Anna saw Edmund's head turn at that; felt the weight of his stare.

General Lacy went on, "So you turned his own scheming against him. And you, Edmund, saw what you wanted to see. That was no more nor less than what happened," he said, "at Poltava. The secret to keeping one's actions concealed from the enemy is, in most cases, to learn what he thinks you will do, and then seem to be doing it, for that is what he'll believe."

Anna saw the sense in that, and would have asked the general further questions if he had not been distracted by the movements of the younger man beside him, setting up the chessboard pieces once again.

"And what," the general asked him, "are you doing?"

"Putting your advice to use." He set the white king firmly on its square behind the pawns, and looked at Anna as a man might look when crossing swords with someone he considered equal to the challenge. "Let us see if Mistress Jamieson can learn my thoughts this time around." The dark eyes were an open dare. "Before I learn her own."

"You have impressed my husband," Mrs. Lacy said to Anna the next afternoon. "He told me if you were a boy he'd have you in a uniform and serving in his regiment before the snow could melt."

Anna smiled, and took her seat upon the stool behind the harpsichord. "In truth, when I was young I often wished that I could be a soldier."

"Oh, my dear, why ever would you wish a thing like that? It is a wretched life. I cannot count how many months my husband has been forced to live away from us, because he was away and fighting, sometimes for a year and more. It is a burden for the man," she said, "and for his family." With a look around the drawing-room—the silk-lined walls, the Dutch tiled stove, the portraits and the curtains, she remarked, "My sisters told me I was mad, to come here with the children. Our estate at Loeser is much more . . . well, it is very grand, and comfortable. Nothing like St. Petersburg. But this is better, all of us together here. Or nearly all." Her smile turned briefly sad before she forced herself to brighten. "I have an elder daughter, from my first marriage. Beata. She is living with her father's family now, in Sweden. She is very near your age. You might be friends, were you to meet."

The words escaped from Anna before she could think to hold them back. "Do not you wish to bring her here?" she asked. "To have her with you?"

It was impudent, she knew, and she should not have asked the question, but the answer seemed of curious importance to her, as though Mrs. Lacy could somehow help reveal what Anna's own mother had felt those years ago. How she might still be feeling.

"Yes," the general's wife said, very quietly. "I wish it more than anything. But where my daughter is, the opportunities are greater. She will make a better marriage there, and have a better life." She looked at Anna as though not supposing she'd be understood. "It is the price of raising children that we must one day release them, sons to their own destinies, and daughters to the hands of others whom we hope will love and care for them. We can but try, along the way, to choose what we think best for them. And no choice," she told Anna, "is an easy one."

In the silence following, it seemed to Anna that the other woman was about to ask a question of her own, and so to change the focus of their talk she put her fingers to the keyboard of the harpsichord and tried to do again what she'd been shown the day before.

"That's very good," said Mrs. Lacy. "Only try to hold yourself as still as possible, and keep your fingers close above the keys. You do not need to give much pressure, you will feel the strings as they are plucked."

She did. It was an odd sensation, but ladies of society were meant to be accomplished in such arts, and Anna knew that the vice-admiral did desire that she become a proper lady, so she played the string of notes a second time, and then a third, trying to follow Mrs. Lacy's soft instruction not to hit the keys too forcefully, nor race too quickly over them.

The lesson lasted nearly a full hour, and by the end of it her back ached and her neck was feeling knotted from the effort. Still, she would have carried on had not the general's wife confessed that she herself was growing weary, and would rest awhile.

"Do as you will now with your time, my dear, and I will call you when I need you."

Time alone was both a blessing and a curse to Anna. On the one hand, it was all her own; but on the other, there was little she could do with it. She could not leave the house without a purpose or an escort. She could only sit and work more on the flowered petticoat and gown, or seek escape through one of General Lacy's many books, but an escape within her mind was not true freedom.

She had been too long indoors. That was the problem, Anna thought, as she wrapped warmly in the fur-lined cloak and hood that had been hers for several winters. For although it was now past mid-March, the days had turned as cold as though it had still been mid-January, painting crackled frost across the windowpanes each morning, with a wind that tore against the shutters, blowing a fine mist of snow that settled in small drifts along the sills.

There was one place at General Lacy's house where she could breathe the outside air without an escort, for she had not truly left the property—the yard, hemmed round on all sides by the high walls of the houses, would provide her room to pace about, and might help cure her aching head.

The servants clearly thought her mad, but none of them said anything as she made her way through the kitchen to the door that led out to the yard. Outside, the cold air struck her like a blade, so sharp it froze her nostrils as it stung her cheeks, but Anna gladly raised her face to welcome it.

And saw that she was not alone.

The children were already out here, legs half-swallowed by the deep snow as they clustered round the doorway of the small grey shed that leaned against the western wall. She was about to call to them and ask what they were doing when a taller figure moved within the shed, and as she recognized the man and would have turned away, the youngest boy, young Pierce, turned, too, and called her over. "Mistress Jamieson! Come see! Come see our bird."

Then all the other heads turned, too, and there was nothing for it but to make her way across the yard and stand among the children while they stared with fascination at the crow held in Edmund O'Connor's gloved hands.

He told them, "Only for a minute, now. She'll freeze if she stays out too long."

The crow, seeming calm, watched them all with a curious eye while the children took turns gently stroking a finger across the black head. All but Helen, the littlest girl, who pressed back against her brother, Michael, in fear. "It's so ugly."

Edmund crouched so that he and the bird were on Helen's own level, and gently agreed, "Aye, she's never the prettiest bird, to be sure. But she's taken that form as a test, to see how well we'll care for her."

Katie asked, "What do you mean?"

"Well, I think what we've captured is not a true crow, but the Cailleagh herself. Do you know of the Cailleagh?" He lifted his eyebrows as all of the children assured him they didn't. "And what has your father been teaching you then? The Cailleagh," he said, "is a very old woman of Ireland, very old, older than time. Every autumn she's born, and she cradles the year as it dies, and she cares for it under the frost and the snow, and through all of the winter she keeps safe the seeds that will turn the world green in the spring. She has powerful ways, but she's not to be feared," he told Helen.

The little girl blinked at him. "And this is her?"

Edmund nodded. "I think so. 'Tis one of the forms that she likes to appear in, to see whether we will be kind to her."

Katie asked, "And if we are? What does she do then?"

"Why, then she brings you good fortune. Go on," he told Helen, and held the crow closer to her in encouragement. "Show her your heart's not so cold."

Helen, biting her lip, reached one small mittened hand out to touch the bird's head, then withdrew it as quickly, but proud of her bravery she smiled up at Edmund, and he smiled back.

"There you are then," he said to the girl, "she'll be bringing the spring to us soon, that's for certain."

Anna, through all this, said nothing, because she'd been suddenly struck by a memory: herself as a child, walking with Captain Jamieson in the dim church of the convent at Ypres while he gave her advice. "Ye'll learn more of a man if ye look at his face when he's looking at somebody else," he had said, "than ye'll learn any other way."

Looking at Edmund O'Connor's face now, while he was looking at Helen, she saw what she hadn't expected to see. Kindness. Tenderness. Patience.

And something more. All down the edge of his jawline, the skin was beginning to whiten, with small crystals forming along it. Without taking time to think, Anna reacted as she would have done were he one of the children—she scooped up a handful of snow and, not asking for leave, rubbed the side of his face with it.

He rose to his full height, evading her hand as he asked, "What the devil was that for?"

His irritation, wholly understandable, but following so soon upon her unexpected glimpse into his other nature, left her for a moment without words. A new experience, for Anna. She could only stand before him and absorb his anger while the children hastened to explain that in this harsh and northern climate any sign of frost upon the skin must instantly be treated so; that she had only rubbed his jaw with snow to stop it freezing.

She could see the change of his expression as their jumbled explanations penetrated, and as fast as it had flared, the anger left his eyes, but there was no more tenderness within them, either.

With a nod he thanked her, and she took his thanks and turned away, still silent.

She had gone halfway across the yard before she felt the impact on her back as something hit her. Turning, she had scarcely time to see the ball of white approaching before snow exploded on her face, a thousand stinging needles.

Edmund O'Connor, having presumably put the bird back in its cage, stood with both hands now free, by the door of the shed. "I'm only returning the favour," he called, "Mistress Jamieson." Raising one gloved hand, he brushed his own cheek before pointing to hers. "You were looking a little bit frosty, just there."

She saw the challenge in his stance, and would have dearly loved to have got something of her own back, but she did not wish to show the general's children an unladylike display. So instead of taking up his gauntlet she convinced herself to turn again, with dignity, and carry on towards the house.

But even so, it gave her satisfaction to see all the children pile themselves upon him as she left, well-armed with snowballs of their own, their shouts and laughter as they brought the dark man to his knees a thing of beauty to her ears.

Katie fell ill during Holy Week, and though her fever had broken when Sunday arrived, she was yet far too ill to have gone with the rest of the family to church Easter morning, so Anna stayed home with her.

Truthfully, Anna was happy enough to keep out of the crush of the day's celebrations. Russian Easter was a very big affair, the most important holy day in all the year, so much so that the empress had sent heralds with their trumpets and their drums all through the city to announce that, for all Holy Week and Easter Sunday, too, the men were not to wear full mourning dress but put on coloured waistcoats with their black coats and black breeches, and the ladies of St. Petersburg were all to wear white hats.

The general and his wife and all their other children had looked very fine as they had headed out this morning to the little church on Greek Street, with the brown-robed friar following behind them.

Father Dominic had sat with Anna earlier that morning and had led her through the prayers that were best suited to the day, so that her soul would not be any way neglected from her absence at the church. To do likewise for Katie, Anna sat now at the bedside of the little girl and read to her the words of the apostle John, to help her understand the day's importance.

She'd begun her reading with her favourite part, the night of the Last Supper and the promises that Christ had made to those whom He'd so loved, and who had followed Him: "And if I shall go, and prepare a place for you, I will come again, and will take you to myself; that where I am, you also may be."

When Anna had first read those words herself, she had felt her eyes fill suddenly because it was a lovely promise, one that Captain Jamieson had made to her, and one she'd badly wanted to believe. It would not happen now, of course, but still the words felt warm within her heart, and gave her comfort of a sort, as did Christ's words two chapters on: "So also you now indeed have sorrow; but I will see you again, and your heart shall rejoice; and your joy no man shall take from you."

Those words reminded Anna that she *would* see Captain Jamieson again, if not in life then in that place where none were ever to be parted, where his daughter and her father had already gone before.

She turned the page, and went on reading. At the moment of the crucifixion, Katie raised a protest.

"But," she said to Anna, "He did nothing wrong. Why are they being cruel to Him?"

The concept of Christ's suffering in payment for the sins of others wasn't something Anna could make Katie understand. No matter how she tried explaining it, the little girl seemed more and more perplexed. "But why?" she asked again.

There was no simple answer, Anna reasoned, but she sought to put it into simple terms. "Because He loved us very much. And when you love somebody very much, you do what you must do to keep them safe."

A sudden loud explosive boom made all the windows rattle in their frames, and Katie gave a shriek and clapped her small hands to her ears.

Smiling reassurance, Anna quickly set the Bible to the side and reached for Katie's hands, to draw them down and hold them fast within her own. "There's nothing you need fear. 'Tis but the guns of both the fortress and the Admiralty, set off at once. Did you not hear them earlier this morning?"

Katie shook her head, still wide-eyed and uncertain.

Anna told her, "Well, I heard them well enough, for it was only four o'clock and fully dark outside. I leaped so high out of my bed I'm half amazed I am not on the ceiling, still."

That brought, as she had hoped it would, the first suggestion of a giggle from the little girl, but did not take the worry from her eyes. "Why do they fire the guns? Is there a war?"

"Of course not. No, the first time that the guns went off this morning, it was only to make sure we all did waken for this special day. And this time, it was telling us the empress and her family have all finished with their service at the church, and it is time for all the people of St. Petersburg to come and pay her court now, at the palace."

From memory, Anna painted a bright picture with her words so that the child might see the whole of what was happening right now—the merry groups of noblemen and ladies all descending on the Winter Palace, where the empress and the princesses were waiting to receive them.

Katie asked, "And will my father go there, too?"

"Yes, for your father is a most important man."

Katie looked well pleased by that, and snuggled back into her bed while Anna carried on describing how the Winter Palace would be looking on this Easter morning, with the court musicians gathered all before it, playing drums and trumpets, flutes and oboes, and the kettle drums that rumbled in one's chest behind the breastbone like a roll of regal thunder.

"And," said Anna, "when the people greet each other, there will be the giving of the painted eggs, which is great fun. Do you give eggs to one another in Livonia, at Easter?"

Katie, being little, could not say with any certainty.

"Well, here in Russia, there are painted eggs—some red, and some with all the colours of your mother's jewels, in clever patterns, and most beautiful to see."

"And do you eat them?"

"Yes, eventually. First though, people give them to each other, and receive an Easter kiss. Like this." She held up an imaginary egg, and said to Katie, "First I tell you, 'Christ is risen,' and your answer should be, 'Truly He is risen.'"

Katie parroted the words.

"Good. Then you take the egg from me, that's right, and kiss me three times, starting here." She put a guiding finger to her left cheek, leaning close down to the bed to let the little girl perform the triple kiss, the left cheek, then the right, and then the left again.

"Must you kiss everyone?" asked Katie.

"Yes, it is the custom. If you're greeted in this way, then you cannot refuse the kiss," said Anna. "Nor the egg."

"I wish I had a real egg."

From the open doorway just behind, a man's voice said, "Will this one do?"

The light in Katie's face, all on its own, would have told Anna who it was that stood there, had she not already recognized his voice.

And as she always did in Edmund's presence now, she put on mental battle dress, composed her features carefully to be polite but only just, and straightened without haste to turn and face him.

He had leaned one shoulder jauntily against the door frame, with his black wool coat left open to reveal the yellow waistcoat worn beneath, all edged with braid. She'd never seen him in a colour, only in the plain black coat, or in the plain white of his shirtsleeves; never with this vibrant dash of light that made him seem a bit more human.

In his hand he held an egg that had indeed been painted with a rainbow's colours, red and blue and gold and green. "My landlady did give this to me earlier this morning, with instructions that, as soon as mass had ended, I should give this to the princess, and exchange it for a kiss. And I could think of but one princess in all Petersburg," he said to Katie, "so now, Princess Katie, will you—"

Katie cut him off, blond curls dancing as her face mingled delight and firm denial. "I'm no princess, Ned."

He paused, and feigned confusion. "Are you not?"

She was decided. "No. Your landlady meant the imperial princesses. They're at the palace."

"I see. Are you sure about that? Well, they'll have so many eggs by now," he said, "they'll not miss mine. Here, you can have it."

"No," she put him off again, but for a different cause. "You have to do it properly."

"How's that?"

"Like Mistress Jamieson was showing me. You have to tell me, 'Christ is risen,' then I answer you, and then you give the egg to me, and then I kiss you."

Edmund schooled his face. "It seems a lot of effort," he told Katie, "for a kiss."

"It is the custom," Katie told him, very solemnly, in a near-perfect imitation of the way that Anna had just said those very words, and Edmund's mouth twitched faintly.

With a shrug he came away from the door jamb and crossed to the little girl's bedside, and Anna moved out of their way, standing back several paces to watch while the Irishman bowed very gallantly low to the child and announced, 'Christ is risen.' Now, take the damn'd egg."

"Not yet. First I must tell you, 'Truly He is risen,'" said Katie, and looking to Anna, asked, "Is that right?"

Any notion Anna might have had of telling Edmund not to curse in Katie's presence fell away then, for she saw the child herself was not at all affected by it. Innocence, she thought, was often blind to other's wickedness. And Edmund did not look so very wicked at the moment.

He looked much as he had looked when she had watched him with the children in the yard, nearly two weeks ago: a gentle man, a stranger to her eyes, without a trace of the sardonic, cutting wit he liked to turn on her when they were in a room together.

Seemingly mindful that Katie was still weak from illness, he leaned lower still for his kiss and received it at last, saying, "Three kisses! Sure, that's a generous reward."

"Mistress Jamieson says every egg gets three kisses."

"Indeed? Well, I've no doubt she'd tell you the truth." He was standing again at his full height and looking at Anna, as though he were trying to guess at her thoughts. "Mistress Jamieson, you appear troubled."

She said, "Hardly that. I was only admiring the egg."

"Oh, yes? I've another just like it." Drawing a second egg out of his coat pocket, he held it up in full view as he levelled his gaze on her own, and the glint in his eyes told her she was a fool to have ever believed him not wicked. He said, 'Christ is risen.'"

He was seeking to amuse himself at her expense, she knew, for he'd be well aware that there was no one she'd want less to kiss in friendship than himself. But this had naught to do with friendship. He was offering the egg, but he had not, as any gentleman would do, come near to give it to her. No, his stance demanded that she cross the length of floor that lay between them, put her pride aside, accept the egg, and kiss him, because custom and tradition gave him power to demand it. Anna damned his dark and laughing eyes in silence, taking care to keep her face composed. She would not let him triumph, any more than she would disappoint the little girl who watched them.

With her head up she approached him calmly. "'Truly He is risen,'" she replied, and took the egg from his scarred hand.

He did not bend for her, as he had bent for Katie. He stood straight and tall, his downward-angled gaze an open challenge. She had never let a challenge yet defeat her, so she raised herself on tiptoe and began the kiss.

She would have given all three kisses quickly and been done with it, but needing to stay balanced on her toes she had to slow her movements, and her senses then had time to notice things that Anna would have been more comfortable not noticing. Like how his skin smelt pleasantly of shaving soap. And how his jawline tightened when he . . . what? When he did what? She could not see what he was doing, and so she was unprepared when Edmund turned his own head slightly, at the last, as though by reflex more than conscious thought. She felt the feather of his breath against her own skin as the corners of their mouths just barely brushed.

She could not say which of the two of them was first to pull away from that brief contact, but they both stood rather stiffly for the moment that came afterwards, till Katie, from the bed, asked, "Do you have a third egg in your pocket, Ned?"

"No." He cleared his throat and looked at Katie, and became

himself again. "But if my princess does command me, I shall go back out into the town and kiss as many maidens as I can, to win you more."

He bowed, as Katie nodded eagerly and answered him, "Yes, please."

She had a heaping bowl of painted eggs beside her bed by supper-time, and Anna had the fair beginnings of a headache.

Mrs. Lacy, who had come to sit as well by Katie's bed, said with concern, "I hope you have not also caught the illness."

Anna had since set aside the Bible in exchange for a more adventurous book from General Lacy's shelves, that being Mr. Pope's translation of *The Illiad of Homer*, but she could not seem to concentrate upon it, so she marked her place and closed the book and smiled at Mrs. Lacy. "No, I'm sure that I have not. 'Tis but an aching head."

The older woman, nodding at the bed where Katie lay now fast asleep, said, "Likely it was not helped by her chattering all afternoon."

"I'm pleased to see her well enough to chatter."

"I am, also." Mrs. Lacy's eyes grew serious. "I feared it was the smallpox, to begin with. We've been fortunate so far, to have escaped it, but each time one of the children does complain of feeling ill, or has a fever, I confess I fall to worrying." Her belly was no more than slightly rounded yet, but still she laid a hand on it protectively. "I could not bear to lose a child. In truth, I know not how the Empress Catherine has endured it."

Nor did Anna. Of the dozen or so children that the empress and the late tsar had been blessed with, only three had lived above their first few years, if that long. And of those three, there were but two remaining, now that young Princess Natalya, only seven years of age, had sickened following the tsar's death and succumbed, and had been buried with her father. It had not been the tsar's coffin, with its host of sad attendants, that had tugged at Anna's heart when she had stood upon the river's ice and watched the long procession of the funeral passing by, but the much smaller coffin following behind it, for she'd known well that a mother's hopes lay buried there.

Small wonder Empress Catherine had retreated from her social ways, and kept herself apart from those who earlier had freely gained her company.

"The empress is a very special woman," Anna said, in full agreement. And remembering what Colonel Graeme had once said about the sons he'd lost, she added, "I do pray she'll find some consolation in the princesses yet living."

Mrs. Lacy gently said, "A living child may be a consolation, to be sure, but it cannot replace the child that was lost."

Anna wondered if her mother thought the same, in her home far across the sea with her new husband, her new children. With her head bent she replied, "I have no children, so I cannot know."

"You will have children one day," Mrs. Lacy said, and as though that reminded her of something she continued, "Mr. Taylor of the English Factory greeted us this morning in the street. He is a nice young man."

She could not contradict that. "Yes, he is."

"He's asked permission of my husband to come pay a call to you, one day. My husband told him that, if you had no objections, he'd be welcome." Her sidelong glance held interest. "Do you have any objections?"

Anna raised her head and looked, she knew not why, towards the bowl heaped full of painted eggs that sat by Katie's bed. And then she forced a smile and told the general's wife she could not think of any reason why they should not welcome Mr. Taylor, if he chose to pay a visit. "As you have observed," she said, "he is a *nice* man."

Mrs. Lacy sent another sidelong glance in her direction, but she merely gave a nod, and with the matter settled, moved the conversation on to other things.

"I'll tell you," said the general, full of charm as he upended a decanter of fine claret over Mr. Taylor's cup, "a merchant's life is fine, I'll grant you, but there is no occupation can compare with soldiering."

The afternoon was grey, and in the drawing room the rush-backed chair that Anna had moved closer to the windows, for the light, was growing harder at her back and more uncomfortable to sit in. Had she been a child, she thought, she would have fidgeted. And had she been a man, she would have sat as Edmund now was sitting, all but lounging in his armchair with his legs stretched out at ease in front of him, his elbows propped so that his hands were linked across his stomach, making him the very picture of a man digesting dinner in contentment.

Anna rolled her shoulder slightly to relax the cramping muscle as she tried to keep her focus on the tiny, even stitches she was placing in the fullness of the fabric that would be the petticoat of her new gown, when it was finished. She liked sewing. Liked the steady repetition that allowed her thoughts to drift, and the unequalled satisfaction of creating something functional, and sometimes even beautiful, with her own hands. Embroidery, for her, had never held the same appeal. The whorls and leaves and flowers worked in thread were wasted effort if they did not have a use.

The general's wife, who sat with perfect grace upon her stool before the harpsichord, said, "Leave him be, Pierce. Mr. Taylor surely does not wish to be a soldier."

"No, indeed." He was a pleasant-faced young man, with fair hair slightly tinged with red and clear blue eyes that held no guile. And coming as he did from Perth, he also had a Scotsman's practicality. "I've not the nature for it, I'm afraid. I have no quarrel with most men, which makes me disinclined to choose a path in life that leads me into conflict."

Edmund asked him, "And if conflict came to you, how would you meet it, then?"

"With honour, I should hope, sir, if it could not be avoided." Mr. Taylor sipped his wine, and with a flash of humour added, "But I'd still prefer to be among my ledgers and my books, than on a battlefield."

The general's wife agreed. "So would we all."

Anna said nothing, for it would not have been ladylike to say where she'd have wished to be, in any time of conflict, but she felt herself observed from all sides while the talk devolved to that of trade in general, and the weather, and the rumour that the elder princess would at last be married to the Duke of Holstein.

"He has waited long enough for it," was General Lacy's wry opinion. "And he's been more patient in his suit than many men would be, but patience often wins the day in love, eh, Mr. Taylor?"

Mr. Taylor, diplomatically, chose not to make reply to this. Instead, he paid a compliment to Mrs. Lacy on her home, and one to Anna on her sewing. "I do mind that very silk arriving at the Custom House," he said, "and I said then to Mr. Wayte, 'Just see if we don't have Vice-Admiral Gordon in to buy it,' for I saw it was the colour of your eyes."

Mrs. Lacy smiled approval. "So it is, and she is making a fine job of it. A most accomplished seamstress."

Edmund cut in languidly. "I do confess I've never yet seen Mistress Jamieson remain so still and quiet for so long. Are you quite well?" he asked her.

Biting back the first retort she would have liked to make, she told him, "Very well, I thank you, sir."

"I see my pawns are safe, this afternoon," he said. Then, looking past her shoulder, "Mr. Taylor, will you have a game of chess?"

"I do not play it, I'm afraid."

Edmund made no comment, only glanced at Anna pointedly, then back at Mr. Taylor. "Cards, then."

General Lacy, turning in his seat, said in a murmur, "Edmund."

Mr. Taylor was already answering, "I do play piquet, sir."

"Excellent."

A servant brought the folding table covered with green plush, and cards, which Edmund shuffled rather clumsily, as though he had not done it in a while. He dealt, and Mr. Taylor gathered up his hand while General Lacy settled nearby in a chair to watch, and Mrs. Lacy played a flowing tune upon the harpsichord.

As Anna sewed her seam, she kept one part of her attention on the game. She found it difficult, no matter how she tried, to not compare the men at play. In looks, and manners, and in dress, young

Mr. Taylor should have won, and drawn her eye; so it was frustrating to her that he did not, that more and more her eye returned to Edmund's roguish face, his plainer clothes, the square hands with the scars across the knuckles. And the more she watched, the more she grew aware that he was not as unaccomplished with the cards as he appeared.

His hands were lazy in their actions, and she did not truly see how he controlled the play, and yet she grew convinced he was controlling it. Yet not for his own gain. When it seemed certain that he would not lose, the cards turned very suddenly in Mr. Taylor's favour, and it seemed to Anna she had not imagined the faint smile in Edmund's eyes that vanished even as it formed, as though it were enough amusement for him just to play the game.

He turned his head, and caught her looking. If he guessed at her suspicions, he said nothing, only, "Will you play the winner, Mistress Jamieson?"

"No, thank you. I must finish with this seam."

"Ay, for 'tis of great concern to finish with a gown you cannot wear, in time of mourning."

Mr. Taylor, seemingly surprised at Edmund's tone, said mildly, "But the mourning will not last forever."

Anna gave a nod. "As Mr. Taylor says. Afflictions pass, Mr. O'Connor, just as surely as the winter brings the spring. You ought to know this, with your Cailleagh."

General Lacy roused himself from deeper thoughts, at that, and looked between the two of them. "What's this about the Cailleagh?"

Anna said, "Mr. O'Connor shared a piece of Irish folklore with the children and myself, a few weeks past."

"I was that surprised," Edmund remarked to the general, "they'd never yet heard of it, being half Irish and all. "'Tis a piece of their heritage, surely." His dark eyes touched Anna's with meaning as he added, "People should know who they are."

Mr. Taylor said, "Aye, there is much to be said for tradition." And looking in his turn at Anna, his honest face could not hide how he admired the picture she made in her chair by the window, the fabric spilled over her lap and her needle in hand. Then he turned back to Edmund and asked, "Shall we play one more hand, sir? I must say, I'd forgot just how much I enjoyed this game."

Edmund's mouth curved in a smile that seemed private as he looked down, reaching a hand for the deck of cards. "Aye," he replied, "so did I."

chapter
THIRTY-FOUR

Spring came, and with the thawing of the river the whole city came again to life, the merchant ships returning and the open-air exchange on Vasilievsky Island growing once more crowded with the merchants and their goods, and with the men who kept the warehouses and worked about the docks.

Vice-Admiral Gordon now divided his own days between the Admiralty and Cronstadt, the small island with its castle and its shipyards near the tsar's old house of Monplaisir a half-day's journey distant down the Neva, where the greater ships were forced to put to anchor when they ventured in towards St. Petersburg, and where the warships of the Russian navy often gathered with the galleys before setting out to sea.

From time to time he visited the general's house to see that Anna was well, and just as often carried a small gift within his pocket as he'd done when she was younger. Last week he had brought her a wrapped piece of palest pink silk, for a lining to the bodice she was piecing at the moment, and two days ago he'd given her a handful of dark hairpins, each set with a tiny pearl. "It is the fashion of the French, I'm told, to dress their hair with jewels," he'd said.

So on this morning, when the shoes arrived by messenger without a note, she knew from whom they'd come. Even the general, when he'd seen her with the package, had deduced, "Another gift from the vice-admiral?"

Anna had nodded, still struck speechless by the beauty of the shoes. They were of silk brocade in twists of cream and berry red, with silver buckles, pointed toes, and heels much higher than she'd ever dared to wear.

"He is a cruel man," General Lacy had remarked, in all good humour, "to give such things to a girl who cannot wear them till the mourning has been lifted at year's end. I daresay by that time you'll have those worn out just from looking at them."

Truthfully, she could not take her eyes from those bright shoes. They sat now on the table at her bedside, so whenever her gaze lifted from her sewing she could see them, though she scarce had time to focus with the lively goings-on within her chamber.

Living in a household full of children might have been a trial for some, but Anna loved the near-continual activity, with the boys seeming to never stand still, and the girls going past in a flurry of petticoats, all of them laughing and playing and fighting in turn, as a close group of siblings would do. It reminded her of her own first happy years with the brothers and sisters who hadn't been truly her own, and yet had been. She thought of them all now and then, and she'd minded the promise she'd made to the father who'd raised her to never forget them, but though there was warmth in those memories she rarely felt sadness. She'd let those days go, as the mother who'd raised her had opened her arms and released Anna from them that day with the loving, true words, "Ye never were my own to keep."

Some memories, Anna thought, were like that—only to be held with fondness, never mourned. But still, she liked to hear the children's voices.

Both the boys were at their lessons for the day, with Father Dominic instructing them, and so the girls had gravitated to where Anna was, with tiny Helen winding thread, and Katie keen to protest while her older sister tried to read a book to her. "But I want Mistress Jamieson to read to me."

"But Father said I had to practice reading."

Anna verified this, nodding. "It is true, for I was there when he did say it."

Katie frowned. "You read to Mama."

"She is Mama's companion," said Hannah-Louise, who was twice Katie's age. "Not our governess."

Their mother's cheerful voice within the doorway said, "'Tis well you do remember that, my dears, or you'll have wearied Mistress Jamieson past all reviving, and I do have need of her myself, just now."

She looked refreshed and happy, from her hour of rest. The child within her had announced its healthiness a week before by quickening, and Mrs. Lacy's sickness had now all but disappeared, replaced by a glad energy.

Replying to the summons, Anna fastened off her stitch and bit the thread and set the gown aside. "What would you have me do?"

The older woman smiled. "The same thing you are doing there, but sadly, in reverse. I have a gown that I would wear, but my dimensions have increased since last I wore it, as you see. I wonder, could you let the seams out for me?"

"Yes, of course."

"I would have asked one of the maids, but your work is more skilled than theirs, and it is one of my favourite gowns, sent as a gift from my sister. I'd not see it ruined."

Hannah-Louise brightened. "Is it the green one, Mama?"

"Yes, it is." Then, on noticing Anna's confusion, she smiled more broadly and crossed to the window to open it, letting them all hear the still-distant roll of the drumbeats and flourish of trumpets; the indistinct voice of a herald progressing through all the streets with an important announcement. The general's wife turned round again to Anna. "You will soon have your wish, my dear," she said, "to put off mourning for a short while, for it seems we are to have a royal wedding, after all."

The day had been dazzling. It had all begun, officially, that morning at eleven with the grand procession to collect the bridegroom, with the open phaeton of the wedding marshal in the lead and all two dozen of the groomsmen riding two by two on horseback with the trumpeters amongst them, and the day had grown in richness and in wonders ever since. The Duke of Holstein and the princess, glitteringly royal in their wedding clothes of silver brocade, made a most impressive couple. Anna, being as she was included in Vice-Admiral Gordon's family, had by virtue of his high rank been admitted as a guest, and so had watched with her own eyes the wedding vows be given in the great Church of the Holy Trinity, and joined with all the other guests who'd crossed the river back again by barges to the gardens of the Summer Palace.

Here, close to the corner where the Neva met the smaller Swan Canal, a brand-new banquet hall had only just been built for this one joyous celebration. Designed by one of the chief architects, the speed of its construction had been overseen in person by Prince Menshikov, the late tsar's boyhood friend and closest confidant, who'd even stayed to sleep within it these past days, to make sure that the workmen did a proper job of finishing.

The end result was beautiful—a building with a fine, enormous central room, and more than fifty windows all around it, decorated on the outside walls with rows of pilasters and vases set on pedestals, and on the inner walls with painted murals showing battle scenes, the sculpted forms of Mars and Neptune set to guard the southern doors that opened to the tree-lined pathways of the Summer Garden.

They'd been banqueting for hours, now, on a feast that had begun with two enormous pies set down before the newly married couple, and from those pies two dwarves had sprung, a man and woman who had danced a measure for the entertainment of the guests.

The lively music had continued, and each toast had seemed to draw an answer in the roar of guns fired from the Admiralty, the fortress, and the regiments of guards outside, as well as from the Duke of Holstein's yacht upon the river.

Anna could not mind when she'd enjoyed a better time, in the bright company of both Vice-Admiral Gordon and his daughters and across from General Lacy and his wife, the children having been assigned to the kind eye of Father Dominic at home, since he'd had no desire to come among the common people on the meadow that adjoined the Summer Garden, where those who were not formally invited to the wedding could yet join the celebrations.

Anna had enjoyed the day still more because she had been able to relax, without the ever-watchful eye of—

"Edmund," Mrs. Lacy said, "is missing a delightful day. A shame he could not join us."

General Lacy shrugged. "He will be fed upon the meadow. And it was by his own choice that he is there, and not with us at table."

On the other side of Gordon, next to Nan, Sir Harry Stirling turned his head. A Scotsman of an old and noble family, he displayed the easy elegance of one who had been born to better things. His clothes were always finely cut and fit him well, his wig in keeping with the latest fashion, and his lean face showed the quick intelligence and wit that had attracted more young women than just Nan, though Nan, of late, appeared to be the only one who held any attraction for Sir Harry.

"This would be your kinsman?" he asked General Lacy.

"Aye, that's right. Mr. O'Connor. We'd expected him this morning, but he sent a note to say that he regretted his appearance might reflect ill on the family, for it seems he had an . . . altercation, yesterday."

"He's the man who fought the harlot's husband, then." Sir Harry grinned. "It was the talk of all the merchants' wives last evening."

"But," said Mrs. Lacy, "not the kind of talk we wish to have today." Her tone was gracious, but the look she sent her husband stopped that line of conversation cold.

"Indeed," he said. "I should have liked him here, though, as a witness to my honour." And he tapped, with pride, the scarlet ribbon with its military decoration newly hung across his heart, the star of the new Order of St. Alexander Nevsky, that the empress had awarded to a handful of her finest subjects earlier today, with her own hand.

Anna was well aware that it had wounded Gordon's pride that he had not received the Order also, when two other of the vice-admirals had been so honoured, but he'd masked his disappointment with congratulations, and dry wit.

He looked across at Lacy now and said, "I expect, with all you've talked of it this afternoon, the news will by this time have reached the meadow."

Lacy took that in good sport. "When you've expelled the Swedes from Russia and been wounded in the process, you may have a star upon your chest to talk about as well, Tom."

"I have heard much about this wound," said Gordon, "yet I've never seen the scar."

"And that," said Mrs. Lacy, firm, "is also something most unfit to be discussed at table. And," she added, to her husband, "if you do attempt to show it in this company, I warn you I shall leave."

He hid his smile.

Sir Harry, rising cheerfully to General Lacy's aid, remarked, "Poltava was indeed a victory worthy of remembrance, and a man who had a hand in it should be allowed to crow from time to time."

General Lacy gave a nod that aimed for dignity. "My thanks to you, Sir Harry. And in truth, 'tis only just. I had but little time to crow about it when the battle happened, for three months after that my brother died at Malplaquet." As though remembering the youth of some around him, and what Anna had remarked when he'd first spoken of Poltava at the house, he said, to her, "You were a babe for that one, also."

Yes, I know, she wanted to reply. *My father fell at Malplaquet.*

Instead she held her silence, drew a breath and let it out again, and counted herself fortunate that nobody had noticed how her spoon had frozen for a moment in its course towards her plate, as though the very name of that old battlefield had yet the power to wound her.

It was only when she chanced to look beside her and discovered the vice-admiral's gaze upon her, full of thought, that she felt suddenly compelled to force a smile and change the subject. "I have not yet thanked you for the shoes," she told him brightly. "You'll be thinking me ungrateful. They are beautiful, and near a perfect fit."

His eyebrows drew together slightly. "And what shoes are those?"

"Why, these ones." With one hand she inched the hem of her full damask petticoat a fraction from the floor, to show the pointed toe of one shoe, with its whorls of berry red the very colour of the tiny sprays of blossoms woven in among the white leaves and the golden fern fronds on the sea-green silk that made her gown.

Vice-Admiral Gordon gave a nod. "They are most beautiful, I do agree, but I can claim no credit for your having them."

Her turn to frown. "They did not come from you?"

"Perhaps," he said, "they were a secret gift from an admirer. I can think of one who might have access to such merchandise."

She truly hoped it was not Mr. Taylor who had sent them, for they were a gift too costly and too personal to be so lightly given and accepted. But then, who . . . ?

Sir Harry, on the other side of Gordon, had leaned back in his chair and craned his neck to look at Anna's shoes himself, and told her, "They look very like a pair that came lately from France in a shipment for our Mr. Morley."

The vice-admiral asked him, "Is that a fact?"

"Yes. But they can't be the same ones," Sir Harry said, only a little too lightly. "He lost those while playing at cards, with an Irishman."

She found him in the meadow. She had wondered, at the first, how she would manage it, with all the crowds of people milling round and making merry, and their own group having just crossed over from the Summer Gardens with the newlyweds and empress in their midst, to pass an hour of the evening with the common people. There was ample food for everybody here as well—two full-roasted oxen that she could see, and a variety of roasted birds and rabbits, and two fountains that were running not with water, but with wine, one white, the other red. As with all celebrations here in Russia, people had been taking much advantage of the drink provided, and the sound of raucous laughter, even singing, mingled thickly with the energetic music being played by a collection of court oboeists and flute-players and trumpeters.

The meadow had once been a length of swampland, drained and dried by the construction of canals to either side. Its northern edge reached to the Neva, and its eastern boundary was the narrow Swan Canal that kept this public place divided from the Summer Garden of the empress, with the span of a small bridge guarded by the sentries to decide who came and went.

They'd stood respectfully aside to let the empress and her daughter and new son-in-law pass by, with all the wedding guests behind them, and more guards had stood in ranks upon the meadow—both the regiments of Preobrazhensky and Semyonovsky—offering a musical salute and three loud volleys of their guns that had been fired with such precision each had sounded like a single shot.

It had been during that display that Anna had excused herself from her own party, and for several minutes since then she'd been searching in the crowd.

And now she'd found him.

He was standing not far off from Mrs. Hewitt, who was taking not the slightest care to modulate her voice as she discussed him with the little clutch of merchants' wives around her. Whether he could hear them talking, Anna did not know, but she herself could hear the ugly words as she approached the women.

". . . and my dear," said Mrs. Hewitt, to a younger woman next to her, "the clothes he wears are sorely out of fashion, and quite worn about the sleeves. And no wonder, if he does engage in fisticuffs so often."

"Did he really strike the harlot's husband?"

"Strike him? Knocked him clear out of his senses," Mrs. Hewitt set the facts straight. "I was told the husband found the pair *engaged* with one another, if you take my meaning, and did seek to turn our gallant out of bed, and so was cruelly set upon."

"Disgraceful," said another.

And a fourth among the wives, who had been listening wide-eyed to all of this, now shook her head and said, in righteous tones, "I told you, when he came. Did I not tell you? I was doubtful of his character when first he spurned my Betty at our gathering at Christmas, when he would not dance the minuet."

Perhaps he could not hear them, Anna thought. He stood apart, a cup of drink held cradled in one hand, his gaze fixed idly in a contemplation of the passing ships that ran along the river, and the Duke of Holstein's yacht with all its guns.

She did not notice, to be honest, how his coat was cut, or whether it was worn through at the sleeves. She marked the colour of it—deeply blue—and noted that he wore the yellow waistcoat underneath it, and his hair was neatly tied with a black ribbon at his collar, underneath a fine three-cornered hat. He looked, to her, a gentleman enough.

It was the rush of anger running sudden through her veins that, in the end, undid her. She could very easily have turned around and left him as he was. He had not seen her, and the way he stood there, unconcerned, reminded her he was a man of strength, and had no need of her. Of anyone.

But hearing Mrs. Hewitt and the others speak so rudely of him, Anna felt her temper rise in answer to it. Keeping her reaction in control, she calmly paid her honours to the other women as she passed, then raised her chin with new determination as she crossed the grass.

He turned his head, and watched her come towards him, with no alteration of his stance or his expression. She could see, then, why he had not wished to burden General Lacy's reputation by his presence at the banquet, for the skin across his cheekbone had been split and badly bruised.

She saw the light of curiosity flash briefly in his eyes as she approached him; watched it change to dark amusement as she spoke.

"Mr. O'Connor."

"Mistress Jamieson." His head inclined politely.

In a voice that carried clearly, she said, "I am sent to fetch you, for the empress has herself expressed a fond desire to meet you, having heard so much about you from the general and his wife."

Whatever he'd expected her to say, it was not that. She saw the visible suppression of a smile, the smallest twitch along the hard length of his jawline, but he did not answer straight away, and standing there she felt an echo of the feelings she'd had standing at the Calais gate and waiting to discover whether Gordon would indulge her or expose her, for depending on the way that Edmund answered Anna knew she could so easily be made to look a fool.

He paused, and seemed to weigh his choices. Though he did not look beyond her to the place where Mrs. Hewitt and the merchants' wives were standing, Anna knew he was as conscious of their keen attention as she was herself, just as she knew the more respectful nod he gave her was entirely for their benefit, as was the charming smile he aimed at her, and his well-mannered offer of his arm for her to take.

"Well, lead on, then," he invited her, "for I'd not wish to disappoint the empress."

chapter
THIRTY-FIVE

H e didn't speak until they'd nearly reached the Swan Canal, and then he said, "You haven't got the face for it, you know."

"For what?"

"Deception." His low voice was still amused. "It's a fine thing to announce you have a royal pair of aces, but it is enough to look at you to know you only hold a pair of treys. I doubt those hens back there believed your tale."

The velvet of his sleeve felt warmly soft to Anna's fingers, but the arm beneath was hard. She let it go. "I do not care what they believe."

No longer supporting her hand with his elbow, he let his arm straighten again to his side, but he did not give any more distance between them. "If that were the case, then why bother to charge to my rescue?"

She answered him, "Truly, I have no idea. But if you will speak about cards, sir, allow me to ask what possessed you to play Mr. Morley for such foolish stakes as a pair of French shoes? Here in Petersburg, playing for stakes is not legal."

"For money," he smoothly corrected her. "Playing for money is strictly forbidden, I know, but the late tsar apparently had no objections to footwear, whatever its country of origin. That's why we played for the shoes."

He was such an impossible rogue, Anna thought, always twisting around her best speeches. She tried again. "Wagering *anything* on my account was a risk you should never have taken."

"'Twas no risk at all."

She argued, "And if you had lost? What then would you have owed Mr. Morley?"

"My sword. But there wasn't a chance I would lose."

"You are prideful, sir. And overconfident."

His mouth curved briefly. "Not at all. But I've acquired certain skills in life that on occasion serve me well."

"You cheat, you mean."

"Is this how you say thank you, then, in Scotland? I confess I'm ill acquainted with the manners of your country."

Anna might have made a sharp retort about his being ill acquainted with most manners, but she bit it back and opted for civility. "I thank you, sir, it was most kind, but I cannot accept them."

"Mr. Morley will hardly be having them back now you've worn them all over the town and the gardens." His gaze angled down to the hem of her gown, where the toes of the shoes briefly showed as she walked. "Anyhow, they were made for that gown, so they were. They're the very same colour as those little flowers, there."

She was so surprised to think he'd taken note of such a pointless detail as the shade of the small sprays of flowers, that it took her several seconds to collect her thoughts sufficiently to get her bearings. Both the general and Vice-Admiral Gordon were tall men, resplendent in their regimental uniforms with all the gold braid gleaming in the sun, which made it easier to spot them from a distance, standing not far off from where they had all been when she had left them. "Shall we go and join the others?" she suggested. "I am sure you'll be most welcome."

Edmund stopped, though she'd walked on a few more steps before she noticed he was no longer beside her. When she turned, she found him looking at her strangely.

"You were not sent to collect me." It was not a question.

Anna answered anyway. "No."

"Yet you took the trouble to come find me. Why?"

"Because I did not think it fair you should be so deprived of better company," she told him, adding, "And to thank you for the shoes."

"Aye, well, you've done that brilliantly, you have." His tone was dry. He looked in his turn to the place where all the others stood engaged in lively talk. "As for the company, I would not deem it better, necessarily, nor think I would be welcomed in its midst, with such a face as this."

It was, in truth, a livid bruise, the mark of a disreputable man. She should not have remarked on it, she knew, and yet she could not keep from asking, "Is it painful?"

"Only when I try to smile," he said, and did just that, if briefly.

Anna reckoned that the other man must look a good deal worse, and said as much.

He laughed. "You've heard the tale, then?"

She admitted that she had. "The merchants' wives, just now, were speaking of it. Mrs. Hewitt never can resist a piece of gossip."

"True enough. And what, exactly, did you learn?"

"That you did fight a harlot's husband."

"Also true." He stood there wholly without shame, and unrepentant. "She has lodgings in the house beside my own, and plies her trade there most discreetly, for her clients are most often men like Mrs. Hewitt's husband. Her own husband," Edmund said, "lives by her earnings, which he uses for himself and his own comfort. And he beats her. When he beat her last, I heard it through my own wall. She was weeping. I went over and suggested he remove himself. He disagreed with my suggestion. The result is as you see." He turned that cheek a fraction so she'd have a better view of it, as though to him it were a badge of honour, which in many ways it was. "Is that the tale the merchants' wives did tell?"

"You know that it was not." She did not need to tell the lurid details of the story she had heard, because no doubt he'd heard it, too, and knew it well enough. "Why do you not correct them?"

Edmund smiled, and for an answer gave the words she'd used herself. "I do not care what they believe." And she could well believe it true. "But I am curious," he told her, "why, with all that you'd just heard about my character, you'd seek to be my saviour. I can well defend myself."

"Aye, from a man, perhaps, but never from a woman's tongue. I

did not think it right," she told him honestly, "that they should so de-
fame you when social custom bound you not to make reply."

The smile had left his features, yet it lingered in his dark eyes. "Social custom never stopped me."

There was still a space between them, and he stood regarding her
across it as one soldier might regard another on a field of truce. And
then he tipped his head a little to the side and offered her his arm
again, and asked her, "Will you walk with me?" He did not miss the
small betraying glance she cast behind her at the others, Anna knew,
because he added, with a trace of his old mockery, "Or do you fear to
harm your reputation?"

Anna studied him a moment. Then she told him, "I am not afraid
of anything." And stepping forward, took his arm.

"Indeed," was his reply. "So I'm beginning to believe."

They left the crowds and joyful chaos of the meadow, crossing by
the little bridge over the Swan Canal into the Summer Garden. The
sentries at the bridge gave Edmund's battered face close scrutiny, but
in the end allowed them entry, through the gate in the high fence,
onto the broad and peaceful pathways of this green and private place
that had been such a favoured project of the tsar, while he had lived.

The tsar had patterned his own gardens after those he'd visited in
Amsterdam and Paris, on his European tours. He'd planted oaks and
elms and lime trees; scores of tulips that in summertime gave way to
masses of carnations, with artistic hedges set as backdrops for the countless busts and sculpted figures he had brought from every corner of the
empire and beyond. Sightless faces of white marble watched them while
they strolled, unhurried, down the broad paths edged with trees that had
been clipped and trained to grow as living walls, some even shaped to
arch above the path and cover it in shifting dappled shadow.

Near one of the fountains several officers were sitting smoking long
Dutch pipes of clay, and talking quietly, and in another corner near
a statue of Apollo a small cluster of musicians stood and played their
strings and flutes and oboes as though they were practicing, perhaps
for a performance later on that night.

Apart from that, there seemed to be no one but them remaining in the Summer Garden. Everybody else was in the meadow for the evening, with the empress and the duke and his new bride.

The sense of space, with nothing pressing in on her, felt wonderful to Anna. Had she wished, she could have spread her arms and run the whole length of that empty path and not been seen by any person but the man who walked beside her. She wondered how he would react, were she to let go of his arm right now and do exactly that.

Glancing down, he asked her, "What has so amused you?"

"Nothing."

"That," he said, "was not a smile for nothing."

"I am happy."

"I can see that. I presume it is the garden that is having this effect, and not myself. And fair enough," he said. "It is a lovely place. You blend in nicely." When she looked at him, he clarified: "Your gown. It is all flowers."

"Oh." She'd thought, just for a moment, he was saying she was lovely, too. The gown, though, *was* quite worthy of the compliment. She'd made it a Mantua gown, with a long flat train carefully caught up and folded and looped over silver cords held by the buttons on each side, a trick in itself to arrange, so the hem of the gown brushed the ground at the same length all round, while the back had a beautiful fullness. The sleeves fitted straight to her elbows and ended in turned-back cuffs, softened below by a fall of white lace, and the bodice lay smooth with its pattern so carefully matched to the waist of the petticoat that the gown's front appeared all of a piece.

Other men might have gone further, she thought, and remarked on the way that the frosted sea green of the silk matched her eyes. Mr. Taylor had done so. But Edmund O'Connor did no more than look her once over and tell her, "That gown's an improvement by far on the black one. It makes you look less like a nun."

"That's a good thing, then, is it?"

"It is. Nuns are terrible creatures," he said with a mock shudder.

"Always peering down their noses at you, smacking you with rods and such."

"If you were smacked, I'm sure you did deserve it. For my own part, I knew only love and kindness from the nuns that I did live with."

"Sure, you never lived with nuns, then." When her gaze assured him otherwise, he asked her, "When was this?"

"When I was small." He seemed to study her so long she turned her head to him defensively. "You doubt me?"

"No. I'm trying to imagine it." Whatever he imagined made him faintly smile. He looked away, and asked, "Which way, now?" for the pathway lay divided just in front of them, in one direction angling through an avenue of sculptures, and in the other entering a double row of lime trees. To her eyes, the statues looked too much like people, a reminder of the crowds. She chose the trees, and was immensely pleased she'd done so moments later, when the fragrance of fresh lilac, newly blooming, trailed around them.

"Could we stop?" she asked, not caring if it sounded odd. "Just here, please, for a moment?"

Edmund stopped. "What is it?"

"Lilacs," Anna said, and closed her eyes, and breathed the scent of them. They woke a memory, as they always did, of Scotland and of Slains, of childhood hours spent sitting underneath her favourite tree within the stone walls of the kitchen garden, with the lilac blossoms drifting down like snow upon her face and hair, the old tree's branches shaken by the winds that blew forever from the sea.

It was a happy memory; something to be held, and when her eyes came open to find Edmund watching her, she shared it with him. "There was once a lilac tree I used to love," she told him, "growing close against the castle near the place I lived, when I was but a child. I still do love the scent of lilac."

Edmund said, "So, you were raised beside a castle, and then placed with nuns. And is this commonplace, in Scotland?"

Anna, in her happy mood, was moved herself to mischief. "Aye. Are not you all raised likewise, sir, in Ireland?"

His glance held new appreciation of her wit. "Did you drink the wine," he asked her, "on the meadow?"

"I did not. And if you'd have the truth of it, my first home was a cottage with one room and seven people in it, so you see my origins are humble."

"And what of it? I have patches on my sleeves and do not dance the minuet."

She glanced at him in turn, and saw the way his jaw was set, and knew that he *had* overheard the cutting talk of Mrs. Hewitt and her group of friends, and that for all his show of unconcern he had not been unmarked by it.

She had, herself, been fortunate in life to have Vice-Admiral Gordon's care and his insistence she be taught the necessary things to let her fit in with society. Not everyone, she knew, had that advantage.

Now she said, "As dances go, it is not difficult."

"What's that?"

"The minuet. It is a simple step to learn," she told him. "Shall I teach you?"

"Here?"

"Why not?"

Unseen behind the trees and walls of living greenery, the practicing musicians had begun a slower tune, in triple time, and Anna said, "The music even suits the dance. I'll show you." And she raised her skirts a hand's breadth from the ground so he could see her shoes as she began to demonstrate the simple pattern of the step. "Start with your right foot and step forward, rise and sink again, like this, and then the left, and then step quickly forward with your right and finish with your weight upon the left." It was an easy rhythm: right, and left-right-left, and right, and left-right-left, and right . . . a swaying, easy movement.

Edmund stood to one side, watching her. "You're sure you did not drink the wine?"

She let the insult pass, still too contented in this place among the lime trees with their rustling, heart-shaped leaves and with the scent of lilacs strong about them, to allow him to provoke her into argument. "Are you afraid to dance, Mr. O'Connor?"

Edmund looked at her a moment longer, and his mouth curved slowly to a smile. "I'm not afraid," he said, "of anything."

"Then come, I'll teach you all of it, before the music changes."

Accepting the challenge, he deftly unbuckled his sword and removed it, laying it down on the grass by the nearest tree as he came forward.

She told him, "Stand just there, that's right, and I'll start over here." The path was wide enough—not wide enough to make a proper dance floor in a ballroom, but sufficient to allow them space to start as though they stood in separate corners, as the dance demanded, facing on a line of the diagonal. "We start as with all dances," Anna said, "by paying honours to the top part of the room." She curtseyed, demonstrating, while he turned obligingly and bowed. "Now, do the same to one another." Which they did. He had a gallant bow, she thought, when he so chose to use it, and his hair gleamed very blackly in the shade as he removed his hat and set it on his head again.

"And now," she said, "we move directly to the dance, when the first note presents itself. You go round that way, I go this, and we meet at the top of the room. No, you don't simply walk, sir, you do the step . . . there you are."

When they had met, Edmund looked down expectantly, waiting for his next instruction.

"Now offer your right hand," said Anna. "Up higher, that's right."

Her own hand, though not tiny, felt small when resting in his larger one. His hard palm rasped her skin, but the touch was more gentle than she'd have expected, the weight of his thumb resting over her knuckles deliberately careful.

"And now we dance this way," she said, "in a line. Some men here do a hop, or a bound . . ." Edmund angled his dark gaze to hers, only briefly, and Anna conceded, "And some men do not."

As directed, he let go her hand at the place where she told him, and both slowly danced to their opposite corners and back again, passing each other by twice at the centre of their makeshift dance floor.

The proper form, dancing with partners, she knew, was to keep your face always towards them, so that you looked always towards your left shoulder, thus giving a graceful and eye-pleasing line to the dance for the spectators watching; because, when two people were dancing the minuet, everyone else cleared the dance floor and stood round to give them an audience.

But there was nobody watching them, here. And a good thing, she thought, because dancing with Edmund O'Connor was having a most strange effect on her. Maybe it came from the scent of the lilacs, or from the air softening round them as twilight came on, or the spell of the music, or simply the way that he looked in his blue velvet coat, darkly elegant. Dangerous. Anna was not sure of anything, really, except that the ground was beginning to feel much less solid beneath her than when they had started the dance.

He danced well, with an easy grace, naturally turning in time with the motions, his steps crossing over when custom required, but with none of the flourishes some men employed. When his hands moved they did not bend soft at the wrists but remained always strong, as did he, and when she led him into the circling approach that would see them both meet at the middle, she felt unaccountably nervous.

He did as she'd told him and lifted his arm as a warning that he was about to present his right hand, which he did in one motion, extending his elbow and taking her own hand and holding it as they completed the turn.

Some men removed their hats at this stage, smoothly with their left hands, and replaced it all in rhythm with the dance. He left his on, so that its shadow fell across his eyes, but still she saw them, and her world for that one moment seemed reduced to their brown depths. In time with the dance he let go of her hand and their arms fell again to their sides, leaving only their eyes locked upon one another's as their turning steps brought them closer than they'd been before.

Anna faltered, forgetting to give him directions for what to do next, but he told her, "I think I remember the rest of it."

And with a wink he swung round again, moving without her instructions, too expertly for this to be the first time he had danced this particular dance. When they met in the middle again and he offered his left hand, she tried to rebuke him.

"You lied to me, sir."

"How is that?"

"You said you could not dance the minuet."

His eyes were darkly warm on hers. "I said I did not dance it. Never that I could not."

They were separated by the dance's steps again, and for those moments Anna sought to gain her inward balance, only to lose it again when they met at the middle the final time. This time he held both her hands as they turned, and then stopped, without warning, and stood looking down at her.

Anna said, "Mr. O'Connor . . ."

"The music has stopped."

So it had. She had not even noticed, but now, in this part of the garden, the silence seemed suddenly thick with unspoken things. Anna would have tugged her hands free, but he held them fast.

She raised her chin and said, "You cheat, Mr. O'Connor."

"When it suits my needs."

"What need could you have had," she asked, "to dance with me?"

He smiled a little in the shadows. Then as he was wont to do, he turned her own words back at her, replying as she'd done when he had asked her why she'd searched him out that evening in the meadow. "Truly, I have no idea. But," he added, "when I've got it sorted, you will be the first to know."

He loosed her hands, and let her pull them free this time, and

Anna took a step back, gaining breathing space as she heard someone coming down the path behind them. Several someones, actually, men's muffled voices mingling with the rustle of a woman's skirts.

She saw the change in Edmund's face and turned herself, uncertainly, then dropped into her deepest curtsy as the woman leading the procession stopped, and smiled.

"Good evening, Anna Niktova," said Empress Catherine.

chapter
THIRTY-SIX

Anna, still bent low, could see the full black skirts and petticoat of Empress Catherine's gown, for while the other guests had put off mourning by her own command, she had herself remained in black, although she wore a lovely new white headdress as a show of celebration for the day.

Behind the empress, other skirts and several men's legs had all stopped as well. Aware of all the eyes upon her, Anna replied in the same formal Russian the empress had used. "Your Imperial Majesty, may I offer my congratulations on your daughter's happy marriage?"

"Thank you. But do stand, my dear, that I might see your gown, it is most lovely. You look quite a part of my garden." She smiled. "I am pleased to see that you have worn your very best, to do my daughter honour. Did Vice-Admiral Gordon bring that gown from Paris for you?"

"I believe the silk did come from Paris, yes," said Anna, "but the gown is my own work."

"Indeed." The empress arched her eyebrows. "You are skilled, Anna Niktova. Perhaps I will have you come and sew for me. How would you enjoy that?"

How she truly felt would be of little consequence, she knew, because when royalty asked something of you, there was only one way you could answer. "Very much, Your Imperial Majesty. But I would pray you would not so command me until after General Lacy's wife has had her child this autumn, for I've given her my promise I will stay with her till then, and I'd not wish to break a promise."

It was bold of her to speak so to the empress, and she knew it, but she stood her ground and hoped that she had not offended. One of the ladies who stood by the empress—a lady-in-waiting, presumably—looked wholly shocked, but the empress herself only said, "General Lacy's wife is very fortunate to have engaged such a loyal companion. Have you left the vice-admiral's house, then, to live with the Lacys?"

"I have, Your Imperial Majesty."

The Empress Catherine looked at her with eyes that seemed to see past the simplicity of those few words, to understand some hidden piece of Anna's inner workings. "I, too, was raised in the houses of others," she said very gently.

Anna knew this, naturally, for everybody knew the story of how Empress Catherine had been raised from humble circumstances to the throne of Russia, though the story changed depending on the teller. All agreed she had been orphaned as a small child, and been taken to the household of a parish clerk, and then from thence to service in the family of a minister of Lutheran persuasion, where she'd stayed until arrangements had been made for her to marry a young soldier in the Swedish army. Some said that the marriage had occurred, while others said the soldier had been killed the morning of the wedding, but all were in agreement that the Russian army had then overrun the town, and Empress Catherine, brought before the commandant, had so impressed him that he had found service for her in a house of great respectability, from which she'd passed to service with Prince Menshikov, who'd introduced her to his friend the tsar.

The prince himself came forward now to stand beside Empress Catherine. Anna had not marked him out among the other men before, but there was no mistaking his lean features underneath the white wig that rose high on the crown of his head.

Anna curtsied again, and the prince gave a nod of acknowledgement before he murmured some words to the empress. Since the tsar's death the prince had kept close to her side, and the usual whispers had started to spread. General Lacy had recently said in disgust, of the gossips: "They'd have the poor empress so busy with lovers she'd never be left with a moment to sleep. 'Tis the curse of a woman of influence that she must always be reckoned unvirtuous."

Anna agreed. There was certainly nothing in how Prince Menshikov and Empress Catherine were talking to each other now to imply they were anything more than good friends of long standing.

The empress was saying, "I am well aware, Aleksandr Danilovich, but this will take but a moment." She looked again to Anna. "I trust that General Lacy is as kind as he appears to be?"

"He is indeed a kind man, and a good one, Your Imperial Majesty."

"I am glad to hear it. My younger daughter always has been charmed by him, and thinks him most heroic. And this young man who is with you, this is General Lacy's kinsman, is it not? The one who fights?"

So the rumours had risen to high places. Anna said, "Mr. O'Connor is kin to the general, yes, Your Imperial Majesty, but if you will permit me to correct what you have heard, he was provoked to fight, and only to defend a lady's honour, so I hope you will not think to judge him harshly."

Edmund, she was thankful, couldn't understand a word of what she said, for he did not speak any Russian. He'd have surely been amused to see her rise again to his defence.

The empress looked past Anna to where Edmund stood, his head still bent respectfully.

"Is that his sword, behind him on the ground?" she asked.

"It is, Your Imperial Majesty."

"Why did he remove it?"

"We were dancing," Anna said.

The empress made no comment, only turned her head a little as Prince Menshikov leaned in a second time to tell her something, then she nodded and looked back at Anna with a kindly smile. "Till the next meeting, Anna Niktova."

Dipping in her final curtsy Anna saw the empress give a gracious nod to Edmund as she passed with all her party down the pathway, heading back towards the banqueting pavilion at the north end of the garden.

"Well," said Edmund, moving up to stand behind her, "what the devil was all that about?"

She said, "Nothing of consequence." And then, struck by a sudden thought, "But now you've met the empress."

Edmund laughed. "Aye, so I have. It seems what you did tell me on the meadow was not all a lie. But then, the very best of lies," he said to her, "are hidden half in truth."

And with a smile, he went to fetch his sword.

Rob handed me half of the orange he'd peeled. "Well, I certainly had the impression," he said, "that was only the second time Anna and Catherine had met. Did you think that?"

I'd translated for him the essence of what both the women had said to each other, and thinking back now, I agreed. "Yes, you're probably right. Catherine didn't know Anna had gone to the Lacys' to live."

"So we've likely not missed anything."

"No." At least, not the scene I had glimpsed when I'd first held the Firebird; when Catherine had looked down at Anna and said, "You were never a nobody."

"So," Rob concluded, "we're on the right track."

It had been a long time since I'd walked in the Summer Garden. I could see the changes for the better made by recent efforts to restore it to its former grandeur, though it was much smaller now than it had been in Anna's time. The meadow had long gone, replaced two centuries ago by the parade ground called the Field of Mars, where modern incarnations of the regiments we'd just been watching at the wedding still stood in their ranks and fired salutes for state festivities, and where St. Petersburg's eternal flame burned for the memory of the fallen.

Other things were lost to memory. Of the buildings that had stood around the gardens as we'd seen them on the royal wedding day— the stables and orangeries and sheds, only the palace now remained to stand as plainly as it always had, without pretensions, seemingly unbothered by the busy tourist boats that chugged past on the great canal called the Fontanka. Now, as then, the Summer Palace with its square walls and its rows of simple windows seemed to gaze across the ever-flowing Neva at the gold dome of the fortress, lost in dreams of grander days.

The gardens held a wilder kind of beauty, now, the oaks and lime trees stretching high above us in this green and peaceful world of quiet solitude. The broad path we were walking on was lined on either side by statues, pale and white against the dark trunks of the trees, and in the fading light they watched us pass, like ghosts.

Rob walked beside me, uncomplaining, although I had kept him out and running round the city after Anna for some hours, and it was going on for sunset.

"I enjoyed it," he said now, when I apologized. "I'm starting to like Edmund."

"So is Anna."

"Is she?"

"Can't you see it?" How, I thought, could anyone *not* see it? There were just so many signs, how could he possibly have missed them?

"I'm no good," said Rob, "at reading signs."

I sighed, and said, "You're doing it again."

"What's that?"

"Answering questions before I can ask them."

"You did ask," he countered with logic that was not about to face argument, because to Rob it made no difference whether I spoke with my voice or my thoughts. He looked up at the white marble figure of some smirking god we were passing. "These statues," he said, "must have tales they could tell."

From his casual tone it was hard to tell if he was making an innocent comment or trying to prod me to use my gifts. "Yes, well, the problem," I said, "is that most of the tales wouldn't be of St. Petersburg, would they? They'd be about where all these statues first came from. Ancient Greece, maybe. Italy."

"France," Rob corrected me. "This one's from France." He had finished his half of the orange, but I could still catch its strong scent as he said, "If it's native impressions you're after, though, some of these trees might have been here in Peter the Great's time."

I tipped my head back, looking up at the fine lace of leaves overhead, less distinct now that part of the sky had begun to turn bluegreen as well, bringing shadows.

"I wouldn't know which ones, though, would I?" I said.

"Not unless you touched them, no."

I glanced at him, and our eyes met for a moment, and I saw they held the same unspoken challenge that Edmund O'Connor's had held when he'd asked Anna whether she'd walk with him, there on the meadow, or whether she feared to.

She'd taken that challenge and met it directly.

But I wasn't Anna. I looked away. "Well, they'll be locking the garden soon, anyway," I told him. "And we should eat. And tomorrow, I think we should start back at Lacy's and see if we can't pick up after the wedding, at some point."

Rob didn't judge me. Perversely, that bothered me more than if he had reacted, had called me a coward, had stopped being so . . . so forgiving. So calm. So damned *brotherly*. I didn't want Rob to act like my brother. The force of that shook me so deeply I stopped on the path.

"Right then," Rob told me, "I'll follow your lead."

He was only replying, I knew, to what I had just told him, my plans for the morning, for where we should next look for Anna. I knew that. And yet, as I fell into step at his side once again and we walked through the gates of the old Summer Garden and onto the Neva Embankment, with twilight descending all round us, I had the same feeling that Anna had felt at the mid-point of that minuet—the same sense that the ground was beginning to feel much less solid beneath me than when I had started this dance.

chapter
THIRTY-SEVEN

Captain Hay had returned to St. Petersburg. It had been slightly more than a year since he'd left the tsar's service and gone south in search of a climate that would more agree with his health, and Anna had missed him. He'd been such a regular visitor to the vice-admiral's throughout the whole time that she'd lived there, that truly he seemed like a favourite young uncle to her, and he greeted her that way when he came to dine with the general the last day in May.

It made quite a full table for dinner: the general, his wife, Father Dominic, Vice-Admiral Gordon with Sir Harry Stirling and Captain Hay, and of course Edmund beside her, his shoulder for want of space brushing her own when he reached for the bread.

Anna lost track a few times of what they were actually talking about, but she put her distraction down more to the liveliness of the conversation than to her awareness of the dark man at her side.

Gordon sat at her other side, with General Lacy as usual heading the table, his wife at the foot, and Sir Harry and Captain Hay sitting to either side of the Franciscan, who seemed keen to hear all the news out of Rome.

Anna, living with Vice-Admiral Gordon so long, had grown very accustomed to having the business of King James's exiled court talked about openly, but this was the first time she'd seen it happen here, at General Lacy's own table. She'd known his sympathies, certainly, and that he'd fought for King James in his youth and still passed his glass over the water, but it gave her pleasure to hear him now talking of current affairs with the ardour of one who was still a true Jacobite.

"And did you see Daniel O'Brien, when you came through Paris?" he asked Captain Hay.

"I did, aye. He is well. He said he'd spoken to the Duke of Holstein's agent there, who did assure him that the duke, were he to gain the throne of Sweden, wishes nothing more than for King James to be restored."

Vice-Admiral Gordon nodded. "Aye, the duke says much the same to me."

"I also met with our friend General Dillon, while in Paris," Captain Hay went on, "and found him very desolate. The king no longer holds him in his confidence."

"Why not?" asked Gordon. "Dillon is a good man, and a loyal one."

"The king is well aware of that, but General Dillon," said the captain, "keeps unfortunate companions. Like the Earl of Mar."

The name meant something to the men around the table, for apart from Father Domenic they all seemed understanding of the reasons why the king would have withdrawn his trust from General Dillon.

"Anyway," the captain said, "I did not stop too long in Paris, for even though I travelled with an alias there are too many eyes there for my presence to go unremarked, and knowing I had just come from the king, the rats came out to sniff about. I did not wish to find myself in irons, or worse. O'Brien told me of a former courier, some years ago, who'd come across with money for the king, and who resisted all attempts to turn his loyalties so strongly that the agents of the English had him poisoned. Far from killing him, it turned him mad, so that his friends were forced to bind him, and O'Brien said the man has never yet recovered."

"Who was this?" Sir Harry Stirling asked, with interest.

"Maurice Moray."

Anna let go of her cup of wine and would have spilled it had not

Edmund's reflexes been quicker. As he righted it, she bent her head to hide her face. "I'm sorry."

Captain Hay was speaking, still. "You will have heard about his family, I am sure. Of Abercairney. This Maurice was the youngest of them, I believe."

"Indeed, I know them well," Sir Harry Stirling said. "His elder brother Robert married my own father's widow, for she was still young at my father's death. Robert," he said, "only narrowly missed being hanged after Sherrifmuir, but though he won his release his wife died not long after, and left their five children all motherless."

"Oh," Mrs. Lacy said, "how very sad."

"That whole family has come quite undone, in standing for the king," Sir Harry said. "But then, 'tis true of many families that have done the same, both Scots and Irish."

Edmund put in drily, "We should all do as the English, merely drinking healths to James instead of raising swords for him, for then we might avoid the broken heads and lost estates, as they do."

Anna had blinked back the sting of tears enough to lift her head again, and yet the pain of hearing of her uncles' fates, and knowing full well that her Uncle Maurice would not have been made to suffer anything had she been more discreet and not revealed him to his enemies, she could not keep the bitterness from sharpening her voice. "But it is by our actions, surely, and not by our words, that we reveal our worth."

"I know that, Mistress Jamieson. 'Tis why I made the joke."

"Forgive me, sir, it did not sound a joke to me."

Across the table, Captain Hay watched their exchange with curiosity, as though, surprised by Anna's tone, he sought a closer study of its cause. "Mr. O'Connor, you did lately come from Spain, I understand?"

"I did, sir. I left Spain nearly a year ago, and came here the beginning of November last."

"I only ask," said Captain Hay, "because in Paris I did hear some talk of an O'Connor who had left Madrid last year under suspicion he was Stanhope's spy."

"That would have been myself, sir." Edmund took the accusation full on, straightening his shoulders as he settled back, so that the roughness of his coat brushed Anna's arm. "In faith, I have lost count of all the things I was accused of when I left, but I remember that was one of them."

"And were they right, then, to suspect that you were spying for the English?" Captain Hay asked, pressing, as he liked to do, until he had the truth.

Anna could feel the irritation of the man beside her, even though his voice stayed pleasant. "Surely there's no answer to be made to that, for if I were a spy I'd scarcely own it, and if I were not, my answer would yet be the same as if I were."

The general laughed. "He is no spy, and I myself will own to it, if he will not. Like General Dillon, he has merely had, upon occasion, some unfortunate companions. Is that not so, Edmund?"

Edmund dragged his gaze from Captain Hay's and sitting forward once again remarked, "So it would seem."

Sir Harry Stirling, in his own good-natured way, disarmed the situation with, "I see your bruises have now disappeared, Mr. O'Connor."

"Very nearly, aye, Sir Harry."

"I am glad to see it." With a grin, Sir Harry added, "I have heard the harlot's husband is yet in his bed." He sent a charming look to Mrs. Lacy. "Madam, my apologies for sullying the conversation, but you have a table full of men and I'm afraid we cannot always mind our manners as we should."

The general smiled as well. "Perhaps," he said, "we ought to let our Edmund deal with Captain Deane, when he arrives."

That made the other men, save Father Dominic and Edmund, burst out laughing, and Vice-Admiral Gordon said, "In truth, I'd pay to see him do it."

Edmund, looking round at Gordon, asked, "And who is Captain Deane?"

Anna knew most of the tales about Captain John Deane. She had never much liked him the few times she'd met him, but that had been mainly because he'd so clearly disliked the vice-admiral, and being a child, that alone had been reason for Anna to think poorly of any man.

It had only been afterwards, when he had first been court-martialled, then sent out of Russia, that she had begun to hear the stories that had reinforced her own ill-favoured view of Captain Deane.

Edmund had, before today, heard none of them, and even when the final course was cleared and they had moved into the drawing room, they'd only reached the court-martial itself.

"So he was never tried for Captain Urquhart's death?" asked Edmund, frowning.

Gordon answered, "No. We could not make him pay for that." His voice still held the buried anger Anna knew would always be there when he thought of Adam Urquhart crushed to death beneath the great mast of a ship that foundered on a sandbank close to Cronstadt. Urquhart and a second captain, new to Russia's service and still unfamiliar with the waters, had been led by Deane, who knew that coastline well and had been charged to bring them and their ships to Cronstadt in all safety. Deane had given charts to both the other captains, and instructed them on how to steer their course, then he had steered his own ship on a safer one and let the others founder. Both the other ships were lost, young Adam Urquhart lost his life, and all who heard about the incident did count it no coincidence that Urquhart and the other captain shared one common thing that Captain Deane could not abide: They were both Jacobites.

Vice-Admiral Gordon said, to Edmund, "Urquhart's death was never any accident, but with the charts conveniently lost we had no evidence to prove it. We could prove, however, that Deane had colluded with the Swedes some two years earlier, to sell them back their own ships that he'd captured, at a profit to himself. That was no secret amongst any who had served with him, but none would dare to speak, until . . ." He paused, and shook his head, and finished, "What he did to Urquhart went beyond the pale, for even Deane's own friends."

"And so the tsar dismissed him?"

Gordon nodded. "Banished him at first, into Kazan, then called him back here and dismissed him all in anger, with an order he was never to return."

"Aye, well, he's taken that to heart," remarked Sir Harry, who was setting up the chess pieces.

"The tsar is dead," said Gordon with a shrug. "No doubt the English do believe that Empress Catherine is a fool, or more forgiving, else they never would attempt it."

"They attempted it two years ago," Sir Harry said, "but it was stopped in time by our associates in London."

"Had he come two years ago," said Captain Hay, "the tsar himself, on learning Deane had disobeyed his last instruction, would have met him when he landed and ensured he neither walked nor chewed his food again, and we'd have had no problem."

Mrs. Lacy, who'd been dozing in her chair beside the window, roused herself enough to ask, "And why is it a problem now?"

Her husband answered her, "Because, my darling, Captain Deane is in the pay of England's chief of spies, Lord Townshend, who would send him like a rat among us now, to learn our business. And because Deane is a naval man, he'll see what other men would not."

Sir Harry said, "Not if we find a way to stop him." He had finished setting all the pieces in their places on the chessboard. Now he looked at Captain Hay. "Come, William, have a game."

"Thank you, no. I have a vivid memory of my last defeat."

The general, with a smile of mischief, said, "Play Mistress Jamieson."

Anna had not sat beside the window, as she often did. Instead she'd picked a chair well in the corner, cast in shadows, from where she had sat till now and watched, outside the conversation, keeping to herself. On any other day she might have asked what they were worried Deane might see, here in St. Petersburg, but she was thinking still about her Uncle Maurice, and felt far too miserable to play an active part in the discussion. "No, I thank you," she replied, before Sir Harry even framed the question. "Do forgive me, but I do not wish to play."

Sir Harry said, "A lucky thing for me, I think, for I have heard Miss Gordon say that you defeated the vice-admiral on occasion, and I know he is a formidable player."

Gordon took Sir Harry's measure with a father's eyes. "My daughter seems to tell you much."

"She does, aye," said Sir Harry. With a smile, he looked the older man directly in the eyes. "Can you be tempted to a game?"

"Indeed I can."

As Gordon moved to sit across the chessboard from Sir Harry, Captain Hay asked General Lacy, "General, you're the best tactician. How would you suggest we deal with Captain Deane?"

"Do we know yet when he will arrive?"

The captain said, "It could be any day now."

"Then we do not have the luxury of time." The general's gaze fixed thoughtfully upon the chessboard for a moment, then slid still more thoughtfully to Edmund.

"What?" asked Edmund. "Are you wanting me to beat him for you, after all?"

The general's wife said, intervening, "No, Pierce. That will never do."

The general reassured them all, including in his gesture Father Dominic, who'd moved to protest. "That was hardly my intention. And from what I do recall of Captain Deane, he can be vicious on his own part, when provoked." He said, to Edmund, "There is more that could be said about his character before he came to Russia. He was already notorious as captain of the *Nottingham* that wrecked upon Boon Island fifteen years ago, but that tale has some details I would spare my wife."

"Boon Island." Edmund frowned. "Was that the shipwreck where the captain called himself a hero, and his crewmen said he had betrayed and badly used them? Where the men surviving ate the flesh of their dead cook?"

"Yes, thank you, Edmund, that would be the very detail that I wished to spare my wife," the general answered in a dry tone.

Father Dominic had crossed himself in horror at what Edmund said. "For such an act, your Captain Deane will burn in everlasting fire, no matter what you do to him."

"Aye," Sir Harry told the monk, "I've no doubt God will deal with him accordingly, but till he is committed to God's hands, I fear we have him on our own."

The room fell silent once again, and Anna noticed Edmund had turned slightly and was watching her. She looked away, but still he asked her, "Are you feeling quite well, Mistress Jamieson?"

Anna nodded, which appeared to leave him unconvinced.

"And have you no opinion on how we should deal with Captain Deane? No wisdom from the nuns that you would share with us?"

He'd meant to make her smile. It did the opposite.

Vice-Admiral Gordon turned. "What nuns would those be?"

"Why, the nuns she was placed with when she was a child," Edmund said, and then stopped when he saw Anna's eyes.

Gordon looked at her. "Where was this, Anna?"

The general, on the far side of the room, looked to the monk and said, "'Tis well you do not wager, Father Dominic, for you would have my money. You were right."

The mild Franciscan said, "I saw the signs of it at once, in how she prayed, and in her manners."

"Irish nuns, they must have been, for her to have such grace," the general teased. "Were they then Irish, Mistress Jamieson, these nuns who did instruct you?"

Still Vice-Admiral Gordon held her gaze, his hand above the chessboard as he asked again, "Where was this, Anna?"

Trapped, she looked at Edmund with reproach and answered all of them, "I'm sure it was so long ago, I've quite forgotten." And then, because her eyes had fast begun to fill with tears, she closed them, bent her head a moment and collected her emotions, and then rose. "You will excuse me," she said calmly, "but I have a dreadful headache."

She walked carefully and unconcerned until she'd left the room and reached the corridor where none could see her. Then she let the tears come, and she ran.

S he'd told them one thing true: Her convent days at Ypres were long ago and past, but still she felt the bars. She felt them even here, today, more strongly in the yard, where she could see the sun and breathe the open air yet on all sides was caught by walls that she could not escape, and whose deep shadows ever chased her heels.

It seemed that for her sins, the penance God had chosen for her was the bitter curse of memory, and that, too, created bars that she could not escape. She saw her uncle's face through them, the face that might have been like her own father's, and she heard his voice demanding of the nun, "Whose child is this?"

They had done better, Anna thought, to tell him she was no one's child.

The tears spilled over once again. She turned her steps towards the shed, to seek at least the sympathetic company of one who knew the feeling of captivity, but when she reached the cage she found it empty with the wire door swung open on its hinges, all abandoned.

She was not completely sure when she first noticed she was no longer alone, but she was well aware of it for several moments, and of who it was that stood behind her, before Edmund spoke.

"I must apologize," he said, and she could not recall when she had heard him say those words as he did now, without an edge of mockery, but perfectly sincere. "I did not know that you had not . . . I did not know it was a secret." He was standing not three steps behind her, speaking very quietly, so none could overhear them from the house. "I must confess," he added, "that the very fact you *did* tell me convinced me it was not a secret, for I hardly guessed you'd hold me in your confidence. Believe me, had I known it to be otherwise, I never would have mentioned it."

She drew a slightly shaky breath, and steadied it, and asked, without forgiving him, "What happened to the bird?"

"Her leg had healed, so I released her."

"Did you never tell the children?"

"They had lost all interest. Truly, they'd forgotten she was here."

"But you had not."

"'Tis not a thing I'm likely to forget."

She thought on this a silent moment. Then she said, "I'm glad she flew away."

"Aye, so am I. Some things weren't meant to live in cages." He paused, too, then said, "I'm truly sorry, Anna, that I so betrayed your confidence. I promise it will not be done again."

She did turn, then, and faced him. "No," she said. "No, it will not. I should never . . ." Her voice, against all her best efforts, still broke on the words that were more about what she had done in the past and could never undo. "I should never have spoken."

Edmund's gaze searched her pale face. "This cannot be entirely my fault. You were upset by something long before I made my comment."

She had wiped away the wetness from her eyes, and yet she knew she could not make them clear of shadows, so she told him with faint stubbornness, "I have a headache."

"Do you? Well, I have a cure for that," he said. "I'm sent to Vasilievsky Island, on an errand for the general. Will you come with me?"

She looked at him, to see if he were serious or teasing her. "Why should I?"

Edmund shrugged. "Because I'm sorry and you know it and you wish to show forgiveness. Or you're sorry in your turn that I have none else who can bide me, and you wish to show me charity. Or maybe, Mistress Jamieson," he said, "because you need to."

She'd have sworn that, when he looked at her like that, he saw her inner self stripped bare of its disguises and defences. Yet she did not know if he were speaking of her nature or his own, when he remarked a second time, with force, "Some things weren't meant to live in cages."

All she knew was, when he held his hand to her, she took it willingly, and went with him.

Rob grinned. "A sneaky way of getting ice cream for your breakfast."

"Well, he did say that his errand was on Vasilievsky Island, and we could hardly have just followed them across. There were no bridges, in those days. They'd have to cross by barge." With that justification, I leaned happily against the waist-high granite wall that ran along the Strelka, and looked out across the Neva to the Hermitage, its windows brightly glittering with morning sunlight.

Clouds were hanging low off to the west, above the distant Gulf of Finland, past the far edge of the island, but the day so far was starting fair, and warmer by a few degrees than yesterday. I didn't need my jacket.

Rob, his own ice cream in hand, and looking more awake than I was, leaned beside me. "There's your mobile," was his warning in the instant before it began to ring.

I told him, "Show-off," and the crinkles showed a moment at the corners of his eyes as I took the call.

When I rang off, Rob had finished his ice cream.

I said, "That was Yuri. They're hanging the rest of the paintings this morning, but Wendy Van Hoek won't be there until three, so I'll meet with him then."

"At the Menshikov Palace?" he asked. "Which is where?"

"Just down there."

"On this island?"

I nodded, and Rob said, "Well, that gives us plenty of time." In a casual voice, he remarked, "You've had no calls at all from your boss, in a while."

"No." I'd noticed that, too.

"Does he ken that I'm with you?"

"Of course not." I said that a little too quickly, then kicked myself, trying to make it sound less rude by adding, "Sebastian and I don't share details about our own personal lives, as a rule."

Rob accepted this with a brief nod. "Well, I guess he can manage without you, when he puts his mind to it."

I tried to *not* try to read deeper meaning in that, nor to wonder if he spoke from his own experience. I only shrugged and said something about the new receptionist suiting Sebastian, and how we were none of us so irreplaceable.

"Speak for yourself," Rob said lightly. "I'm one of a kind. You'll find no other man who would work all these hours for so little food."

I'd find no other man like him ever, I thought. Full stop.

"Nick?" He was watching my face. "Are you ready?"

It took me three seconds to realize that he was just asking me if I was ready to try to find Anna. I nodded, and turned so he'd not see me blush like an idiot.

Only a few steps behind where we stood there were white benches ringing the Strelka, beneath the clipped line of the trees, and we chose the one second along the curved path, with a lamp-post beside it and little inquisitive sparrows that scattered around our feet when we sat down.

"D'ye want to give this one a go?" Rob asked.

I shook my head. "Sorry," I said. "All new gravel and ground, all young trees . . . I've got nothing to touch."

"Have ye not?" he replied. And then made me a liar by laying his arm on the back of the bench so it settled in warmth on my shoulders.

I had searched out the paintings and sketches and coloured engravings last night, in my grandfather's book, that showed how different places had looked in St. Petersburg in the first quarter of the eighteenth century, so I already expected to see the great Custom House, and the long warehouses, guarded by soldiers, that stood all along the exchange, where the merchants all met to do business each day. The exchange looked a lot like a very long, very wide promenade built all of wood, that extended out over the edge of the land so it served as a broad landing stage for the smaller ships moored all along it, their masts bobbing gently in time with the current, all waiting to take on new cargo or discharge the ones they had carried upriver.

Anna stepped carefully onto the wooden stairs set at the waterline, lifting the hem of her petticoat clear of the river as Edmund, who'd climbed up first out of the boat, bent to help her, his hand strongly holding her own.

"I am not like to fall," she assured him. "I've spent half my life getting on and off ships and small boats."

"'Tis your blood," Edmund said, "same as mine."

Anna let go of his hand as she stepped to his level, and smoothing her skirts asked him, "What do you mean, sir?"

"You Scots and we Irish, and even the English, we're islanders all." Edmund looked to the river, alive with its traffic, and narrowed his eyes to the sun. "We're surrounded by seas and we'd seek to know what lies beyond them, and where those wide waters might carry us."

Anna could not but agree with him, for from her earliest memories she'd looked to the sea and the distant horizon. She never had outgrown the thrill of sailing the half day downriver with Vice-Admiral Gordon to the naval port of Cronstadt, where the great ships of the Russian fleet all jostled at their anchors and the Gulf of Finland stretched away towards the larger Baltic Sea. She'd always loved the sound of creaking timbers and of sails that snapped and fluttered as they rose and filled with wind; the ropes that strained and stretched as though the whole ship were a living thing impatient to be free upon the waves.

She looked at Edmund now, his face still turned into the wind, and wondered if he felt the same. "And where would you be carried, if you had a ship that you could steer?" she asked.

He answered without hesitation. "Home," he said. "To Ireland."

And then, as if he felt that showed a weakness, he looked down at her and found his old sardonic smile. "But I cannot attempt it. I'd be hanged before I left the beach, or else transported off to the Americas, for having served King James. I have heard tell the Prince of Hanover, whom some would call King George, is not forgiving of the men who chose the Stewart cause, so I shall have to see our own king back upon the throne before I ever see my home again."

She said, "I'm sorry."

"Why should you be like to pity me?" he asked. "You are as homeless as myself, and have no true kin I can see to give you comfort."

Anna bristled at his bluntness. "Aye, I have a home. And family, though they may not be my own by blood."

"I did not mean—"

"There is a strength, Mr. O'Connor, in a family that is chosen, and not merely thrust upon us. From my birth I've lived with others not my kin, but not by sufferance, by their choice and invitation, while Vice-Admiral Gordon's late wife's daughter, Jane, had family who were hers by blood and high of rank, yet were most cruel to her, and treated her with nothing but neglect, and it was not their arms that held her when she breathed her last. Vice-Admiral Gordon," Anna said, "would do the same for me as he did do for Jane, and well I know it, so you will forgive me, sir, if I do not agree that I've no family."

Edmund stood beneath her speech with all the dutiful attention of a schoolboy being lectured, but his eyes took a keen interest in her features, and when she had finished speaking, his reply was only, "Do you know, that when you're in a temper, your Scotch accent grows more strong?"

She gave a feeling sigh. "I should have stayed at General Lacy's house."

"But then you would have missed the peaceful pleasure of my company." The brown eyes danced. "And look, here comes good Mr. Taylor. Surely, you'd not wish to miss the chance to speak to him?"

Anna sighed again, and turned, and greeted Mr. Taylor with a curtsy while he bowed, but he seemed in a hurry and in no mood to converse. He asked her, "Is Sir Harry still with General Lacy?"

Anna told him, "He was there when I did leave, not half an hour ago."

"Good. Is this your boat? May I engage it? I have news to give Sir Harry, and it cannot be delayed."

With interest, Edmund asked him, "Is it news of Captain Deane?"

The Scotsman turned to look at him. "It is, aye. Do you know of Captain Deane, then?"

Anna said, "He was a topic of discussion over dinner."

Mr. Taylor told them, low, "I've just had word that he's expected into Cronstadt on the day after tomorrow, so Vice-Admiral Gordon will be wanting to sail there himself, I should expect, so that he can delay Deane if he's able to."

"The vice-admiral," Anna said, "was also dining at the general's house, and was there still when we did come away."

"Then you'll excuse me," Mr. Taylor said, and gave a hasty bow to them, "I will away myself, and pass the message."

Edmund watched the boat depart, then turned and gave his arm to Anna. "He's a good man, Mr. Taylor."

"Yes, he is."

"And Scottish, like yourself."

"He is."

"And I daresay that he does hop and bound, when he does dance the minuet."

Her mouth curved, though she turned her head so that he would not see it. "Yes, all gentlemen of quality," she said, "do hop and bound, sir."

"So I'm told."

They crossed the broad exchange, and left the timber walkway for the hard-packed ground of the great square that stretched between the line of warehouses on one side, and the longer line of colleges that faced it to the west, where General Lacy came each day to work, as did the other great men of the city.

There were soldiers here as well, some standing guard while others strode amongst the throngs of people and the carriages and wagons. Anna looked at Edmund. "Where must we go now, to do your errand?"

"Mr. Trescott's tavern."

Anna stopped. "You're never serious."

"It is all right." He urged her on. "We are not going in."

The tavern stood, a low and wooden building, at the edge of all that was respectable. The smells of stale tobacco and spilled wine and drunken men came wafting outward through the door each time it opened, and the men who spilled out also looked unsteady on their feet.

Anna did not mind their looks—they were as likely to be clerks and writers from the colleges as seamen from the wharves—but it was not the sort of place she cared to stand alone, so she was reassured when, having looked but once at Edmund, all the men in the vicinity retreated by a pace or two.

He smiled at her, and said again, "We are not going in." And with a coin he paid the nearest man to vanish through the door and re-emerge with Mr. Trescott in his wake.

The owner of the tavern was a pleasant man, an Englishman, with traces of the West Country still clinging to his speech. His head did not quite reach to Edmund's shoulder though his arms were thick with muscle and, in his own day, he'd earned a fearsome reputation as a fighter. "Now then, Mr. O'Connor, and Mistress . . ." He had forgot her name, she knew, though likely he remembered her attachment to Vice-Admiral Gordon, for he was acquainted with the best part of the naval men. "In what way can I serve you?"

Edmund told him, "General Lacy asks if he could buy an anker of good brandy, if you have one going spare, for there are like to be some meetings at the house."

"Oh, yes? And what is the occasion?" Mr. Trescott smiled at both of them. "A coming marriage?"

"No, a visitor."

The tavern owner asked, "Would you be speaking, then, of Captain Deane?"

Edmund had obviously never yet experienced the speed with which news travelled round the docklands. "Is there anyone who does not know him?"

"All men round here know good Captain Deane."

"I am myself in doubt about the 'good,'" said Edmund, "for in truth I never knew a man so hated and ill spoken of as he was this day at the general's table, by those men that knew him. Will that do?" He handed coins to Mr. Trescott.

"Aye, it will, sir, very nicely."

"And will someone bring it out? For I would not leave Mistress Jamieson to stand here unattended."

From behind them a man's voice said, "I'll attend her, if you like."

She turned, because it had been several months since she had heard that voice. "Charles!"

"Cousin." He stood tall and straight as ever in his regimentals.

Anna said, to Edmund, "May I introduce Lieutenant Gordon, the vice-admiral's nephew. Charles, this is—"

"Mr. O'Connor," said Charles. "I have heard much about you."

"Indeed."

They were well-matched in height, and in simple belligerence, Anna decided. They squared off in silence a moment, then Edmund said, "Will you then stand with your cousin, while I fetch the brandy?"

Not certain if he had been speaking to her or to Charles, she said, "Yes," and stood fast in her spot while he entered the tavern.

Charles said, "You'll have heard Captain Deane is returning?"

She nodded. "Your mother will have him to tea, I've no doubt, to sustain him in seeking to ruin your uncle."

Charles smiled at her tone. "She well may. But my mother knows nothing," he said, "of my uncle's affairs. Do not worry. If Deane comes to tea, he will gain nothing by it apart from a pain in his stomach from Cook's indigestible scones."

Anna laughed, just as Edmund came out again with a small barrel held balanced on one of his shoulders. He glanced with unreadable eyes at the pair of them.

Charles, not noticing, told Anna, "I shall be sure to keep Mother distracted as well as I can do. And how is my uncle's health? I heard that he was—"

"This is, as it happens, incredibly heavy," said Edmund, "so either take hold of an end of it, sir, or find some means to walk while you're talking, for I've no great wish to stand long with this load."

And with that speech he started back by the same way they had come. Anna, smiling at Charles's expression, said, "Come, then," and both of them fell into step behind Edmund.

Charles looked at her. "What are you doing?"

"I'm walking."

"That's not what I mean."

"Then you'll have to be clearer," she told him.

Whatever his thoughts were, he held them in silence until they had come to the wharf again. As Edmund lifted his arm for a boatman, Charles said to him, "May I congratulate you, sir?"

Edmund turned, and Anna inwardly groaned, for she knew what came next.

"And my cousin," said Charles, in the same charming way that he'd used in the winter, when he'd said the same words to poor Mr. Taylor. "I was not aware that you two were engaged to be married, but since you would act as her escort in public, I must assume that is the case."

Edmund turned for a moment to carefully lower the barrel of brandy down into the hands of the boatman, and Anna was certain she saw him suppress a slight smile. Then he looked back at Charles with a face that gave nothing away, and said, "Sure if we were, it would be our own business and none of your own." Then he held out his hand towards Anna.

She took it, in full disbelief that he'd said what he'd said, and allowed him to hand her down into the boat while Charles went from stunned silence to full-throated laughter.

"Now this one," he told Anna, "*this* one, I like."

chapter

THIRTY-NINE

All Saturday the storms had raged, with wind that tore at all the
rooftops and flung rain in clawing sheets against the houses, keeping everyone indoors, and on the next day Captain Deane had come
into St. Petersburg.

He'd come at noon, and overland, complaining rather loudly that
he'd been detained for several days at Cronstadt. When she'd heard
that, Anna had felt satisfaction, because then she'd known that Gordon had succeeded in his purpose. He had sailed to Cronstadt on the
morning after that disastrous dinner at the home of General Lacy, and
had stayed away all week, and when he'd next come to the general's
house, the very evening of the Sunday Deane arrived in town, he'd
looked as men must look when they had been to battle.

Anna had been playing a duet with Mrs. Lacy, very poorly, on the
harpsichord, and was no doubt not meant to hear the men's exchange,
but she had heard it notwithstanding.

"Do we have Apraxin?" General Lacy had asked Gordon.

"Aye," the other had replied, "we have him firmly on our side. He
got us this." He'd held a piece of paper up, subsiding wearily into a
chair as General Lacy took the paper from his hand.

"What's this?"

The vice-admiral had closed his eyes and, leaning back, had told
him, "Read it."

"'I, whose name is underwritten, do declare . . .'" The general had
glanced up at Gordon. "Surely you're not serious."

"Go on."

"' . . . do declare to His Excellency the General Admiral Count

Apraxin, that on the ninth of May last past, the Right Honourable the Lord Viscount Townshend, did give me permission when a favourable opportunity should present . . . '" The paper had been lowered as the general had asked, even more incredulous, "Deane *wrote* this? He admitted that he came here on a private mission from the English court, by the spymaster's direction?"

"And we have the written proof of it, all signed in his own hand. When he did first arrive in Cronstadt, and Apraxin asked him why he'd come, he answered he'd brought goods here to dispose of, with a mind perhaps to settle here in Trade."

"What did Apraxin do?"

"He told Deane that he lied, and made it plain that if he did not tell the truth of why he'd come, he'd never make it into Petersburg. I'm told Apraxin yelled at Deane a goodly time. I have doubts I myself could stand against the Lord High Admiral, if he came at me full volume. Have you heard him?"

"I have not."

"'Tis fair impressive. Even so, it took him fully until Friday to convince Deane to write *that*."

"Well, God bless and keep the Lord High Admiral," General Lacy had remarked. "It is a damning document. And who has seen it?"

"Tolstoy. He was not much pleased, as you can well imagine. I have made a second copy for Sir Harry, to be circulated well among the members of the Factory, for you know how warmly they view any interference out of London. And I thought," he'd said at last, "to give a copy to Galovkin, for both he and Tolstoy, sitting in the College of Foreign Affairs, do take an equal view of foreign meddling. It seemed hardly fitting to show this to one of them and not the other."

"No," the general had agreed, and smiled. "It would indeed be most discourteous. I should imagine both of them will have some questions for our Captain Deane, before they grant him leave to stay here."

Gordon had asked, "And where is Deane now, have you heard?"

"I have. Apparently he wrote to Nye, the shipbuilder, and asked him to find lodgings for him somewhere in the town, so he is now lodged with a captain of the guards, and will no doubt begin his prying at the break of morn."

"No doubt. When he discovers William Hay has now returned here, and from Rome, Deane will be sniffing like a dog that's lost its bone to learn his business, mark my words."

"Oh, I believe you." General Lacy had leant back himself, the paper in his hand, and said, "I'm sure that is exactly what he'll do."

And so it proved.

The next few days were busy ones, and Anna was as often sent on business for the general now as for his wife. It was, she knew, because she could pass by without attracting much attention, and if anyone outside their own community of Jacobites had wondered why she ventured quite so frequently to where Sir Harry Stirling lodged, a nudge and word from Mrs. Hewitt soon reminded them that Mr. Taylor had now more or less become Sir Harry's private secretary.

Mr. Taylor took great pleasure in escorting her whenever he was able, though it was more often Edmund who was strolling at her side.

He was at her side this morning, Thursday morning, as she made her way across the broad expanse of the great square on Vasilievsky Island, heading to the colleges. "So then you liked him," Anna said.

"You'd twist my words. I did not say I liked the man, I only said that, had I met Deane as I did, at Trescott's tavern, without being warned about his character, I would have liked him well enough, that's all I said."

"I think you do feel sorry for him."

"Why would I do that?"

She said, "Because he has a reputation that does go before him, as does yours, and you feel moved by that to grant him all the benefit of doubt that you are oftentimes denied."

"Of all the . . . woman, you exhaust me, do you know that? Yes, you're right, you have exposed me. I do feel a sense of kinship with the man."

"You see? I knew it."

"One day," Edmund warned, "I'm going to fall down dead, stone dead, right in the middle of the street, and when I meet St. Peter at the gates he'll ask me, Edmund, what became of you? And I'll say, I did walk with Anna Jamieson a mile too far, that's what."

She told him, calmly, "You're assuming it's St. Peter you'll be meeting."

"Up or down," he said, "the sympathy will no doubt be the same."

They walked some paces more, and then she said, "A man like Captain Deane seems charming at the first, but he is charming for a purpose, and in truth he values nothing but himself. So long as any other man can be of use to him, if only to pay homage to his high opinion of his value, he will let them think he is their greatest friend and ally, but let any man oppose him, even question him, and he will show the venom that does flow within his veins." She looked at Edmund. "You must watch his face, when he is watching someone else, for then you'll truly see the workings of the man."

"Now that," said Edmund, "sounds like an instruction from your nuns."

"Not from the nuns." Her smile was faint. "From someone who was all that Captain Deane is not."

"And have you ever tried that trick with me?"

She took a sudden interest in a passing cart, and Edmund grinned.

"You have! Pray, who was I then watching when you saw my inner self?"

She told him, "Helen, if you must know."

"Helen Lacy? Little Helen?"

Anna nodded. "You were telling her about the Cailleagh. Telling her she need not be afraid."

"And you discovered me from that?"

"I think I did, yes."

He stayed silent after that until they'd nearly reached the line of colleges. And then he asked, "Why do you not say 'aye'?"

She turned her head, a little puzzled by the question, and it must have showed because he carried on, "When you are angry, you say 'aye.' But not at any other time."

"'Yes' is more ladylike." The answer came with automatic ease, as she'd been hearing it for years. "It was the wish of those who raised me I should always act as though I were a lady."

"And is acting for your whole life something that will give you pleasure? For my part, I could not do it."

Anna told him, "No one ever would suspect you, sir, of acting like a lady."

Edmund laughed aloud at that, a sound that drew the stares of people round them, and one figure moved through all the rest and came at them with black skirts billowing like sails.

"Good morrow, Mistress Jamieson," said Mrs. Hewitt, "and Mr. O'Connor."

"Mrs. Hewitt." Anna watched the woman warily as they exchanged their honours, for it was a rare thing for the merchant's wife to seek her out, when Mr. Hewitt and Vice-Admiral Gordon had been openly at odds this year upon the matter of a rented house.

"You know my husband is at Moscow," said the woman, "but today being his birthday I did think to hold a supper in his honour at the house. Not an assembly, mind, for in this time of mourning that would never do. More like a gathering of friends. And I'd be honoured if you'd come, Mr. O'Connor."

Edmund, who'd been taking interest in some goings-on across the square, not paying true attention, brought his gaze back with a lifting of dark eyebrows. "Me?"

The woman nodded. "Captain Deane did ask me, in particular, if you would be there, and we are so short on men. He said . . . ah, here he is now. Captain Deane, good morrow to you, sir."

The captain on this day, as ever, made a most attractive figure, with a face most women did find handsome and compelling. His black suit had been tailored to the very latest fashion, like the thick white wig tied neatly with a ribbon at his collar, underneath a fine, expensive hat. He was quite tall, and strongly built, and straight of back, and gave the full appearance of a man of all accomplishments and power, one whom others would do very well to follow.

And his smile, as always, showed teeth of a perfect, even whiteness. Like a wolf's, thought Anna. For although there was no outward cause to fault the captain, there was something she found wanting in his eyes, a strange detachment mixed with cunning that put her in mind of the grey beasts that prowled the untamed forests just outside St. Petersburg, and sometimes came within the city's streets to seek their meals.

And wanting Edmund, now, to see it, too, she did not hide her feelings when Deane greeted her, for well she knew his mask slipped much more easily when he did not receive the adulation that he took to be his due.

"I should imagine, sir, you find St. Petersburg more welcoming than you did find it when you left," she said.

His smiled stayed, although his eyes grew colder. "Yes," he answered, in his smoothly English voice, "I do."

"It is a shame that you did not return while yet the tsar was living, for I should expect your welcome then would have been even warmer."

He dismissed her with a glance, and would have said something to Edmund had not Anna drawn him back with, "Tell me, when do you take up your new position?"

"What position do you speak of?"

"Why, as consul, sir."

The smooth voice showed a sharp edge. "Mistress, you are misinformed. It was, in good measure, my private affairs that induced me to come. Though of course, if I can be of any assistance to those of my countrymen here in the Factory, by virtue of my own connections, I'll offer it gladly."

"That is very kind of you, Captain," she said, "for I hear your connections are most high, indeed." She left it there, and looked at Edmund to discover that his eyes were not on Deane's face, but her own, as Mrs. Hewitt interjected with,

"I'm sure our men would all be pleased to have the benefit of your advice and prudence, Captain Deane. 'Tis sure you've lived a wide and varied life."

He gave a gracious half bow of his head, to show acceptance of her compliment, then turned as he had done before, to Edmund. "And what of yourself, Mr. O'Connor? What is your own background?"

"Varied and wide, to be sure." Edmund smiled. "I was lately in Spain, but have been here in Petersburg now several months."

"Doing what, may I ask?"

"Very little of anything, Captain. The general has offered to find me a place as lieutenant in one of his regiments, but 'tis a junior position and one I'm not sure suits my temperament."

Anna, who'd heard nothing of this till now, glanced at Edmund, her brow furrowed faintly.

Deane asked him, "And what would you otherwise do?"

"I had thought of returning to Spain," Edmund told him, in serious tones that revealed he was telling the truth, "for if I am bound to live ever in exile, 'tis better to be where the weather is warmer, and living is not so expensive."

"You've just missed your passage then, surely," said Deane, "for when I came past Sweden I saw three ships, Russian ships, just coming out of the Baltic, and word was they might have been destined for Spain." Then he said, "The Pretender's affairs are quite highly supported in Spain, are they not?"

Anna bristled, as she always did, at the disrespect shown by anyone calling King James "the Pretender," as though the king's enemies, sitting in parliament, could with one dishonest vote so subvert God's design and the natural order of things to deny James the throne that was his right by birth. If anyone was to be called "the Pretender," Anna reasoned, it must surely be the foreign prince who'd taken James's place by such deceit, and dared to style himself "King" George.

She might have even said as much had Edmund's hand not lightly touched her back as he replied to Deane, "I do not take much notice, sir, of politics."

"You're kin to General Lacy, I believe you said?"

"I am."

"The general," Deane said, "always did impress me as a man who threw his whole self into service of the country that employed him, and did not let foreign influences meddle with his purpose."

Anna knew that he had cast that out as careful bait, to see if Edmund could be lured to disagree and so provide an insight into General Lacy's thoughts, but she could do no more than hold her breath and wait to see if Edmund had observed the ploy.

Without a change of tone, still sounding friendly, Edmund answered, "Aye, 'tis sure the general always knows exactly whom he serves."

"I would that I could say as much," said Deane, "for many of the merchants here. I have been speaking to their chaplain, and he tells me he is heartily abused here. Mrs. Hewitt, is it true one of the members of this Factory even threatened once to have the chaplain caned, on learning he had sworn the oaths to serve His Majesty our king?"

The merchant's wife confirmed it. "Yes, and there are several in the congregation, Captain, I'm ashamed to say, who spit during the service when King George's name is mentioned."

Captain Deane shook his head in disbelief. "I observe things are still as they were when the tsar lived, with Jacobites being caressed here upon all occasions, whilst good honest Englishmen are forced to bow and cringe off at a distance."

"Can Jacobites never be good honest men, Captain?" Anna asked.

Deane said, "I've never yet met one. Indeed, had more care been put into the choice of our Factors, things would not have come to that miserable state they are now. We might have had a set of sober-thinking men, who would have added something to the credit of their native country, instead of men sadly debauched both in morals and principals. Generally speaking," he qualified, smiling towards Mrs. Hewitt. "Your husband and others excepted, of course."

"Of course. You are coming tonight to my supper, I hope?"

"I would not wish to miss it. But I first must attempt again to get my goods and baggage entered at the Custom House, for that is all my business at the present. And after that," he told her, "Mr. Nye has very kindly said he'll tour me through the shipyards, where he says they are now building several pinnaces. But after *that*, I'll surely come to you."

The merchant's wife was clearly flattered by his smile, and his attention. "As a navy man yourself, I'm sure the shipyards will prove most diverting. Truly, there has been so much activity of late upon the river, I believe our squadron may be setting out to sea at last."

"It would appear so." Deane looked out across the river to the Admiralty, and his keen eyes narrowed slightly with an aspect Anna did not like.

She said, "I take it you no longer do command a ship yourself, then, Captain Deane?"

His cold eyes angled downward to her own. "I have acquired other interests, Mistress."

Mrs. Hewitt said, "The captain told us, Mistress Jamieson, that he is writing a new and complete account of his heroic rescue of his crew upon Boon Island. I'm sure it will be most exciting."

"I've no doubt." This time she paid no heed to Edmund's warning hand upon her back, but said, "I will be glad to read it, Captain, for I've heard such differing accounts of that adventure."

There, she thought, she had succeeded in her purpose. Edmund surely could not help but see the captain's nature now, for Deane's annoyance with her plainly showed behind his icy smile.

"I have been ever plagued by enemies," he said, "whose only purpose is to slander my good name."

And there, thought Anna, was the venom, plainly evident. She met his gaze directly with her own. "A good name, Captain Deane, must first be earned, before it can be slandered."

And not bothering to curtsy as a proper lady would, she just as frostily excused herself and carried on her way towards the colleges.

"She never did!" The general laughed, and leant back in his chair behind the heavy desk that sat before the windows of his offices within the College of War.

"She did indeed," said Edmund. "I was there, and had the very devil of a time making excuses for her afterwards."

From where she stood beside the window looking to the square below them, Anna said, not turning, "I've no need of anyone to make excuses for me."

General Lacy shared a look with Edmund before folding up the letter he'd just written. "Here, then, take this to Sir Harry, if you will. And are you going, then, to Mrs. Hewitt's supper, Edmund?"

"Sure I'd rather swim with sharks. I told them I did fear that I was otherwise engaged." He paused, and asked, "Have you sent ships to Spain?"

"Why do you ask?"

"Deane said he saw three Russian ships, just heading out as he was coming in the Baltic. He believes they might be on their way to Spain."

The general asked, "What else has Deane been noticing about our ships?"

"He has observed the squadron is preparing to set out, and that the shipyards have been busy building pinnaces."

The general nodded and looked faintly satisfied, though Anna could not see it was in any way remarkable. The Russian squadron always sailed to sea, this time of year.

So she was puzzled when, a few days later, Captain Hay and Gordon were again discussing ships.

"Deane did observe you at the shipyards, though?" asked Gordon.

Captain Hay said, "He'd have had to be a great fool not to."

Gordon nodded. "Good. That's very good, then. Mr. Elmsall tells me he and several others of the Factory were called to the College of Foreign Affairs last night, to answer questions about whether Deane had been their choice for consul, and whether they'd known he was coming. Apparently, they answered no, on both counts."

Captain Hay grinned. "So then that's an end to it?"

"Hopefully, aye. Count Galovkin has little affection for English spies, and quite a lot for King James, so I should not be very surprised to see Deane told to pack his belongings and leave, very soon."

"That will be a relief to me," Captain Hay said, "for he's been like a hound on my trail these past weeks."

The next morning, the College of Foreign Affairs ordered Deane to depart, and the news spread like fire through the Admiralty and the exchange. He'd been given a week to arrange his affairs, and still made himself visible in the community, only he now was less likely to show charm to anyone, and much more likely to find fault with those whom he claimed had so bitterly wronged him.

When Anna had pointed this out at the table to Edmund, she'd found Father Dominic nodding agreement.

"St. Francis would teach us," the monk said, "that we cannot know a man's nature when all does go well with him, but when those people he thinks will assist him oppose him instead, then we know, for a man has the patience and humility that he shows then, and no more."

General Lacy agreed. "He is at his most dangerous now, William," he had advised Captain Hay, "so you keep your head down."

The vice-admiral had gone a step further, and sent Captain Hay with Sir Harry to Cronstadt.

"To what end?" the captain had asked.

"When he does leave St. Petersburg," Gordon had told him, "he'll head first to Cronstadt to make his complaints to Apraxin, and when he arrives, I want you and Sir Harry to inspect as many ships as you're both able to. Make sure Deane sees you do it."

And with a nod, Captain Hay had agreed. "But it will be for nothing," he'd warned, "if the empress remains out of reach."

Anna saw the vice-admiral's frustration at that.

He'd been trying for weeks, since the day Captain Hay had arrived, to arrange for an audience with Empress Catherine. He'd had such a cordial relationship with the late tsar that, a year ago, he'd have had only to ask and the audience would have been granted. But since the tsar's death, the whole court had closed in round the empress—some said to protect her, some said to control her, and those who would speak to her had to first pass by Prince Menshikov.

Gordon was still in high favour with Catherine, that much was made plain, but her mourning was deep, and she showed little interest in meeting with anyone.

Vice-Admiral Gordon tried once more that week, going all on his own to Prince Menshikov's palace to make his petition, but when Anna, making her way to the College of War with a letter for Lacy, and Edmund again as her escort, came over the river, she found the vice-admiral just leaving the palace, and frowning.

"She's in there," he told them. "She's in there right now, but he says she'll not see me."

"You cannot just send in the letter alone?" Edmund asked.

Gordon withered him with a look Anna knew well, for it meant the vice-admiral was nearing the end of his patience. "This letter," he said, speaking low, "does come straight from the hand of King James. Captain Hay has risked much to come north, for this purpose alone, and the king does depend upon us, upon *me*, to fulfill his request and deliver it into the hands of the empress. The fate of a nation does ride on these words, and the way they're received. So no, sir, I cannot 'just send in the letter alone.'" Drawing breath, he collected his temper and lowered his head, with his hands on his hips in a posture of utter disgust.

Anna looked at him for a long moment. And then she said, "Give it to me, then."

The vice-admiral lifted his head. "What?"

"I'll take it. The empress is mourning the loss of a husband and child," was her reasoning. "Men and their matters of politics may not hold interest for her, but I'm no man. She'll see me, I think, if I ask."

Edmund nodded, when Gordon looked doubtful. "'Tis possible, sir, for I've seen Empress Catherine speak privately with Mistress Jamieson, and she paid little heed then to Prince Menshikov's counsel."

The vice-admiral stood for a moment, and looked down at Anna with much the same look he had given her those years ago in Calais. Then he nodded, and gave her the letter. "Take Mr. O'Connor as escort," he told her. "As far as I know, Captain Deane has no spies in Prince Menshikov's house. But if you do encounter one," he said to Edmund, "I trust you will know how to serve him."

Edmund gave a nod of understanding, but already Anna was a step ahead of him, and heading for the great doors of the palace, and the guards who stood outside it.

chapter
FORTY

Rob stood behind me, his hands in his pockets, not pushing me. "Rob, I just can't." I looked up at the brilliant dark yellow facade of the Menshikov Palace, restored to perfection, the multiple panes of its old wooden windows reflecting the clouds drifting over the Admiralty dome on the opposite side of the river. The palace, which had in its time been the finest in all of St. Petersburg, stretched like a great sleeping lion along the south shore of the island, with two grand wings lying like paws to each side of the three-storied, most ancient part at its centre, its pediments topped by imperial crowns.

We were standing in front of the four massive pillars supporting the porticoed front entrance, while traffic raced at our backs up and down the long road that now ran between us and the water, and women clicked by in high heels on the pavement.

"I can't," I repeated.

He said, "It's your choice. Seems a waste, though. We know Catherine's in there, and every time Anna meets Catherine it might be *the* time."

"Yes, I know." I looked up at the deep yellow walls and felt something of Gordon's frustration. "I know, but I can't do it now. I'm supposed to meet Yuri and Wendy Van Hoek here at three. That's in barely an hour. And besides, there are people inside, Rob. It isn't like walking around on the sidewalks, or sitting outdoors on a bench, this is . . ." Helplessly, I shook my head. "This is different."

He gave me no argument. Only repeated, "It's your choice."

I sighed. "Maybe we could come back here tomorrow . . ." But even as I spoke the words, I could hear the futility of them, for even tomorrow this palace would still be a public museum, with people inside it, and with or without the time pressure that I felt today, my core problem would still be the same.

"I'm not saying I will," I said slowly, "but if I did want to, could you pull us out before Yuri and Wendy arrive?"

"Aye."

"You're sure of it?"

"Aye."

I bit down on my lower lip, thinking. I tried to remember the layout, inside, of the Menshikov Palace, to think of a place where we might sit or stand without anyone noticing. "Maybe," I said, "if we stayed in the entrance hall, under the stairs. There are big columns there, and we wouldn't be quite so conspicuous. What do you think?"

"It's your choice."

"Will you stop saying that, please?"

"Well, what would ye wish me to say? Aye, it's worth the small risk you'd be taking?" he offered, in level tones. "Aye, you should stop wasting time and go in?"

"That's exactly what I wish you'd say. Thank you."

"Happy to help," was his final reply, as he followed me round to the actual entrance.

We paid the full fee, both because I had never liked freeloading on my position, and because I wasn't too keen to announce my arrival to anyone upstairs who might know my name, or know Yuri Stepanovich might be expecting me.

"Rob," I said, "when Yuri does come, I haven't . . . that is, I think he thinks I'm here on my own, and . . ."

"I'll blend with the tourists," he promised. "You'll no ken I'm here."

There were several groups of tourists here to blend with. We slipped the shoe protectors on that everyone who visited the palace had to wear, to keep from ruining the floors, and made our way through the enticements of the gift shop with its prints and reproduction drawings and the ever-present amber jewellery, and up the back stairs to the ground-floor rooms, where we moved quickly past the reconstructed kitchen, through the turnery, the sailors' room, the chamber full of tapestries—and came into the graceful vaulted space of the Large Corridor.

This would have been the entrance hall in Anna's time, the first place any visitor would see when they'd been ushered through the massive double doors that had originally opened onto steps that met the river. Any visitor back then would have been awed, as I still was, by the sheer scale of this great room, its stone floor laid with large square tiles, a double row of Tuscan columns holding up a ribbed and painted ceiling arching in enchanting vaults, the side walls painted shades of quiet green and sand and made to look like marble, set with arching niches in which statues of Greek goddesses and gods stood fixed in contemplation of those passing by, between the candles on reflective gold medallion backings hanging on the walls to either side.

Rob looked around. "So what in here's original?"

"I'm sorry?" Then, as I took in his meaning, "You can't be thinking I can do this? Oh, come on. We haven't got that sort of time."

He looked down at his watch. "We've nearly fifty minutes. And if you're wanting me to stay alert, it's easier," he told me, "if you're driving. So then, what in here's original?"

There were a few things that I knew of, but it had to be something that I could touch. "The stairs."

They curved up, broad and grand, to either side of the large statue of Apollo at the farther end, and framed the double doors that would have led out to the formal gardens. Made of water-seasoned oak, their darkly polished treads displayed the heavy wear of centuries, concave along their centres where so many feet had climbed.

The stairs had been roped off, so tourists wouldn't try to use them, but if I stood very casually beside them, and pretended I was looking at Apollo, with Rob beside me, shielding me from view, I could just lay one hand discreetly at the railings, and . . .

I closed my eyes.

It came so very easily, this time. I didn't know if that was from the fact that I was feeling rushed, and maybe pushing myself just a little more because of it, or if it was because I really wanted to be able to explore this, and to test what I could do. But for whatever reason, I slipped comfortably and quickly to that place where all the images began to run, and blur, and shift in focus.

There, you've got it, Rob assured me. *Go.*

And I found Anna.

They'd been ordered to wait. The antechamber into which the guard had led them was too large to let Anna feel comfortable. She'd paced the inlaid floor at first, until she'd realized Edmund could not sit while she was standing, and so now she sat and fidgeted on a large Spanish chair, whose leather seat was fastened on with thirty copper-headed nails, a number she knew well because she'd spent the last ten minutes counting them.

Edmund, sitting solid and relaxed in his own chair beside her, commented, "See now, this is why I could not picture you with nuns. You never can be still."

"I can."

"I've only seen you do it when you're feeling all unwell," he told her, "or with Mr. Taylor, though perhaps the two are intertwined."

She tried to wither him, as Gordon had, with just a look. "That is unfair to Mr. Taylor, and you know it. He's a good man."

"Aye, he's nothing like myself, I'll give him that. But you are nothing like yourself, when you are with him, Mistress Jamieson. Why is that?"

Anna looked away. "I have no time for playing games today, Mr. O'Connor."

"Now, that's a shame, for I was thinking to divert you while we waited." He shifted in the chair as though removing something from his coat, and Anna heard the sudden slide and shuffle of a deck of cards.

Her gaze came sharply back to see the cards held in his hands. "You keep them with you?"

"Always. Cards can serve me better than a purse of coins," he told her, "and they often have."

"I know no games."

He smiled. "I was not going to play you. Here." He spread the deck into a fan and held it out towards her. "Choose one."

"Any of them?"

"Aye," he said. "And hold it to yourself, don't let me see it. There, now put it back."

He closed the fan and shuffled once again. His hands were expert and their movements were so fast she couldn't follow them. "Now, cut the deck in two," he told her. "Anywhere you like, and turn the top half over."

Anna did, and stared in pure astonishment.

"Is that the card you chose?" asked Edmund.

"Yes."

"The ace of hearts." He smiled again. "Of course it is. All right then, put it back again, let's see where it ends up."

Six times the ace of hearts returned into the deck, and six times Anna drew it out again at Edmund's bidding, always in a different place and by a different method.

"How," she asked him, "do you do that?"

"Are you finding it impressive?"

"Yes."

He grinned. "Well then, I'd be a fool to tell you." Shuffling the cards once more, he himself flipped the ace of hearts over with casual ease, put it back and reshuffled and cut and produced it again, did it over and over till Anna was thoroughly awed.

"Were you born with those cards in your hands?" she accused him.

"Aye, cards in my hands and my fists up."

She looked at those hands and gave voice to the question she'd wanted to ask since the first day she'd met him. "Your left hand, sir . . ."

"Aye?"

"Did those scars come from fighting?"

He turned the ace of hearts out of the deck and put it back again, and studied his own fingers while he did it. "No," he told her, "those I got from being whipped across the knuckles as a lad, for thieving, by the steward of the lord who kept the manor where I lived. They left my right hand untouched, as you see, so I could use it in my work."

"What did you steal?"

His dark eyes met hers briefly in a glance that slid away as he looked down again, and half-smiled without humour. "I stole nothing, Mistress Jamieson. It was another boy who did the thieving, not myself."

"And was he also whipped?"

"He would have been, had I revealed him, but I saw no point in it," he said. "He was a smaller boy, whose need was greater than my own."

"That hardly makes it just, for you to have to bear his punishment," said Anna with a frown.

His shoulders lifted in a shrug. "'Tis often easier, when someone will suspect you of it anyway, to take the blame."

She found she did not know how to reply to that, for any words she thought of sounded glib and superficial in the face of such a declaration, and although he'd said it very casually, she had the sense, from how he concentrated his attention on the cards directly afterwards, that he had just revealed a key component of his character that few besides herself had ever learned.

She drew a breath as though to speak, let it escape, and then drew another one. "Mr. O'Connor, I—"

Hard footsteps rang out behind them, approaching the door, interrupting her. Edmund in one motion gathered the cards in a neat stack and held them secure in one hand while the same guard who'd told them to wait swung the door open wide.

"Her Imperial Majesty says she will see you," he told Anna, adding, to Edmund, "The girl only. You may wait here."

Edmund, not understanding the Russian instruction, asked Anna, "What did he say?"

"That the empress is wanting to see me alone."

"I'll wait here, then." He stood with her, not from respect alone, Anna thought, but to provide her a bit of encouragement. As the door closed at her back, he was taking his seat again, and she could hear the small tap as he straightened the deck of cards, starting a new shuffle.

Head up, she followed the guard through a room where the ceiling and walls were all covered in blue-and-white tiles, like the Dutch ones in Vice-Admiral Gordon's house, and beyond that into one of the most stunning rooms she had ever seen. Not an enormous room, but an exquisite one, panelled all over in richly burled wood with five windows that looked to the Neva.

She'd heard tell of Prince Menshikov's walnut study before, from the vice-admiral, who had been in it, but seeing it firsthand was like being inside a richly made jewel case, and the empress herself was the jewel at its centre, serenely composed on a three-cornered armchair, with two of her ladies- in-waiting behind her, and the great Prince Menshikov himself leaning on the edge of his desk.

The tick of a long-case clock standing against the wall just behind Anna was all she could hear while she curtsied as low as her gown would permit.

"Well then, Anna Niktova," the empress said, "what brings you here on this fine day to visit me?"

Anna, not rising, replied, "Your Imperial Majesty, please do forgive me, but it is a matter most private."

The prince said, amused, "She has come to apply as your seamstress, no doubt, as you lately invited her to."

Anna heard the small whispers and quickly hushed giggles that told her the ladies-in-waiting were enjoying the joke, too, at her expense, but she ignored them and waited for Catherine's reply.

"Aleksandr Danilovich," said Empress Catherine to Menshikov, "may I have use of this room for a moment, to hear this young woman?"

"Alone?" The prince did not sound shocked, so much as curious at this strange breach of protocol.

"You were not always a prince," she reminded him, "and I was never a princess, but though we were common, the tsar gave us both the great honour of his private audience when we had need of it. How can I do any less, when I'm asked?"

In the small pause that followed, Prince Menshikov must have smiled, for when he spoke next his voice had warmed. "How indeed?" Standing away from his desk, he said, "Come with me, then, ladies, into my chamber next door. I daresay we can do something there that will keep us all well entertained."

The ladies-in-waiting, with more giggles, followed him, as did the sober-faced guard. When the door had swung shut and the great latch had clicked, Empress Catherine told Anna to rise.

"Now," she said, "tell me, what is this matter so private?"

Straightening her shoulders, Anna reached into her pocket and produced the letter, holding it towards the empress. "This. Vice-Admiral Gordon had it given him by Captain William Hay, who travelled here for no cause but to bring it to you. It is from King James," she said, "in Rome."

The empress did not move to take the letter, only looked at it in Anna's hand a moment and then nodded at the desk and told her, "You may put it there."

"I fear I cannot, Your Imperial Majesty." As the empress's eyebrows began to lift, Anna went on, "This comes from the hand of my king, by the efforts of men he does trust, and I would not be doing my duty to any of them if I left it where others might see it, and did not deliver it properly into your hand."

The empress still sat in her chair, without moving. "If that letter touches, as I should imagine it does, upon some new endeavour of his to return to his throne, for which he has need of us, then it should properly go to Prince Menshikov, or to the young Duke of Holstein. They are more accomplished in affairs of state."

"But this is not addressed to either one of them," said Anna. "It was written to the tsar, and—"

"I am not the tsar," the empress cut her off. And then, more softly, with a trail of sadness running through her tone the way a raindrop ran down window glass, "I'm not the tsar." She looked away, towards the desk. "I was not meant to do such things as this, Anna Niktova. I was meant to be a mother and a wife," she said, and on a not quite steady breath revealed, "now I am neither."

Anna's heart ached of a sudden for the empress, who was set so high with all the court at her command, and yet seemed so unbearably alone. It was not fitting, Anna knew, to speak familiarly to such a woman, yet she could not help but try to ease her pain by saying, "You have daughters."

"One is gone, the other grown, and all the others in their graves, with all my sons. And with their father." Empress Catherine closed her eyes for one brief instant, and when she reopened them they glistened with a brightness Anna recognized from all the tears that she herself had ever gained control of.

And it was the memory of those tears and why she had so often nearly cried them that emboldened her to say what she was thinking.

"But the daughter grown yet needs you," Anna said, "as do your people, for they too have lost their father, and they need to know that they're still in their mother's thoughts, and heart."

"And so they are, but thoughts and heart accomplish very little, Anna Niktova. As we say in Russia, we will know the bird by how it flies." The empress brought her gaze to Anna's, kind, and yet still sad. "I may now wear the feathers of an eagle, but my flight betrays me. I am still the little wren who nests beside the door," she said. "My only purpose, all my life, has been to care for those I love, to feed them and look after them. The tsar, my husband, knew this well. He did not leave his throne to me because of my abilities, but only to be sure that I would live when he was dead, that his successor would not have me killed or sent into Siberia. It was a kindness, that is all." Her voice held quiet certainty. "I cannot be the ruler that he was, Anna Niktova, and that letter is not meant for me, but for the Duke of Holstein, or Prince Menshikov, as I have said. Your king requires an eagle for his purpose, not a wren."

It was a speech intended to dismiss her, Anna knew, and yet she stood and gathered courage. "If you will permit me . . ."

Empress Catherine's eyes revealed a mild surprise, but she prepared to listen.

"If you will permit me," Anna started for a second time, more surely, "I believe His Imperial Majesty left you his throne out of more than just kindness."

"You are very young."

Anna tried hard to sort her words properly, say what she wanted to say. "Your Imperial Majesty, if you will look out these windows, in any direction, you'll see what the late tsar has built here." *My Russia*, he'd called it, that night last November when all in a rage he had broken the mirror—*all that I have made, my whole life's work.* She minded well how he'd described how easily it all could be brought down again, and ruined. "I believe," she told the empress, well aware that she had now gone past propriety, "the late tsar left the throne to you because he knew your flight so very well, and he needed the wren by the door to look after what someone else might have destroyed. He knew, you see, you would take care of his Russia. That you would continue what he had begun."

Empress Catherine had turned, and was staring at Anna with such an astonished expression that Anna dropped into a penitent curtsy and stayed there, her cheeks flaming colour. "Forgive me, I shouldn't have spoken, I don't have the right. I am nobody."

Slowly, the empress stood, and with a few measured steps crossed the distance between them. Her hand lightly touched Anna's hair, travelled soothing and cool from her cheek to her chin where, quite gently, it made Anna tilt her face up till her gaze met the empress's.

"My darling Anna," she said in her elegant Russian, and smiled. "You were never a nobody." Letting go of Anna's chin, she took the letter from the younger woman's hand in a decided motion. "Tell Vice-Admiral Gordon I will read this letter from your king, and tell him when I've done so I will send for him, so that we may discuss its contents further. And tell him," she said, smiling still more deeply, "that this little bird that he has raised flies very like a falcon, with a true and honest eye that does him credit."

Anna had no certain memory, afterwards, of walking from the room, although she knew she must have managed it. She had no memory, either, of the guard escorting her out of the chamber of Prince Menshikov and back to Edmund, waiting in the antechamber.

"Well?" asked Edmund, rising to his feet, his dark eyes keen upon her still embarrassed face, "What happened? Did she take the letter?"

"Aye," said Anna. "Aye, she took it. She—"

I lost her, then.

More properly, Rob yanked me clean away from her, and thrust me without ceremony back into the present. He was standing with his back to me, quite close so that he blocked the line of vision of the man and woman just now coming into the Large Corridor. It gave me needed moments to restore my equilibrium.

Okay? he asked, not looking at me.

Yes, okay now. Thank you.

Rob stepped away and, with what felt like nothing so much as a friendly hug, wandered off casually into the next room as I turned to Yuri and Wendy Van Hoek.

chapter
FORTY-ONE

Of all the things I'd been expecting Wendy Van Hoek to be, a kindred spirit wasn't one of them; and yet before ten minutes had gone by, we'd formed an easy and immediate rapport with one another, moving from topic to topic as though we'd been friends for years. Yuri was watching the pair of us like someone watching the finals at Wimbledon.

Physically, Wendy was not what I'd thought she'd be, either. From how Sebastian had spoken about her, I'd pictured a middle-aged, rigid-faced woman. In actual fact, she was not that much older than me, and incredibly pretty, with eyes that took an interest in the person she was speaking to, and long, straight hair the lovely golden-blond shade emblematic of the Netherlands.

Her accent was American, and while it had been clearly shaped by summers in the Hamptons and a college in the Ivy League, its tone was fresh and pleasant. And she laughed more than I'd thought she would.

"And then he spilt wine down the front of my dress," she concluded the count of the many disasters that had marked her first encounter with Sebastian. "Red wine, all over my new Valentino," she said, "and he stood there and laughed. I mean, honestly, you name a bone-headed move, and your boss made it."

That didn't sound like the suave man I worked for. "He laughs when he's nervous," I offered.

"Well, I must have made him incredibly nervous, then, because he laughed at me all weekend long. We just didn't—and don't—get along very well."

Just like Anna and Edmund, I thought. Only, their animosity had always masked something else, a much deeper awareness, developing under the surface. I wondered if maybe Sebastian and Wendy were feuding because they subconsciously felt the same kind of attraction.

"Anyhow," Wendy said, "he was smart to send you."

"Well, I'm better behaved. I'm more likely," I said, "to spill wine on my own frock. That's why I drink vodka martinis at parties. They don't leave a stain."

She smiled. "So go on, make your pitch," she invited me. "Why does Sebastian St.-Croix want my Surikov?"

"It's for a client of ours," I explained, and while we made our slow way through the ground-floor rooms that had been set aside for temporary exhibitions, watching while museum staff attended to the hanging of the final bits and pieces of the Wanderers exhibit, I tried telling her about Vasily, and why he had always been my favourite client.

". . . and even after that," I finished off, "with all the things his family suffered in the war, and under Stalin, I don't think I've ever once heard him complain. I asked him one day, why it hadn't left him scarred, and he just pointed at his paintings and said that was all the trick of it: He took away the ugliness by choosing to remind himself each day of what was beautiful about his country, and that healed him."

Wendy sent a thoughtful sideways glance at me. "You're good." She gave a little smile and asked, "But why the Surikov?"

"Because the Cathedral of Christ the Saviour, down in Moscow, was Vasily's parents' church," I said. "It's where they met, and where they married, and he told Sebastian that, since Stalin blew the church up and the murals were all lost, to have this one small piece would be like saving something of his parents. A reminder of their life, and love."

She looked at me in what was almost disbelief and groaned and looked away again, her hand upon her heart. "And I'm supposed to stand against a tale like that? Of course," she said. "Of course this lovely man can have my Surikov. But only when the exhibition's finished. We can sort the terms out then, all right?"

I shook her hand, well pleased. "All right."

"You'll have to have Sebastian send you to New York, for that," she told me. "You and I can spend the weekend shopping on Fifth Avenue."

I was still smiling happily when one of the museum workers brought the painting out to hang it, and when Wendy asked me if I'd like to take a closer look, and when, at her request, I helped her turn it so that I could see the signed authentication on the back, written by Surikov's own daughter.

But I touched the canvas. Only very lightly, but I touched it, and inspired by my earlier success at viewing Anna's life, I closed my eyes to get a glimpse of Surikov himself. For after all, I thought, why not? No one would know, if I was quick about it.

And I saw the artist. Saw him standing in a paint-stained shirt and trousers while he deftly added light along the edge of the long scroll held in the hands of Bishop Gregory. Except the artist I saw wasn't Surikov. Could not have been.

A television straight out of the 1960s sat behind his easel, and his clothes were of that period as well, and on his arm he wore a wrist-watch.

"Something is wrong?" asked Yuri, watching me.

I told him, "No." And then I said, "It's nothing," and I gave the painting back. "It's very beautiful."

But now I had a problem.

We'd only been here for a couple of days and already the servers at Stolle knew Rob and his preferences, and at the counter they met him halfway with the language, and filled in the Russian words he didn't know. Not that they needed to help much. He really was making re-markable progress in learning the phrases, and his Russian accent was spot on.

"It's nothing so special." He modestly shrugged off my praise as we sat. "I've been practicing, that's all. You're bound to get better at any-thing that way." We'd snagged what was quickly becoming our "usual" table, and I thought I'd never be able to eat here again without picturing Rob with his back to the wall, tucking into his fish pie and Baltika Krepkoe strong lager.

"And when do you get time to practice?" I asked.

"When you're working, like. Having your meetings. I talked to some very nice people today at the Menshikov Palace." I must have stayed silent a moment too long after that, because Rob moved from small talk to something a bit more substantial: "So, what will you do now?"

"Sorry?"

"Nick." He said no more than that, but from his eyes I knew that he knew.

With a sigh, I set down my fork. "I thought you told me I was difficult to read."

"Aye, well, I've had a bit of practice lately with that, too." He took a drink of lager. "Will you tell her?"

"Wendy? Yes, I guess I'm going to have to tell her, aren't I? I can't buy the painting, not when it's a forgery." I let my disappointment show. "I really liked her, too, you know? I would have liked doing this deal."

"Aye, I got that."

"She wasn't at all like I thought she would be."

"Sometimes people surprise us." I didn't know why he was looking at me when he said that. I couldn't think what I'd have done that Rob wouldn't have guessed I would do, but he didn't elaborate. "When were you thinking to tell her? Tonight?"

"No, tomorrow, before the reception. I'll deal with it then."

"So we've got time tonight, then, to follow your firebird."

Nodding agreement, I said, "But we've lost the trail, haven't we? I was so hoping, this afternoon . . . I mean, that *was* the scene I saw, Rob, word for word."

"And according to you, they did talk about birds."

"Not our bird, though." I frowned. "And so now we don't know where or when Anna's going to meet Catherine again."

"So we'll go back to Lacy's," he said with a shrug, between forkfuls of pie. "Try to get some direction from there."

"Best go easy on those, then," I said as he tipped back his lager. "I can't do the driving tonight, if we're going to Lacy's, there's nothing to—"

"—touch. So you've said." He looked at me the way my brother eyed a new sudoku puzzle, trying to see numbers in their proper combinations, to decide what ones were missing. "Have you ever tried?"

"Tried what?"

"To see things without touching them."

"No." I shook my head with certainty. "I can't."

"How d'ye ken that a thing is impossible, if you've not tried it?"

"I've never tried to make myself invisible," I told him, "but I'm certain that's impossible, as well."

The brief smile in his eyes was warm. "That's not a good analogy, for you." Then, when I looked at him blankly, he said, "You're aye trying to make yourself invisible."

"I'm not."

"All right, trying to keep yourself hidden, then."

I didn't think that entirely fair. As I looked down to sugar my tea, I said, "Everyone hides, in their own way."

I still felt the weight of Rob's gaze on my face for a moment before he reached back for his lager and said, "Aye. You're probably right about that."

She had helped Mrs. Lacy to bed for her mid-morning rest, and had read Matthew Prior's poetry aloud until the general's wife's tired eyes had closed and the sound of her breathing had let Anna know she was peacefully sleeping. And now Anna had a spare hour to herself before dinner.

They were to have guests, Mr. Taylor among them, and afterwards she was to play a duet at the harpsichord with Mrs. Lacy, so truly she ought to have spent the time practicing that, as her playing was not all it should have been. But she was using the time now instead to attempt to decipher the musical notes on the paper she'd carried from Ypres, with the words of "The Wandering Maiden" still written upon it as clear as the day Captain Jamieson had marked them down for her in his fine hand.

She had learned and remembered those words through the years, but she found she'd forgotten the tune, having heard it just once. And so now she had learnt to play music, as he had advised her to do, and she finally could pick out the notes on the keyboard and play them.

The tune, written down, was a simple one—only the melody, all on its own, and her hand could not capture the lilt of it, but it still brought from her memory the captain's deep, comforting voice, singing gently to soothe a small girl in the darkness. When she'd played it three times there were tears in her eyes, and to keep them from falling she looked swiftly up from the keys and saw Edmund, who'd entered the house without any announcement, and stood in the doorway.

His head briefly dipped in a gentleman's greeting. "And what song is that?"

He was already leaving the doorway and coming across to the harpsichord, and short of snatching the paper up rudely and stuffing it safe in her pocket again there was little that Anna could do but allow him to look at it.

"May I?" He lifted the paper. "'The Wandering Maiden.' I am unfamiliar with this one, although I've heard some very like it." He read through the words. "Not a happy song."

"Not till the end."

"And is this what you're playing," he asked, "after dinner? To keep us all well entertained?"

"No," she said. "Mrs. Lacy has planned a duet."

Edmund smiled at whatever her face had betrayed. "And 'tis plain that you relish the prospect."

His smile did not mock, but was meant to be shared, which she did in a small way as she replied, "I have no skill at this instrument that would allow me to do so. As you will discover."

"I'll stop up my ears," Edmund promised. "Perhaps I should teach you a trick with the cards. You could do that in silence."

"I have no great skill with cards, either, sir."

"Right, you did tell me." He seemed to have taken more care than he usually did when preparing for dinner. His face had been recently shaved, his hair carefully combed and tied back, yet for all that he still had the air of a rogue. "Do you truly not know any card games at all?"

"I do not."

"Come, I'll teach you one." Setting the song sheet back down on the harpsichord, he gave a sideways nod towards the small plush-topped table still set up between two chairs, only a few steps away.

"What, this instant?" she asked him.

"Why not?"

He was clearly not going to sit till she'd crossed to take one of the chairs, so she did.

"Now," said Edmund, removing the cards from his pocket, "this game is called Fives. 'Tis the game of my country and simple to learn, quick to play. It is how your red shoes were won."

Anna refused to give in to the charm of that smile. "I would doubt that the shoes were won fairly."

"Then you'd be mistaken. I played all upon the square for those shoes, so I did, for Mr. Morley is an honest man."

She watched him while he shuffled. "Do you not cheat honest men, then?"

"Honest men cannot be cheated," Edmund said. "They've a conscience that speaks to them, leads them away from a game that might harm them. No, a man who will fall for the play of a sharper must first have the heart of a thief himself, under his fine clothes and all his respectable airs. Very often you'll find he's a liar besides, spinning tales to impress you. The thing is, he wants something from you himself, whether it be respect or your money, and right till the end of the game and beyond it he'll think in his heart he's the one cheating you. There you are, then." He dealt her five cards, and himself the same, then explained how the game worked with its trumps. "So, the five of trumps, that's the best card you can have, then the ace of hearts—which is your own special favourite, as I recall—then ace of trumps, then the knave. Follow that?"

Anna nodded. They started to play. For the first hand, he played along with her, and showed her what moves she should make. At the start of the second hand, which Anna dealt in her turn, he quickly looked over her cards and, on seeing that she held the ace of diamonds, shook his head. "No, that's truly the worst card of all you could possibly have. Give it here," he said, taking it from her and giving her one from his hand in exchange. "There now."

Sighing, she told him, "That still counts as cheating."

"Does not," was his argument. "Not if my intent is good."

In her third hand, her cards were so perfectly good that she knew he had dealt them on purpose. She looked at him. "Stop it."

"Stop what?"

"I had rather play poorly and lose by my own efforts," she said, "than win by dishonesty."

"Sure that's a very fine sentiment," Edmund replied, with his eyes on his own cards, "but life does not always allow us to do as we'd please."

Still, he won both of the following hands, and when dealing the next gave her cards that did not seem to be pre-arranged. Anna played them with full concentration, unable to guard her own features as closely as Edmund did while he was playing, for she could not help the satisfied smile as she played her last card. "I believe I've just won."

Edmund, looking down, too, gave a nod. "Aye," he said. "Ace of hearts wins the knave."

His eyes lifted and met hers and held them, the smile in his own fading slowly to something less readable, though no less warm, as he told her, "And *that*, I'll allow, you did all on your own."

Something changed in the way the air settled between them, and had they been walking outdoors, Anna might have believed that a storm was approaching. It brushed on the back of her neck and her spine and made everything at the periphery darken a shade, so that Edmund's half smile and his face and his eyes were the things most in focus.

And then he was standing, and taking the cards from her hand, and the whole world came back in a rush as she heard, from the hallway, the sound of male voices and laughter.

The rest of the guests had arrived.

chapter
FORTY-TWO

D inner was a miserable affair, and her duet was a disaster.
Anna doubted whether anybody else had even noticed, but
for her the trouble had begun before the bread was served. She had
at first been truly pleased to see that Nan and Mary had come with
Vice-Admiral Gordon this time, in a bid, no doubt, to better even
out the sexes at the table. But with Nan all tongue-tied sitting at Sir
Harry Stirling's shoulder, being no help whatsoever when it came to
conversation, and Mary on the other side of Edmund, talking nonsense with the dark-haired, dark-eyed Irishman, Anna had been left
adrift.

Ordinarily she would have taken an interest in the lively inter-
change between the general and Vice-Admiral Gordon, at her own
end of the table. Gordon, who'd been sitting just across from her, had
tried to draw her in on two occasions that she'd noticed, but she'd been
distracted by the sound of Edmund's laughter mixed with Mary's, and
as ever, she had been aware of Mr. Taylor's obvious regard.

She had been bothered more today than she had ever been before that her own feelings could not equal Mr. Taylor's, for in truth
he was exactly as a man should be. His looks were pleasant, and his
manners even more so, and he was a good and even-tempered man
who'd be, she had no doubt, a faithful husband and good father. He
had prospects, he had friends, and he was clearly half in love with
her, and yet her heart would not return the sentiment, no matter
how she willed it to. A heart, so Anna had decided, was a cruel and
stubborn thing.

And then, midway through dinner, when the general and Sir Harry had been speaking about Captain Hay, who was just then arranging for the passport that would let him leave St. Petersburg, Sir Harry had looked straight across at Edmund and asked, "And have you decided, yet, the date of your departure?"

Edmund, with a shrug, had answered, "No, but it would look to be the middle of July, just at the moment." Only that, and nothing more was said, as though the matter of his leaving had been common knowledge to them all.

It had affected her. It shouldn't have, she knew, yet after that one short exchange she'd found it difficult to focus, and when all of them had moved into the drawing room and she had tried to play the harpsichord with Mrs. Lacy, she had played so very poorly that the faint applause that followed had, she thought, been more from gratitude the piece was finally over than from praise.

Nor did she think it a coincidence that Father Dominic excused himself immediately after that to see to his devotions.

She made light of it. "Perhaps if I had played for Captain Deane, he'd have departed Russia earlier than Sunday last."

The others hastened to assure her she'd done better than she knew she had. Except for Edmund, who before this had been watching her with what approached impatience, and who now appeared the only one well pleased that she had failed at her performance.

"'Tis the song," he told the gathering. "It speaks of home and hearth and things domestic. Sure, our Mistress Jamieson wants something more adventurous. Where is your song," he asked her, "of 'The Wandering Maiden'?"

She had folded it already and returned it to her pocket before sitting down to dinner, but she only said, "I do not have it."

"It was well loved, from the look of it. Do you recall the words? For our hostess knows so many tunes, she may know that one, too."

Mrs. Lacy, to Anna's relief, had not heard of "The Wandering Maiden." "Is it to the tune of 'The Wandering Young Man'?" she asked Edmund.

"It is not," he replied, then unfolded himself from his lounging position to stand as he said, "But play that, if you will, for it is a good tune on its own."

Mrs. Lacy looked delighted as he crossed the drawing room towards the harpsichord. "And will you sing it for us, Edmund? We have not heard you sing since Christmas."

He did sing it, standing next to Mrs. Lacy while she played, with Anna sitting just beside her. She had guessed that, from the deepness of his speaking voice, he would not be a tenor when he sang, so she was not surprised to hear the richer timbre of a baritone, nor was she much surprised that he sang well, for singing seemed, in truth, to run within the blood of many Irishmen.

The song surprised her, though. Where "The Wandering Maiden" was weeping and sad, this song spoke of a man who'd been pushed to the brink of frustration by what he perceived was the torturous treatment the woman he loved had been giving him, and to that end he addressed his song, not to some wide and uncaring world, but directly to his lady love.

Edmund, singing in the role of the young man, aimed all his words in turn towards the women in the room, so that he seemed to be accusing Mrs. Lacy at the first of being beautiful and cruel, before his gaze moved on to Anna with the lines,

> *"'Sometimes your eyes doth me invite,*
> *But when I enter, you kill me quite,*
> *and the more increase my fire.'"*

His gaze did seem to hold a dark and languid heat as it held hers a moment longer than it needed to before it moved to Mary, making her the object of the young man's next reproach, then Nan, till all the others in the room were well amused.

"'Tis thee alone can kill or cure,'" he sang to Anna next. *"'Send me one gentle smile.'"*

But she could not, although the others did. She could not smile; she could but sit there silently and feel the words and wish that she did not, because it seemed as though he sang for her alone, when at the end his gaze returned full force to hers.

> *"'If I may not enjoy the bliss,*
> *Bestow on me a parting kiss,*
> *I'll wander all my days.'"*

The sound of clapping jarred her back into reality, reminding her that there were others with them in the room. She blinked, and roused herself enough to pull her gaze away from Edmund, to find Mary Gordon watching her with undisguised surprise, and a small, knowing smile that Anna looked away from, too.

But Mary would not let her escape with such ease. Later on, when they'd all gathered into the lobby to say their farewells, Mary caught Anna's elbow and drew her aside and said, low and delighted, "But I thought you hated him."

"Hated who?"

Mary just gave her a look that would not be fooled, and with a kiss and embrace said, "You must tell me all, the next time I come visit."

To be so discovered by Mary, who knew her so well and could read her expressions, was not unexpected, but Anna still felt thrown off balance, and when Mr. Taylor was saying goodbye to her and she saw Edmund himself looking on with a frown, Anna could not remove herself quickly enough from the lobby, relieved that the general had, at the last minute, called Edmund aside for a private talk, so she would not have to wait to farewell him.

The air in the yard was much warmer than that in the stone-walled house, but there was light and the feeling of freedom that washed through her troubling thoughts like a tonic. At least, for the minutes she spent there alone.

When she heard the door open and close, she instinctively straightened her back, her arms folding as both a defence and a means of protection. Not waiting for him to approach, she turned round.

"Was there something you wanted, then, Mr. O'Connor?"

"A great many things, Mistress Jamieson. But for the moment, my purpose was only to find you."

"And why would you go to such trouble?"

He said, "'Twas no trouble at all, for I knew where to look." With a glance round the yard and a faint upward lift of his chin to the clouds he remarked, "This is your bit of sky, is it not? Where you'd fly, had your wings not been clipped."

"You talk nonsense."

His own arms crossed over the width of his chest. "Mr. Taylor will do more than clip those wings for you. He'll tie them."

"You've no right—"

"I need no right," he cut her off, his voice gone hard, "to tell you what a fool could see, and what you seem determined not to."

Anna stood her ground in all defiance, though she hugged herself more tightly. "Do you seek to provoke me, sir?"

"Aye, Mistress Jamieson. That is exactly what I seek to do." Edmund took a step closer. "For it's when you're provoked that you show your true nature, the one you would hide from the world and your tame Mr. Taylor."

"He is not—" She cut herself off, that time, taking care to calm her temper. "He is not mine."

"Not yet, but he would like to be. And you encourage him, allowing him to call on you and be your escort."

"This is a small community," she told him, "and it would soon be talked about were I to snub him. You have been my escort also. Do you claim I then encourage you?"

His mouth curved faintly. "Never that."

"Good, for in truth I only act as any other lady would, in the same circumstances."

Edmund took another step, his eyes fixed on her face. "You are no lady."

Anna felt the sting of that as though she had been slapped. Incredulous, she stared at him a moment before striking back. "And you, sir, are no gentleman."

His own impatience briefly flared as he continued his approach, his gaze increasingly intense. "You think I meant that as an insult? Faith, it was a compliment."

"To say I'm not a lady?"

"Aye." He was too close, and well he knew it, pushing her as always, stopping just beyond her bounds of comfort. With his dark head tilted down so he could look at her, he said, "You are more rare than that. You are a fighter, like myself."

She was not sure which she found most unsettling—having him so near, or knowing he could see so clearly to her core.

She somehow found her voice. "Well, if I am, it is for naught. A woman cannot be a soldier."

"Not a soldier. No, you are not that. A soldier fights by someone else's orders, but a fighter," Edmund told her, "answers only to his passions, and his heart. And you have both in great abundance, Mistress Jamieson. I saw it clearly, so I did, the day you took on Captain Deane. You told me I should watch his face, remember? But I watched your own, instead."

"Oh, aye? And what did it reveal to you?"

The corners of his mouth turned upward once again, if briefly, at the surge of her defensiveness. "I do believe," he told her, "had you been a man that day, and in possession of a sword, you would have run the captain through."

She could not argue that, and so she simply stood with her face tilted up to his, and gave no answer.

In the silence Edmund grew more sober. "Do you honestly believe he'll make you happy? Christ, you cannot even be yourself when he is here. You barely spoke three words together all this afternoon."

He was looking at her now with all the heat that had been in his eyes when he had sung those verses of the song to her; when he'd sung that she could either kill or cure him, and it stirred an answering emotion deep inside her that felt very much the opposite of anger.

Lowering her gaze, she told the buttons of his waistcoat: "It was not because of Mr. Taylor that I did not feel like speaking."

"Was it not?"

She might have better planned her next words, she thought later, but they tumbled out before she could restrain them. "When did you intend to tell me, sir, that you were leaving?"

Anna knew, as those words dropped between them, that she had revealed too much. She was not surprised when Edmund turned her face up to his own once more, so he could search her eyes and try to judge the thoughts behind them. But she did not guess that he would kiss her till his mouth was on her own.

She'd recently imagined what a kiss would feel like, Edmund's in particular. She'd thought it would be fierce, as he was fierce, and just a little unforgiving, but to Anna's great surprise it was not hard at all, but gentle. Careful, even. Stealing her own breath until she doubted she'd have still been standing, had he not been holding her. His hands were on her upper arms, and she had the impression he was holding her away from him as much as doing anything, as though he did not wish to have her cross some unseen line between their bodies.

In the end, it was herself that crossed it, putting her own hands against his chest in search of something steady. When his coat seemed in the way, her hands slipped underneath it to his waistcoat, seeking out the shoulders that felt warm through the thin linen of his shirt.

His own hands moved, then. One spread wide against her back to bring her hard into his body while the other travelled up her neck to tangle in her hair, and for some minutes after that she felt the fierceness that she'd felt in all of her imaginings since they had danced the minuet together in the Summer Garden.

Groaning in his throat he broke the kiss and took her hands and set her back from him, his breathing out of rhythm as his fingers, for a moment, closed round hers. And then he let her go.

"Forgive me, Mistress Jamieson," he told her in a voice she did not recognize. His dark eyes briefly touched her own, their fire banked but burning still. And then, more low, he said, "Forgive me, Anna."

Turning, he strode back across the yard towards the house, his shoulders set and squared as though he were determined not to look behind. He was retreating, nobly and with honour, so that she could keep her own.

And had she truly been a fighter, Anna knew, she'd have gone after him.

Something felt different, this time, when I came back out into the present. I couldn't quite place it at first, but it felt unfamiliar enough that I stood for a moment, both hands in my pockets, and tried to decide what it was. Then it struck me. Both hands. In my pockets. Not holding to anything.

Turning, astonished, I looked round for Rob. He was standing some distance off, under a streetlamp, his collar turned up to ward off the night wind. When his head lifted, I couldn't see his expression but I sensed his smile, and the current that rippled between us was rich with the boyishly satisfied air of a man who's done mischief.

But . . . how? I had trouble collecting my thoughts. *How long . . . ?*

Nearly the whole time. He stayed in the light as I crossed through the shadows to meet him, his smile clearly visible now I was nearer.

I asked him again, not believing it, *How?*

I let go of your hand.

But you kept on controlling it, right? I mean, that was still you, doing all of that . . . wasn't it?

Slowly, he shook his head, watching what I knew must be a wide play of emotions cross my face as I absorbed this.

But . . . how did you know I'd be able to do it?

I didn't. His answer, as always, was honest. *That's why I let go.*

And what if I hadn't been able to—

Rob's calm logic cut across my worries. *Everyone's afraid to fall, but sometimes you just have to take the stabilisers off your bike and try to ride on two wheels.*

I was left to ponder that while we walked back to the hotel, and for those minutes I knew something of what Anna must have felt, with Edmund pushing her and prodding her and battering away the careful shields she had constructed. And like Anna, tonight I felt all in a knot with my feelings.

I blamed it on what I'd just witnessed—the depth of emotion in that final scene between Anna and Edmund; the way they had argued, the way they had kissed. If I felt more aware of Rob now it was largely because of that, and because, in the same way Anna stood to lose Edmund when he left St. Petersburg, I knew that I would lose Rob the day after tomorrow, when we flew back home. He'd be heading north, and I'd be stepping back into my regular life. Only I wasn't sure I could ever go back, now, to how things had been.

If I'd loved him two years ago, I was falling *in* love with him now in a way that I'd never experienced, ever, with anyone. Something had shifted between us, beyond my control, and it had me so twisted inside that, when we finally came to the corridor outside my room and Rob turned round to tell me good night, I could say nothing back to him. All I could do was nod silently, struggling inside to know what to do, how to tell him I didn't yet have all the answers, but I couldn't seem to stop asking the questions.

He gave me a brotherly kiss on the cheek before turning away.

I stood miserably, holding my room key. If I'd been less of a coward, I thought, I'd have asked him to stay. Another man might have stayed anyway, whether I'd asked him or not. But not Rob.

Rob was always a gentleman.

Five paces off, he stopped dead in the corridor, still with his back to me.

Then, as it had on that first night in Eyemouth, when I'd seen him coming to shore on the lifeboat, his dark head turned slightly, as though he'd just heard something. I heard the heavy exhale of his breath.

And in one sudden motion he turned and came back, and the force of his forward momentum swept me up along with it, bringing me up hard against the closed door of the room at my back. With his hands on my shoulders, his face filling all of my vision, his eyes locked with mine, Rob said softly, "Not always."

And lowered his mouth to my own.

chapter
FORTY-THREE

He was right. He didn't kiss me like a gentleman.

He kissed me like a man who had been taken to his limit and beyond it, with a wordless, urgent passion that made anything but breathing seem impossible; and even breathing wasn't all that easy.

I had no remembrance whatsoever of how we got through that door, or how it locked behind us, but I had a vague awareness of us being in the room now, in the semi-darkness, with my back pressed up against a wall and not the door.

I *did* remember Rob's shirt coming off, because the sleeves had stubbornly got stuck around his biceps and I'd heard the tearing sound as he had yanked the fabric free, before his hands had roughly pushed the jacket from my shoulders, found the buttons of my own shirt; dealt with that, as well.

It tore a little, too, but at that point I didn't care. And then he leaned in once again and settled onto me more carefully, his skin against my own, his forearms braced against the wall beside my shoulders, both hands buried in my hair as though he sought to hold me there and never let me go.

This kiss was gentle, deep, and left no walls to hide behind. His thoughts lay fully open to me, but they had no form—they were pure feeling, crashing into mine and over them and through them till I couldn't tell which one of us was thinking what, or feeling what, or whose sensations made it seem as though I were no longer held by gravity, but spinning in a void.

Rob's voice, that calm and sane and quiet voice, became a thing of heat and want and desperate need, and I did what it asked of me.

We didn't even make it to the bed.

Our thoughts were the last things that we untangled, in the aftermath, and even then we did it with reluctance. Rob's head slowly tilted forwards till his forehead rested heavy on my shoulder, and I slid my own hand upwards from his neck to grasp his dampened hair and hold him close.

I guessed that he was having the same difficulty I was having sorting out my thoughts from his, because he used his spoken voice to tell me, thickly, "Sorry."

My voice wasn't working all that well, yet, either. "Don't be."

"Not exactly how I planned it."

If I turned my head a fraction, I discovered, I could brush my lips against his shoulder. Doing this, I answered him, "I thought I was the planner. You're meant to be the spontaneous one."

"No." His head changed its angle, his voice rumbling low down the sensitive skin of my neck. "No, for this, I had plans."

"Did you?"

"Aye." I could feel that faint smile, and my fingers curled into his hair as his one hand slid slowly the length of my side. "Very definite plans."

Then he dragged his mouth back to my own and his smile disappeared in another deep kiss as he wrapped both arms strongly around me and lifted me up, and we crossed the few feet to the bed, where he set me down gently and followed me into the blankets. And showed me.

"I'll be putting on weight," Rob accused me, "with you and your ice cream for breakfast."

"You're not the type to put on weight. You're far too fit."

He slid his arm along the back rail of the white-painted bench, slanting a look down at me. "You're blushing, now."

"I'm not."

He only grinned and looked away again, his level blue gaze settling on the gold glint of the church spire showing in between the curve of trees, above the fortress walls along the river's edge.

"Anyway," I said, "it's more like brunch. It's gone eleven."

"And what time is your reception?"

"Not till three o'clock. We've loads of time." Contentedly, I leaned against Rob's side and let my head rest back against his arm as he adjusted it to cradle round my shoulders.

Looking down, he said, "I have to say, you're being very calm about it."

"About what? Telling Wendy Van Hoek that her painting's a forgery?"

"Aye, that," he acknowledged, "and telling her, too, how ye ken it."

"Well, she doesn't have to know that, does she? I mean," I explained, "it *is* a forgery. The evidence of that is already physically there, in the painting. I only have to say I have my doubts about it, and let Yuri's experts do the rest and run the tests to prove it. No one ever has to know that . . . what?" I asked, as I felt Rob go motionless beside me.

He lifted his arm from my shoulders, and then from the back of the bench altogether as, shifting, he straightened away from me.

"Rob?"

I was hit by a hard wave of something like hurt, then he closed off his thoughts. To the static, I said again, *Rob?*

It was no use. He'd shut me out. Raking a hand through his hair, he said carefully, "I thought, when you said you'd tell her . . . I thought . . ."

I caught up in a rush. "You thought I was going to tell her what I saw?" I read the answer plainly in his eyes. "Oh, Rob, I'm sorry. Really sorry. But I can't, you know I can't. Besides, there isn't any need to, like I said. I can convince her it's a forgery without all that."

"Convenient." There was bitterness in that one word I hadn't heard from Rob before.

I said, "This isn't like you. You're supposed to understand."

"Aye, well, I thought I did. I thought I understood, last night." He exhaled hard. "You're right, you can be difficult to read, sometimes. I got it wrong."

"That isn't fair."

"I'm done with fair."

"I'd lose my job," I told him bluntly. "All the clients, all the people that I work with, and Sebastian, they'd all think that I was lying, or they'd think I was a—" I bit back the word, but Rob supplied it.

"Freak." The hard twist of his mouth was nothing like a smile. "Was that the word that ye were wanting?" When I didn't answer, he went on, "Ye ken this for a fact, then, do you, that they'd all react so badly?"

"I can't take that chance."

"Aye, you can. It's a choice. We choose most things in life, ye ken. Whether we live it or watch it go past. Even whether we're happy."

I looked down. "It's easy for you."

He gave a hard laugh. "Because this is so easy." He threw his unfinished ice cream in the bin at the side of the bench, and asked, "If I had some other ability, if I could sing, or put a football in the net, would you have been ashamed of that, as well?"

"I never was . . ." Words failed me for a moment, and I focused on the sparrows that had gathered round our feet until my voice returned. "I'm not ashamed of you."

"You're feart that I'll embarrass you," he said. "That's why you've kept me hidden from these people that you work with here, because you're feart I might just be myself, and read a mind or two in public."

He'd hit close to home with that, and I could tell he knew it when he saw my face. I turned defensive.

"Would it really be so hard," I asked, "to hide what you can do? To keep it private?"

Rob looked down at me. "Short term? Like this? No, not so hard. But over time? Aye, then," he said, "I'd find it near impossible. It's what I am." He held my gaze. "It's what you are, as well."

"I hide it."

"Aye," he said, "and look how well that's working for you."

Round our feet the sparrows hopped and chattered, all oblivious to what was going on between us. For a moment Rob looked down at them in silence, too, and when he spoke again there was no anger in his voice, nor even bitterness, but just the smallest hint of something sad.

"If we cannae be what we were born to be, the whole of it, we die a little on the inside, every day we live the lie. I'd die for you in every other way," he told me, quietly, "but not like that. I'm sorry, Nick."

I thought that I'd known every kind of pain, until I watched Rob walk away from me. He didn't touch me, didn't kiss me, didn't say goodbye. It would have been a touch of melodrama if he had, I guessed, since we'd be flying home together on the plane tomorrow. But I knew he'd left me, all the same.

The whole world blurred. I felt the searing heat of tears and closed my eyes as tightly as I could so that they wouldn't fall, and out of nowhere I was struck by a deep stab of anguish answering my own, yet not my own.

I thought at first it might be Rob—that his control had slipped enough to let me in for that brief instant. But it wasn't him at all. The pictures rose and raced by in a blur behind my eyelids, stopping of their own accord and widening so suddenly the bright light left me blinded, till it flared and settled into the warm sunlight of a summer afternoon.

I was above the Strelka, wheeling like a bird upon the wind that smelt of salt and sea and ship timbers and canvas sails. Below me lay the Custom House, the line of merchants' warehouses, the long and broad expanse of the exchange, and to the west the row of colleges. Between them, in the dusty square, the people walked in pairs and threes. A carriage drawn by four matched horses, with a little dog that ran behind it, swung by jauntily and passed a heavy wagon, moving slower with its creaking wheels and plodding team of oxen.

And as always, there were soldiers in the square. As I gradually came down to their own level I could see them clearly, many standing guard around the Custom House, and others strolling on patrol, and one lieutenant talking to a younger woman who stood very still and straight amid the chaos, in her black paduasoy gown.

• • •

Anna held herself with care. "Charles, it is not true."

His eyes held sympathy, but they were sure. "I had it from a man who had no reason to invent it. He was there."

It was a strange thing, Anna thought, how her world could so completely shatter in the small space of one brief heartbeat, and with sunshine warm upon her shoulders, and the flow of people all around, uninterrupted. She tried to hold the broken pieces in their places, as though willing it could make it whole. "He often is accused of things he did not say or do. You know he is."

Charles said nothing to that, only looked at her as though he wished there were some way that he could have spared her what kindness and duty had bound him to say.

Anna focused her gaze on the masts of the merchants' ships, just past his shoulders, and blinked at the brightness. "This friend of yours . . . is he entirely sure Captain Deane was the man to whom Mr. O'Connor was speaking?"

"He knew Deane himself, from before. Well, not knew him, exactly, but yes, he's entirely sure."

"And why did he not say something earlier? Deane has been gone from this place for a month."

Charles defended his friend. "He did not know that I was acquainted with Mr. O'Connor. It was not until this past hour, when we dined at the tavern, and Mr. O'Connor was there, that my friend told me what he'd observed. What he'd heard."

Anna nodded, still watching the masts of the ships as they danced on the river, not wanting to think of the details of what Charles's friend claimed he'd overheard in Trescott's tavern, the day before Deane left St. Petersburg: that Deane and Edmund had talked as though friends, and that Edmund had told Deane, without any prompting, that Captain Hay had come from King James's court with instructions for Sir Harry Stirling to buy several ships here, supported by money from Spain and the pope, and that Edmund was sure he'd have more information in time he could pass on to Deane.

Charles watched her. "Anna, I—"

"Maybe your friend heard things wrongly, and misunderstood."

"Anna. Look at me." When she did, he told her, very soberly, "Deane tried to buy me, too. Trescott reminded him of the divisions between the vice-admiral and my mother, and Deane approached me, to see if I'd spy for him."

"What did you tell him?"

"I told him to go to the devil. But he was an active man, while he was here, and I know he found others more willing," Charles said. "Mr. Trescott, for one. I am told he agreed to find probable men for Deane's purpose and make introductions."

She would not have thought Mr. Trescott dishonest. "For payment?"

"Not in money, but Deane promised him an English education for his son," Charles told her. "Even good men can be made to turn from their own conscience for a price."

"What was Mr. O'Connor's price?" Even asking the question was painful.

"I do not know. Faith, I'd have called him outside on the spot and discovered it, but I thought only of coming to find you, and tell you. My uncle should know."

"Yes." Her eyes stung again, and she blinked fiercely as Charles went on.

"I did not think to find you so close," he said. "What business brings you across to the island?"

She had to think hard, to remember herself. "Mrs. Lacy is large with her child and she finds it uncomfortable sitting so long. She desired an outing, and having not yet seen her husband's new office she thought to come visit it." That seemed an age ago. "She's with him now."

"Well, it was my good fortune you waited out here, else I might not have found you."

She gave a distracted nod. "Yes, very fortunate."

"Are you all right?"

Anna nodded a second time.

Charles said, "And so you will tell him?"

"Tell whom?"

"Tell my uncle," he said, "about Mr. O'Connor."

She nodded again. Then she thought for a moment and asked, "Will you do something for me?"

"Of course, if I'm able to."

"Will you wait here in my place? If the general's wife comes, and I have not yet returned, please see she gets home safely."

"Anna . . ."

"Charles, please. Please just do it. For me." And she gave him no choice but to do it by turning away from him, crossing the great square with blindly swift steps that by chance and pure providence steered her without any incident through the confusion of feet, skirts, and carriage wheels.

She did not slow her pace till she had reached the tavern. Then she stopped, and searched among the faces of the men who stood outside it for an honest one, and offered him a coin. "Sir, if you please, there is a man within to whom I must speak urgently."

The man brought Edmund out to her.

He came out laughing, dark eyes gleaming just enough to tell her he'd been drinking, with his jacket wafting scents of whisky, wine, and pipe tobacco. When he saw her, though, the change in his expression let her see he was not altogether drunk.

"What is it? What has happened?" In concern, he took a step towards her. "Mistress Jamieson, what's wrong? Is someone injured? Mrs. Lacy, or the children?"

That his first thoughts should be for the general's family made her instincts war more desperately against her reason, for it seemed impossible that such a man could do what she'd been told he'd done.

She shook her head. "They're well. But I must speak to you."

He looked around. "This hardly is the proper place to—"

"Edmund, please." Her words came with more force than she'd have liked, but nonetheless they reached him, for he frowned and came the final steps towards her, reaching one hand out to guide her by the arm along the path that led towards the river's edge.

"What is it?" he repeated.

She could not reply yet, only walk along with him in painful silence, as though with every step she trod on knives.

He brought her to the shore, where marsh reeds bent before the currents of the river, and the spindly trees leaned out across the water, and small birds sang while all around them unseen insects buzzed and hummed like nature's summer orchestra.

Exactly where the soft ground changed to mud, he turned her to him and asked once again, with gentleness, "What is it?"

"I have heard something." She gathered up her courage and then took a breath and looked him in the eye. "I have heard something that I do not believe, nor will I yet believe it until I have heard it from yourself, sir."

She'd imagined it, she told herself. She'd only just imagined that he'd stiffened in response to that, the way a man might brace himself against a coming blow.

She said, "I'm told that you did talk to Captain Deane, the day before he left St. Petersburg. And that you did inform him of some things that you should not have, and did promise to inform him further."

Edmund let her go, and turned a little from her so she could not see the whole of his expression, though she saw enough to know his face was serious. "Who told you this?"

She asked him, "Does it matter?"

He looked down at that, and she could see the faint edge of that half smile that was not a smile, the one that held no humour. "No," he said. "I don't suppose it matters much at all."

Her voice betrayed her with a tremor. "Is it true?"

He turned his head then, and his eyes found hers. "You really don't believe it?"

"I confess that I cannot."

Why that should make his eyes turn sad at first, then darken into anger, Anna could not claim to know, but he controlled the anger as he asked, "And why is that?"

"Because," she started, but he had turned fully back towards her now and come a slow step forwards, and she faltered. "I . . ."

"Because you saw me looking at a child once, and you think you know my nature?" Leaning in, he brought his face to hers and told her, "Look again."

She still saw only Edmund, but she felt the heated pricking as her eyes began to fill, and with an oath he straightened to his full height.

"'Tis the truth. You've heard correctly."

Anna forced the tears back with an effort, looking up at him, unable to look elsewhere for a few long, painful seconds. When her hand moved, she was almost unaware of it. Until she heard the slap, and felt the stinging of her palm, and saw the red mark spread along his jaw. She slapped him once again, still harder, and he stood there silently and let her do it.

Nothing in his face changed, nor his stance, and Anna had the strong impression that he would have stood there for as long as she desired to hit him, without ever moving to defend himself. She wondered if he'd stood like that, so stoically, when as a boy he had been whipped in punishment until his hand was cut and bleeding, for a crime that was not his. Except this time, she told herself, he was not being noble. This time he deserved the blame.

She let her hand drop. Turned away before the tears spilled over.

She did not ask for details, for in truth it hardly mattered. But there was one thing she wished to know. "What did he offer you?" she asked. "What was your price?"

The silence stretched. And then he said, "A pardon, Mistress Jamieson. A pardon from King George."

She gave a nod, and in a small voice told him, "Well, then. Now you can go home again."

And without looking back, she walked away.

The reception was nearly half over before I arrived. I had spent a long time in the shower, just standing there, letting the water wash over me, thinking. I'd spent even longer deciding what I ought to wear. But the longest time had been spent willing my own feet to carry me, step after step, from the hotel and down to the river and over the long bridge back onto the island, the same way I'd walked there this morning with Rob.

I had not seen or heard from him. I knew he'd closed himself off and he wanted to keep it that way, so I hadn't intruded. I didn't know whether he knew that I'd done a whole vision without him, alone. Had it happened a day ago, I'd have been wanting to tell him about it, exchanging my pride for his praise, but today it had been such a hollow victory, and what I'd seen had been so sad, I'd felt no sense of triumph or accomplishment.

And now I stood in the beautiful Great Hall upstairs in the Menshikov Palace, a full and untouched glass of wine in my hand, and tried taking an interest in what everybody was saying, and I couldn't do it. I couldn't.

"Hey." Wendy Van Hoek nudged my shoulder. "Are you okay?"

With her striking looks and a pair of truly amazing high-heeled shoes, she managed somehow to make a plain cream-coloured pant-suit look more glamorous than my black cocktail frock. Even though my wine was white, I held it with new care, remembering Sebastian's disaster.

I forced a smile. "I'm fine."

"Good. Your timing was perfect, you've missed all the speeches," she said with a smile. "We'll be heading downstairs in a moment, to tour the exhibit."

Terrific, I thought. I *did* drink the wine, then, if a little too quickly.

Downstairs, Yuri took his turn giving the guests several insights into the selected works, slipping from Russian and French into English with laudable ease so that everyone there had a chance to appreciate what he was saying.

"This was a great strength of the Peredvizhniki, their portraiture. They moved it from the realm of privilege, the family portrait or the portrait of great persons, to the universal, yes? Their art was not for private viewing, it was for the public, and their subjects were the ordinary Russian people. This was very new, very exciting. Here you see it, in this study from a mural done by Surikov." He stopped, to my dismay, in front of the one painting in the whole room I'd been doing my best not to look at. "When he painted this, Surikov was just beginning, just from the academy, but you can already see what will come in his portraits. This face, this is not done for anyone's vanity, is it? It's real."

Rather too real, I thought. Bishop Gregory, reading his famous oration at Constantinople, in front of the people who'd shunned what he had to say. Bishop Gregory, who'd told the council, when he had resigned, that he would gladly be another Jonah, bringing news that nobody was keen to hear, like Jonah in the Bible—the unlucky prophet who had chosen not to give the message God had sent him with, because it was too difficult to tell. And who had suffered for his choice.

I heard Rob telling me in anger, "It's a choice. We choose most things in life . . ."

And standing here right now in all my misery, I knew I'd made the wrong one.

Breaking into Yuri's speech before I could think better of it, I said, "It's a forgery."

You could have heard a pin drop. If I'd never felt a fool before in all my life, I felt one now. But still I pushed ahead, with all eyes on me, and continued, "It was never done by Surikov. A forger made it, sometime in the 1960s, I would say."

Beside me, Wendy turned and arched an eyebrow, looking not at all impressed. "My father had this piece authenticated."

"Then he was misled."

"And how," she asked me, "would you know a thing like that, when all you've done is look at it?"

I drew a breath, and said, "Because I touched it."

"And?"

"I see things about objects, when I touch them."

I heard the French guests speaking low to one another, no doubt trying to translate my words, and then I heard a laugh.

"What, like a psychic?" Wendy asked me.

I could see what she was thinking, but it struck me at that moment, as I stood there, that it didn't matter all that much what anybody thought about me, anymore. I'd lost the only person whose opinion truly mattered. So I told her, "Yes, exactly like a psychic. It's a kind of ESP that's called psychometry."

Wendy stared. "You're joking, aren't you?"

Yuri, who through all of this appeared to be assuming that he must have heard me wrong, asked me in Russian to repeat it, which I did, and then he stared at me as well, as though I were a sideshow oddity.

I said, "I know it sounds a little strange . . ."

"A *little* strange?" asked Wendy.

"But," I finished, "it's the truth."

Her eyes were searching on my face. "You touch an object, and you see things?"

"Yes."

A moment passed. I really could have used another glass of wine, but then again, my face was already so flushed from the effects of both embarrassment and alcohol that likely it was just as well I didn't have a second drink.

"All right, then." Wendy pointed out another painting hanging nearly opposite the Surikov. "Touch that one. Tell me what you see."

This was a larger canvas, done by Ivan Shishkin, of a quiet forest path with fallen trees. I went across to it, aware I had become the party's entertainment, seeing all the guests shift round to watch me, most amused. I closed my mind to them, and closed my eyes, and touched the canvas.

Thanks to Rob, and what he'd shown me how to do these past few days, and how he'd pushed me to do more, I didn't only see a narrow scene this time, I was immersed in it, as I had been whenever I'd watched Anna.

I stayed there like that for several minutes, then I stepped away again, and turned to Wendy. "You won't ever sell this one," I said.

"And why is that?"

"Because you bought this painting with your father at the first auction he ever took you to," I told her plainly, "in New York. It was November, you were maybe about eight. You wore a dress with pink stripes on the skirt, and you had a small butterfly pin here, just at the neckline." With a hand to my own collarbone, I showed her where. "It had a yellow stone in it. Your father gave you that, as well. He let you hold the auction paddle, told you when to bid, and you were so excited . . ." I could see I'd said enough, from how her eyes had changed, and so I gave a shrug and tried to smile and summed up with, "You'll never sell this painting, it's too special."

Wendy stared at me in disbelief. "My God. There is no way . . . I mean *no* way at all that you could possibly have known . . ." She blinked, and looked at me more closely, and incredibly, returned my smile. "That really is amazing."

The mood had shifted in the room. The French guests murmured once again, and nodded, and looked on with newer interest now as Wendy moved towards the Surikov.

She looked at it, and then at me. "So tell me what you saw, when you touched this one."

When I came out of the palace at the end of the reception, I was still a little wobbly from the wine. It was just six o'clock, still light, not really evening yet, but with the bank of clouds that had moved in to block the sun and raise the wind it felt as though the day had ended.

I was glad my frock had sleeves, and that I'd thought to bring a coat. I hugged it round me now and started walking up the pavement to the bridge.

I nearly passed him.

He was standing close against the hedge that ran along the pavement here, his back set squarely to the wind, his head up. Waiting for me.

I stopped walking. Faced him with a mix of hope and hesitation. *Hi. I was . . . I've just been . . .*

Aye. I ken what you've been up to. He crossed the space between us with what seemed a single motion, strong and sure, and caught me hard within his arms and held me there, the cold wind a forgotten thing that could no longer touch me as he kissed my hair, my neck, my face.

I'm sorry. I released it like a litany. *I'm sorry. I'm so sorry, Rob.*

I love you, Nick. His mouth found mine then, and for several minutes after that I could not frame so much as a coherent thought, let alone answer him, but when he finally pulled away to breathe I found that I was smiling, though my eyes seemed wet with tears.

I love you, too.

He touched my face, his strong hands gentle. Wiped the tears away and bent to kiss my forehead before setting me away from him. *Right, then.* He gathered my hand into his, our fingers interlaced. *Let's go and finish this.*

"I shall be very glad to see this summer done and over with," said Mrs. Lacy. They were sitting in the drawing-room, an hour after suppertime, and she was having difficulty finding somewhere comfortable to sit. "This child of yours will be a giant, Pierce, you mark my words."

The general, midway through a game of chess with Anna, smiled. "It is a boy, I think. Both boys were big, like that, and made you most unsociable."

His wife said, in complaining tones, "I wonder Edmund does not come to see us. He will leave soon, will he not?"

"Aye," General Lacy said. "Tomorrow, or the next day, I believe."

"'Tis very bad of him to not come say goodbye."

The general slid his queen across the board and glanced at Anna. "Check, again, my dear."

She tried to concentrate. Two days had passed now since she had left Edmund standing at the river's edge, and she was wrestling with her conscience, still, not able to tell anyone. She could not tell the general, to be sure, for Edmund was his kin. And the vice-admiral was away at Cronstadt, so she had been told.

It hadn't helped that she'd received a note from Edmund yesterday, delivered by a ragged boy who'd waited in the street for her. She'd thought to send it back to him unopened, but against her better judgment she had taken it and opened it, alone and in the privacy of her own room. It had been just a single sheet of paper, folded neatly round two playing cards.

You will hate me, he had written, *and God knows you'll have a right to, but in truth I had no choice.* He'd signed *Your Servant*, and his name, and that was all. She'd held the two cards in her hands, and looked at them: the ace of hearts, her card. And his, the knave.

And she had fought the tears again without success, and held the guilty knowledge to herself, and let it shrivel her inside so that she might have thought she had no heart at all remaining, had it not reminded her by sharply twisting every time she heard his name.

She breathed the pain away, and moved her bishop to protect her king. At least, she thought, he would be on the road soon and away from them, where he could do no further damage.

Mrs. Lacy said, "And why must he away so soon? Did he not tell you?"

General Lacy smiled and told her, "Men, my darling, do not share their thoughts with one another in the same way that you women do."

His wife rose, found another chair, and settled in it with a sigh. "Oh, well I know it. You men and your secrets. All your letters, and your meetings, and your visitors. Vice-Admiral Gordon has brought back new visitors from Cronstadt just this afternoon, I've heard." She looked towards her husband. "Do you know them?"

General Lacy said, "I could not say. It is the first I've heard of it."

His wife sighed once again, with feeling. "Secrets."

"Some, my dear, would call it privacy." He moved his queen another square and said to Anna, "Checkmate."

So it was. She should have lain her black king on his side, admitting the defeat, but for some reason she could not, and so she took the king with care into her hand as General Lacy leaned back in his chair.

He told his wife, "At least, for Gordon, and Sir Harry, Edmund's leaving is convenient, for he can now carry letters for them."

Anna looked up sharply. "Letters?"

"Aye, there are few avenues to trust, out of St. Petersburg, as well you know. Whatever Gordon and Sir Harry give to Edmund he can take directly to the right people at Hamburg, or at Amsterdam, wherever he might come ashore."

"And have they written letters, do you know?"

"I know they meant to." General Lacy's gaze upon her face grew curious, and thoughtful. "Why?"

She could not give an answer, for her mind was in a tumult. *You will hate me*, Edmund's note had promised. *You will hate me*. In the future tense, and not the present.

With the black king still clutched tightly in her hand, she rose and mumbled some excuse to them, and left the room, and ran. She ran across the lobby, through the door, and out into the street, and ran down that as well, and did not care it was unladylike.

Dmitri answered to her urgent knock at Gordon's door, and stood aside to let her in as though he'd been expecting her.

"Of course he's here," he told her when she asked. "He has come back this afternoon, and brought—"

She did not wait to hear about the vice-admiral's new visitors. She raced ahead and through into his chamber, so intensely focused on her purpose and on him that she paid no attention to the other man who rose to stand, too, as she burst upon them.

"Do not let him take your letters," she told Gordon breathlessly.

He steadied her with both hands on her shoulders. "Anna."

"Please, you cannot give them to him. He will—"

"Anna." Gordon spoke more firmly, and his tone was the same one he'd always used to let her know that he would have her pay attention.

Anna paused, and did just that, as she had done from the first days that she had spent under his protection. Gordon's eyes, grown older now, smiled down at her with an expression that she did not understand. He moved a half-step sideways so that she could see the man who stood behind him, past his shoulder in the corner of the room.

A man with brown hair and no hat, and eyes that would, she knew, have crinkled at their corners had he smiled. He was not smiling now, but stood there looking at her steadily, as though he held his breath and was not sure how she'd receive him.

"Anna," said Gordon, "your father is come."

Captain Jamieson stumbled a little beneath the full force of her running embrace, but he held to her tightly and did not let go. He was wearing a coat of fine brocaded silk now and not a rough uniform, but the hard sheltering warmth of his chest was the same, just the way she had fought all these years to remember it.

She did not think to correct the vice-admiral, to tell him the captain was not her true father, because at this moment, in her mind, he was. He had promised her, all those years past, he would find her. And now he was here.

"You came." She could not seem to stop the tears, and his head lowered more so his cheek rested warm at her temple.

He gathered her closer, as though, like herself, he had long had a hole in his heart of her size and her shape and was feeling it fill now, if slowly.

She said again, hoarsely, "You came."

"Aye." His voice, when he answered, rolled over her like a great comforting wave, so familiar it left her heart aching. "I told ye I'd return for ye."

For a while they stayed silent, as though neither wanted to undo the magic. And then a faint sound in the next room drew Gordon's attention. A look passed above Anna's head. Captain Jamieson stroked his hand over her hair; brushed the tear-dampened curls from the side of her face, and more gently still, said, "I told ye I'd do something else, I recall, and I'm not one for breaking a promise." He tilted her face up and smiled and the years rolled away and she felt eight years old again, holding his hand in the church of the convent at Ypres. "Will ye come meet your mother?"

The woman who sat in the vice-admiral's parlour had hair that, although it had lightened, still held the same brightness as that in the curl tied with ribbon that Anna had carried for all these long years. She was lovely and slender, with beautiful eyes that could not seem to leave Anna's face. When the two men had entered the room, bringing Anna between them, the woman had gone very still, as though fearing to move, and her mouth had lost form for a moment and trembled, her eyes growing bright.

Now she blinked, very hard, and her smile was a thing of great beauty.

Gordon said, "Anna, this is Sophia McClelland. Your mother."

She ought to have curtsied, she knew. It was how she'd been taught to greet strangers. But Anna stood speechless, her manners forgotten, her mind whirling helplessly, all of this strange day's events making ordinary action impossible.

This was Sophia. Her mother.

She formed that thought over, more clearly. Her mother.

Then memories rushed in, all unbidden, small fragments and bits that flew randomly round and made little sense, never connecting: a frill of silver lace, a fire, the softness of grey silk, a breath of cold, a woman's voice that asked her, gently, "Which one is your favourite?"

And it seemed to Anna, then, that it was natural for her to hold her hand out to this woman she had never met, and open it to show the chess piece, lying still within it, that she'd taken from the general's chessboard and until this moment had forgotten she was holding.

Time slipped backwards for a moment while she watched her mother's eyes.

Sophia looked at the black king, and in the silence raised one hand and pressed it flat against her heart, as though she wished to hold it in its place. It seemed to Anna that the older woman was about to weep, but then instead she smiled—a smile that wavered only slightly as she said to Anna, quietly, "My favourite pieces always were—"

"The pawns," said Anna. "I remember." And she felt her own eyes fill then, as her voice became a whisper. "I remember you."

It did not matter, then, that she misplaced her steps as she came forward and began to fall, because her mother's arms were there to catch her, and to hold her, as though they'd been made for that one purpose.

It was several minutes before either woman moved, or let the other go. Their hands stayed linked though, when at long last Anna took a chair beside her mother's, for it felt as if they should not now be made to separate when they'd already been so long divided.

Both the men, by this time, had moved off a discreet distance and were sitting now discussing something that appeared to be of some weight, judging by their faces. Anna noticed Captain Jamieson still held his one leg straighter than the other, as if it did not bend easily, remembering its wound. She noticed something else, as well, and faintly smiled.

Her mother, following her gaze across the room towards the captain, asked, "What is it?"

"He still wears the stone," said Anna, "with the hole in it."

"Aye, he has worn that always since I gave it to him," said Sophia, "before you were even born. I found it on the beach at Slains, the summer we were married, and I gave it to him on the night he did return to France, and . . ." Her words trailed into silence as she studied Anna's face, her own face suddenly incredulous. "You do not know."

All in confusion, Anna said, "I gave the stone to him."

"And where was this?"

"In Ypres, while I was in the convent. Colonel Graeme gave the stone to me, and told me it had been my father's, and I gave it to . . ."

Then Anna, too, had let her voice trail off.

Her mother looked again across the room towards the men, and interrupted them by saying, "John?"

The captain turned.

Her mother asked, "Will you come here a moment, please?"

He rose and walked towards them with the limp that she remembered, and the face that she remembered, though he'd shaved the beard away. But now as Anna watched his face she knew why he had worn that beard in Flanders, where her father had so often fought, and where he'd fallen; and she knew why, when she had first seen her Uncle Maurice from the back, she'd thought he was the captain. Still, it seemed a thing impossible, until he'd crossed the whole room and he stood there looking down at them.

Her mother asked her, "Anna, will you tell me who this man is?"

Captain Jamieson, she nearly answered, but she knew the full truth now of what Sister Xaveria had told her at the convent, when she'd asked the nun about Dame Clare. "We rarely see the things we don't expect to see," had been the answer. And as she looked up now at the captain's eyes, his eyes that were the colour of the winter sea, just like her own, she knew the truth at last.

"He is my father."

Gordon, as he always did when faced with things emotional, had rung for tea. He sat back now while Anna poured it out for everybody, as she'd done so many times when she had acted as his hostess, and he told her, "Well, I saw it the first moment I laid eyes on you, that morning in Calais, when you looked up at me with those eyes, yes, like that. It was like looking at a ghost," he said. "Or so I thought." He sent a look towards the captain.

No, thought Anna, not the captain any longer, but the colonel, for that was her father's true rank, and how she must learn to see him now—not as her old friend Captain Jamieson, but as her father, Colonel Moray.

He'd explained already why he'd let his family, friends, and foes alike believe him to be dead, and why he'd left the battlefield of Malplaquet a different man, and how he'd ended up in Ulster on the northern coast of Ireland, and how the name McClelland fitted into everything, but to be honest, Anna had been more absorbed in watching both her parents than in listening to any tale they told.

She had marked, though, why he'd assumed the name of Jamieson the year he'd fetched her out of Scotland. With a shrug he'd said, "I could be neither Moray nor McClelland if I fought for James at Sherrifmuir, and I could not have raised my head again had I not fought, so it seemed fitting, then, to call myself the son of James."

And after that she'd fallen back to watching him, half-listening, more interested in the way that he and the vice-admiral interacted. It was clear they had a history that had not been without conflict, though they seemed to view each other with respect.

Moray smiled and said, to Gordon, "Having buried me already once at sea yourself, you should not have been much surprised to see me resurrected."

"No, perhaps not. But I was surprised to think you might have had a child." He took his cup of tea from Anna, thanking her. "The priests who were pursuing her did call her Anna Moray,, though she would not own the name. I did allow she might have been your brother William's girl, or Robin's, but I could think of no good reason why they'd send their daughters out of Scotland, when they were themselves both there still. And the more I knew her, I confess I could not think of her as anyone's but yours. Not in her face alone," he said, "but in her habits and her manner, and her speech." He smiled. "She all but dared me, in Calais, to take her part."

Sophia said, "And I am glad you did."

There could be no mistaking, Anna thought, how Gordon's features softened when he gazed upon her mother. "Would you like a different drink?" he asked her, with a hint of humour. "I recall the last time you drank tea with me it was not to your liking."

The small smile that she returned to him held memory, too. "No, thank you, Thomas. Tea is fine." And at her prompting, he continued.

"Well," he said, and looked again at Moray, "if you were indeed her father, as I did suspect, then I could think of but one woman who would be her mother, for considering the girl's age, I remembered you had eyes for but one woman at the time. And I knew where I'd last seen her. So I wrote to Slains," he told them. "To the Earl of Erroll."

Anna, with her own tea in her hand, returned to sit beside her mother. "When was this?" she asked, because it was the first she'd ever heard of it.

"At Candlemas, our first year here. But what I did not know was that the earl had died the autumn just before that."

Anna frowned. "But he was not an old man."

"No. No, it was indeed a tragedy. His letter was returned to me unopened by his sister, the new countess, who assumed it spoke of business for the king, which might be private. I assured her, in the letter I wrote back to her, my business was of quite a different nature." Gordon drank his tea, the way he always drank it, without sugar to smooth any of its bitterness. "I asked the countess if Sophia Paterson, who once had lived at Slains, did live there still, and if she'd ever had a child. I got my answer the next spring. The countess, like her mother, is a woman of discretion. She said, no, Sophia was no longer there, and yes, there'd been a child, but all she was at liberty to tell me was the child had left that place with Colonel Patrick Graeme some few years before, and if I truly had a right to know her whereabouts, then I would also know the colonel well enough myself to ask him." His eyes, in good humour, admired the countess's cleverness as he went on, "So I did. I learned where Colonel Graeme lived in Paris, and I wrote to him. And then had no reply until the letter you yourself did see me open," he told Anna.

She remembered.

Moray levelly remarked, "My uncle died nearly five years ago."

"I know," said Gordon soberly. "I'm sorry. News is slow to reach us, sometimes, in this place. It was his son, the Capuchin, who wrote to me November last, to say he had just then found time to sort his father's things, and found my letter yet unopened, and had read it."

Anna pictured Father Graeme, with his father's laughing eyes and bearded face, and asked, "And was he well?"

"The monk? Aye," Gordon answered, "he was well, but very curious as to why I would ask about Sophia's child." He settled back. "Till then I had been guarded also, with my information, for I would not for the world, my dear, have put you in harm's way. But when I had this letter from the Capuchin, I knew from how he wrote that he did have an urgent interest in your welfare. So I answered him, and told him I believed that I did have you here, with me. I told the tale of how I'd found you at Calais, and then—"

"And then my cousin, Father Graeme, wrote to me," said Moray, neatly picking up the narrative.

"To us," Sophia said.

He granted the correction, with a sideways glance towards his wife. "His letter reached us . . . when?"

"The seventeenth of May," she told him, quietly. "At half-past three."

Her gaze had drifted downward and he reached across to where her hands were tightly twined upon her lap, and covered them with one of his. A little gesture that would have gone unremarked by most, but Anna saw the strong unspoken flow of comfort pass from Moray to her mother. Then he raised his eyes to Anna's.

"We'd come to think the worst. When ye were lost," he started, and then stopped and had to start again, as though his voice had failed him. "When ye vanished from Calais, I was where word could not have reached me. It was not until the summer, when we'd seen the king moved safely into Italy, that I had leave to go, and I came north, to Ypres."

"To keep your promise."

"Aye. To fetch my wee brave lass, and bring ye home with me to Ireland, where your mother and your brothers were awaiting ye. Where ye belonged."

Her smile was sad. "Except I wasn't there."

He shook his head. "And I learned why, and that ye'd gone with Patrick—Father Graeme—to Calais. So that's where I went, too." He looked then, at Vice-Admiral Gordon. "Did ye ken Rebecca Ogilvie was also at Calais, then?"

"Aye, I did. In fact, I had just crossed the channel in her company," said Gordon. "I confess I took no small delight in making it a most unpleasant voyage for her." He was smiling at the memory.

"Well, the Ogilvies and I have an acquaintance of long standing," Moray said. "When I went across to Scotland twenty years ago with Simon Fraser, they were in the boat behind, and being captured when they landed, neither one did hesitate to string the noose around our necks to save their own. They've intrigued for the English ever since," he said, "and when I heard that Patrick, all unknowing, had left Mrs. Ogilvie alone with Anna . . ."

Whatever he'd thought when he'd heard that was destined, it seemed, to stay private, because he looked down and away from her then, and this time it was her mother's hand that moved gently from underneath his to lie calmingly over the top of it, weaving her fingers through his as she clasped his large hand within both of hers, lending him strength.

"We believed you'd been taken," she told Anna, softly. "Your father spent some months in Paris, and he and his cousin and your Uncle Maurice and good Colonel Graeme together did search for you, but there was nothing." Her voice dropped in volume. "Just nothing."

Recovered now, Moray turned back to her. "Why did ye run from Calais?"

Anna tried to explain, though the words sounded sorely inadequate now, the attempts of a small, lonely child to protect those she loved by surrendering all hope of happiness, as it had seemed to her then.

When she'd finished, Sophia was once again holding a hand to her heart. "Oh, my dear. Oh, my love."

Moray did not say anything, but his eyes had the same reddened bright look they'd had long ago when she had kissed him goodbye at the convent. Abruptly, he pushed himself out of his chair and crossed over to one of the windows and stood looking out, with his back to her.

Gordon, affected as well, drew a sharp breath and looked to the side, to a candlestick set on the bookshelf, as though it were suddenly wanting his keen observation.

"But really, it all worked out well in the end," Anna told them, attempting to fix what she'd broken. "I've had a good life. Not just here, but before this," she said to Sophia, "at Slains, and at Ypres. I have had a good life."

Moray said, "Not the life ye were meant to have, Anna. The life that we wished for ye."

"No, perhaps not, but . . ." She paused, and her forehead creased lightly with all of the effort of trying to say what she wanted to tell them, to lessen their pain. She said, "I should have been very sad, to have missed any part of it."

Vice-Admiral Gordon sniffed loudly, and coughed, and said, "Well, then."

And all of them sat there in silence a moment.

Sophia was first to speak. "Thomas, I cannot begin to—"

"Then don't." In his charming smile, Anna could see how he might have appeared as a younger man. "There is no need. I owed you that much."

Moray told him, "I'm thinking ye've paid any debt to us over more times than ye needed to."

Gordon's gaze travelled from Sophia's face to her daughter's, and looking at Anna he said to her father, "In this instance, Colonel, 'twas I who was paid."

"You've done well by her, Thomas," Sophia said gently. "You've made her a lady."

That word struck a discordant note within Anna, and twisted her heart in a way she had almost forgotten, with all that had happened this evening. But now she looked sharply at Gordon.

"Your letters."

"What letters would those be, my dear?"

"I was told by the general that you and Sir Harry had both written letters of late, touching things of importance. If I'm to return into Ireland now with . . ." She broke off and glanced at Sophia, in case she assumed too much, but when she saw how her mother was watching her, looking so hopeful and happy, she said, ". . . with my parents, I pray you allow me to carry those letters, instead of the man you have asked."

Gordon lifted his eyebrows. "Why? What's wrong with Mr. O'Connor?"

She stopped up her ears to the voice of her heart. And she told him.

chapter
FORTY-SIX

It only took four days to get her passport, little time to see to everything that needed to be done; to say goodbye to all the people she'd
grown up with and grown fond of, and would miss.

The trunk she had brought to the Lacys' had been packed again,
only this time more full, with a pair of red shoes at the bottom that
she'd been unable to part with, for reasons she did not examine.

There'd been other gifts. The general had insisted that she take the
chessboard with its pieces, "For it rarely has been used so much as
when you have been here, and I do fear the chess men will grow bored
and idle after you have gone, so you had better take them with you.
Every army," he had told her, "needs its general." Father Dominic had
given her the grace of the Seraphic Blessing of St. Francis, placing his
hands gently on her head while he had prayed, "May the Lord bless
you and keep you; may He make his face to shine upon you, and be
gracious to you; may He lift up his countenance upon you, and give
you peace." And then he had told her, "Remember the faith you were
raised in, my child, and love not in word or in tongue, but in deed and
in truth; and whoever may come to you, either a friend or a foe, or a
thief or a robber, receive them with kindness, for each man must walk
on the path to which he has been called."

She'd promised to try, though she knew she had not the monk's
way of forgiveness.

The children had made her a drawing in pencil, with all of them in
it, and labelled in Michael's fine hand.

"This is you," little Katie had said to her, "catching the bird. And that's Ned." She had pointed to one of the sketched figures, taller than the rest. "He's gone away now."

"Yes, I know."

She had let Gordon tell the Lacys what she knew about their kinsman and his dealings with the English spy, for she'd not had the heart to do so. None of them had spoken of it to each other since.

In time, thought Anna, she herself would cease to think about him, and she would no longer see his smile or hear his voice within her memory quite so often. He'd be relegated to that same dim place as Christiane, and she would count it well that she had never lost her heart to him. Or so she'd reassured herself, as she had packed her things away, but for some reason when she'd taken up the note and playing cards he'd sent her, and prepared to tear them through and so dispose of them, her fingers had been unable to do it, and instead they'd gripped the ace of hearts and smiling knave more tightly, and had wrapped his note around them and thrust all into her pocket.

Mrs. Lacy knew, she thought, for in the older woman's eyes as they were saying their farewells Anna had seen a light of sympathy. "Men and their secrets," Mrs. Lacy had said, and she had shaken her head and given Anna one more kiss and had assured her she'd be perfectly all right with Mary Gordon coming now to keep her company until the baby's birth.

Mary herself, and Nan, had been harder farewells, and there'd been weeping all around, but Anna knew now, from her parents' own example, that a parting did not always mean a permanent goodbye. She had remembrances from each of them—a pair of pearl earrings from Mary, and an amber brooch from Nan. And even Charles had paid a visit to Vice-Admiral Gordon's house, to sit for tea and talk and say his own goodbye.

Gordon had remarked to him, "I hear you're bound for Moscow soon, with General Bohn."

"Yes, sir."

"You have done well, my lad. I'm proud of you, as would your father be."

Charles had returned the smile and said, "Your own pride, Uncle, is enough for me." To Anna, he had added, "I expect you now to write to me, and tell me your adventures, Cousin, for I trust you'll not forget your family."

She had given him her promise.

And in truth, she seemed to have more family round her now than she knew what to do with, for she'd scarcely moved these past few days without her father walking by her side, or else her mother sitting next to her, and all within their circle had by now been told the story of their coming, or at least the public version of it, for to everyone her father had been introduced as Captain Jamieson, who'd left his daughter in Vice-Admiral Gordon's care while he himself had been away and fighting for the French, and now had come to take her home again.

Sir Harry was the only one among their friends who knew the perfect truth of it, because he knew her father's family well and had been quick to recognize him when they'd first been introduced, although he'd held the secret close and played along in public with the common version of the tale.

Sir Harry had himself arranged the sloop that was to carry them to Cronstadt, where they were to meet a larger ship to take them first to Amsterdam, and then from there to Ulster, where her parents had their home. And it was now Sir Harry who was personally seeing to the loading of their baggage on that sloop, while he and Moray stood together on the solid timber planks of the exchange, beneath a sky whose sun was hidden behind swiftly running clouds.

"And how are both your sisters?" asked Sir Harry.

"Very well, I hear."

"Amelia was always great fun. They did both marry Grahams, your sisters, did they not?"

"Aye. Our family's well bound to the Grahams."

"We're all interwoven, I think," said Sir Harry. And then, as though that had reminded him, "I was sorry to hear that my stepmother, your brother's wife, had passed on. Has he married again?"

Moray shook his head. "No, I'm told Robin manages well enough now, with the children grown older."

"It must be very difficult, to not have any contact with them. You were always close, as I recall."

"Aye." Moray gave a nod so short that Anna knew by now, from watching him these past days, that it hid a deep emotion. "My youngest brother, Maurice, knows I live, for I did see him while he was at Paris, but I doubt he does remember that."

"I'd heard he was . . . not well," Sir Harry said. "So he has not recovered?"

Moray gave a shrug. "He is much improved, I'm told, from what he was. But he will never be again the man we knew."

Sir Harry gave a feeling sigh. "Aye, well, the world has turned us all, and which of us will ever be the man that we once were?"

Moray's eyes grew slightly crinkled at their corners. "I do see the world has turned you into a philosopher."

"A merchant, if you please," Sir Harry said, and smiled. "And with much business to attend to." While they'd shaken hands the men had shared a brief embrace, like brothers. "A safe journey to you, John. 'Tis good to see you look so well. Come, Mr. Taylor," called Sir Harry to his secretary, "it is time we were away."

As Mr. Taylor passed, he gave a final bow to Anna. "God speed, Mistress Jamieson."

"I thank you, Mr. Taylor."

They had spoken briefly earlier, and Anna had, with some remorse, said, "I am very sorry if I gave you cause to hope, sir, that—"

He had not let her finish. "Any hopes," he'd told her, "were my own. Your behaviour, Mistress Jamieson, has always been most proper and most ladylike, and quite above reproach."

That had been earlier this morning. Now, he only wished her well and bowed and took his leave.

As Anna watched him walk away down the exchange, her mother came to stand beside her. "He does seem a nice young man."

"He is," said Anna. "He is very nice."

Her mother smiled, and straightening the seam at Anna's shoulder said, "If I could give you one piece of advice, my dear, it would be that you should never give your hand to any man unless he also holds your heart."

What hope for her, then? Anna wondered, for her own heart was already held by one who had no right to it and who did not deserve it, but who would not let it go. "Then I suppose," she said, in a small voice that did not fully seem to know that it was saying things aloud, "that I shall never give my hand."

Her mother did not make reply to that, but gave her arm a reassuring squeeze and turned away to say farewell to the vice-admiral.

Gordon looked most fine this morning, in his uniform with the black armband, and his sword hung gleaming at his side. He raised Sophia's hand and kissed it in a gallant gesture, and for that unguarded instant Anna saw the longing in his face, as of a man who'd loved and lost and, while resigned to it, had never yet forgotten. "This," he told her mother, quietly, "I did not do for duty, either."

And Sophia seemed to understand, because she gave a nod and told him, "I am glad that it was you."

Moray, when he said goodbye to Gordon, was more formal than he had been with Sir Harry.

Gordon handed him the thick packet of letters. "You will see that those are properly delivered?"

"Aye."

Beyond that, there were no light words, no brotherly embrace; only a silence that appeared to say much more than any words could have attempted, and at last, as though it were a gesture that had been a long time coming, Moray held his hand outstretched, and Gordon took it, and above their solemn handshake Moray gave a curt and quiet nod, and that was all.

When Anna's turn came, she found, as her father must have done, words seemed inadequate. She looked up at Vice-Admiral Gordon, and he looked at her, and she suddenly realized the words did not need to be spoken at all. Not out loud.

He said, "I have a parting gift."

"You give too many gifts."

"'Tis not from me. It was delivered to my hands this morning, from the palace. From the Empress Catherine." From his pocket he drew out a parcel wrapped in silk, about the size of his own hand, and strangely rounded. "The messenger who brought the gift spoke only Russian, so Dmitri translated. He said that what you hold was made by the late tsar himself, and was a gift to Empress Catherine in the days before they married. She would have you keep it now, to mind you of the day you gave an empress back her purpose, and to help you know your own." As she took the gift and started to unwrap the silk, he asked, "Does that make any sense to you?"

She nodded, looking down at the small wooden bird, a plain thing carved by a great man who'd always taken pleasure in creating things with his own hands. "She's telling me, I think, that I should seek to be none other than myself, and so fly always like the bird that I was born to be."

"Then," Gordon said, "you will fly very high, my dear. And very far." His blue gaze travelled up towards the sails of their small ship, and Anna looked where he was looking.

"It has been a long time since I've been aboard a ship without you being at the helm," she said. "Will not you pilot us to Cronstadt?"

"I had better not." His smile was slow. "I might be tempted not to come to shore."

When their lines were cast away, he was still standing by the water on the broad exchange, as tall and dashing as he'd been the day she had first seen him, and the way she knew she always would remember him. They stood on deck, the three of them, and watched him till he'd passed from view. Then Moray's arm came round her and, as he had done when she was very small and they had come across from Scotland into Flanders, he drew her back a safer distance from the rail and said, "The wind is cold. Come down below."

The crew's cabin was to the fore, but Moray led her aft to the captain's cabin, swinging the door open so she could enter first. Inside, the curtains had been drawn across the window and the light was lost in shadow, so she did not see the man until he straightened from the place where he'd been sitting. Clothed in black, he looked himself a shadow as he stood.

Her father, all calm, took the packet of letters that he'd just been given by Gordon, and passing them over to Edmund O'Connor said, "These, I believe, would be yours. Whether she is, as well, is for her to decide."

And his gaze briefly travelled between them before he went out again, closing the door.

chapter
FORTY-SEVEN

She did not move.

The ship rolled with the current and she somehow kept her balance, but it was not such an easy thing with Edmund standing suddenly in front of her, and her own father having done a thing she could not fathom.

Yet with all the things she did not understand, the one thing she could say with utter certainty was that her father never would betray the king. Which meant that her perception of his actions must be wrong; that she had somehow missed the movement of some small but vital piece upon the chessboard.

She cast her mind backwards, while Edmund stayed silent and watched her.

She had not acknowledged him, did not dare look at him. Everything round her—not only the timbers beneath her, but everything— felt at that moment as if it were moving and in the wrong place, and she feared if she let herself focus on Edmund she might lose whatever small hold she still had on the things that were real. Anna wanted him there and she wanted him gone and she wanted, above all, to know what was happening.

"He gave you the letters," she said, well aware there was no need to actually say it, for it was self-evident, but she was working things through in her thoughts. Then she met Edmund's eyes and her thoughts grew confused, and she simply asked, "Why?"

"Because they are my burden. I'm the only one can carry them."

She dimly saw the missing piece then, though she could not fully comprehend the purpose of its move. "You are no traitor."

That, he did not answer. But she knew.

She said, "Vice-Admiral Gordon and Sir Harry, they *want* Deane to read those letters."

Edmund smiled faintly in the shadows. "Christ, your mind is quick."

"But why?" And even as she asked the question she believed she knew the answer. "They are trying to deceive him."

"He was sent here by the English as a spy, in search of secrets. We are giving him a secret. That it happens to be false," he said, "is more your fault than anyone's."

"My fault?"

"Aye. When you trapped me with your ruse upon the chessboard," he reminded her, "that evening at the general's, and he told us of the crossing of the river at Poltava, it did set him thinking of a clever way to deal with Deane."

She thought back to that evening, and the general's reconstruction of the way the Russian army had convinced the Swedes they planned to cross the river in one place, while all unseen they made their crossing in another.

Edmund said, "The thing is, here in Russia, as in Spain, the English always have their eyes upon us, waiting to thwart any new attempt King James might make to claim his throne. And the general knew that, when they learned that Captain Hay had come here, and from Rome, they would not rest until they learned the reason why."

She did not ask what Captain Hay's true business on behalf of King James might have been, for even had he known it she would not have asked him to share such a confidence. But she remembered what she'd heard from Charles, that painful day. "You said to Deane yourself, I'm told, that Captain Hay had come to give Sir Harry new instructions to buy ships here, with the backing of the Spanish and the pope himself."

"I did."

"And that was all a lie."

"A lie the English would believe," he said, "because it was exactly what they thought we would be doing. Misdirection, Mistress Jamieson, can be a useful thing."

She gave a nod towards the letters. "And so those are meant to misdirect Deane further?"

"More to misdirect his masters in the government of England. When I meet Deane in Amsterdam and we do break the seals together of these letters, they will tell him most convincingly of how the Duke of Holstein and the empress have conspired to send ships to Spain. I don't doubt he'll believe it, for in truth did he not see three ships himself, just heading out as he came in? So he'll believe that there are surely more to follow. In those letters, there will also be a good account of how we plan to so alarm the Danes by our manouevres in the Baltic, that the Danes will beg the English to assist them. Deane will further learn that, once the English fleet has thus been lured to Denmark's aid, King James will deal a blow from Spain with his new fleet of Russian ships, while Empress Catherine strikes them from behind, and Sweden from above." He gave a half smile. "'Tis in truth a cunning plan."

"And false, as well?"

He shrugged. "I would myself know little of such things, for I am not a naval man. But Deane is."

"Captain Deane," she said, "is many things."

"But not a fool. He is a naval man of long experience, and when he came to Cronstadt he'd have seen within the space of half a day how things do truly stand."

"I do not follow."

Edmund said, "The Russian squadron is not fit for sea, and ill provisioned, and things are not in the order that they would have been in had the tsar not died. However much the empress and the Duke of Holstein may support King James, this year is not the one to try to set him on his throne again, and all of us do know it. But we cannot let the English know it, else they might make use of their advantage. They could do much damage while we try to build our strength. Unless—"

"Unless they do not see that we are weak." She gave a nod, to show she understood. At least, she understood that part of it. She looked away and asked him, in a different voice, "Why you?"

He did not answer for a moment. It fell quiet in the cabin, with the rolling of the ship beneath them and the half-light in which she could not have read his eyes if she'd been looking at them. Then he asked, "And who else was there?"

"Anyone."

"None else Deane would believe could turn a traitor to his kin." The hard and mocking edge had crept back in his tone. "Your Mr. Taylor offered."

She did bring her head round then, and looked him in the eye. "He is not mine. And if he offered, why did you not let him do it?"

"Because whoever carries these damn'd letters into Amsterdam will lose his reputation altogether, Mistress Jamieson. A month from now, when I am well away and none can fetch me back or stop me, there's a harlot in St. Petersburg will swear that, while I lay with her, I told her of my plans to meet with Deane, and after that there will be none, except a very few, who do not know me as a traitor."

As he faced her, she could see his closed jaw lift and set again at a defiant angle, as though he were waiting for her once again to strike him, but instead she kept her gaze on his and asked him, very calmly, "Would this be the harlot who did live next door to you? The one whose husband beat her?"

Edmund stared at her.

"I'd think," said Anna quietly, "a woman who is grateful would say anything you asked her to. Would she have told the same lie about Mr. Taylor, then, if he'd been carrying the letters in your place?" She knew the answer to that, also. "So you would not let him bear that shame, yet you yourself would shoulder it?" She studied him. "You need not always stand and take a whipping you do not deserve."

He went on staring at her, saying nothing, as though he could not believe he'd heard her properly. And then he left the shadows; took a step towards her, cautiously.

"I am always as I am. People will see me as they want to see me. But never before in my whole life," he told her, "have I had a person who wanted to see me as good." He stood and looked down at her, searchingly. "How do you know I've not lain with the harlot?"

She answered him honestly. "You would not take such advantage of someone who had been so wounded."

He shook his head slightly, his eyes never leaving her own. "How would you know how I deal with wounded things?"

"You healed the bird."

"How do you know? You never saw me let it loose. For all you know I killed the thing and had it for my dinner."

"You did not."

"How do you know?"

"Because you told me." All this talk about the bird reminded Anna she still held the silk-wrapped carving from the empress, and she looked now for a place to set it down. There was a table just beside them, with a chair where Edmund had sat earlier, and waited for them, playing at some single-handed game whose object seemed to be to end with all the cards arranged in their four suits.

She lightly touched the cards. "What game is this?"

"It goes by several names. Some fancy it can tell your fortune, tell you if you will succeed or not in what you venture."

Anna asked him, "And what have these cards told you?"

"Their advice is undecided, for the deck is incomplete." Not content to stop their argument, he cornered her again with, "Why is my word enough for you?"

There was no way to answer that, thought Anna, not in speech, because the words did not exist to tell him why. She found another way to do it. Reaching deep into her pocket she drew out the cards he'd sent her, and she set the ace of hearts face-up upon the table, in amongst its fellows.

"I am happy to return you this," she said, "for I believe that it is yours, and has been for some time, and very likely always will be." As his eyes found hers she forced herself to finish. "But if I may," she told him, "I should like to keep my knave."

He raised his scarred hand to her face, and touched her very softly. "I'm not good with fragile things," he said. "I'm careless, and I break them, and I lose them, but I . . ." He broke off, as though to gain control of some emotion, and when next he spoke his tone was gentler than she'd ever heard it. "I'd take care of *you*."

"That is not true," she told him, and before he could misunderstand, she carried on, "You're not so rough with fragile things. You carried twenty painted eggs within your pockets just to please a child, once," she reminded him. "And I am not so breakable."

She saw his dark eyes glisten in the instant just before he closed them, tightly, as though warding off a pain. And then she raised herself on tiptoe and she kissed him, and his arms came round her as he kissed her back. It did not matter that the world was all unsteady then, because with Edmund holding her she knew that she was safe.

He raised his mouth a little from her own, though she still shared his shaking breath and felt the warm curve of his smile.

"Your father is a fierce man," Edmund said, "and he did warn me if I were to lay a hand on you I'd lose the hand."

She moved her hand to where his own was tangled in her hair, and closed her fingers round his larger ones, and felt the hard line of the scar beneath her palm. "Ye'll not," she said. "Ye'll never take a punishment because of me."

"You're fierce as well, then, are you?"

"Aye. All fighters are, I'm told."

The second kiss was deeper than the first, and lasted longer. When he broke it this time he drew back to look at her. "I must still go to Amsterdam."

"I know."

"As long as Deane believes he pulls my strings, I must pretend to dance to them."

"I know," she said. "I'll wait."

"It might be months."

Why was he talking? Anna wondered. Reaching up she kissed him lightly on the hard line of his jaw. "Ye'll have your pardon, as Deane promised, will ye not?"

He gave a nod, his own mouth lowering.

"Well then," she said, "I will return to Ireland with my mother and my father, and I'll wait for you," she told him, "to come home."

And that, to Anna's satisfaction, was the last thing Edmund let her say for quite some time.

The sun had set, the wind was blowing strong across the Strelka, and in front of me Rob stood against the waist-high granite wall and turned his gaze towards the river where the fortress lay in floodlights. There were lights, too, coming on all down the line of the Embankment and across the long green bridge, reflecting in the water of the Neva, but Rob's face was half in shadow.

"What did he say?" he asked me as I pocketed my mobile.

"He was angry." Then, as he looked round, I added, "That I hadn't told him earlier. Apparently I could have saved him time and money, telling him what items were worth bidding on at auction."

"And what did ye say to that?"

I shrugged and smiled. "I told him what I do will never be accepted as a true authentication."

"Not the now, at any rate," said Rob. "I'd not say never."

As I joined him at the wall, he changed the angle of his body slightly so he blocked the worst part of the wind, and told me, "But you have your job."

I gave a nod. "It seems that way."

"That's good, then."

When I nodded for a second time, not answering, he slanted a quick glance at me and asked, "So why the frown?"

"I'm disappointed. I was really hoping we could prove the Firebird had come from Catherine, but I don't see how we can. Can you?"

He thought a moment. Shook his head. "No."

"And that means, after all this, Margaret Ross won't get her cruise."

Rob shrugged in his turn. "Well, I'd not assume that, either. She could always sell her books."

My frown grew deeper. "What books?"

"The James Bond books in the bookcase in her sitting room," said Rob. "Did ye not see them?"

Thinking back, I had a memory of Rob bending to examine Margaret's bookcase, and the vintage hardbacks with their garish covers. Her father's books, she'd told us.

Turning round myself so that I faced him more directly, I asked, "What about them?"

"Well," he said, in that calm, nonchalant tone that I knew by now was anything but innocent, "a first edition James Bond hardback sells for a fair bit at auction. First editions of the very first book sell for nearly twenty thousand pounds. And she's got the entire set, all signed by Ian Fleming."

I was staring at him and he knew it. I could see the faint suggestion of a smile that he took care to straighten out again before I asked him, "Does she know this?"

"Well, she will after you tell her."

"Rob."

"This place," he said, "is growing on me. I can see why it's your favourite spot in all St. Petersburg."

"Rob."

"Aye?"

"You knew about the books before we left Dundee," I told him, "didn't you? You knew she didn't have to sell the Firebird to take that cruise." A little hurt, I asked, "Why did you never tell me?"

He looked back towards the fortress, so I couldn't see his face. "And if I had," he said, "ye would have had a different journey, would ye not?"

I thought about it for a moment. Thought of all the paths I never would have taken, all the turnings I would never have discovered, all the things I would have missed. "I guess I would have."

Quietly, Rob told me, "It just seemed a thing worth following, your Firebird."

I watched his back, the way he held his shoulders, and I knew that like the heroes in the varied versions of the Russian fairy tale, the treasure I had ended up with when I'd chased the Firebird was not what I'd set out to find, nor what I had expected it to be, but something better, beyond price.

His voice was even. "So, what happens now?"

I stumbled on the answers. "Well . . . I guess we try to sort it out, somehow. I mean, it's going to be a bit of an adjustment for me, I expect, but—"

Rob's head came around and he cut me off. "Will ye stop doing that?"

"Doing what?"

"Answering questions afore I can ask them."

His smile stopped my heart. Then my own heart replied with an answering smile as I realized what I had just done.

You did ask it, I told him.

If I had not loved him before, there was no way I could have resisted the way that he looked at me now.

Aye. His thoughts flooded into my mind like the river below us, and left no more corners of emptiness. *Maybe I did.*

He reached for me then, and he wrapped his arms warmly around me, and kissed me, a long thorough kiss that stole most of my power to concentrate. When it had ended I drew back to look at him.

"Rob?"

"Aye?"

"I still have to go back to London."

"I ken that."

"I'm sure I can get things arranged with Sebastian so I can work partly from Scotland, but that might take time."

Rob repeated, "I ken that."

"I mean, it might take a few months."

Then I heard my own words, and I suddenly realized how closely they followed the last ones that Anna and Edmund had said to each other. I knew Rob had noticed it, too, because I saw the smile in his eyes as he lifted one hand to recapture a strand of my hair that had feathered away in the wind. As his fingers closed round it, he brought his hand warm to the side of my face, and his touch held a promise.

"I'll wait," he said, gently, "for you to come home."

And to my satisfaction, that was the last thing he was able to say for some time.

About the Characters

This book began with one character, stubbornly standing alone on the page and refusing to let me forget him. Long after the other characters from my book *The Winter Sea* had gone about their business, Colonel Graeme stayed alive in my imagination, standing in the doorway of a cottage on the northeast coast of Scotland.

Those who've read *The Winter Sea* will doubtless have remembered Colonel Patrick Graeme, former captain of the Edinburgh Town Guard who, like so many other Jacobites, had followed King James the Seventh into exile, and returned in secret in the months before the 1708 invasion attempt that is at the heart of my earlier novel.

Although I found no record of what Colonel Graeme did between that failed invasion and his death at Paris twelve years later, I'd come to know his character enough to know that, if he had been able to take part in the 1715 rebellion, he would have done. And so I chose to put him there, along with his nephew, John Moray—another real-life character, and one I'd grown so fond of that I didn't let him die in 1710 as history demanded, extending his life instead and providing him with a fictional wife and children, including young Anna. That John and Colonel Graeme would return to Slains to protect Anna in the dangerous last days of the 1715 rebellion seemed natural to me, and that they would then take her to the convent of the Irish nuns at Ypres, a place John Moray knew himself, made equal sense.

But while Anna Moray might have been my own creation, along with a few other minor characters—the Logan family in their cottage close to Slains; the neighbours of the nuns, and Christiane, at Ypres; Dmitri, Father Dominic, the Winter Palace guards, and Mrs. Hewitt in St. Petersburg—most of the people in the eighteenth-century story were real, and I didn't want to take too may liberties with their lives. To that end, I have tried to place people where they actually were at that time in the past, keeping where I could to the original documents and records, and when possible, to their actual words.

I was generously helped in my efforts by people like Sister Maire Hickey of Kylemore Abbey, County Galway, one of that same community of Irish Benedictine nuns who shelter Anna in my novel. Those nuns remained at Ypres until their convent was destroyed by bombing in the First World War. Forced to leave, they spent a few unsettled years before finally purchasing Kylemore Castle, in the west of Ireland. There, on the shore of a beautiful lough, surrounded by the Connemara mountains, they have lived since 1920, and it was from Kylemore that Sister Maire not only answered my questions about the history and daily routine of her community, introducing me to Reverend Dom Patrick Nolan's book *The Irish Dames of Ypres* (an indispensable source of information on the specific nuns who lived there in 1716), but also, as a further kindness, took the time to proofread my finished chapters dealing with the convent, to help me ensure my portrayal was accurate.

The convent at Ypres may be gone, but the details—and drawings—of John's memorial stone in its church are preserved in the papers of his family. As an amateur genealogist myself, I find one of my greatest pleasures in writing historical fiction is researching the families of my characters and restoring their lives, in a way. Although his brother William, being Laird of Abercairney, makes the history books, John's sisters and his other brothers Robert (Robin), James, and Maurice are more frequently ignored. Since Maurice, as noted in correspondence kept among the Stuart Papers, was actually passing through Flanders at the time of my story in 1716, it seemed fitting to let him stop in at the convent to pay his respects to the grave of his brother. His account of his family's misfortunes, and of his own crossing, I took from his letters, and his mission to Paris for King James the Eighth was real. His sudden and unexplained madness is recorded in the Stuart

Papers, and whatever its cause, he presumably never fully recovered, as at the end of his life in 1740 he was dependent on the charitable care of his nieces and nephews in Scotland. He apparently never married.

It never fails to fascinate me just how many of the people in the past, who seem at first glance unrelated, were in fact connected to each other in their lives, through blood or marriage, and these relationships can often make it easier for me to understand the real-life actions of the people in the story. It also gives me scope to create motives for my characters in any situation I invent.

The fact that Father Graeme was not only Colonel Graeme's son, but cousin to the Morays, made him useful to me when I needed to transport young Anna to Calais from Ypres. And here, I did take liberties. With Anna being fictional, the journey Father Graeme takes to Ypres and back is fiction, too. His character, though, including his former service as a soldier, and the reason he became a monk, are all recorded history, and he was at that time living in Calais. He loyally provided information to King James for the remainder of his life. And while his journey to Ypres was my invention, his relationship to Mrs. Ogilvie was not.

Rebecca Ogilvie and her husband, Captain John Ogilvie, had in fact been apprehended and taken into custody by British authorities in 1704, when they'd come across from France in the wake of John Moray and Colonel Graeme (who were on an earlier mission for King James, in what became known as the Scots Plot). Brought before a special committee of the House of Lords, Captain Ogilvie not only turned informant, revealing the names of others who had come across from St. Germain, but went a step further and offered to spy on the Jacobites, an offer which was apparently accepted, as he then entered into a correspondence with the British spymaster Harley, who paid Ogilvie a "royal bounty" of one hundred pounds.

The Ogilvies then returned to France, and Father Graeme, at least, appears to have been unaware of their change of loyalties. As both he and Captain Ogilvie had served in Catalonia, perhaps their friendship was an old one. As late as 1739, the trusting Capuchin monk mentions receiving letters from the captain. And in that spring of 1717, when I have him bringing my fictional Anna Moray into Calais, Rebecca Ogilvie had in fact just arrived from England, and mentions in a letter to her husband that Father Graeme came to see her. It was happily convenient for me that, in real life, she did make the crossing to Calais with Captain Thomas Gordon (whom she also mentions, less agreeably, in that same letter).

Captain Gordon also featured in *The Winter Sea*, and I was more than pleased to have him reappear in this book, and take charge of little Anna.

I had known from my previous research that Gordon had gone into Russia, and had risen to be Governor of Cronstadt after years of distinguished service in the Russian navy. I'd also known that he'd remained a Jacobite, but I am indebted to the historian Rebecca Wills for her book *The Jacobites and Russia, 1715–1750*, for giving me a broader window on the active Jacobite community at St Petersburg, and for directing me, through her detailed footnotes and bibliography, to a wealth of useful primary resources for my own research.

My favourite sources are always the letters and diaries of the times, and one of the most fascinating of these remains the detailed diary of Friedrich Wilhelm Bergholz, who was himself only in his mid-twenties when, as one of the courtiers of the Duke of Holstein, he kept an almost daily record of the happenings in St. Petersburg. His diary, which has been published in German and Russian (though sadly, not yet English) proved a treasure-trove of details, from the days on which mourning for the tsar was lifted, to the wedding feast and celebrations of the duke and princess, and the way the meadow looked upon that day.

Bergholz also gave me little glimpses of my characters, from time to time, recording small moments like the morning when, while he and the duke were standing in the naval yard discussing ships with then Vice-Admiral Gordon, the talk turned to the galleys. Like most galleys throughout history, the Russian ones were rowed by slaves and criminals condemned to man the oars, and Gordon remarked that "the British, as free people, do not want to hear about them at all," to which Bergholz appended, "From his words, it was easy to see that he viewed these ships unfavourably, and was no friend of Vice-Admiral Izmailovich, who commands the galleys here" (translation mine). I must confess, this only made me fonder of Vice-Admiral Gordon.

John Deane's thorough report to Lord Townshend on his aborted spying mission to St. Petersburg in June of 1725 paints, as one might expect, a less flattering picture of the Jacobite community there. The fact that I've portrayed Deane himself less favourably than many other historians is not something I did lightly or with malice; rather, it represents the personal conclusions I came to after reading, not only this one report, but several of his other writings, and those of the people who knew him, from his early life and the shipwreck on Boon Island, through his later career as British Consul at Ostend, until his death in 1761, at home in England. I owe thanks to my friend, Maureen Jennings, author of, among other things, the Murdoch mysteries, who also spent almost thirty years as a practicing psychotherapist, and who generously read through Deane's writings and agreed Deane might have suffered from either narcisstic or borderline personality disorder, an insight that helped me immensely in crafting his character.

For all that Deane hated the Jacobites, his report to Townshend is nonetheless valuable in that it records, in minute detail, the timeline of his visit, what he observed while in St. Petersburg, whom he met, and what they spoke of. Without Deane, I might not have known that Edmund dined every day at General Lacy's house, and more minor characters like the inn-keeper Thomas Trescott might have slipped my notice altogether. (Whether Mr. Trescott's son ever did receive the English education Deane had promised him, I do not know, but one of Trescott's sons, John, after graduating from the Russian Academy gymnasium, became a skilled cartographer and the only Briton in the eighteenth century to be made a full member of the Academy of Sciences; and another son, Thomas, did complete a five-year apprenticeship with the British instrument-maker Benjamin Scott.)

Deane remained particularly fixated on ferreting out the reason for Captain William Hay's return to St. Petersburg. He would no doubt have given much to have had the chance, as I did, to read Thomas Gordon's letter book.

Letter books, in which a person's private correspondence was drafted and copied, are a rare and wonderful resource for any historical novelist, and I treasure the week I was able to spend in Edinburgh reading Gordon's letter book in the National Archives of Scotland's Historical Search Room. I will forever be grateful for the tireless assistance of Alison Lindsay, head of the NAS's Historical Search Section, who was—and continues to be—an invaluable help to my research.

Gordon's letters, written to everyone from his closest relations to King James the Eighth himself, provided me with a wealth of information, not only about the political intrigue and day-to-day life within the Jacobite community, but of his own home life. The household supplies that he ordered each year to be shipped to him from Amsterdam are listed in fascinating detail, down to the various fabrics for his daughters' clothes, and his favourite types of tea. His letters also revealed family connections and personal details that I'd never found elsewhere, including the deaths of his son and his stepdaughter Jane, and the existence of his half brother and his nephew Charles.

The daughters who were living with him in St. Petersburg, Mary and Ann (whom I nicknamed "Nan" in this novel, to avoid any confusion with Anna), both married into the Jacobite community there—Mary to the merchant William Elmsall, and Ann to Sir Henry (Harry) Stirling, a match that Gordon wrote, in a letter to his cousin, was "the greatest satisfaction that I have on earth." Fittingly, Ann and Sir Harry's granddaughter, another Anna, married into the Morays of Abercairney, thus continuing the interweaving of the families that seems to so dominate the lives of those I write about.

As of this writing, I don't know what became of Sir Harry's

sometime secretary Mr. Taylor, although I presume he remained active in the English Factory at St. Petersburg, together with the merchants Mr. Wayte and Mr. Morley. Whether there ever was a Mrs. Hewitt, I cannot say, but there certainly was a Mr. Hewitt, with whom Thomas Gordon had a falling-out around this time, though they appear to have settled their differences a few years later.

The military exploits of General Pierce (Peter) Lacy are easy to follow, thanks in large part to his journal, but his personal life in St. Petersburg proved more difficult to piece together, and I had to rely on the writings of others to fill in the gaps in his household. His wife, despite being a woman of quality and wealth, receives little mention anywhere, and depending upon which source one trusts, I may have left him short one daughter.

The birthdate of his youngest son, Francis, is recorded at St. Petersburg in 1725, just after the events of this novel, and it is known that Michael was the eldest son, and Helen the fourth daughter, but I was forced to make my best guess as to the relative ages of the other children, based on the documents I had. I offer my apologies to them and their descendants if I've got them out of order.

The girls all married well, mainly to high-ranking officers, and little else seems to be known of what became of them. The boys all followed their father into military service with foreign armies. Michael became a cavalry officer and was killed in 1735; the younger Pierce served the King of Saxony and lived a long life, dying in Belgium in 1773. Francis (Franz), rose to the rank of field marshal in the Austrian army, and died well respected in 1801.

As for General Lacy himself, his heroism at Poltava was eclipsed by his even greater victories in the Russo-Turkish wars of the 1730s. He remained a favourite of Peter the Great's daughter Elizabeth, who became empress in 1741. She allowed Lacy to return to his beloved Livonia, where he served as governor-general and commander of the military forces there.

Lacy remained in Livonia for the rest of his life. When a fire broke out in a house dangerously close to the city of Riga's stores of hemp and gunpowder, Lacy roused himself and, though in his seventies by this time, stood all night in the cold on the roof of the gunpowder store, directing the efforts to put out the fire. His bravery saved the city from an explosion, but he suffered a fever as a result, which in his doctor's opinion was the cause of the steady decline of his health afterwards. Lacy fought from the time he was thirteen years old, and death found him at last, not on the battlefield, but in his own bed, surrounded by his family, in April of 1751.

Edmund O'Connor, his kinsman, appeared at first glance a much less noble character.

From Edmund's own statement (recorded by the secretary of the British spymaster Lord Townshend), we know the dates that he arrived in, and departed from, St. Petersburg; that he brought letters from the Jacobites in Spain addressed to Gordon and Sir Harry, and on leaving, carried letters from those same men into Amsterdam, where as arranged, he met with Deane, and the letters were opened.

Edmund made a good impression on Townshend, who found him "plain in what he says." Deane was less sure of his loyalties, and having examined the facts, I found myself siding with Deane.

The letters Edmund carried from St. Petersburg, and that he showed to Deane, spoke of invasion plans, and Edmund himself, in some detail, related the Jacobites' intent to purchase Spanish ships and lure the British navy into battle in the Baltic.

But the deeper I dug with my research, the more it appeared that those plans might be false, and be meant to deceive.

Although Townshend himself took them seriously, and seemed particularly bothered by the three ships Deane had seen leaving the Baltic, apparently headed for Spain, no one in Townshend's far-flung web of European agents was able to find any evidence to back Edmund's claims. Britain's agent in Sweden went so far as to say, in a letter to Townshend that very October, "one would almost suspect the letters from Petersburg to be a fiction."

I began to agree with him. And if that were indeed the case, then in my view, it left only two possible options: either the Jacobites at

St. Petersburg had known that Edmund O'Connor was a traitor, and had deliberately given him false information to unwittingly deliver to the British, or Edmund was a willing participant in a very clever sting operation.

I cannot know the motives of a man who has been dead more than two hundred years. I only know that, when he gave his information to the British, Edmund told them next to nothing about Gordon and Sir Harry and the Jacobites he'd lived with in close quarters at St. Petersburg the past nine months, claiming he "never heard anything of Business from them." Perhaps he really did know nothing. Or perhaps he kept what he knew secret, to protect his friends. I chose to think the best of him. I'm happy with my choice.

At any rate, he got his royal pardon. I still hope to find some record of what he did, after that.

As for the three ships that Deane had observed and that had so alarmed Townshend, they eventually arrived without incident in Spain, offloaded their harmlessly commercial cargoes, and reloaded with nothing more incendiary than oil, salt, and raisins before sailing north again. Townshend, firm in his belief of the plot, continued to expend the government's time, funds, and energy in gathering intelligence and trying to prepare for what he felt sure was an imminent invasion.

If the Jacobites had wanted to gain time to plan and regroup, while making the British waste valuable resources, they had succeeded.

I cannot claim to know what they intended. But I do know that, on August 8, 1725—the day before Edmund O'Connor left St. Petersburg to carry his tale and the letters to Townshend and Deane—King James the Eighth himself sat down and wrote a somewhat different story to his trusted friend Lord Atterbury. "By my accounts of the North," wrote the king, "I perceive the Czarina was willing to hear my proposals, and that the fleet was not like to undertake any thing this year; all which will afford time both for negociation [sic] and execution against the next; and I own I never had better hopes in general."

These hopes stayed high till Empress Catherine's death, just two years later. What she might have done to aid James in his efforts to regain his throne, we'll never know. The next tsar was not sympathetic to the Jacobites, and after a few more years of attempting to gain assistance from Russia, James and his followers were forced to turn their hopes westward again, to their older allies Spain and France.

But that is another story.

A Note of Thanks

In addition to Alison Lindsay, head of the Historical Search Section at the National Archives of Scotland; Sister Maire Hickey, OSB, of Kylemore Abbey, Connemara, County Galway, Ireland; and my friend and fellow author Maureen Jennings, all of whom I've mentioned in my notes about the characters, and all of whom deserve a second mention here, I also owe thanks to the two researchers at the National Archives of Scotland who kindly took time to share with me the more extensive catalog of records from the Stirling-Home-Drummond-Moray papers; to Charles Hind, FSA, Associate Director and H. J. Heinz Curator of Drawings for the British Architectural Library Drawings and Archives Collections at the Victoria and Albert Museum in London, who was my guide in St. Petersburg; to the two women working at the Municipal Museum in Ieper, Belgium, on the day that I walked in, who helped me track down the location of the former convent of the Irish nuns; to John G. Kruth, Executive Director, and Christine Simmonds-Moore, PhD of the Rhine Research Center in Durham, North Carolina, who vetted my details concerning the ganzfeld procedure and parapsychology research; and as ever, to my editors and agents, and my mother—my most critical developmental editor.

Above all, I owe special thanks to Margaret McGovern, of Eyemouth, Scotland, my onetime landlady and longtime friend, who not only gave Robbie his bye-name but helped me make sure that his voice was authentic. I couldn't have written his story without her, and wouldn't have wanted to.